PRAISE FOR SOPHIE WHI

'A sharp, funny story of female friendship at its best, with characters you'll fall in love with'
Beth O'Leary

'One of the best flawed heroines in Irish commercial fiction since Rachel Walsh in Marian Keyes' ground-breaking *Rachel's Holiday*'
Sunday Times

'A modern, witty, razor-sharp page-turner'
Emer McLysaght

'White's pages fizz with earthy wit and [Marian] Keyes fans will definitely find plenty to enjoy here'
Sunday Independent

'Fresh, current and thoroughly enjoyable'
Eithne Shortall

'Witty and wonderful – I devoured this in a single sitting'
Image

'Whip smart and very, very funny'
Sarah Breen

'White's sharp-eyed take on modern life couldn't be more on target'
Irish Independent

'Unsettling, sharp ... strikingly witty'
Irish Examiner

Sophie White lives in Dublin with her husband and three sons. She writes regularly for many Irish publications, including her weekly 'Nobody Tells You' column for the *Sunday Independent LIFE* magazine, and also co-hosts two podcasts, *Mother of Pod* and *The Creep Dive.*

Also by Sophie White

Fiction

Filter This

Unfiltered

The Snag List

Where I End

Non-fiction

Corpsing

Recipes for a Nervous Breakdown

My Hot Friend

SOPHIE WHITE

HACHETTE
BOOKS
IRELAND

First published in Ireland in 2023 by
HACHETTE BOOKS IRELAND

1

Cataloguing in Publication Data is available from the British Library.

ISBN 9781529352757

Typeset in Arno Pro by Bookends Publishing Services, Dublin
Printed and bound in Great Britain by Clays Ltd, Elcograf S.p.A.

Hachette Books Ireland policy is to use papers that are natural, renewable and recyclable products and made from wood grown in sustainable forests. The logging and manufacturing processes are expected to conform to the environmental regulations of the country of origin.

Hachette Books Ireland
8 Castlecourt Centre
Castleknock
Dublin 15, Ireland

A division of Hachette UK Ltd
Carmelite House, 50 Victoria Embankment, London EC4Y 0DZ

www.hachettebooksireland.ie

For Vivi, who welcomed us into her beautiful home during the writing of this book, thank you from the bottom of my heart.

This book contains passages and scenes pertaining to mental illness and suicide. There are also references to disordered eating. Please see the resources below should you need support.

Samaritans
Phone: 116 123 *Email: jo@samaritans.ie*

Pieta House
Phone: 1800 247 247 *Text HELP to 51444*

Bodywhys
Phone: 01-2107906 *Email: alex@bodywhys.ie*

St Patrick's Mental Health Services
Phone: 01-249 3333 *Email: info@stpatsmail.com*

CHAPTER 1

'Claire! You're back in bed! It's four o'clock. Can you put your phone down for two seconds? We need to get going! It's *your* mother we're visiting!'

Jamie, Claire's boyfriend, was standing in the bedroom doorway, looking amused despite his exasperation.

'Sorry! I'm up. I'm up.' Claire straggled to her feet still clutching her phone, open as always to WhatsApp.

Jamie's eyes flickered to the phone. 'All okay?'

'Yes!' Claire conjured a smile to reassure Jamie, but her mind was still lodged firmly in the phone – specifically in the girls' group chat titled 'The Bitch Herd'. None of them had replied to her Happy New Year's message. Not even a casual emoji or GIF. It'd been eighteen minutes.

Concern lingered in Jamie's wide grey eyes. He was always concerned now – *how could he not be?*

Claire swallowed her guilt and scouted for something to say to distract him. 'I am okay! I'm buzzing for Christmas Dinner the Sequel!'

'Insisting on re-celebrating Christmas on New Year's ... Your mother is nothing if not a complete loon!' Jamie winced. 'Sorry! Not a loon. A ... you know ... a very intense person.'

Jamie pushed his dark hair back and made his way towards Claire. The tiny bedroom of their city centre flat was filled to absolute capacity with their small double bed so he had to shuffle carefully along the narrow channel (clogged with Claire's discarded clothes) between bed and wall to sit on the bed. He leaned over to hug Claire.

'I'm really sorry that my parents' split is dominating the festivities this year,' Claire grimaced.

Christmas Part II was her mother Marian's response to the fact that David, Claire's dad, had won the coin toss deciding which parent Claire would have Christmas with.

'Don't be sorry,' murmured Jamie, nuzzling Claire's neck before heading back over to the mirrored built-in wardrobe that ran the length of the opposite wall. There was such a dearth of floor space, he had to kneel on the bed to get the doors open.

Claire watched as Jamie pulled out a plaid shirt and dark jeans, then shimmied back towards the door and tossed the clothes out into the living room. They often got dressed out there; that's how tight the bedroom was. Claire felt a little bad. On Jamie's Google salary they could probably have afforded something a shade bigger, but Claire had insisted that they split the rent equally. And unfortunately, working as a childminder, she didn't make nearly as much as Jamie did, even though her bosses Norah and Sean Sweeney were generous.

'At least your parents actually WANT to see us.' Jamie was matter-of-fact. 'All my mother has done is send me pictures of their Alaskan cruise, proclaiming "best Christmas and New Year's ever". Subtext: "We should have ditched you kids long ago"!'

While Claire was an only child, Jamie was the middle one of five boys. His brothers were lovely, though even after three years with Jamie, Claire still couldn't quite get a handle on who was who. They had a host of English names like Edward and Colin and were all perfectly nice but too similar for Claire to have any hope of differentiating them. Jamie, with Claire in tow, had only gone back home to Tunbridge Wells a handful of times since leaving for a job in Google's Dublin offices. And now, because the brothers were all married off, procreating at a fierce rate and spending the holidays at their various in-laws, Jamie's parents had decided to abandon the customary family gathering and take themselves off on an extended holiday.

The timing was brilliant, as it meant Claire would have Jamie as a wingman through this first torturous Christmas with her 'separated' parents. Though there was nothing 'separate' about their current set-up. Her mum and dad were both still living in the same house, as they hadn't a hope of affording a second place. Rent in Shanganagh, the small village an hour from the city where Claire had grown up, was exorbitant. And so her dad was cowering in the old guest room down the hall from her mum. Claire was pretty sure that they'd eventually get back together. She fucking hoped so.

Claire sighed. 'At least your parents have some sense of boundaries.' She really only had one foot in the conversation: she wanted to check her WhatsApp but didn't want to seem like she was obsessing; that would set Jamie on edge. 'I just don't know if I can do another episode of the Marian and David Shitshow so soon after the last one. My dad shedding a few tears into the stuffing while my mum blasts Wham! from down the hall is not what memories are made of.'

'Hmm.' Jamie nodded in sympathy. 'Look, remember we have a game plan. We get in, we get out. We're back here in time for midnight and couch.'

By mutual agreement, they'd decided to watch disaster movies to honour the passing of what had to have been the most apocalyptic year of their relationship so far. Claire shook the thought away and tried to smile.

'Is this thing grafted to your hand?' Jamie held up Claire's right arm, still clutching the phone.

'I wish it was – that would be so handy!' Claire quipped, attempting to sound playful, to be more like her old self.

'We'll probably see it in our lifetime,' said Jamie with a rueful shake of his head. He slid the phone from Claire's grip and pulled her down onto the duck-egg blue throw and matching pillows. They kissed and Claire tried to stay in the moment, but her thoughts kept straying back to the silent WhatsApp group where still no one had responded to her Happy New Year's message.

Why is no one replying? It's the New Year. Surely everyone lashes the standard Happy New Year text into all their WhatsApp groups?

Jamie was kissing her more urgently and it was very nice, but Claire could not focus while the group chat was lying dormant.

Why is NO ONE replying? It's New Year's everywhere, for fuck's sake.

The phone buzzed in Jamie's hand and Claire had to resist the urge to forcibly push Jamie off and grab it from him.

'I should check that,' she said lightly, trying not to betray her eagerness.

They broke apart and Jamie stood, smiling. He tossed the phone to Claire. 'I guess it's for the best – you're just too nice a distraction and we REALLY need to go! You have fifteen minutes to get ready.'

Claire smiled and watched him leave before pouncing on the phone. The rising excitement abruptly ebbed as she realised it wasn't a reply in the Bitch Herd group but a voice note from her mother. It was seventeen minutes long.

Resigned, she grabbed her earpods from the shelf above her side of the bed. Marian wasn't one of those parents who didn't get technology; she was more up on these things than most young people, having worked in PR up until taking early retirement the year before. Since she had more time on her hands, her Voicys had doubled in length and Claire suspected she was actually dictating her memoirs via WhatsApp.

Claire connected her earpods to the phone, selected double speed – that way it'd only take half the time to listen – and pressed play. Next, she scooched over to her side of the wardrobe and shimmied out of her joggers and jumper; then she began wrestling with the strappy silver slip dress she'd picked out earlier. All the while her mum raged in her ears.

'Claire, pumpkin. I know I'm seeing you shortly, but you won't believe what that effing bee Darina has done to me now ...'

Marian didn't use curse words but instead the first letter of a bad word, which meant she had her own lexicon of swearing. Bee was bitch, effing was fucking, and so on.

'... She was supposed to bring meringues to the afternoon tea we're having for Noleen tomorrow and then at the last minute with no effing notice she announces that she's doing a lemon drizzle.'

Claire laced up her Docs and pulled on a big, chunky black

cardigan – one of the many things she'd made to channel some of the nervous energy that plagued her. Knitting calmed her mind, along with the cornucopia of pharmaceuticals she was supposed to take. Shit. That reminded her …

She crawled back over to her shelf and the pill sorter sitting on top of her stack of craft books. She examined the little compartments and took out Friday's trio of meds. The previous two days were still stocked with pills: she must have forgotten to take Wednesday's and Thursday's. *It's very hard to keep track of all the adult admin*, she reassured herself. She took out the pills she'd missed and popped them into her knitting bag, which hung from the bed post. She didn't want Jamie to see the missed days when they restocked the sorter together on Sunday night; she'd put them back in the bottles before then.

In her ears, her mother was still on a roll. 'Now I'm up S-H creek with berries and cream and no meringues to put them on. This is just so typical of her.'

Marian's ability to obsess over the minutia was incredible though Claire sometimes worried that this trait might be genetic. Sure, she didn't care about cake politics as much as Marian did, but her focus on the various machinations and micro-slights of her friendship group was, even Claire could see, not dissimilar.

'Then of course I hear that Darina is having a dinner party on Sunday night and has invited everyone except me. And you know why that is, of course.' Marian paused for breath for the first time since she'd begun speaking.

Claire knew what was coming and tensed slightly.

'It's because I've split with your father. I know it. They're so effing uptight. They think, "Oh, we can't have Marian because she's not with David any more so the numbers will be uneven."'

As Jamie had said, Marian was intense and it was extremely intense being her only child, especially since the split, when her Voicys had become ever more unhinged.

Though with everything that had happened this year, Claire figured she was in no position to call anyone unhinged.

Claire flicked away from WhatsApp and resumed the episode of *Your Hot Friend* she'd been listening to earlier. It was her favourite podcast – two best friends, Lexi and Amanda, just chatting.

Jamie did not get it. 'Are they discussing interesting topics?' he'd asked. 'No! It's just chaotic chit-chat – it's fun,' Claire had replied.

Claire sat on the edge of the bed to face the mirrored door and grabbed her little make-up bag. Lexi was talking about the night she'd met her boyfriend, Jonathan. This brought a smile to Claire's lips as she remembered the night she'd met Jamie three years ago, at, of all things, a ceramics class. It was Claire's twenty-eighth birthday and she'd been pretty down, because Aifric, her best friend since they were four, had bailed on the class at the last minute. Claire wasn't exactly thrilled about going on her own, but she'd paid for the course. And in a way it worked out better that Claire was on her own. She probably wouldn't have been as open to chatting to the tall, angular Jamie with his messy pile of dark hair if Aifric had been there. Jamie had brought his sales team, trying to foster a bit of bonding among his charges.

Claire smoothed a little tinted moisturiser on her creamy pale skin, scattered with freckles, and grinned at the memory of Jamie completely ignoring his colleagues the second he saw Claire. Jamie was confident, and before their bowls were thrown, he'd asked Claire to come for dinner.

While Lexi and Amanda bantered back and forth on the podcast, Claire leaned into the mirror and added a deep plum lip that worked well with her red hair. Two subtle little flicks of eyeliner in the corners of her brown eyes and she was ready.

Claire approached the driveway of her childhood home warily. These days it was hard to know what she'd be walking into when she arrived. On any given day, Marian and David could be entirely ignoring each other's existence or vocally railing at one other from either end of the house. It was so hard to predict with them; she got emotional whiplash every time.

The estate was packed with extra cars: New Year's parties were gearing up all around them. The grassy park in the centre of the estate was frosty and almost navy green in the approaching darkness. The white bungalows, still festooned with Christmas lights, circled this patch where she and Aifric had graduated from Tip the Can to Kiss Chase and eventually to languid sunny afternoons reading *More!* magazine and eating Icebergers.

At the foot of the driveway of fourteen Dundeela Crescent, she and Jamie paused, looking at the latest evidence of her parents' pettiness: a heavy chalk line demarcating one side of the driveway from the other, with the words 'You park here!' Her mother's banged-up Volvo estate was sitting just to the left of the line and her father's little red Fiat to the right. Claire rolled her eyes at Jamie as they slipped past the cars to the door.

Just as Claire reached for the bell, she heard her mother's voice ring out from behind.

'Why are you so early?'

She and Jamie turned around to where Marian was standing, half in, half out of a taxi that had just pulled up.

'We're only twenty minutes early!' Claire narrowed her eyes at Marian's extremely fancy outfit: a black velvet tuxedo jacket, matching trousers and a diamante-studded black hairband in her tousled salt and pepper hair.

Marian leaned in to thank the driver, then shut the door gently.

'Well,' she beamed shyly, walking towards them. 'You caught me! I'm a dirty stop-out! Would you believe it, I'm still out from last night!'

'Delighted for you,' Claire squirmed. 'Absolutely no need for any further details.'

Marian ignored this: 'His name's Peter; he's forty-two. A little lash.'

'Mum! That's very young.' Claire was momentarily impressed, but this was immediately dampened by a glance up at the curtained window on the right of the bungalow where her dad now dwelled. Poor Dad. Marian was fifty-four – she'd had Claire in her early twenties – while David was about to turn sixty. He couldn't compete with a forty-two-year-old.

'Well, I don't want to have sex with an old man. Who would?'

'Not me,' Jamie grinned gamely.

'And OLD men …' Marian wrinkled her nose. 'Well, let's just say there's a lot of loose skin in the crotch when they're YOUNG … never mind when—'

'Okay,' Claire interrupted. 'I need to line my stomach if you're planning on giving any more details on this front.'

Marian pulled Claire into a hug and Claire basked in her mother's comforting smell, unchanged in thirty-one years: Coromandel, a fancy perfume David replaced every birthday and Christmas. *That'll probably be my job now,* Claire realised. Her mum's birthday was in September: if her parents stayed separated, her costs were going to rise significantly.

'Right, inside, you two. Let's get the oven on; I had the foresight to prep everything yesterday evening before I went out.'

In the kitchen, while her mother set the table, Claire examined the recently instated roster stuck to the fridge – a colour-coded timetable of who was using the kitchen when. David was yellow and Marian was green. She'd grown up with them fighting; she'd thought that was what all parents did. Still, she couldn't quite believe that they were calling it a day – also the timing of it seemed pertinent, though they both insisted it had nothing to do with what had happened last year.

Suddenly, after over three decades of sticking each other out, they were sleeping in different rooms and refusing to explain why. Every time she'd tried to get an answer, they'd fobbed her off, saying it was between them and not something for her to worry about.

Claire grabbed a bottle of white wine from the fridge, inside of which everything was labelled with green and yellow Post-its.

'So how are you feeling?' Marian was putting plates in the oven, where a tray of roast potatoes was crisping up.

'Great!' Claire said brightly.

'Fab,' Marian nodded with a firm smile.

Claire felt sorry for her. Imagine only having one child and for it to be such a dud.

'And how are you, Jamie?'

'I'm good.' He was distributing Christmas crackers. 'I've loads of training seminars lined up across the European teams when we get back to the office, so I'll be going all over the place!'

A sudden slant to the mouth betrayed Marian's worry, but her tone stayed bright: 'Well, Claire, you can come out here any time and stay with us if you're ... lonely or whatever!'

'Oh sure. Thanks, Mum. It's pretty far with work but yeah, maybe.'

She didn't have the slightest intention of it. She'd be on the train for two hours a day if she was going back and forth to her parents' from the Sweeneys' place in Stoneyhill where she worked. Things would have to reeeeally nosedive for her to do that.

They did before ... The thought rose unbidden and Claire turned from it. *It's different now. I know what's wrong with me. I know how to handle myself.*

'So is Dad ... like ... gonna pop in and say "hi"?' Claire said, eager to change the subject.

'No.' Marian pursed her lips. 'I wasn't allowed to encroach on *his* time on Christmas Day—'

'We asked you if you wanted some trifle!' Claire persisted.

'And you recall I declined,' came Marian's prim response.

'Sure,' Claire replied, defeated.

'Now. Any news? How is Aifric? And the girls? I ran into Connie.' Marian turned to Jamie. 'Aifric's mum and I still do bridge together, even though they're long gone from the estate. Moved down closer to town after the girls went off to college,' she explained. 'Anyway, she was telling me that Aifric's doing some huge rebrand for a drinks company. She's so dynamic.'

'Yeah, she's mad busy.'

Too busy to answer a text, Claire thought darkly. The silence in the Bitch Herd WhatsApp group felt somehow pointed.

By the time midnight was approaching, Claire and Jamie were mercifully freed from the awkward dinner and back cozied up on their black faux leather couch watching *The Day After Tomorrow*. Claire often wondered if there was some kind of mandate that all extortionate Dublin rentals must have at least one horrendous pleather couch. Claire had often made the mistake of sitting on it in shorts – disastrous. If you got up without carefully unpeeling yourself, you'd be nearly skinned. *We need to get one of those universal couch covers; it'd bring the room together,* she thought, adding it to her ever-lengthening mental to-do list. She looked around the room. It was bleak. As if the Dublin rental market wasn't depressing enough, there was orange pine everywhere and main lights blaring above. *We need some lamps,* she noted.

Nadia had mentioned lamps she got somewhere ...

The thought brought her full circle back to the Bitch Herd group chat where the lamp-mention had occurred. Someone must've replied to Claire's text by now. She unlocked the phone and checked. Not a word. She sighed and Jamie looked over.

'What's up? You also pissed off that Dennis Quaid is criminally underused in this movie?' he grinned.

'An excellent point, but no. It's just … I sent a Happy New Year's text to the Bitch Herd,' she said quietly. 'There's like fifteen minutes left in 2022 and no one's said a thing. Not. A. Fucking. Word. I feel like …' She hesitated slightly, not wanting to sound pathetic, but then Jamie cut in, giving voice to her concerns.

'You think they're all out together somewhere? Without you?' he said gently, frowning.

Claire looked across to the telly, where a tidal wave was ploughing through New York City. *There's some dumb metaphor here*, she thought.

'But Claire …' Jamie stroked her hair. 'Did you say you were going to your mum's? Maybe they made a plan and just didn't say cos they knew …' He trailed off. Jamie knew the Bitch Herd were more than capable of letting Claire down.

Claire rustled up a smile. 'Yeah, actually, I think you're right,' she said vaguely, so that they could drop the subject. Jamie could get quite outraged on her behalf.

Claire tried to focus on the movie, but her brain thrummed with theories about her friends. They were having dinner, or maybe they were out at a gig. The not knowing was the worst part.

Maybe one of them's posted something on Insta? Surely they will have. She picked up her phone. *Everyone has to 'gram their fun, how else can they bask in it? Fun unwitnessed by internet followers lacks a certain umami.* She'd know, she thought bitterly. She was usually the viewer supplying said seasoning. Whenever she did go out with them all, *she* did the basking, folded into group selfies and feeling the warm glow of belonging.

She opened Instagram and went to Aifric's profile first.

Aifric was the alpha. She'd been the alpha of every group she'd ever been in since they started Montessori together. Even the teachers seemed to just *get* that Aifric was better than them. She was their superior, essentially. When she insisted that she play both the Virgin Mary and the Angel Gabriel in the nativity play (she wanted to be the lead but she also wanted to wear wings), they obeyed, completely cowed by her, which resulted in a strangely avant-garde take on this quintessentially Irish Catholic rite of passage.

Jamie, being both English and Jewish, thought Claire was taking the piss when she told him that in Irish primary schools, the children do an elaborate re-enactment of Jesus Christ's BIRTH every Christmas. Claire was always a shepherd. She just had that kind of vibe: some people are shepherds, some people are main players and some people – Aifric – are both the lead AND an angel. As children, Aifric's blonde hair and blue eyes and innate instinct for what was cool meant others flocked to her – she pioneered the rip-off trouser craze in fourth class and was an early adopter of the Juicy Couture joggers in second year.

Claire's proximity to Aifric in primary school meant she could bask in some of her reflected light. When they started secondary, new friends appeared – Nadia, Helena and Gillian – all orbiting Aifric like planets do the sun and Claire became just another planet. And as the years went on, her orbit felt further and further from Aifric, especially when Claire went to DIT to study Montessori teaching while they all went off to UCD together.

Now, as an adult, Aifric's hair existed in a permanent immaculate blow-out and her clothes were tailored and chic. Claire's hair was in a permanent bun and her clothes were often covered in glitter and paint after a day with the Sweeney kids, Lila, Frankie and

Sonny. They just didn't seem to have as much in common as they used to.

Aifric's Insta story flicked past. She was certainly out. But it looked like it was a romantic dinner for two with Paul, her equally alpha boyfriend.

Claire went back to the Bitch Herd group chat and held her thumb down on her own Happy New Year's message, just hanging there like a bad smell, then hit 'Info'.

√√ Read
Nadia
4 hours ago
Helena
5 hours ago
Gillian
5 hours ago

√√ Delivered
Aifric
8 hours ago

They've ALL READ IT! What the fuck? Well, except for Aifric.

Somehow it was very *Aifric* to not have read something: banal activities like reading messages were beneath her; she was born better. But the others. They could reply, at least.

Claire flicked back to Insta and was immediately assailed by a shocking, just-shared image. Aifric. An immaculate manicure. And a diamond ring.

'Oh my god!' Claire squealed. She was flooded with equal parts excitement and relief. Aifric wasn't *not answering,* she was *getting engaged.*

Jamie was startled. 'What the hell!'

'Aifric is engaged!'

'Ahh!' Jamie smiled, a little tightly. He had his feelings about Aifric and the Bitch Herd.

'I can't believe one of us is getting married. I've never been a bridesmaid before. Eeeeek!'

'Has she asked you to be bridesmaid?' Jamie's words were careful.

'Well, she hasn't *asked* me yet, but like, I'm her oldest friend.' In Claire's hand, the phone purred with WhatsApp notifications, no doubt the Bitch Herd collectively gushing over Aifric's news. 'There's so much to plan. The dress! The hen! My maid of honour speech!'

'Hmmmmm.' Jamie offered up a tepid little smile, which Claire chose to ignore. She returned to the phone to add a burst of joyful emojis to the cascade of excitement.

'I feel like this gives a whole new vibe to this new year. We'll be doing dress-shopping and countless amounts of prosecco-ing. It's gonna be so fun.'

CHAPTER 2

'Well, if it isn't my sister, the rising star of the Irish podcasting scene!' Abi, Lexi's youngest brother, plonked himself into the passenger seat of her battered grey Saab.

'Alright, no need to mock me, or you can walk to Dad's.' Lexi tucked her long dark hair behind her ears, checked her wing mirror and pulled away from the decidedly unattractive house-share in Inchicore that Abi had moved into just before Christmas. He'd just moved home, after returning from Glasgow, where he'd been studying marine biology for the last few years.

'I'm not mocking,' he insisted. 'I'm merely quoting the article.'

Lexi turned left out of the estate and started down the canal towards the Naas road that would bring them to Hereford, the village where they'd grown up, an hour and a half outside Dublin. The roads still had the deserted post-New Year's vibe, though in another week life would no doubt be kicking off again at its usual frenetic pace. All going well, this year would be her busiest yet. Lexi could feel the anticipation gathering: there was so much to look forward to career-wise. Especially if the piece in *The Cut* was anything to go by.

She just needed to get today over with. The fifth of January was hard every year. *I should be used to it by now. She's gone eighteen years.*

'Lexi?' Abi was looking over.

'Sorry! The article! Yep! I haven't read it, to be honest. You know how it is. They can be so … judgy.' Her podcast, *Your Hot Friend*, wasn't for everyone. The iTunes reviews were either one-star or five-star; nothing in between. Everyone felt strongly about *Your Hot Friend*. It was either 'setting feminism back 200 years' or it was the 'funniest, rawest, say-what-we're-all-thinking' show on the internet.

Lexi was particularly shocked that the piece seemed to have gone so well. She needn't have wasted most of the Christmas break fretting over all the ways the journalist who'd done the interview, a conscientious young Gen Z-er, would pick apart their occasionally controversial show, routinely dubbed 'problematic'.

'She called you the female Joe Rogan.' Abi grinned. 'Which is I'm pretty sure a bad thing, but she also said ye were …' – he consulted his phone – 'probably the last no-bullshit, authentic podcasters on the internet'.

'Yikes! Don't tell me any more – I don't want to know.' Lexi wasn't a fan of reading back over their press. So often it was car crash stuff. Her co-host slash best friend, Amanda, was a liability. Within the confines of their platforms, Amanda's divisive commentary was warmly received. Their listeners, the 'Hotties', applauded Amanda's willingness to say whatever she liked, consequences be damned. The people she offended – everyone from the RTÉ weatherman with whom she had a long-standing beef to the Auschwitz Memorial Museum – labelled her ignorant at best and downright hateful at worst.

'The Jane Rogans!' Abi was shaking his head. 'Guess that's what you and Amanda signed up for.'

Lexi reached over to mess up Abi's dark curls. 'Thank you for the sympathy.' Abi was more like her twin than a brother; there was barely a year between them. They were the youngest of five, though their three older brothers had all scattered for university – Andrew to London, Paulie to Canada and Tristan to Melbourne. They seemed more like strangers on the rare occasions when they did all get together now. Even family Zoom calls were awkward, given that the time-zones didn't even align.

'You don't need sympathy, Lexi! According to *The Cut*, you're one of the "ones to watch" of 2023. Well, you and Amanda. Mad! I take it she's not coming today?' He gestured to the empty back seat.

Lexi smiled. 'Oh, she is. We all had a late one last night and Amanda crashed at mine and Jonathan's, so they're following in Jonathan's car. They'll be down for dinner.'

'You, Jonathan and Amanda are like a throuple!'

Lexi giggled. 'Yuck. Weird. It's more like Amanda is my and Jonathan's wayward child.'

'God,' Abi snorted as he thumbed his phone, playing Tetris. 'Imagine you and Jonathan with a child!'

Abi had never been much of a fan of Jonathan's, not even when they first got together. She'd met Jonathan at a media event five years ago, when *Your Hot Friend* was in its infancy. She and Amanda had been downing free drinks in a committed fashion and Jonathan and Lexi fell into conversation late on in the night.

'She your co-host, then?' He'd nodded at Amanda, who was lolling like a bladder on a stick on the couch beside her.

'Yeah. She's not usually like this,' Lexi had lied. She was always like this – a drink, a line, a pill, and Amanda was away. 'She didn't have dinner.'

'Right,' Jonathan had grinned. 'Listen. Don't let her change. She's your golden goose. Controversial, hot, messy. People won't be able to look away.'

Lexi was a bit miffed at the 'hot' bit, but he quickly followed up.

'Not as hot as you, of course.' He'd stared down at her. She was wearing her trademark cropped band tee, no bra and grubby trackies. She'd basked in the laser focus of his attention. Jonathan wasn't everyone's idea of hot – he had a quiff of grey hair and sharp features, but his confidence was magnetic. He was thirty-four then – nine years older than her – and he made her feel gorgeous.

That night, Lexi and Jonathan had fucked in a hurry in the jacks while Amanda remained splayed on the couch outside in the dim lounge, music blaring.

'Is a baby SO hard to imagine?' Lexi shot back at Abi, frowning at the featureless motorway rising ahead of her. 'I'm thirty; he's nearly forty. We're looking for a house together. It's not that crazy.'

Even though screwing in a toilet was a slightly squalid beginning, they'd soon found out that they had a lot in common. Jonathan's mum was gone too, though unlike Lexi's, she hadn't died: she'd left the family when Jonathan was nine. He'd barely seen her in the years since. Lexi suspected that this early trauma was what had given Jonathan his toughness, but his slightly brash exterior belied an unexpectedly caring side. After a few dates, he'd started to relax and Lexi found herself falling for him. He was particularly encouraging of her career, which no one in her family had shown any interest in. In the first year, he travelled tons, managing tours for some of the biggest acts in the pop world, but as *Your Hot Friend*'s listenership grew, he suggested he become their manager. That way he could stop touring and they could move in together and actually live like a normal couple, plus they could get serious about the show, which Jonathan believed had the potential to go international. He even made a formal pitch to Lexi and Amanda, with a comprehensive plan for their world domination. And so his role in Lexi's life expanded from boyfriend to boyfriend-manager.

'Baby? What does that mean ... ?' Abi had turned to examine her face. 'A baby, Lex ... fuuuuuck.'

'Well, no, we're not ... trying or anything.' Lexi shook her head. 'It definitely would not play well for the show; it's already bad enough that I've been coupled up for so long.'

Abi laughed. 'Gotta keep the listeners happy! Also, you've already got enough tied up with Jonathan: boyfriend, manager ...'

Abi had questioned the wisdom of this joint occupation of Jonathan's before, but since Amanda, who was the one most at risk of getting screwed by the set-up, wasn't remotely worried about it, Lexi had dismissed his concerns. And it was undeniable that Jonathan was the best thing to have happened to the show. They'd started the podcast for a laugh, just recording their post-night out drunken conversations, and were initially as surprised as everyone else when they immediately gained a dedicated following. Back then it had all been pretty slapdash – they weren't making any money off it and had no idea how to – but once Jonathan had come on board and started brokering sponsorship deals, they'd both been able to ditch their day jobs pretty quickly. Since graduating, Lexi'd worked in marketing and Amanda had worked in a restaurant called Chez Sandrines alongside doing a bit of modelling, which in Ireland at the time largely consisted of slightly embarrassing photocalls: posing in bikinis on Grafton Street with a variety of bizarre objects. Jonathan had negotiated brand deals for them. Organised their live tours. Even sorted their taxes every year, as their earnings jumped from a paltry few hundred a month to a decent five figures.

About halfway home, Lexi pulled in for petrol and for Abi to grab snacks. She tried to ignore the waft of his deli chicken-fillet roll as she got the green juice marked 'Thursday PM' from the cooler bag in the back seat. Before Christmas, Amanda had announced that Lexi was getting the 'love chub' from having been with Jonathan too long and had signed them both up to the service. Every day you could have two juices and one meal.

'Not fucked up at all,' Lexi had quipped when Amanda first introduced the idea. Still, Amanda was right: the fact was, 'hotness' wasn't just a 'state of mind', as they endlessly proclaimed on the podcast. It took work. Lexi knew Amanda wasn't being mean; she was being practical. So, every day, Lexi picked which meals she would be 'drinking' and which she'd be 'eating'. *It's not the worst – everyone has something about their job that they hate,* she reflected. *We're having dinner with Dad tonight,* she told herself sternly. *That's today's food.*

She and Amanda always made sure to eat around people; it wasn't something they'd discussed explicitly, but there was an understanding. Diets weren't on trend any more. Lexi and Amanda were the hot girls that ate! Their *Your Hot Friend* feed on Insta was full of them necking milkshakes and tonguing doughnuts. They never finished any of it, of course, and lately Amanda had read an article about some influencers using diabetes medication for weight loss and had been pushing for them to try it.

Lexi was sick of the whole thing. Never eating enough meant she was always thinking about food and on nights that Jonathan was out, she often gorged.

Lexi's WhatsApp buzzed with a picture message from Jonathan and she grinned at the sight of her two favourite people, Amanda and Jonathan, pulling faces in Jonathan's car.

Absolutely hangin' but hittin' the road cuz we love you so much! (Don't forget to share the Ones to Watch piece on social!!!!)

Lexi moved away from the car and pulled out her phone to do a quick story for Insta.

'Hey guys! Super exciting news today! *Your Hot Friend* has been named one of the "ones to watch in 2023" by *The Cut*! Eeeeek, can't believe it. We'll definitely be hittin the voddies during our record later so expect an even more chaotic episode than usual!!'

She finished the story and added the link to the article. Then, frowning, she dragged a filter across her smiling face on the phone. The voddies would probably have to wait till they were back in Dublin. It would be better not to drink down home.

Her dad, Eamon, had been drinking again over the Christmas period. Thank god for Abi and Jonathan and Amanda. Without them, going home this weekend would have been way too bleak. It was becoming harder and harder every year to cope with the cycle of drinking and quitting, drinking and quitting. With four brothers, in theory, she could share the burden of her dad, but Andrew, Paulie and Tristan rarely came home, claiming they were too tied up with work, so in the last few years she'd often had to go on her own And as they'd all been contributing financially since Eamon, who was now seventy, retired from teaching, Lexi felt she couldn't complain about it.

At least Abi was back in the country now. They'd gone down together for Christmas and had to watch as their dad got steadily more bleary and maudlin in front of the TV.

'Are you and Amanda catching up with any of the school crowd later?' Abi cut across her thoughts. 'Eddie and Deano are doing a thing in Malloy's for their engagement.'

'Oh yeah! Me and Manda have to record an episode real quick but then will deffo head down. It has been so long since I've seen anyone.'

She and Abi arrived just before four p.m. and let themselves in the side door. Inside, the light was already sliding from the small rooms in her dad's cramped bungalow and Lexi's chest tightened. When her mum Angela had been alive it had been nice, though always small for their family of seven. After Angela was gone it deteriorated and Lexi was ashamed to bring school friends over; only Amanda ever came.

Though her apartment with Jonathan in Dún Laoghaire was gorgeous – white everything and views over the harbour – when she and Jonathan finally bought a place, it'd be more than just a foot on the ladder, it'd be the first time since she was little she'd have somewhere that actually felt like home. Of course, they'd been outbid on every house they'd tried for and their savings, while decent, could be better. They'd come close to securing a big deal with a huge podcasting platform, Podify, the previous summer but it seemed to have fizzled and died, though Jonathan said he'd follow up with them soon.

In the living room, Lexi took off her big Puffa jacket and leaned down to hug her dad, who hadn't even stood when they came in. 'Hiya, Dad.'

She did a speed-scan of the room but saw no bottles or cans anywhere, though it was as dingy as ever and the ashtray was brimming. He also smelt fine: his usual Pears soap and tobacco scent.

Abi shuffled around her to hug his dad and a micro-glance passed between her and her brother, the shorthand used by children of drinkers to communicate that things seem fine, though always with the implication that at any moment things might turn suddenly.

'How were the roads?' Eamon asked stiffly.

'Grand, Dad.' Abi chucked his coat over the balding corduroy couch and started gathering up the scattered newspapers and abandoned post.

'I'm gonna start dinner,' Lexi announced, her bright voice a stark contrast to the leaden feeling in her limbs – it was a heaviness that always settled over her the second she arrived in her childhood home and wouldn't lift until she was back on the motorway.

While she was relieved to have the distraction of making the dinner, it was also unfathomably sad cooking in the kitchen that used to be her mother's domain. Nothing had changed in eighteen years. The same utensils crowded the drawers. The same appliances stood on the creamy-beige plastic countertop.

Though the room was preserved, frozen in time, a stubborn layer of grease coated everything and charted the room's neglect.

The grease skin had begun to form in Lexi's early teens and all her attempts to clean were futile, as her dad refused to join the effort. Lexi was convinced the room had actually got smaller from the build-up of fat on the walls. On every visit she tried to beat back the advance of filth, but the next time she came it would have once again gained ground.

Lexi sorted through the bags she'd brought in from the car – they were having a roast leg of lamb with garlic and rosemary potatoes and minty peas. She turned on the oven to get it warming and started to peel the potatoes, remembering the time she'd told Amanda about how the counter was so dirty the tea towel had stuck to it. Amanda had been flummoxed. 'Just wipe it, Lex!' she'd said. Lexi hadn't bothered to go into how cleaning historical filth was not a simple task. Amanda had a very nice, ordinary family who would not need a power sander to clean the kitchen counter.

As she started to fill a large pot with water, Lexi noticed a strange smell seeping into the room. It was coming from the oven and her heart sank, realising immediately what was producing the slightly rotten, burning odour. Holding her breath, she opened the oven, her suspicions immediately confirmed. Her dad had left the Christmas leftovers there. She slammed the oven closed again, turned it off and hurried out to the side door for a few gulps of air. *Fucking rank,* she fumed. *I told him once it was all cooled down to wrap it and put it in the fridge. He's like a fucking child. Christmas was nearly two weeks ago.*

'WHAT is that smell?' Abi appeared in the hall behind her, covering his nose and mouth with his arm.

'He left the goddamn meat tray from Christmas in the oven.'

'Oh, Jesus.' Abi grimaced. 'Though at least …' He dropped his voice. 'At least, there's no sign of cans or anything.'

Lexi wasn't in the mood for any 'look on the bright side' bullshit. She was pissed off. 'We have to get this sorted before Amanda and Jonathan get here.' Even though Amanda and Jonathan knew about her dad, she couldn't bear to expose him like this. It was humiliating.

'Is something burning?' Her dad had ducked his head out of the living room.

'Yeah, the rancid meat you left in your oven, Dad!' Lexi snapped.

His face froze, then crumpled. 'Ah, Jesus, Lexi, I'm so—'

Lexi didn't want to hear it. 'You two can go get some stuff from the Indian in town when it's time for supper. There's no way I'm cooking in this oven. I'll take care of it.'

After Lexi had finished the disgusting task of ridding the oven of spoiled meat, she checked the balance in her current account and decided then and there to shell out for a deep-cleaning service she'd read about. Any time in the past when she'd tried to convince her dad to get a cleaner, he'd argued, but this time he couldn't pretend it wasn't necessary.

She found the website, which described their service as 'trauma cleaning'. *Pretty apt,* Lexi thought. They cleaned up homes where bodies had been left undiscovered for days. The body in her dad's house had been gone for years, but the trauma remained.

Her mum had died at home. Angela had withered over a miserable, wet autumn, no longer bustling around cooking and singing along to the radio. The cancer had driven her out of her kitchen and into the hospital bed that had been set up in the 'good' room. When Angela died, they swapped the bed out for the coffin and waked her over the course of a bright though sharply cold January day. The loveliness of the weather had felt obscene to Lexi.

This shouldn't be happening today, she'd thought petulantly from her spot on the hall stairs. She hadn't had a hope of getting in to see her mother with all the relations and neighbours clogging up every doorway and inch of space.

'Why do we have to have all these people here?' she'd complained to Aunty Joan, who just shushed her and told her she was too old for 'this attitude'.

The men from the funeral home brought the coffin to the church the next morning, but Lexi couldn't shake the feeling that her mother had been left behind in the house. On the third night of being a girl without a mother, she went downstairs at two a.m. and sat in the 'good' room, where fathomless shadows draped every corner. On some level, she was looking for her mum, but the gap where the bed and then the coffin had stood was so stark and empty it triggered a rising panic in her body.

Gasping, she had fled to the kitchen, where the light was so bright, it took her eyes a few minutes to adjust. Then she saw a strange thing. The second drawer in the old pine dresser was hanging open. She went to close it and saw a collection of the battered utensils her mother had always cooked with. She remembered having the thought: *Ah, here you are.*

She had felt bad for reducing her mum's life to a bockety old whisk and a few wooden spoons. But time and grief steal people's memories and now the whisk and spoons seemed more real than her mother did.

Once Lexi had completed the online booking form for the

cleaners, she went over to the pine dresser and pulled out the spoons and whisk – while she hated being in the old kitchen, she did like holding the things her mum once held. She put them in her bag.

When I find my home, I'll put these in my drawers, she promised herself.

An hour later and the smell had mostly gone. Building a fire in the living room helped drive away lingering whiff, and Lexi, Abi, Eamon, Jonathan and Amanda were happily settled on the sofas, cradling warming bowls of rogan josh and butter chicken.

The house felt transformed with the bustle of Amanda and Jonathan gabbing away, and even Eamon seemed livelier.

'It's very exciting about the article.' He picked up Lexi's hand and gave it a squeeze and she thawed a little. She knew part of why she was so annoyed was because she felt guilty. *I should've stayed longer over Christmas. I should be down here more often.*

'Your mum would be very proud too.' He smiled sadly.

'Course she wouldn't have a fucking breeze what a podcast is!' Abi mugged.

'Sure I barely do!' Eamon chuckled. 'But I'm proud. Very proud.' He raised his glass of Fanta.

'We should toast to Mum too.' Lexi raised her own glass. 'We miss you, Mum, and we love you.'

After dinner, she and Amanda grabbed their mics and left the men to watch *The Late Late Show*.

In Lexi's bedroom, they assessed the acoustics.

'Maybe the wardrobe?' Amanda gestured at the small walk-in, still packed with Lexi's teenage clothes and belongings.

'Yah, we'll have to sit on the floor, but at least the clothes will limit any echo.'

Amanda produced some vodka from her bag and poured out two generous helpings. Then she noticed Lexi's face. 'Oh, would you prefer if we didn't? Cos of ...' She nodded to the bedroom door and the house beyond.

Lexi chewed her lip, then picked up her glass. 'Sure, in here is fine. Dad will be gone to bed by the time we're done, plus it'll get us in the mood for the pub later!'

'Oh ...' Amanda leaned over and started plugging her mic into their portable recorder. 'I texted Deano and said we probably wouldn't make it with the record and all.'

'But it's only like nine.' Lexi checked her phone. 'We'll be done by ten?'

'Yeah, but ...' Amanda looked unenthused. 'Can you really be arsed? Chats with the "down home" crowd. It's all a bit stale, no? They'll all be shiteing on about mortgages and getting their gardens done.'

'But—'

'AND,' Amanda cut in, her bored expression switching to glee. 'We've got the Club Electra opening tomorrow night! We have to be on form for that. Paid appearance and a chance to mingle with the media sluts – that producer who was talking about the *Your Hot Friend* documentary will be there.'

'Oh god, that'll never happen – TV people are all talk!' Lexi laughed. 'But stop changing the subject. We should go. We never see anyone ...'

'Let's play it by ear!' Amanda picked up her mic and switched abruptly into her pod voice. 'Hey, Hotties, happy new year blaa blaa, it's your fave hot friends here, Lexi and Amanda, with another free-wheeling, no-holes-barred show! Though my holes are never barred—'

Lexi grabbed her mic and slid effortlessly into *Your Hot Friend* mode. 'It's HOLDS-barred,' Lexi interrupted. 'Trust you to think it's holes.'

'Well, whatevs, bar up your holes, Hotties, and buckle in, cos we're doing a "New Year, New Me" special, though obviously with the *Your Hot Friend* sauce. We're doing self-betterment but with a difference. We're letting you, our dear listeners, tell us where we're going wrong and what we can be doing better.'

'Yep,' Lexi picked up the thread. 'We're going to trawl through the comments on Rants.ie and take advice from some of our biggest haters. It's gonna be Feelings Roulette and I'm scared.' She laughed.

'Okay, you're first up, Lexi.' Amanda was scrolling on her phone. 'Here we go. @CameForTheTea says, "Anyone noticed how safe and boring Lexi's become? She's got this adult persona and she never like SAYS anything any more, it's all just talking about couples' getaways with Jonathan. Probably all spon, though she never says it. Bet they never have sex even, have you seen him?"'

'Okay ouch!' Lexi laughed, hoping it sounded convincing.

You get the audience you deserve, Lexi often thought, especially when a bit soul-searchy after a few voddies, but *Your Hot Friend* was paying for the voddies and every single other thing in her life. Besides, who else got to have a job where they hung out with their best friend all the time? It was the dream.

And she and Amanda were untouchable in terms of listenership figures in Ireland and the UK. Their crossover to UK audiences – thanks to a few well-placed celeb fans in Amanda's old modelling agency – meant that no small-fry Irish podcast could ever come close to their success.

'Well, Lexi?' Amanda was twirling her messy bleached hair and smirking over at her. 'Have you become an adult, aka a boring bitch?'

'Fuck off! I have just become less "twenty-five"!' Lexi defended herself. 'I'm over talking about giving blowies on the back of the 46a all the time.'

'Don't worry, babes, here's a Hottie defending you and your boring ways.' Amanda read on. '@LisaC says: "Lexi's not boring, she's the straight man. Amanda needs her. If they were both 'Amandas', the podcast would be chaos. Imagine the shows! It'd be depraved." There now! That's nice to hear. You being boring is actually making the pod better.'

'Alright, backhanded compliment much?' Lexi pulled up her own phone. 'Your turn. @SeeYouNever says: "Amanda is like a car crash, a complete mess but you cannot look away. Did you see her twerking on the lads collecting for charity on Grafton Street last week? She's like 30, morto for ya luv." Amanda? Thoughts?'

'Those little rascals loved it. And I got their consent!'

'They were transition-year students!' Lexi howled. 'You'd have needed written permission from their parents!'

'Oh shite,' Amanda giggled. 'Alright, so our first goal for 2023 is for you to be less boring and me to be more boring. Jesus, the Hotties are impossible to please.'

Lexi laughed along but she couldn't ignore the familiar wriggle of dread, like eels slithering over one another in her stomach.

'Amanda, maybe we should edit that,' she said quickly. 'I shouldn't have said they were transition-years; it sounds really bad.'

'What?' Amanda looked irritated. 'Oh my god, it's so obviously a joke, bébé. The Hotties know that. And who gives a fuck if a few uptight wagons get het up and start calling me a paedo? Don't let them wreck our buzz.'

'Okay, okay, I won't cut it.' Lexi glanced at the recorder to make a mental note of the timestamp: five minutes eight seconds. Lexi did most of the editing and Amanda never listened back, so she wouldn't know that Lexi had taken it out.

Amanda was right, of course: it was just a joke and you didn't host a free-wheeling, unfiltered twice-weekly podcast without something you'd said on mic blowing up every now and again. However, it was happening with an exhausting frequency as their following grew and as Amanda got more kamikaze with her ranting.

'I think people are sick of all the nicey-nice basics all the time,' Amanda continued into her mic. 'The Hotties aren't here for bland bullshit. If they wanted that they could go listen to one of the wanky wellness pods the other influencers are doing – *The Holistic Hole* or whatever they're called.' Lexi took another look at the time stamp. No way was she letting any of this go out on the show.

With the podcast, Lexi could at least curtail some of Amanda's more outré comments, but on her social media Amanda was a law unto herself. Only a week ago she'd announced on Insta that she was sick of waiters being so uppity all the time because 'Hello!!! It's the service industry, you're serving me, honey.' Fuck me, Lexi thought at the memory of the ensuing debacle. The tweets cascaded for two days straight.

> @sweetasfry: That c*nt on *Your Hot Friend* down on wait staff is sick-making, they're underpaid and undervalued by spoilt bitches like her.
>
> @benjiplatt88: Next level ignorance from the *YHF* one this week though when are they NOT spewing ill-informed nonsense.
>
> @jeno-d-w-y-e-r: Ewww. They are the WORST. Unsubbed long ago.

There was even a Twitter account called @YourThickFriends dedicated to chronicling their various crimes and misdemeanours.

Lexi was very conflicted in these scenarios. She didn't like all the things Amanda said and she did sometimes correct her on mic but if something exploded, no matter how much Lexi might agree with the angry responses, she couldn't ever come out and say that. She couldn't abandon Amanda and leave her on her own to deal with it. What are friends for if not to suffer through endless micro-cancellations with you? Though the pile-ons definitely didn't make Amanda as anxious as they did Lexi.

'Okay, okay.' Lexi repositioned her mic. 'Let's not have you slapping us straight into a Twitter furore when the year has barely even begun.'

'Awwww, Lexi, the listeners are right, you're no fun any more.'

Another hour and the show was wrapped.

'I am wrecked,' Amanda announced, tidying up the mics. She

flopped onto Lexi's bed. 'Let's just cosy up and watch *The Hills* like old times. We need a night off to replenish.'

'I feel bad, though.' Lexi scrolled through their school group chat, where people were posting pics from Malloy's. Abi was down there – because they were so close in age, they had a lot of the same friends. Still, despite the guilt, Lexi felt utterly drained and the thought of hitting the pub did not appeal.

'Okay,' Lexi agreed. 'I'll go tell Jonathan we're sleeping in here.' Amanda was right, nights with the school friends did feel a bit forced; their lives were just so different.

Moments later she and Amanda were tucked under the duvet, with the laptop balanced between them, and Amanda was posting a pic of them to Insta.

> Cuddled up with the only gal I need @LexiLexiLexi @MyHotFriend #TheHills #NoughtiesTeens #BFFS

'Does every last second of our friendship have to be mined for content?!' Lexi laughed lightly.

'That's being a celeb-besty, bébé,' Amanda kissed her on the cheek.

CHAPTER 3

'I cannot believe you won't be in work with me on Monday!' Joanne's friend Aoife was driving them around the IKEA car park. It was completely jammers on the chilly first Friday afternoon of January. 'I would fucking kill to take two months off,' Aoife said as she swung down another row of parked cars.

'It's maternity leave.' Joanne laughed, pushing her short blonde hair behind her ears. 'From what I hear, it's not exactly a holiday. It's not even a particularly long maternity leave, but it's all we can afford.'

Her impending leave and the baby that would be coming with it was the reason they were in IKEA. Aoife was going to be the muscle while Joanne lumbered around pointing at the various things the internet told her she'd need to operate a baby: towels, changing mat, cot.

'Any opportunity to stay in your pyjamas all day is a holiday,' Aoife insisted. 'You're so lucky you won't be on the Bantry Butter campaign any more. If I have to design one more logo for them to shit all over, I will scream or do some kind of dirty protest with their stupid Cork butter.'

Six years ago, Aoife and Joanne had landed their dream gig as the two-woman graphic design department in the Your Story advertising agency, straight out of art college. Bar annual leave, they had barely had a day in work without each other.

'Hmmm, a greasy protest!' Joanne giggled. 'Murder to clean up. Look, there's a spot.' She pointed to a parking space.

'It's a family space, though.' Aoife frowned.

'Eh, hello!' Joanna pointed to her gargantuan nine-month bump. 'This thing is practically cooked; I think we qualify.'

'How many more weeks? Three?'

'Nearly three.' Joanne chewed her bottom lip and tried not to betray the sudden surge of fear that accompanied any mention of D-day. Being pregnant was a mind fuck: she'd had no idea you could be so terrified and so excited all at the same time; what a cocktail. 'Three weeks till my baby tears me a new one.' Joanne tried to sound relaxed.

Aoife flicked a glance over at her, then steered them into the spot. 'It's all gonna be fine,' she said soothingly as she spun the wheel.

Joanne smiled. You couldn't pretend with your best friend of ten years.

'You're going to be the best mum,' Aoife continued. 'And the baby will have all the aunties with me and the gals.'

'I know, I know.' Joanne opened the passenger door and began the process of heaving herself out of the car, with Aoife giving a jokey push from behind.

Aoife pulled her shiny straight blonde hair into a ponytail and hopped out of the car. 'Remind me again what contraception you and Bert were using? So I don't screw myself over!' she called.

'Diaphragm and pulling out.' Joanne righted herself. 'I'm a cautionary whale.'

Joanne had met Bert when she was in art college with Aoife and their other pals, Kate and Aideen, who also specialised in graphic design. Bert, fresh out of culinary college, had actually worked in the campus cafe. They started seeing each other and within the month, much to the disbelief and chagrin of all their friends, they'd moved in together, to a miniscule bedsit in Rathmines. She was twenty, he was twenty-two, and from the get-go they were inseparable. They shared everything: their single bed, money, friend groups, weed. And now, eight years later, they were sharing DNA! It wasn't planned as such, but it was hardly a big surprise either. They weren't exactly militant about birth control.

'We were always gonna have kids,' Bert had explained to the college gang, bursting with excitement, the night they announced the news in their little rented cottage in Portobello. 'We're just hoppin' on the train early'.

Twenty-eight isn't even that early, she reminded herself. Her mother, Emer, had her at twenty.

Bert was thrilled and quite impressed with his virality – as he told everyone from the guy who came around to clean the windows of the houses on their street to the woman in the laundrette.

In a mild panic, Joanne had googled 'abortion'. And she may even have gone through with it had Bert not announced the pregnancy to his mother during one of their weekly 'state of the nation' phone calls before Joanne could bring it up with him.

The news had charged through the family WhatsApp, sparking a burst of joyful GIFs, so she'd kept schtum about the fact that her thoughts had ever drifted in that direction, and as the weeks passed she found that excitement had started to overtake her anxiety until she was eventually kind of glad that it had happened like that. In a way a 'happy accident' was easier than consciously deciding to have a baby would've been.

Upstairs in the showrooms, Aoife pushed the trolley through the various 'mock rooms'. 'Are you guys still talking about moving?' she asked.

'Definitely not soon.' Even though the cottage was tiny, Joanne didn't think she could take any more change. 'Mum says babies are grand in a small place. It's not till they're walking and wrecking the gaff that you really need more space.'

'It's already tight for you and Bert, though. Rude of him to be six foot four!'

Joanne giggled, assessing a changing table and wondering if they could get away without one. Where the hell would it go? The cottage was sweet, but there were only four rooms: bedroom, toilet, kitchen and living room.

'We'll be fine.' Joanne didn't really like to think about moving. Renting anywhere bigger would have to be further out of town and away from their friends and both their jobs. Bert cheffed in the Morton, a five-star hotel on the quays, and the Your Story office was five minutes from their front door.

'Would you move in with your mum?'

Joanne winced. Her mother, Emer, had a lot on her plate with Joanne's three younger half-sisters, who were all teenagers and all at tricky moments in the hellish adolescent journey.

Joanne was her mother's own happy accident. Joanne's dad had been over on holiday and he'd been long gone by the time she realised she was pregnant. Emer was extremely touchy about the fact that she hadn't caught his last name; she wasn't even clear on whether he was French or Belgian. 'He could even have been French-Canadian,' she'd wail whenever the subject came up – usually when Joanne was good naturedly slagging her mum.

Joanne hadn't missed having a dad as such, though she occasionally wondered if it was a buried trauma that would one day rear its head. She had her stepdad, Ronan, who had come into their lives when Joanne was ten. She'd loved him from the start – he was a calm and capable type – and when baby Jess was born, Joanne felt as though they were pretty much the same as any other family in the estate.

'I couldn't do that to her! Mum's in a pit of volatile teenagers. Jess has the Leaving this year, Sylvia's doing the Junior Cert and Dawn has entered her Bitch Era. She's halfway through first year, hating it and taking it out on everyone in a four-mile radius. Plus Skerries is ages from work and all you guys.'

They were now through the showroom and hitting the warehouse part of the IKEA journey. Joanne held the trolley steady as Aoife heaved in the flat-pack wooden cot and threw a sheer white canopy after it.

'Definitely don't need that,' Joanne remarked.

'It's to shield the poor baby from you and Bert getting carnal!'

'Then I won't be needing it before 2040. Also what do you *think* of us? We won't do it with the baby in the room; we'll put the baby out in the yard when we're getting carnal!'

Both their phones buzzed with a notification in their girls' group chat, currently called Fuck Keto, though the name changed every few months with the ebb and flow of various in-jokes.

Joanne chose two sets of sheets for the cot while Aoife checked her phone.

'Oh my god.' She looked up. 'Kate says they've a spare ticket for the Pillow Queens!'

'Cool.' Joanne smiled. Standing at a gig sounded horrendous; she couldn't wait to get home to her lovely couch and a few episodes of *One Born Every Minute*.

'Thing is, though …' Aoife was looking a bit awkward. 'I'd probably have to get out of here pretty sharpish. It's in Malahide Castle. And it's five already. I need to go home beforehand … and the traffic …'

'But you drove.' Joanne looked at the loaded trolley. 'How will I get home? The whole point of this is you help me carry stuff and drop me home.'

'Yeah … but …'

Aoife was now looking mildly pleading and Joanne felt a flare of irritation.

'Could Bert come and get you?' Aoife asked. 'It's just yours is in the complete opposite direction and like, yanno, it's not every night that the Pillow Queens are playing.'

Joanne gazed stonily down at the floor, her bump completely eclipsing her feet.

'Fine. I can call Bert.' What else could she say? And maybe Aoife did have a point. *It's not like she's bailing to go to the pub or something. Gigs are one-off things … though the Pillow Queens are from Dublin, they'll play again …* Aoife's smothering hug snuffed out Joanne's aggrieved little thoughts.

'Will you at least get me checked through the tills? I can't lift these.' Joanne knocked on the large, flat box containing the cot.

'Of course, of course.' Aoife took over the trolley again. 'You call Bert. I'll find the drawers.'

Once they'd got through the checkout, Aoife couldn't escape quick enough.

'You sure it's okay if I head on?' she called, backing towards the car park lift.

'Yeah.' Joanne gave a sulky shrug, which Aoife either didn't notice or was opting to ignore.

'And I'll see you for the baby shower tomorrow night!' Aoife was now stabbing the button to call the lift. 'I'm sure Bert won't be long.' She waved.

Bert arrived two hours later.

Joanne had passed the time moored on a deeply uncomfortable chair, seething to an almost aerobic level. *Why say you're going to help then fucking leave?* She could feel tears building and that made her even more enraged. She was not usually a crier, but pregnancy hormones were no joke. She felt like she'd been slightly off her face on feelings for ages now. She could barely remember what it was like to be 'normal'.

'Hey-hey!' Bert appeared and bent to give her a hug.

Joanne stiffened. 'Bert, I know this is going to sound unfair and irrational, but I am liable to lash out right now. And it's not about you. But I just think it would be best if you don't touch me or speak to me until I am home, on the couch, eating chocolate.' She hauled herself up to standing.

'Totally understandable.' Bert nodded, raking a hand through his auburn curls and then, like a man with a death wish, continued to talk. 'Can't believe Aoife fecked off.' He steered the trolley towards the lifts. 'Not on. *I* could've come to help. I *wanted* to come on the IKEA trip.'

'Bert!' They stepped into the lift and Joanne pressed the button.

'Ah yes, ssssshhhhh!' He put a finger to his lips. 'Gotcha. Love the sound of silence. It calms the mind.'

He continued talking as Joanne stepped neatly back out of the lift.

'Joanne? Where are you—'

The doors closed on him and Joanne headed for the stairs. She'd meet him down there; she didn't trust herself in a confined space with him in this, her own current Bitch Era.

'Nothing's going to change,' Joanne declared the next night at the baby shower from hell.

'Of course it won't, darl.' Aoife's response echoed slightly, the acoustics of the toilet bowl amplifying her voice and giving it a slightly ominous undertone.

Joanne rejigged her grip on Aoife's hair to pull her head up a bit from where it was sliding further down into the toilet bowl. She wasn't overly gentle. *Hope the gig was good,* she thought darkly. Aoife spat, then her body shuddered as another gush of regurgitated slop hit the water.

'Oh god.' Joanne turned her head away. Nobody actively enjoyed assisting at a drunken vomiting session but it was particularly difficult given her gag reflex had remained sensitive even after the morning sickness was supposed to be over. Also crouching on the floor with an eight pound baby stuffed into your bladder was far from ideal.

'This is so fun, I'm so glad we did it,' Aoife said, eyes closed.

'Yeah,' Joanne agreed without enthusiasm, watching a string of murky saliva latch onto her friend's chin.

A little snore escaped Aoife and Joanne decided to knock off on friend duty. She struggled to her feet and, leaving Aoife draped over the toilet, made her way to the bedroom of the large hotel suite they'd rented to surprise her.

The start of the night had been wholesome. They'd had sweets and cake. Aoife had shaved Joanne's legs as she now couldn't get down past her belly. They also painted her toenails for the same reason. Her friends then proceeded to consume a lot of prosecco and some cocaine which they had absolutely delighted in snorting off her bump. 'Just what precious memories are made of,' Joanne had remarked dryly. Now a mere six hours later, half the girls were passed out and the other half were deep in frenetic coke-fuelled heart-to-hearts – unbearable for anyone not on drugs to participate in.

They could have toned it down for my fucking baby shower, she thought as she picked her way towards the bedroom.

They weren't crazy into drugs but they had a tendency to get carried away on occasion. So did Joanne to be fair but pregnancy had completely put paid to that. Now she was the sober responsible one. Weird.

Joanne had known it was going to descend into chaos the second the espresso martinis were ordered after dinner in Miro's, the hotel restaurant. That was when they'd announced that they were having a 'sleepover' in a suite they'd booked. Joanne, seeing where the night was headed, had wanted to leave immediately.

'Come home,' Bert had urged her on the phone. 'You know what they're like. It'll devolve into absolute debauchery and you'll be left catching someone's sick in your bare hands.'

His prediction hadn't been far off, in fairness.

'What are you even doing home?' she'd asked.

Not to be outdone, the lads half of their gang had organised a baby shower for Bert too.

'Ah I've been home hours, the lads were going on to Sketchers for more messing but I wanted to get back and get some of the IKEA stuff put together. Wait till you see the cot. It is so cute! C'mon back and I'll make you tea and a crisp sandwich.'

'I have to stay,' she'd told him. 'I don't want them to think that everything's going to change all of a sudden.'

'Everything *is* going to change,' he'd replied with enthusiasm. 'Little Bert or Bertina is coming and we're going to be parents!'

'I'm aware,' Joanne had snapped.

She wasn't trying to pick a fight, she was just testy – worn out because along with her excitement at being pregnant had come unexpected and *debilitating* worry. Round and around her head all day, the questions stabbed at her brain like little knives: What if I'm a crap mum? What if it's a crap baby? What if it ruins our relationship?

In the bedroom of the suite, Joanne found that Erica and Iseult were asleep on the bed. Fucking brilliant. She walked to the side where Iseult was lying and rolled her friend up onto her side, then lay down at the edge of the bed and let Iseult flop back down on top of her like a fleshy meat blanket.

I am never doing this again, she vowed. Bert was right, it was obvious things were going to change whether she wanted them to or not. She just wished she could see how and prepare mentally. Her chest felt constricted. Every time she thought about the birth and beyond, it was just an expanse of unknown and she was hit with a kind of emotional vertigo. *Everything's going to change.*

Each word seemed to twist the vice around her chest tighter.

CHAPTER 4

It had been over a week since the 'New Year, New Me' episode in which Lexi had vowed to get less adult and boring and yet here she was, on a steely mid-January Saturday morning, doing the most adult thing she could think of: house viewings.

Jonathan was beside her, pinballing between apps. He'd been on his phone since they'd parked the car back on Thomas Street in Dublin's city centre.

She gazed at him. 'What's going on?' With soundbites from their shows constantly being circulated out of context (and, let's face it, sometimes in context) on social media, Lexi was always poised for a take-down. But his expression was one of excitement – thank god.

'Nothing, nothing! I will tell you all in the fullness of time.' He flashed a grin.

'So there's something to tell?! You've been so mysterious all week. Is it a new sponsor for the pod?'

'Now, now ...' He rounded on her and pulled her close. 'Don't be spoiling the surprise! I have a whole bit planned.'

'Fine.' She feigned exasperation and then brushed his lips with hers.

They resumed walking, following the blue dot on the Maps app that would lead them to a fairly ho-hum apartment block, where they'd be looking at a boxy one-bed not much bigger than their current place. But this was what they could stretch to; everyone had to start somewhere.

They made their way through the streets of red-brick terraced cottages that criss-crossed Dublin's Liberties behind the iconic Guinness brewery.

'It's gorgeous here, isn't it?' Jonathan pointed down to their right towards a cobbled square with a railed-off grotto to the Virgin Mary in the centre.

'It's like it's from a different time.' Lexi followed his arm.

'So many great spots for Insta posts,' Jonathan remarked, nodding at a wall of very slick street art ahead. 'You should get a few snaps for the socials after we're done at the viewing. Though you're looking a bit basic ...' He took in her outfit – chunky boots, black jeans and a petrol-green leather bomber with a fur-trim hood.

'Thanks!' Lexi summoned a stiff laugh. She didn't always love his 'feedback', it was a downside of him being both her manager and her boyfriend. 'Just say I look nice like a normal boyfriend!' she admonished him.

'Lexi, if you're letting the brand down in terms of aesthetics then it has to be said,' came his pragmatic reply.

'You were the very one who said to keep a low profile at the viewings. "Don't want the Hotties finding out – home ownership is not relatable."'

Jonathan held up his hands to placate her. 'Fair point, fair point.'

Of course it wouldn't matter if they kept getting outbid. The Dublin housing market was a shit-soup and they were lucky to be even putting a foot on the property ladder. If and when they eventually got something, they would be keeping it firmly under wraps. Amanda and Lexi's appeal had always been their relatability, but it was getting harder and harder to maintain this as their star continued to ascend far beyond their sexy, scrappy image. Their wardrobes were now fully stocked with designer 'pieces'; they ordered in for every meal. When they were on a session, their drugs arrived in Teslas. Neither Lexi nor Amanda had particularly enjoyed being broke-ass bitches. Still, Lexi had fond memories of the two of them screeching on the bus into town when they'd lived in their first grotty house share post-college, drinking shoulders of vodka to save money in the club. So much craic before all their craic became content for their show.

'Five more minutes.' Jonathan quickened his pace, turning down another fairy-tale street of red-brick terraced cottages. It was their goal neighbourhood, teetering on the brink of gentrification, a process they were no doubt throwing yet more momentum behind.

'Hey, hey! Bingo.' Beside her Jonathan stopped and cocked a finger at a pewter shopfront with discreet signage that whispered the word 'sigh' (all lower case). The interior was entirely matt black, with an imposing granite counter floating in the centre. 'That'll be our Saturday morning coffee run.'

'You can barely tell that's a coffee shop. It looks like the toilets of a high end club!'

He laughed. 'The more minimal the decor, the better the blend.' They carried on. 'Left up here,' he pointed, tracking their progress on his Maps app. 'Nearly there.' He slipped his big warm hand in hers, leading her round the corner.

'Hang on.' Lexi consulted her own phone. 'We've gone the wrong way.' She looked up, trying to spot an apartment building.

'No, no.' Jonathan pulled her on. 'I just thought we'd check out another place first.' He nodded ahead, where a clutch of people were milling on the path in front of a two-up two-down Georgian cottage with a lovely bay window, a small patch of grass and a low painted steel fence in front.

'Jonathan, nothing on this street is in our price range,' she hissed.

He put his finger to his lips.

Lexi tried to see into the houses they were passing. Beyond the generous bay windows, there was every variety of living room: chintzy furniture with nest tables crowded with pictures of grandchildren; slender-legged mid-century 'sideboards' and tasteful art; or toy-strewn sofas and flat-screen TVs. They all hinted at occupants in wildly differing life stages. Lexi and Jonathan's life stage was probably right between the mid-century modern people and the can't-move-without-stepping-on-Lego people.

They came to a stop at the edge of the throng of would-be buyers who were starting to stream through the open door – a lovely cherry red. Lexi could hardly bear to look at the house. It was so perfect.

'Jonathan, we've gone over the money stuff twenty times. Unless some distant rich relative has died …' She gestured helplessly at the house.

'I know,' Jonathan nodded. 'I mean, who d'you have to kill to get one of those distant rich relatives.'

Lexi laughed. 'The problem for Irish families is all the fecking siblings you've to share it with. If I had a distant rich relative die, I'd have to kill all my stupid brothers. And, like … I'd miss Abi.'

Jonathan laughed, rocking on his feet slightly, and Lexi narrowed her eyes. 'You are positively high. What is it?'

'Okay …' He spoke in a low voice, glancing at the house, where an estate agent in a pencil skirt was standing at the door. 'Remember the deal I was trying to negotiate back last summer?'

'Ye-es?' Lexi took a breath, trying to calm the swell of excitement. She didn't want to get her hopes up. The deal with Podify, the biggest podcast platform in the UK, had seemed too good to be true – they'd wanted to host *Your Hot Friend* exclusively on their platform AND give them a ton of money for the pleasure. There'd been a flurry of meetings, then it had come to nothing.

'What if I told you that *Your Hot Friend* has been offered a deal that would get us this house?'

'Shut the fuck up,' Lexi blurted loudly, drawing a look from the pencil skirt woman.

'I will not.' Jonathan laughed, grabbing her into a jubilant hug. 'Look, look.' He put her down and thrust his phone into her hand. 'This is the offer.'

She looked at the numbers and baulked at the figures. 'These numbers are …' She stabbed at the screen. 'Money, like … ?'

Jonathan grinned. 'MAJOR money! It's a million-euro deal, babes. As in a million for each of you, Lexi. You and Amanda. A fucking million. Well, eight hundred and twenty-five grand after my cut and solicitors, et cetera, but seriously, did you ever think it?! This year is going to be the biggest turnover yet. There'll be a bit more pressure for targets and so on – Podify will definitely want their pound of flesh – but it is going to be amazing.'

'Targets?' she murmured anxiously as Jonathan steered her over the threshold, nodding hello to the estate agent. 'We've never had targets.' She looked around at the high ceilings and black and white tiled floor and the nerves dissipated as she imagined coming home to this.

'So?' Jonathan leaned in to whisper. 'Will we make an offer? Subject to survey, obviously. The owner wants a quick sale, according to the agent I talked to. We won't have the first instalment of the Podify money in hand till next month if the deal is agreed, which it will be, but yer one won't know that and if our bid gets accepted we can just stall. These things take ages anyway.'

'We should probably look around the place first.' She laughed, then fell silent as her gaze travelled up the stairs to where a stained-glass fanlight glowed above the return. 'It's so beautiful,' she breathed. She flashed on the dingy house in Hereford where she'd grown up and shook her head. Anticipation swelled inside her and she hugged Jonathan closer. She was almost scared to believe this was possible, it felt like a dream.

CHAPTER 5

More than two weeks had passed since Aifric's Instagram post and no major developments had occurred, or none that were shared on the WhatsApp group, anyway. Strange. You didn't get engaged and then not shite on about it endlessly.

They've formed a side group. The thought prodded at Claire as she stepped onto the tram and into the gross body fug that rose from the rest of the slightly dead-eyed morning commuters. Was there anything worse than trying to summon the enthusiasm for work on a mid-January Monday?

An initial flurry of champagne emojis and ring chat had spilled out in the Bitch Herd thread, but soon more routine chat resumed: links to interesting articles, dissection of *The Real Housekeepers of Kensington* (a relatively new addition to the Reality TV canon) and screenshots of embarrassing influencer posts. The thing that was bothering Claire was the long pauses between messages. Sometimes she found herself posting several messages in a row before one would finally elicit a reply.

She edged through the resigned crowd, folded herself into a seat and extracted her phone from the chaos of her *Your Hot Friend* cloth tote.

Claire had a bunch of craft projects on the go in there as well as the brand-new badge-maker she'd ordered for her and Lila. They'd make some later, after she collected her from school. Claire checked the time: seven forty a.m. Her work day was long. She was out of bed at seven every weekday morning. Up to the Sweeneys' house in Stoneyhill by ten past eight, in time to walk Lila to school at eight thirty and drop Frankie to Montessori. The morning was spent either in the park with the baby or tidying the uber chic warehouse-turned-family-home, refurbished to the hilt and full of 'objets' perched around the shelves and ripe for Sonny to pull down onto his cute little sixteen-month-old face.

Lila's mum, Norah, was an actress and her partner, Sean, was a theatre director, meaning at any given time at least one of them was gone off on a job and Claire was the de facto co-parent to whichever of them remained. Pick-ups from school and Montessori broke up the day. Then it was lunch and snacks and whatever entertainment was the flavour of the week. Dinner was usually on the table before Norah or Sean arrived in from work. Occasionally Claire did the elaborate bedtime – apparently a requirement for all children – and didn't get home until her own bedtime. Her hours had been way better when she worked at her old creche, but she hadn't hesitated to jump five years ago when the Sweeneys poached her to mind the then six-year-old Lila full time.

Even though the work was full-on, she loved being a part of their family. Norah was like the big sister Claire had always wanted growing up. They gossiped and often shared a glass of wine after the kids went to bed. And of course they were so good to her during last year's 'blip' – as Claire called it. Norah and Sean had paid her full wages through the six weeks she'd had to take off. They had hired a replacement to cover for her and made it abundantly clear that she could take as long as she needed. Of course she'd been dying to get back to normal and put it all behind her. She was lucky the Sweeneys still trusted her after everything.

The tram swayed through the grey morning as Claire flicked through her podcast app. The new *YHF* was out. The Monday episode was called 'About Last Night', where Amanda and Lexi did detailed rundowns of their weekends and read out funny messages from other listeners.

'Hey, Hotties! How the fuuuuck are ye?' Lexi had a gravelly voice and always spoke in a slow drawl.

While she listened, Claire checked back in on the Bitch Herd thread. Still no responses to her gambit about the housekeeper's shambolic trip to Waitrose for cleaning supplies in last night's episode of *Housekeepers of Kensington. If someone else was texting they'd all be jumping to reply*, she thought gloomily.

In her ears, Amanda trilled, 'Manda and Lexi here, hoes! Your fave hot friends. We're back with this week's 'About Last Night' to make you feel less alone with your Monday Morning Fear!'

Claire wished her Monday Fear was about something more fun, but whatever day of the week it was, her Fear always seemed to be focused on her friends.

'I had the funniest fuck this weekend,' Amanda giggled.

'Oh yes! I love this shit,' Lexi returned. 'No one I know has more random sexcapades than you, Manda. Every encounter starts like some stupid ass porno and then descends into pure farce!'

'I know!' Amanda giggled. 'I swear I'm the butt of the universe's most evil joke.'

'Okay come on. Tee it up. Give us the topline.'

'Okay, okay.' Amanda paused. 'Dude crying – CRYING – cos he couldn't get his skinny jeans off.'

'Oh my god,' Lexi groaned.

'There may have been some "mental health" involved – EYE ROLL!'

'MANDA! Stop!'

A Bitch Herd notification interrupted the girls' chat and Claire immediately pounced on it.

It was Nadia asking if anyone had a recommendation for a good car repair place.

Claire regarded the chat thread with suspicion. This 'Utility Chat' had never been the way with the Bitch Herd. They used to gossip and have a laugh. Now every third message was one of them looking for some boring life-admin shit. Claire switched to her Notes app and noted the time, date and culprit:

Nadia – Car garage recs – January 16, 7.50am
NB: Third Utility Query from Nadia in the past month.

She scanned the list above. Similar bland crap. A few days ago, Helena had asked for a good Indian restaurant to bring her mother to. At the beginning of January, Aifric wanted to know if anyone had applied for some house-related grant, and so on as far back as September, when Claire had started keeping a record. September was when the idea that a side chat had formed began to prod at her with ever-increasing insistence.

The list was maybe a little obsessive – and she certainly hadn't mentioned it to Jamie – but she'd wanted some proof that the vibe wasn't all in her head. She also had significant evidence that overall the group chat was increasingly quiet. She'd catalogued the frequency of messages for the entire month of October and then done the same again for December, and the decline was noticeable. It went from an average of eighteen messages a day to six. Six! And that was *with* the brief uptick in group chat activity in the lead-up to Christmas, when they were collectively bemoaning their office parties and organising their annual Christmas afternoon tea.

The tram doors opened at her stop and Claire joined the forward surge, her mind still pacing back and forth on the troubling utility messages. Had they taken their 'real talk' to another group chat?

Out on the platform, she paused, letting the crowd disperse. She racked her brain for a message they couldn't ignore. She pulled her orange and navy Puffa closer round her, against the blast of wind sweeping the narrow cobblestone street.

On Insta, she skimmed the morning's posts from some of their favourite hate-follows. Hennessy Evans was an influencer of the wellness variety and aways good for a screenshot. On her stories, she was giving her cat a turmeric enema for its depression. Perfect. Claire took the screener and posted in the Bitch Herd chat with the caption 'Henners back on her bullshit'.

That would surely raise a few responses. Saving the rest of *Your Hot Friend* for later, Claire snapped her earpods into their case and began to jog up to Clement Street. Lila hated being late for school. Or anything. Claire figured this was why she and Lila got on so well; neither of them had ever been 'chill' about a single thing in their whole lives.

It wasn't till her teens that Claire realised most people didn't spend their whole childhood being told to stop overthinking and to calm down about stuff. She wished she *could* just calm down about stuff. She'd dedicated many hours to researching and collating data on how to be more laid back, which she sensed might be the most oxymoronic activity of all time. She veered right down the lane that ran behind several restaurants on the hiptastic Clement Street, rammed with cheese boutiques, cafes with tattoo parlours in the back and laundrettes that doubled up as diners. Light-filled, slightly industrial apartments occupied the upper stories of the buildings. From what she'd gleaned from Insta, Claire was pretty sure Amanda from *Your Hot Friend* lived in one of these. From her stalking it seemed Amanda lived alone, which suggested that despite their 'cool girl, we're just like you' personas, Amanda and Lexi were coining it on the podcast. Stoneyhill was not cheap.

The Sweeneys' house was anomalous. No other family occupied an entire building in the area, but Norah and Sean had been among those jammy people whose timing had always been immaculate. They'd graduated college in the nineties, worked in theatres in London and New York, then bought the old warehouse on Clement Street when the area was still pretty forgotten.

They made enough in the boom years to pay the whole thing off. Unreal. Now it was probably worth two million, if not more. It was Claire's dream house. She tapped the code into the keypad beside the heavy steel gate that led from the lane into the back garden. They'd stopped using the front door in the years when the neighbourhood had been a bit dodgy and so it was kind of a back-to-front house. To Claire's right was the home studio, a low, long structure which housed two work spaces for Norah and Sean. An outdoor seating area under a timber pergola lay just outside the big glass and steel doors to the kitchen.

Inside, Lila was barking orders at her little brother.

'Jacket on, Frankie, we're leaving the second Claire's here.'

'Morning!' Claire called, stepping up into the kitchen.

'Oh thank god!' Golden-haired Lila skipped over to the sitting area to retrieve the pram into which the squishy, rosy baby Sonny was already strapped. 'Norah! We're leaving!' Lila yelled back into the rest of the house. 'Come on, I want to be early to get situated.'

'Of course.' Claire grinned. She could relate. *Obviously*.

She straightened out the sleeves of Frankie's jacket as she scanned the compartment under the buggy for all the paraphernalia required to shift a small child from place to place: wet wipes, nappies, bottles, rice cakes and the obligatory smushed banana.

'Morning, Claire.' Norah strolled in, draped in several worn-but-lovely cardigans over a long dress with a geometric print.

Goddamn. She is so chic, thought Claire.

'Hiya.' Claire returned the air kisses Norah had blown her way.

'How was the weekend?' Norah started filling the kettle.

Long. Anxious. Tense, Claire thought.

'Great,' she announced.

She'd never got the attraction of the weekend. Too much time to think. And wonder about what everyone was off doing without her.

'So, Claire, honey ...' Norah, holding a sharpie, had turned to the new calendar hanging on the wall to the right of the fridge. 'I'm right in thinking you're still leaving early on Wednesdays to see your lady, Ella, yeah?'

'Oh, eh, no, actually. We ... I ...'

Norah turned to her, a slight tension in her eyes. 'You are still going to her, Claire?'

'Of course,' Claire said quickly. 'We've just changed the day. So, no more leaving early on Wednesdays!'

'Okay.'

Claire busied herself with Sonny's hat, but she could feel Norah's gaze and, in the pause, sensed that Norah was gearing up to say something further.

'We better get going.' Lila, to Claire's relief, cut them off abruptly and the moment passed.

'Cool.' Norah suppressed a smile. 'Don't forget to have a bit of fun today, Lila, in between getting "situated".'

Claire pushed the buggy out to the lane, then attached the little ride-along scooter for Frankie, and they set off like a slow-moving, many-headed beast. Once out of the lane, they turned right, away from the river in the direction of the Stoneyhill Educate Together school. It was only a ten-minute walk, but pushing the boys while keeping up with Lila's rapid-fire questioning was a workout.

'How's Jamie? Have you picked out any lamps yet? What are we doing after school today? Will you buy the dried mango this time? I hate the apricots.'

Claire wanted to check on her phone to see if anyone had responded to her screenshot, but she needed both hands to steer them all around the hassled, suited and booted people en route to office jobs and early meetings.

All her friends did that kind of work. Meetings around boardroom tables. Meetings with free food! Pastries and fruit platters that remained untouched. Untouched! Coffees in hand, they talked about important stuff. Or stuff they deemed important. They were the kind of jobs that people described being 'in' as opposed to 'doing'.

Aifric was *in* marketing.

Nadia was *in* finance.

Helena was *in* law.

Gillian was *in* pharmaceuticals.

You couldn't be *in* childminding. It sounded off.

'I'm bringing Sonny to the health store, so I'll get the mango. And the badge-maker arrived, so we can make some badges.'

'Deadly.' Lila beamed.

At that moment an incoming commuter, buried in her phone, nearly collided with them.

'Hey!'

Lila was incensed, while Claire's stomach flip-flopped with the strange sensation of seeing someone you know out of the usual context. The hassled commuter was none other than Nadia (in finance, looking-for-a-good-car-garage Nadia).

'Nadia!' Claire stepped around to hug her and she limply returned the embrace.

Claire knew that she and Nadia would never have been friends naturally. Theirs was a friendship of circumstances; Nadia was a proximity pal. They were in the same group, but they didn't direct message each other and would strenuously avoid sitting beside one another at brunch. They just didn't have a whole lot to say to each other; privately, Claire couldn't really see how Nadia had managed to hang on in the group so long.

'How are you?' Claire asked brightly. 'How was your weekend?'

Why does she look so uneasy?

'Great, great,' Nadia murmured vaguely, her eyes darting around, still trying to draw away. 'Just the usual, you know yourself. Listen …' She'd nearly edged past Claire and the buggy. 'We really must get a coffee soon.' And then she was gone.

Oh, MUST we?!

Claire narrowed her eyes at Nadia's back. When did people decide that 'We must get together' was a reasonable way to end an interaction? And was there anything more damning than someone announcing that they 'must' see you, like it was some onerous thing they HAD to do?

Lila was pulling at her sleeve but Claire was distracted by Nadia striding away making odd, jerky movements – a sort of sequence of flailing and pointing gestures.

Lila followed Claire's gaze. 'What's your friend doing?'

'I have no idea.' Claire scanned the street beyond Nadia.

'She looks like she's directing someone,' Lila observed. 'Wait … there!'

She grabbed Claire's arm and turned her slightly to point out a young woman in a beanie crossing the street towards Nadia. Nadia was vehemently trying to head her off, a fact that was obvious to everyone except the girl, who Claire realised was Gillian. Gillian in pharmaceuticals, who worked nowhere near town! What the hell? Her offices were in a business estate on the edge of the city. It couldn't be a coincidence that Nadia and Gillian were just running into each other.

Claire could see them coming together, bowing their heads and having a brief exchange, during which Gillian glanced back at Claire. *They must be going for a Monday morning catch-up. That's all. That's no big deal.* Gillian and Nadia were hardly her best friends; it wasn't like running into Aifric going for coffee without her.

'Hi, Claire!' Gillian called breezily as they walked back towards her having obviously decided to stop and chat. 'And who's this gang?!' She smiled down at the boys and Lila, who impatiently tapped her Apple watch at Claire.

Claire suppressed a laugh and introduced the kids, matching Gillian's breezy tone. 'We're on our way to school. Where are you guys going?'

'Em, we're going for a little coffee and a catch-up,' Nadia replied.

'Just the two of you?' Claire couldn't help but probe.

'Yep, just us,' confirmed Gillian – a little too quickly, Claire thought.

'Oh, is that so?' Lila piped up sceptically, tapping her little foot. 'Just the two of you? Really? Do you swear on my baby brother's life?'

'What?!' Nadia blurted.

'Well, eh, I don't see how that—' Gillian spluttered.

'Just answer the question,' Lila snapped.

'Lila!' Claire laughed and pretended to give an admonishing little shake of the head. 'But really ...' She swung back to Gillian and Nadia. 'Are you guys, like, doing anything nice?' She tried not to sound like a person on the verge of an existential spiral.

Are they meeting the others? Are they all hanging out without me?

'Well, we're just having a little get-together of the ...' Gillian was clearly treading carefully around her words. 'Of the ... of Aifric's bridesmaids.'

'Her WHAT?'

Claire struggled to catch up. How could Aifric have bridesmaids already? Nothing had been said at all. AT ALL. The group chat had been totally silent on the matter.

'It's just to start tentative discussions of plans, et cetera,' Nadia rushed to add.

'So ...' Claire tried to quell her rising upset. Blinking rapidly, she made a valiant effort to compose herself. 'Has Aifric ... like ...

officially made the call? On the bridesmaids? I thought she was still deliberating.'

They looked awkward. 'I don't really know, Claire. I suppose not everyone can be bridesmaids, see?' Nadia was delivering this gently, as though Claire was some erratic child.

'She feels really bad that she couldn't have everyone,' Gillian added.

She feels really bad? So they've been discussing me? No doubt wondering 'What'll we do about Claire?'! Like I'm some kind of nuisance. The Claire Problem. God, this is so humiliating.

'It's like the layers of the onion, isn't it?' Gillian had a pleading look now, as though willing Claire to not make a big deal of it. 'If she had you as well, then she'd have to ask Helena. And then Rachel'd be hurt ...'

'But Rachel and Helena aren't even her best friends! They're peripherals!'

Nadia and Gillian exchanged a look and Claire burned with embarrassment at what was being left unsaid.

Oh, so I'm obviously a peripheral now too.

'Well ...' With superhuman effort, Claire mentally pulled herself together. 'Have a great planning session.' *Keep it light, Claire,* she silently coaxed herself. 'I can't wait to see what you guys come up with. It's gonna be so fun. Better get going with this gang. Bye.'

'Bye, Claire.' Gillian gave a frantic, vaguely desperate wave. 'We must get coffee soon.'

'Oh, *MUST* we?' Claire's sarcasm seemed to go unnoticed by the other two, who were already backing away, clearly relieved that the disastrous stop 'n' chat was done.

Claire resumed pushing the pram up towards school.

Lila looked up at her, concerned. 'Maybe Aifric will still ask you,' she suggested in a small voice.

'Hmm.' Claire didn't want to hold out hope. Hope made her feel even more pathetic. 'Thanks, Lila,' she added. 'God, I'm sorry – that completely derailed us. We've gotta get you to school! I've totally eaten into your situating time!'

'It's okay, Claire. A valuable lesson was learned: stop 'n' chats are NEVER a good idea,' Lila replied sagely.

'We should put that on a badge later.' Claire mustered a laugh.

After she waved Lila into school and watched Frankie totter into the Montessori next door, Claire grabbed a coffee and a vegan sausage roll – there wasn't an animal by-product in at least a five-mile radius of the Sweeneys' bougie neighbourhood. Then she steered Sonny's pram into the park behind the Montessori and found a bench. The small green square was shared by a neat enclave of Georgian houses. She smiled at the three mothers with prams strolling under the bare branches. To her right were a couple of older women, gabbing and ignoring their two dogs, who were scrapping at their feet.

Claire pulled out her phone to check on her active threads. A few lols and eye-rolls in the Bitch Herd chat at her Hennessy Evans screenshot. It was something, at least. She was just popping her earphones back in to resume *Your Hot Friend* when a Voicy dropped into her WhatsApp thread with Aifric. Claire leapt on the notification. Aifric hadn't direct-messaged since Claire's carefully crafted congrats text when the engagement was announced. She could see her text above the new Voicy. She'd spent a good bit of time writing and re-working it in her Notes app before sending it:

Aifric!!! Oh my god, congratulations!!! I am so happy for you. I have to say I am actually so emotional thinking of my best friend in the whole world taking this step. Eeeeeek. I was only looking at piccies of us from school the other day. Such babies! Remember we used to pick our wedding dresses in magazines!??!?!? Lol! Anyway cannot wait to be with you picking the REAL THING so soon!!!! XXX Love Claire.

Aifric had replied with two blowing kisses emojis. A bit of a generic response, Claire had thought at the time, but the engagement no doubt had her busy.

Very VERY busy, evidently: it had been two weeks and two days since this last interaction. But now here was a forty-seven-second voice note.

The timing was … interesting. Had Nadia and Gillian been on? She cringed at the idea of them discussing her: *The Claire Problem.*

She hit play and Aifric's confident voice filled her ears.

'Hey, darl! How's life? Oh my god, so sorry I haven't been on. Things have been SO HECTIC on my end, you can't IMAGINE. Anyway I just wanted to let you know that I've just this second put in place a plan for the official wedding party. I hope you know I would love to have you involved but we're really tight on numbers and so I've gone with Nadia and Gillian to be bridesmaids. Just cuz, you know, they've both done it before for cousins and stuff. And I guess I thought maybe you could help out in a different way. Like making the party favours or something! You're so crafty! Have a think about what you want to make. It's looking like late June! Eeeek, so soon but, fuck it, long engagements are so over! There's about two hundred and seventy guests at the moment and I just think something for everyone handmade by one of my oldest friends would be SO SPECIAL. Okay. Chat soon. Byeeee!'

She's just this second put the wedding party in place? Claire knew that was bullshit.

But she wants me to do the wedding favours! the more optimistic side of her argued. *That is huge! She's trusting me with gifts for her guests. In a way this is even more special than the bridesmaid gig.*

Bridesmaids had a lot of lowly menial labour. Depending on the level of meringue wedding dress Aifric opted for, Gillian and Nadia would probably even have to 'help' Aifric take a piss. Ick.

No, it's definitely way more special making the favours. Claire continued to hard-sell the idea to herself, trying to ignore the little bruise of hurt inside.

She blew some kisses back to Aifric in the thread and then typed her reply:

It truly means SO MUCH to me that you're trusting me with this. I can't wait. I'll start researching ideas right away.

CHAPTER 6

With one week left until her due date, Joanne was rushing up the back stairs of the maternity hospital to the antenatal class. It was the last one and in the six weeks that they'd attended, Joanne had been late every time.

'I think you're trying to self-sabotage,' Bert had said, psychoanalysing her. 'Maybe not on a conscious level but seriously, I think this is an extension of your whole head-in-the-sand approach to our impending baby.'

He wasn't wrong. On the first day of class they were supposed to meet outside and when she'd rounded the corner and seen Bert standing there waiting for her, she'd immediately ducked back and hidden. The class was an hour long so she'd decided to sit in the park and kill twenty minutes on TikTok; then she'd only have to go to the second half. Bert had tried to call and then texted, admonishing her for being late for this of all things. She'd told him she'd fallen over and he was immediately all concern. Since then she'd had a broken-down bus and several client meetings that ran long – neurotic clients were the bane of everyone's life in advertising. Last week, she'd been so desperate for an excuse that she'd actually stooped to claiming she'd pissed herself and had to go home and change.

She hung back at the door of the class. Peeking through the big square window, she could see the other parents-to-be watching on as a couple at the top of the room were apparently being tested on some particulars of parenthood. This was the graduation, though it was unclear what the ramifications of NOT graduating would be. Would they be confiscating the babies? Bert was in the front row, feverishly churning through his notes. She was lucky he was so into it all; she hoped it would make up for her occasional anxiety about this unplanned detour into babydom.

'Joanne, we can see you, you know,' Mary, the midwife in charge of the class, called through the door.

Joanne mobilised, bustling into the room, feigning a slight limp.

'Another fall? Desperate,' Mary said, sounding completely unconvinced.

Joanne slid into the chair beside Bert, who rolled his eyes at her but gave the bump a friendly little pat 'hello'.

'Right, Bert and Joanne!' Mary called to them. 'You're up.'

Bert bounded to the top of the class and Joanne trailed after him.

'First question: The baby is crying but she's fed and changed and only just up from a nap. What do you do?'

'Wind her!' Bert shouted.

'Okay, Bert, well done. You clearly know your stuff. Next one's just for Mum. What have you got on your birth plan, Joanne?'

Joanne froze. Was this a trick question? She'd been under the impression that birth plans were about as useful as armbands in a tsunami.

'Ehm, well ... I suppose the plan is mainly just ... get the baby out?'

'Excellent, Joanne! You're absolutely right. Plans are wonderful for giving Mum a sense of preparedness ahead of the birth, but very often the things on your birth plan do not pan out. It's important not to put too much pressure on yourselves to adhere to the plan. The main thing is to get the baby out … SAFELY.' Mary turned back to Joanne and Bert. 'Congratulations, you two! You're as ready to be parents as you'll ever be.'

Joanne smiled, but maybe Mary saw something in her face, because she then leaned over and clasped Joanne's hand.

'You'll be fine,' she whispered. 'These classes aren't for everyone. Maybe avoiding them was what *you* needed to do to prepare.'

Caught off-guard by this unexpected empathy, Joanne watched as Bert returned to his seat amid a cacophony of whoops and applause, mainly from the other dads. Maybe this was their way of coping with the looming chasm that Joanne imagined waited for them beyond the pregnancy. The men wanted to think parenthood could be 'won', while the women were barely able to think beyond whatever symptoms were holding them hostage at any one time.

One woman in the second row was chugging directly from a bottle of Gaviscon, while another was spooning Dijon mustard directly into her mouth, looking as weirded out as anybody by the strange craving.

Suddenly, belatedly, Joanne regretted not engaging in the class more. These were women going through the same thing as her; these were women she could have been bonding with and swapping phone numbers with. Instead, she'd been trying to keep up with her friends, pretending that being on the session with them while dying from trapped wind was still fun.

Joanne continued to hold Mary's hand, long beyond the socially acceptable duration. 'Will you be at the birth, do you think?' She tried not to sound desperate.

'Maybe.' Mary smiled kindly, extricating her hand gently. 'I might be on shift, I might not – it's the luck of the draw with these things. But, Joanne …' Mary looked intently at her. 'You will be fine.'

Ten hours later and Joanne was about as far from fine as she'd ever been. She and Bert had gone to bed at ten thirty and she'd felt a bit crampy and uncomfortable, but she was thirty-nine weeks pregnant: uncomfortable was her constant state. By eleven thirty, however, she was clinging to the mattress and gritting her teeth through each terrible contraction while Bert fannied around trying to hook up the TENS machine to her back – they were trying to get it on before they got in the car to drive to the hospital. It was a small contraption which looked a bit like a Game Boy, with wires that you were supposed to attach to the lower back to emit small electric shocks. Apparently to counter the pain. *What pain relief involves the use of an electrical current? Make it make sense,* Joanne wailed internally. *Why does NOTHING about pregnancy make sense?*

'Why are we still growing people inside people?' Joanne howled. 'People don't fit inside people and they sure as fuck don't fit out of a hole the size of a polo mint.'

'I know, babe.' Bert was lifting the back of her tee-shirt and consulting the instructions of the TENS.

'Fuck off, Bert!' It seemed Joanne was at the point of labour when any unnecessary touching of her body could result in a homicide. 'Either get it going or burn the fucker,' she snarled.

Bert had become hopelessly tangled in the machine, managing to get one of the sticky pads glued to his beard while two others had become steadfastly stuck to his left hand. He pulled at the beard pad. 'Ahhh, shit, it's pulling out the hairs. Oh my god, it's agony.'

'Bert! If I could, I would rip it off myself.'

'Joanne,' Bert looked hurt, 'I am not a hirsute man. You know better than anyone, every inch of this beard-growth is extremely hard won.'

'Fuuu-uuu-uuuuck.' Coherent words had apparently left her. It felt like she was being cracked open. The contractions were relentless. According to Bert's timing, they were coming every five minutes, though they felt faster than that. Midwife Mary had said there'd be some respite between them but it felt like each wave of pain only just peaked before another rolled in behind, cleaving her apart from the inside.

Luckily, except for being glued to the TENS machine, Bert had everything in hand. He had the bags in the car. One was for the delivery room and contained everything she'd need for the birth, plus a little nappy and onesie to put their brand new baby in. The other bag was for the days she might have to spend in the hospital recovering.

Bert helped Joanne off the bed, wincing every time the TENS wires snagged on things and the pads pulled at his beard. 'Ahh, ahhhh,' he whimpered. 'It's so tender.'

In the car, Joanne was practically clawing the ceiling as another wave wrenched her in the passenger seat. At one point, Bert had to brake a little sharply for a red light and a voice she barely recognised as her own growled, 'I swear to fuck I'll kill you.'

'You're doing amazing, sweetie.' He was hunched up over the

steering wheel, driving with a focus that bordered on maniacal. 'Nearly there. I love you.'

'Shut. Up,' a voice (again, hers apparently) hissed.

At the next lights, Bert tugged feebly at the sticky pad, wincing. 'You wouldn't believe how sore this is – beard hair is so, so sensitive.'

Joanne reached across and viciously tore it off.

'Jo,' he whimpered, cradling his face.

'I regret nothing.'

Finally, they reached the hospital. Joanne staggered through the reception area as Bert ran ahead with their paperwork. A selection of people sitting in the waiting room politely averted their eyes when Joanne crouched down to grind out another contraction.

'Fuuuuu-uuu-uuu-uck!' She balled her fists and squeezed her eyes shut. The pressure of this one felt worse than the others. *Where is Bert? I need him.*

'Jo! Jesus.' He rushed to kneel beside her. 'I'm sorry. I was just getting us checked in.'

Another contraction wracked her body.

She heard a deep lowing sound and could see from the alarm in Bert's face that it had come from her.

'Jesus, Jo. What do you need?'

'I need ... your ... baby ... the ... fuck ... out ... of ... me.'

'They're on their way with a trolley to bring you up to the delivery room. It's gonna be okay.' He began searching frantically through the delivery room bag. 'What about ...' He pulled out the pricey Eau du Calme face mist he'd bought.

Joanne ignored him as another pelvis-shattering tremor of a contraction rumbled through her.

Her whole body contorted and spasmed with it. And this apparently seemed to Bert the optimum time to begin spritzing her.

'Stop. It.' Just as she managed to slap his hand away, she felt a sudden pop and then a gush of significantly less elegant fluid between her legs.

'Your waters. We have to catch some.' Bert leapt forward with cupped hands. 'At class, they said to try and bring a sample.' Bert called over to the waiting-room people all continuing to stare intently at the TV, even though the sound was turned down. 'Will one of you get the plastic box out of that bag?' He gestured, his hands brimming with amniotic fluid. A timid man slid over and retrieved the Tupperware, into which Bert tipped the liquid.

Several pairs of feet and the wheels of a trolley now came into Joanne's field of vision.

'Thank fuck,' Joanne whispered to Bert, who was clutching his box and now rhythmically rubbing her back. 'I feel like I'm going to shit myself and I really don't want to do it in reception.'

'I'm so proud of you. You're doing amazing.'

'Stop touching my back.'

The owners of the various feet were lifting her carefully onto the trolley as she heard Bert asking if there was any chance of a local anaesthetic for his beard.

Now they were on the move. Another hammer of pain bore down on her while above her fluorescent lights whizzed past.

The pain was starting to cloud her thinking. Time seemed to jump. The ding of a lift. A bright room. More pain. A woman in a mask was introducing herself. *I don't care about your name! I'm being ripped in two!* Joanne couldn't tell if she'd just thought it or said it.

Next, she spotted Bert leaning in to speak to a masked man dressed in blue scrubs, showing him the murky fluid in the box. Bert looked worried. It sent a cold trickle of fear through her. Bert never looked worried.

'What's wrong?' Joanne demanded. 'Bert?'

Now someone was checking between her legs. She squirmed. Near the door, the masked man was saying something she couldn't make out. More pain. Fuck, this fucking hurts! A woman was strapping some device around her bump and now they could see their baby's heart beating on the monitor.

Suddenly Bert's nervous face eclipsed the fluorescent lights above her. 'Joanne, they're saying they should do a c-section. There was meconium in your waters and you're not that dilated so far. They want to deliver the baby quickly to be on the safe side.'

'Is the baby okay?' A lash of fear struck her.

'Yeah, they have it all under control.' He pointed at the monitor.

'Meconium? You mean the little shit shat in me?!'

Bert smiled at her and Joanne tried to smile back, though she sensed she looked more like a rabid dog baring its teeth at this point. Then the doctor appeared and repeated what Bert had said, only in more complicated language, while Joanne writhed with another contraction.

Then it was back out to the hall, lights above whipping past and then the clatter of the lift once again. In a new room Joanne was shifted onto a bed, rolled onto her side and given an epidural. From there reality seemed to tilt and distort. The people dashing around her felt very far away. A doctor was working on her lower body, obscured by a blue curtain. The light was so bright. She was sure she saw a blade glint in the doctor's hand. From her viewpoint, he looked like he was sawing something in a frenzy. Joanne wanted to scream but couldn't make a sound. Then came the odd sensation of someone rummaging down inside her. *Please make it stop. Make it stop.* She closed her eyes as the terror engulfed her.

'Joanne? Joanne?' Bert's voice.

She wanted him to hold her, to comfort her, but she was pinned flat to the bed; the drugs had immobilised her.

'Look! Our baby's being born! Isn't he wonderful?'

She looked and it was strange, not wonderful. The doctor was holding a splayed creature covered in blood and some kind of white scum. Its neck was skinny, its eyes screwed shut. From its pursed lips came a squall. The doctors whisked the baby away then and Joanne felt a momentary rush of relief before it hit her: *That thing is mine; it's coming home with me.*

Now a nurse returned with a bundle and held the baby beside Joanne's head for her to see it. The little thing was a livid purple and still squalling but looked considerably more baby-like to her. Thank god. The nightmarish taint of a few minutes before was dissolving and things were feeling a bit more normal. Joanne was shaken, though.

'Your little boy. Congratulations!'

Bert burst into tears as the baby was then laid across his arms. 'Jesus, he's perfect.'

The nurse showed Bert how to do skin-to-skin with the baby. 'It's very important,' she told him, laying a blanket over both of them.

She smiled at Joanne. 'You can do it once the epidural wears off.' Then they wheeled her into another room to recover.

Every five minutes, she asked the nurse attending to her if she could leave.

'I barely saw my baby,' Joanne pleaded. She had an almost primal desperation to get back to him. Even if he looked like a little wet reptile, he was her little wet reptile.

The nurse smiled and lifted up Joanne's right leg. 'Can you feel that?'

'Yep,' Joanne lied and the nurse narrowed her eyes.

'Five more minutes, pet,' she said kindly. 'I just want to see a little wiggle of these toes.'

When Joanne was reunited with the baby it felt like taking a deep breath after a long time under water.

She held him and stared and stared. He was perfect. He was beautiful. He was a stranger. She'd expected to recognise her baby, but he was an alien. She was in love. But it was love with fear stirred in. What a strange, strange new world it was.

An hour later, they were settled in to the maternity ward.

'Are you okay?' Bert was buttering her toast.

'I am ...' Joanne was at a loss. 'I don't know what I am. It's a bit raw. I'm a bit raw.'

Her body felt scooped out and her hand shook as she took the toast Bert proffered. Dawn was beginning to break outside the tall windows in the large ward. There were eight beds, separated by blue curtains. Were all the other women in the room feeling this messed up?

'I can't believe this little guy.' Bert was kissing and stroking the baby and Joanne had never ever seen him look happier. 'You're perfect, you're perfect,' he told the baby.

A weird sensation crept over Joanne. She was on the other side of a pane of glass looking in at them but unable to reach them.

'Joanne?' Bert was looking at her with concern. 'Seriously, are you alright? That was an insane night. You did amazing.' His words dissolved the barrier between them and she was back in the room, with her family. She took the baby's hand. Tiny fingers curled around her own and she drifted away again, this time to a blank, exhausted sleep.

When Joanne woke up, Bert and the baby were gone. Panic seized her. As she tried to pull herself up, her c-section wound seared with fiery pain, but she barely felt it; she had to find the baby. His absence felt profoundly wrong.

At the sight of Joanne pushing back her blanket, a passing midwife immediately veered towards her.

'Don't, don't! You've a catheter in still.'

'What?' Joanne was alarmed. How did she not feel it? She looked over the side of the bed, where the woman had indicated. There was indeed a bag of piss dangling there.

The midwife knelt to inspect it. 'It's quite full,' she remarked. 'I'll come back to change it in a tick.'

She stood to go but Joanne reached for her, grasping the hem of her neat little white jacket like a drowning person. 'My boyfriend left and the baby's gone,' she whimpered. 'I know I sound deranged but I need the baby back. Where is he?'

'Ah, pet. That's not deranged at all. Sure, up till a few hours ago the baby was inside you! Your boyfriend's probably changing him –

we change and bathe the babies across the hall. You'll be able to get up tomorrow and I'll show you. You and the babser will probably be here for a few days – it's Tuesday now, so Saturday, Sunday at the latest.'

Bert suddenly appeared around the curtain, the baby over his shoulder like a tiny sack of spuds. 'You're awake! This thing just did the most insane shite. I took a photo for you!'

'Amazing, thank you.' Joanne took his proffered phone as the midwife slipped away.

'So names!' Bert chirped. 'I was thinking Caligula.'

'What?'

'Relax, it was a joke. You still keen on Ted?'

Joanne studied the tiny lump snoozing on her boyfriend. 'Yeah, Ted is good.'

On the ward, the next four days bled into the nights, which bled into the days until Joanne was so addled by lack of sleep that it really just felt like one long continuous day. Her mother and sisters FaceTimed, but Joanne was wrecked and at points literally drifted off on the calls. Bert appeared and disappeared like an apparition – the dads had to respect the visiting hours – and Joanne really didn't care that he couldn't be with her and Ted. His presence exhausted her. Everything exhausted her. Except the baby. The baby was the most fascinating, beautiful thing she'd ever seen.

The nightmarish feelings of the c-section and immediate aftermath had for the most part evaporated, but she was still getting stabs of panic now and then, when the magnitude of having a baby would suddenly hit her full force.

I can't have a baby – I still feel fifteen! her internal monologue would wail.

This baby is depending on me for EVERYTHING.

Me!

A person who still has to google how to spell 'necessary' and probably will forever.

Then the baby would do something fairly unremarkable like yawn and the flood of love would return, overwhelming her.

She was not feeling any flood of love towards Bert, however. His visits grated.

'He doesn't like being swaddled so tight,' she'd crabbed at him as he fussed about the baby.

'Stop rocking him so much. I only just fed him.'

'Let me do it. I know how to wind him.'

She'd definitely been a bit snappy; she couldn't help it. He had no idea what she was going through. He went home every night and slept in a quiet house. He wasn't hobbling around trying to learn how to operate a baby just days after a surgical procedure.

On the last night in the hospital, Joanne paced the dimly lit corridor with a stubbornly awake Ted. Her eyes burned; he'd been feeding for hours. She felt like she was at the bottom of a hole. Cluster feeding, said the midwife. *Clusterfuck,* thought Joanne. Now she was swaying and humming, trying to lull him to sleep.

Down the hall she saw Elaine coming. Her favourite midwife – the one Joanne desperately wanted to take home with her.

'How are you, hon?' Elaine smiled. 'Is he not settling?'

'Nothing's working.' And to her surprise, Joanne was suddenly crying, giving in to the tears that had been threatening all day. 'Sorry.

I don't know why I'm crying.'

'It's day five, pet, the day of the Big Cry. We all get it – it's a big whack of hormones. Don't worry. The first weeks are very intense and it's very, VERY normal to feel overwhelmed. You love your baby but your whole life has changed in a matter of days. Why don't I take Ted to the nursery for a little while so you can have a sleep?'

Joanne hesitated. She still got very agitated when Bert took Ted, even just for a few minutes.

'I'll come and get you if he needs to feed.' Elaine's comforting smile convinced her.

'Thank you. That would be really great.'

A few hours later, as morning dawned, Bert's slightly accusatory voice roused her.

'Where's Ted? Joanne?'

Joanne pulled herself from a deep, luxurious sleep. 'Wha—?'

Her grogginess ebbed abruptly. Shit – where WAS the baby? He needed a feed. She bolted upright. Her boobs were bursting and had leaked in the night.

Then she remembered that Elaine had taken him to give her a break and her anxiety receded.

'It's okay, he's in the nursery,' she explained. 'Elaine took him for a few hours.' She pulled her legs from the tangled sheets and stood up gingerly.

Bert had already turned and was striding out towards the corridor.

He reached the glass window of the nursery ahead of her.

'He's crying in there.' Bert looked back at her reproachfully and then accosted the midwife on duty at the door. 'My baby is here. Can you please give him to me?'

'I was really exhausted,' Joanne muttered as she caught up with him. Sickly shame rose in her. *Poor Ted. How long has he been crying? How could I have left him alone?*

Bert took the baby and swept back to their cubicle. She staggered after him, trying to ignore the burn of her wound.

He turned to face her. 'I don't get it, Joanne. You hardly let me hold him during the day, but then you leave him down there all night?'

'It wasn't all night. It was a couple of hours. I was so, like, depleted.'

Bert shook his head. 'I was here yesterday. I can mind my son, you know. I could've taken him while you took a nap. I actually *went* to the antenatal classes, remember? I was the one who actually wanted this baby.'

His words landed like a punch and she could see in the way his face caved in that he was immediately regretting them.

'Jo—'

'Bert. Piss off.'

They stared at each other.

'I'm sorry. I shouldn't have said that.'

Bert swayed Ted, but from the way Ted was gently bashing his face against Bert's chest, it was clear he was looking for Joanne and a feed.

'You shouldn't have *said* it? Or you didn't *mean* it?' Joanne unhooked her sodden nursing bra and took the baby, who latched on immediately. *He needed me and I was fucking sleeping.*

'Joanne … You're acting like you're the only one this is happening to. I get it, you've just had a baby, but so have I. ALSO …' He raised his voice to stop her cutting across him. 'I watched you get cut open. It's scary seeing the most important person in your life out of it on an operating table.'

'Hello!' A chirpy voice came from behind the curtain. 'Knock, knock.' It was Elaine. 'Just checking that you're nearly ready to be discharged. Dad, why don't you get the paperwork underway out at the nurses' station?'

Bert looked reluctant to leave but clearly knew they could hardly continue snarling at each other in the middle of the ward. The curtains were doing nothing to hide the row.

'Sure, sorry, okay ...' He took Joanne's big green file from the bedside locker and left.

With Ted cradled in one arm, Joanne flipped open the top of her weekend bag and started to toss in her clothes.

'Sorry about that,' she muttered to Elaine.

'Very normal,' Elaine whispered. 'It's a big transition for your relationship. A lot will change over the next few months.'

Joanne nodded mutely, as a stone settled in her chest.

CHAPTER 7

'Morning gals! It's the first of February and I am officially ready to get back into my good habits.' Lexi grinned at her own face reflecting back at her from her phone.

She was LIVE storying her morning to her 540k Instagram followers as she walked from the train station down to the north quays, bound for a quick workout before the big meeting to sign the Podify deal. She couldn't believe how fast things were moving: it was only two and a half weeks since Jonathan had surprised her at the house on Orchard Terrace. They might even be hearing back on their latest offer on the house that very day.

She continued chatting, narrating her life in the way that nearly everyone did now. 'I'm heading to my regular mindful cardio class at SoulFit, which is literally the only thing keeping me from having a full-scale nervous breakdown every damn day.' She was buzzed and was making a conscious effort not to let the usual stream of judgy comments streaming in below her face ruin her mood.

@LuaNua: Being flippant about mental health is not a good look. Idiotic girl.

@EmilyYoga: She hasn't said a single thing about the migrant crisis, so sick of these self-obsessed influencers.

@DaniJay: Lexi your hair is so gorge, where do you get your stenos.

@Sharon24: As if she'd admit to stenos, her and Amanda are so fake.

@Poppy_F: Well for her hopping off to the gym or whatever shite in the middle of a Wednesday. Some of us have jobs. She's as spoiled and entitled as they come.

Lexi never acknowledged the comments on her live videos. If she replied to the nice ones, the people posting harsh ones would just call her shallow, and if she tried to defend herself against the mean ones – who the fuck wants to hear her thoughts on geopolitics? – she knew she would tie herself up in knots. Best to act like she couldn't see them and never let on that they sometimes kept her up at night.

'It's just an unfortunate part of the job, Lexi,' was Jonathan's refrain.

'Those pathetic bitches hate their lives. They're probably ugly,' said Amanda, who couldn't conceive of a fate worse than ugliness.

The worst part was that Lexi, in the pits of anxious nights, often thought many of them had a point. *Your Hot Friend* didn't contribute much to the world. And they probably *were* perpetuating negative stereotypes. Ugh.

She shook off the thought.

Ignore them. You work hard. You entertain people. Other people's opinions of you are not facts. She mentally scrolled through the mantras given to her by her internet coach, Aine, who she'd started working with in the early years of the pod when her following was just starting to grow and she was trying to adjust to the strange form of low-grade celebrity that came with being chronically online. Aine was trained as a psychologist, but her USP was that she was steeped in online culture. Lexi's previous therapist had been a man in his early fifties who hadn't understood what she meant by followers and had urged her to go to the police.

Aine was an entirely different animal and fluent in the realities of being a person of influence (as was the preferred term nowadays) and how that could be so corrosive when it came to one's mental health – Lexi's anxiety could spike at the slightest things, even nice comments made her feel misunderstood sometimes. The overall feeling of being watched was not pleasant and Aine was an amazing mix of sympathetic and practical. She was also about to be even more essential once the Podify deal was launched and even more eyes would be on them.

Lexi continued on down the river, shimmering in the crisp morning, and was buoyed once more by the thought of the deal and the day to come.

'After SoulFit, it's a day of top-secret meetings that I cannot wait to tell you all about!' she told the phone.

A call from Amanda appeared at the top of her screen. She cheerfully signed off the Insta Live and tapped the green accept button.

'Happy Money Day!' Amanda squealed.

'I know!' Lexi yelped back. 'I can't even story properly, I'm so fuckin' happy!'

'I mean it does feel a bit like we're selling out. Marrying Corporate Satan and all. But do we care?'

'Hell, no!' Lexi giggled. 'If I am selling out, I do not give a fuck. We are Satan's sister wives now. Though …' Lexi paused. 'Is all the talk of listener figures and targets giving you the slight heebie-jeebies?'

'Nah! Sure, look, it won't kill us to work a bit …' Amanda laughed.

'Okay, I have to go – I'm at SoulFit. See you at the Corporate Satanic wedding!' Lexi blew a kiss and ended the call.

SoulFit was the studio for whom she, Amanda and about 16 other influencers were brand ambassadors, meaning she needed to chronicle every minute she spent there for her followers. She pulled up her phone again and started filming. She'd record this morning's session and edit it down to a succinct five-minuter for TikTok and Insta.

'Here we go, girlies,' she purred. 'SoulFit is a wellness experience like no other.'

She winked at the camera and filmed herself pushing open the brightly painted warehouse door, leading to a huge marble hallway with an eight-foot waterfall at the end, just behind the reception desk.

'Another amazing morning here at SoulFit.' Lexi swung her phone around to capture the place as she made her way down the hall. 'I just feel so lucky to have this job that gives me these opportunities to work with companies that nourish my whole being.'

Toby, the assistant manager, was sitting at the desk talking to her phone – shouting really – as the 'water feature' gushed behind her. Despite the tie-dyed bodysuit covered in peace signs and the hippyish plaits, Toby was stern.

At the sight of Lexi, she slammed the phone down.

'Lexi, you're way behind on your posts. Mel told me to remind you of your obligations here.'

'Sorry.' Lexi held up her phone in a pleading gesture. 'I'm filming right now, I swear.'

'You need to do at least two reels during today's class to get back on track.'

'I know, I know.' Lexi nodded, turning right into a long windowless corridor with floor, walls and ceiling in red rubber. A subtle audio thrummed in the darkness. A heartbeat.

Mel, SoulFit's owner, called it the birth canal. Every *soul*, as Mel called her clients, had to pass through the birth canal to get to the changing rooms. It was a whole thing.

Once Lexi was spat out into the changing rooms, she was whacked with the full force of nine different TikTokers doing their thing. It was pretty raucous: some of their 'things' involved dancing and singing. Others were just filming clips of their workout gear and the various bits of culturally appropriated decor around the space: prayer mats, buddhas, a huge dharma wheel hung on one wall that you could actually spin like a game show. Around it were smug mantras of the 'be grateful' variety and whichever one it landed on was the intention you were supposed to 'take into your day'.

Lexi would rather have just gone to the gym and done a few weights, but Jonathan had set up the SoulFit deal as, he vigorously argued, they needed to be 'always elevating'.

'The Hotties look to you two for inspo. You always need to be at the vanguard of the next big thing in Dublin,' he insisted.

Lexi put on her nude crop top and matching leggings, pulled her hair up into a bun and then slipped through the throng to get the obligatory workout selfie. A wall of full-length mirrors was specifically set up for this purpose. Each mirror had a touchpad to adjust the lighting and an extendable arm with a phone holder at the end. Lexi got the snap, uploading it to her Insta as she made her way through the doors to the studio.

'Hey, Lexi!' Inside, a few of the influencer girlies who were gathered in front of the large windows overlooking the river called to her. 'Quick few group shots?'

'Of course.' Lexi joined them. She didn't know all their names, but they were all girls she posed with countless times a month at different influencer events. Everyone's workout gear was in earth tones, except for one girl on the end who was wearing a fluoro bodysuit. Lexi thought she looked gorgeous, but after a few minutes of uncomfortable silence the girl seemed to realise that the group, as a whole, were unimpressed. She was disrupting the tonal cohesion.

'I'll, eh … sit this one out,' she said sheepishly, slipping away.

An assistant gathered up everyone's phones and methodically captured more or less the same shot on each device.

Next, Lexi grabbed a mat over in the corner furthest from the altar where Mel taught. Over to her left, the sound bath practitioner was setting up his bowls and all around her the group were updating their phones on where they were, what they were doing and how excited they were about it all.

Lexi duly propped her phone up on one of the tripods provided, hit record and started her stretches.

'Everyone! EVERYONE!!!' Mel clapped her hands to bring the room to attention. 'It is so wonderful to have all you beautiful souls with me to usher in this bountiful Wednesday. I am so looking forward to creating a soul-enriching space in which we can all move with mindfulness and intentionality. And look good by the end, of course! Today's a special day. Why?' She looked around, presumably noting with satisfaction how many phones were pointed in her direction, capturing this profound moment. She breathed deeply. 'Say it with me, souls.'

'*Every day* is a special day,' everyone obediently chanted.

'Right! First, Elijah will begin the sound bath …' She wafted her hands towards him and he began to run his tool around the singing bowl, creating a melodic vibration. Mel dropped to a crouch and started banging on the floor. 'Right, it's Chakra Crunch time. I want eighty – GO! GO! GO!'

The tone shift was always jarring, Lexi thought, as she began the gruelling workout. The whole class was the furthest from mindful you could get. Not only was Mel's screaming competing with Elijah's sound bath; at any given time at least ten people were talking to their phones – describing what they were doing or taking calls from their 'crystals guy' or just watching other people's social media feeds.

Ironically, Mel didn't allow earphones because they were antisocial and 'disrupted the communal experience'. But phones were, somehow, totally fine. *All the better to 'gram with my pretties!* Lexi grinned to herself.

In the main, Lexi was actually pretty good at tuning the cacophony out. Tuning out cacophonies was basically a requisite for EXISTING in 2023. Tuning out dire warnings about how we're edging towards disaster in every direction: climate, human rights, war crimes. Tuning out the people in the comments berating her for not putting her 'platform' to good use, for not discussing extremely complex injustices about which she had no knowledge or direct experience.

She did try sometimes, but Jonathan was disapproving of her getting 'bogged down' with 'that kind of thing'.

'It's not your brand, Lexi,' he'd stressed. 'Stick to bouncing your tits on your Insta story and shit-talking influencers. If you get sincere, you'll get eaten alive.'

It stung to hear that her own boyfriend didn't rate her opinions but he wasn't wrong. The Hotties could be scathing.

Lexi focused on the next set of instructions from Mel: 'Okay, souls, we are grounding our third eye and we are going for fifty groundings. Let's give it our all! We only have twenty minutes left of class.'

Grounding the third eye – or press-ups, as the rest of the world called them – was a bitch. Lexi was slowing by the thirty mark, her muscles like molasses. She mugged at her camera, taking care to hold her expression for a good twenty seconds so that after the video was edited and speeded up the expression would still land with the viewer. *What a way to live!* She grinned at the thought. *All worth it!* Even the anxiety and the endless bitching about her online would be worth it when they signed this deal and finally got their house. No more precarious renting. They could even finally get a dog!

The sound of her own name amid the chorus of chatter and sound bath droning interrupted her thoughts. She strained to hear. Was someone calling her?

No. She quickly realised it wasn't anyone in the room but a voice coming out of a phone a couple of rows in front of her.

'Lexi didn't say a single thing to her and frankly I am disgusted with them both. Lexi is practically worse than Amanda because she just sits there and laughs along. They have gone too far this time. I really hope their listeners and sponsors get a grip and see them for what they are: toxic bitches.'

Lexi froze.

The all-too-familiar anxiety seized her; a creeping iciness bloomed in her chest and slid down each arm. *Oh god, what now?*

Lexi struggled to hear what else was coming from the phone because the sound bath was hitting a crescendo, but she noticed a few of the other *souls* sneaking surreptitious looks in her direction.

She mentally ran back through the most recent episode of their show. They'd said a lot, but nothing that had massively stood out; she often left records feeling edgy about Amanda's 'takes', but Thursday's had seemed uneventful. A few weeks back they'd had that awful bit about the guy crying because he couldn't get his skinny jeans off, but they'd agreed Amanda would cut that. It wasn't on to make fun of someone's mental health. Though Lexi hadn't listened back to check she had.

Lexi ended the video she was filming on her own phone and brought up the *Your Hot Friend* Twitter. The latest tweet from the account had been sent seven minutes ago and had racked up 874 comments and too many quote-tweets to count. Lexi felt sick at the words Amanda had posted.

> @YourHotFriend: All the men's mental health campaigners complaining about last month's episode need to relaaaax. Don't cry about it, babes. Depression is just the fashionable thing to have these days. Bored of it TBH.

Oh my god. Clutching her phone, Lexi lurched to her feet and bolted for the door, nausea swamping her.

I am going to vom!

She launched herself into the changing rooms. Realising that she wasn't going to make it to the loo, she stumbled to the wall of wooden lockers and pulled one open. *Please be empty, please be empty.* She hurled the full contents of her stomach into the little cubby, wishing she hadn't had smoked salmon and scrambled eggs that morning. Her eyes streamed and her body bucked of its own accord as another wave of bile rose inside her.

She pulled away and managed to get to the bathroom for the rest. She didn't even have time to rinse her mouth out: she needed to clean up the mess and get out before anyone came in. She tried to clear her nose of clumps of regurgitated food – the most disgusting part of getting sick, as Amanda had once pointed out on the pod. Lexi winced, remembering that Amanda had followed it up with 'It's so gross I actually don't know how bulimics do it'. Jesus, that had been a bad one.

She searched around the changing room for a bin to aid the clean-up, but there was no sign of one. Class would be over in minutes. *Shit, shit, shit.*

Lexi pulled her bag over to the lockers and took out the essentials: her laptop and charger, house keys and make-up bag. Then she lifted the bag to meet the edge of the locker and with her own balled-up tee shirt swept the entire mess into her beautiful leather Moschino backpack.

If only the backpack was the sole victim of Amanda's latest bullshit. *What if Podify pulls out?* Lexi shouldered the bag and grabbed up her bits. Her phone was now blowing up with notifications. She walked straight out, back through the birth canal and past reception, trying to look as normal as possible. No doubt anyone who saw her right now would be reporting the sighting back to their WhatsApp groups. She had to look unruffled.

They'd long learned that the more you act like it's a big deal, the more it becomes a big deal.

Maybe it'll be okay. Lexi turned right outside SoulFit and beelined for a bin on the next corner. *I should be used to this by now. Just stay calm. Maybe it'll be one of the ones that blows over fairly quickly.*

With cancellations, you could never tell what would really catch fire and what would burn hot for a minute and then fizzle out.

She carefully placed the laptop and other bits in her arms down by her feet, pulled off her bag and assessed the damage. The smell was horrific; the bag was unsalvageable. She pushed the whole lot into the mouth of the bin and scooped up the rest of her stuff.

She pulled out her phone and, ignoring the mounting texts and missed calls, placed an order on the taxi app, selecting her destination: home. She needed to clean herself up and get it together for this Podify meeting. Would the meeting still go ahead, though? She swallowed back her rising dread.

Podify knew what they were getting into with us; they can't be that shocked that we've said something that's got people's backs up. That's kind of what we do.

She checked in on Twitter again. Amanda hadn't posted anything else from the *YHF* account.

Lexi switched to Instagram to find Amanda doing a blasé LIVE of her skincare routine.

'Hotties, I know it's not some big newsflash, but it's SOOOO important to drink enough water if you want your skin to be flawless. So after cleaning, I'm just going to put on my serum.'

She had a white towel around her head and a skinny little cigarette hanging out of the side of her mouth. She looked like Brigitte Bardot.

Real-time comments scrolled at the bottom.

'You. Are. Flawless!!!! HOW?!?!!'

'Yesssss GET IT Amanda don't let the haterz wreck your buzz.'

'Shame on you for smoking on here, young girls follow you and look up to you.'

'Unbelievable scenes on Twitter rn. You've really upset the WokeBaes this time – hilarious!!!'

'It's not right to degrade an unwell man in one of your sexcapade anecdotes. Vile girl.'

On screen, Amanda paused to scan the comments on her phone, apparently amused.

'Haha I see ye're all LOVING the latest Twitter Tanty! Trust men to be such pussies lol. Ooooh, and hi to all the young girls out there who I'm told follow me. Never forget, girlies, smoking is not cool ... it's actually hot AF!'

CHRIST! Lexi's cab pulled up and she threw herself into the back seat.

Back on Twitter, she found a tweet with a clip from *YHF* attached. She slipped in her ear buds. She knew what was coming.

Amanda: So I was on a date with one of those ... you know those guys who make their depression their whole personality, right? So tedious. But anyway, I figured I'd throw him a bone. So we were back at his place and ... well, let's just say that you haven't lived until you've seen a man crying cos he can't get it—.

Lexi: Amanda, fucking hell.

Amanda: *laughing*

Lexi: We're cutting that. We'd be ROASTED. Plus it's really mean.

Amanda: You've gone so soft, Lex – much like our sad lad.

The clip cut out there. Exhaustion swept over Lexi. The taxi sped down the quays, passing the hordes of people heading in towards the city centre, no doubt to jobs that weren't destroying their mental health. Although, god, what job wasn't doing that to some degree?

At last, they pulled up outside her building. *I only left an hour ago. How has this day already imploded?*

'Thanks a mil, have a good day.' Lexi hopped out of the back of the car, her arms full of her belongings. *I loved that bag. Just the latest casualty of Your Hot Friend. Along with my reputation.*

Inside the apartment, she quickly showered, vigorously brushed her teeth and finally felt together enough to look at her phone again. Her DMs were rammed and she made the decision then and there to get Aine to clear them; she couldn't cope with reading through all the rage and judgement of strangers. In her WhatsApp she could see notifications from a few of the groups she was in. *What are they saying?*

She opened the Soul Crew chat, which was full of the influencers she'd posed with at the start of class. No one had posted a message but there were eleven new notifications:

Katja has left the group

Alice has left the group

Siobhan has left the group

Byron has left the group

Casey has left the group

And so on and so on.

Lexi was the only person left. *Fucking great,* she thought, her eyes stinging with tears.

Another group she'd created for a trip she and a bunch of other influencers had been invited on was the same story. Everyone had left. She was the last person in there. It was the same for the apartment building group and the school gang from down home one.

She desperately wanted to call Abi, but he was on a research trip off the west coast and wouldn't be contactable until after the weekend.

A message from Jonathan was stark:

> *Do nothing, say nothing. I rescheduled the Podify meeting. We need this to blow over. Home asap. We'll be doing an apology video for this one. I'm thinking we post a formal statement today: 'we're sorry to everyone hurt by our actions, want to be held accountable' etc etc 'taking a few days to reflect' etc etc. I'm working on the script right now. Then video to follow. We'll take a break on the main feed but better keep the patron content going just keep it fucking light and nothing gets posted without my sign off.*

Lexi went to her phone settings and switched off all notifications. Then she rang the one person she had left to talk to, even though she was fucking livid with her.

'Hey bébé!' Amanda trilled. 'You have a nice session this morning? You didn't post a vid though? Mel's gonna be pissed!'

'Amanda …' Lexi wasn't surprised that she sounded so absolutely fine. *How does it not get to her? Our million-dollar deal is now hanging in the balance. My fucking dream house. Not to mention we sounded like ignorant bitches.*

'OMG, speaking of pissed, Twitter is RAGING with us. Lol.' Amanda barrelled on. 'Jonathan says he's moved the Podify meeting! Surprise day off, girlie. We should get locked!'

'Manda, this isn't a fucking surprise day off. This could be us losing our fucking jobs. Why didn't you cut the bit like I asked you to?'

'I just forgot but like, relax, this is just the internet being pricks. They'll get annoyed over something else in like two days.'

'That's not the point.' Lexi tried not to sound like a person about to start sobbing. 'What we said was really fucking wrong. I think we need to talk this out.'

'We are! We're talking right now. Plus as you know I talk better with a marg in my hand. Will we go down to Tijuana's for lunch?'

Lexi ignored this. Jesus, the optics of the two of them out for lunch and day-drinking while the shitstorm raged would not be good. And there'd be a pretty high chance of them being spotted by fans wanting selfies. They were nearly always recognised when they were together.

'I don't want to go out, Amanda,' Lexi said flatly. 'This is … This is FUCKED. What if Podify pull out? Don't you fucking care? Jonathan is furious. You know we made an offer on the house. Everyone has left virtually every WhatsApp group I'm in.'

Lexi sat down on her bed and stared out at the boats on the

harbour. She could see people happily strolling on the pier. People who weren't reviled online right now. Lexi's anxiety surged again and then the sobs rose in her throat.

'Yeah, Jesus, I saw the school gang one ...' Amanda was at least sounding a fraction more contrite. 'Awwww, Lexi, please don't cry. It'll blow over. I promise it will. Look at Joe Rogan – he's still the richest podcaster in the world.'

'That is not the comforting statement you think it is.' Lexi somehow managed to smile amidst the tears.

'Yeah, bad example,' Amanda said hurriedly. 'Okay, what about John Lennon? Everyone loves him and he was an abusive husband!'

Lexi sniffed. 'Stop trying to cheer me up.'

'Apparently Mother Teresa was a bit of a bitch.'

'Okay stop,' Lexi giggled. 'She's a dead nun. This is not funny.'

'You're the one laughing,' Amanda said in a reasonable voice.

'Shut up!'

'We're bad people together,' Amanda said soothingly.

Oddly, this did make Lexi feel marginally better. Amanda always made things seem a bit lighter, less catastrophic. Lexi could almost imagine none of this was a big deal if she just focused on Amanda and pretended the rest of the world didn't exist.

'Okay,' she sighed. 'You win. Come over. We'll order takeaway. But we're not drinking. Jonathan says this one's gonna need a formal apology. We've to do a video.'

'Okay,' Amanda replied. 'I'll pick up some booze for after.'

Lexi hung up and gazed down at the black screen of the phone. It only took a beat for the thoughts of the rest of the world to rush back in. Living out your life online was such a volatile position to be in. On any given day her phone was either buzzing with compliments …

Your hair is so gorge, Lexi.
I love your trackies.
I wish I had your confidence.
I wish I had your life.
Jonathan and Lexi are like the dream couple.
Lexi and Amanda are kweens.

… or teeming with the loathing comments of strangers:

Lexi and Amanda are everything that's wrong with internet culture.
Absolute lol at her podcast being called *Your Hot Friend*, Lexi is fugly.
Ever notice that Lexi is totally boring, Amanda's the funny one even if she is problematic.
Lexi is so fucking ignorant, read a book you dumb whore.

CHAPTER 8

Claire was hiding in the chilly loos at Miller's, the restaurant Jamie had chosen for their customary Wednesday night date. She'd come straight from work and wanted to spruce before Jamie saw her. That was the thing about living with your person. The mystery drained away pretty quick. Especially in a Dublin flat. Most flats in the city were so tiny, you could flush the loo without moving from the couch. For some reason once you lived together everything felt very bathroom-orientated. Claire would be trying to go to the loo while Jamie shouted through the door, asking where the remote was. Or Claire would be taking a shower and Jamie would blithely pop in to have a wee at the exact same time.

Claire patted concealer under her eyes and checked the time on her phone, propped by the sink. Ten more minutes till Jamie would arrive. She flicked over to her WhatsApp thread with Aifric. Three weeks (technically three weeks and two days) had passed since Aifric had asked her to do the wedding favours and there'd been nothing further. Aifric hadn't even joined the shared Pinterest board Claire had created.

She thinks I'm desperate. Pathetic. She's off talking to Nadia about me.

She knew that Ella, her therapist, would say she was doing Aifric's thinking for her.

Ella.

I need to start going again.

Their last session had been in November. Claire hadn't meant to let so long lapse, December had just been so hectic and now here she was, a week into February and still couldn't bring herself to book in.

Ugh. Why is self-care such hard work?

Claire leaned into the mirror to line her lips. She was doing a new thing where she only over-drew them just at her cupid's-bow; she'd seen Lexi doing something similar in a recent 'Get Ready With Me' reel.

Claire gathered her make-up back into her bag and checked in on the Bitch Herd. No one had responded to the link she'd sent of the *Your Hot Friend* apology video – though *YHF* wasn't exactly their kind of thing.

The clip had only just landed even though the whole shitshow had happened a week ago. The video had been straight out of the shamed influencer playbook. Lexi and Amanda were suitably subdued – minimal make-up, grey hoodies. They claimed they wanted 'to be held accountable'. They were 'owning their actions' and would be donating their February earnings to men's mental health charities. Claire detected a whisper of a sneer on Amanda's face, though Lexi looked genuinely shaken.

Claire was ready to forgive and forget. What fave *wasn't* problematic these days? Still best not bring out the *YHF* tote bag for a few weeks, though, to be on the safe side.

Claire snapped a selfie and sent it to the Bitch Herd group:

Not me trying to make Jamie forget he saw me squeeze a spot this morning #longtermcouplesprobs

A few of the girls sent grossed-out emojis and laughing GIFs, but there was nothing from Aifric.

She cast a last cursory glance around the bathroom to make sure she wasn't forgetting anything and then, satisfied, headed out the side door, pulling up her navy-blue duffle coat with the fur-trimmed hood.

As she headed round to the front of the restaurant, two separate messages from her parents dropped in to her WhatsApp. At the exact same time. Why did that feel so ominous? She opened her dad's text first.

Hi Claire Hope you're well. I miss seeing you though I know coming out to the house is probably not the nicest prospect for you at the moment. Anyway, I'm sure Jamie's taking you somewhere nice for Valentine's but I was wondering if you would maybe like to have dinner the Saturday after? My treat of course! A little Dadentine's Night!

Oh god why was a Dad Text so tragic. She was picturing him painstakingly typing it out on his old Nokia phone, grappling with the predictive text, and she felt like crying.

She x'ed out of his message and into her mother's Voicy.

Claire, I assume you and Jamie have Valentine's plans but on the weekend following, I think we need to book in a Galentine's night for the Saturday. I'm sure your father will be making some pathetic attempt to thwart me on this one but girls need to stick together. We'll be watching the BBC's *Pride and Prejudice* and ordering takeaway.

Good god, Claire didn't have the energy to make excuses then and there but excuses would be made. She couldn't play favourites.

Around the front of Miller's, Jamie was scrolling on his phone. As Claire approached, he looked up and did an elaborate impression of being bowled over at the sight of her.

'Ooooooh,' he murmured appreciatively, taking in the black crop top and stretch mini-skirt that Claire had changed into before leaving the Sweeneys' house. 'You look so beautiful!'

Claire feigned preening and then kissed him.

'Don't rush to say how gorgeous I look or anything.'

'You look gorgeous too.'

'Okay.' Jamie pulled away. 'As delicious as you are, I'm starving!'

'I know, I could eat a baby's arse through the bars of its cot,' Claire chirped, leading the way.

'Fucking hell!' Jamie looked stricken.

'My god!' Claire looked back, laughing. 'You can be so English sometimes!'

Inside, the restaurant was jammers with couples. They took their seats and began the complicated task of ordering while the waiter stood patiently as they squabbled over who was getting what. Then, while Jamie drew him into a lengthy debate about the various craft beers, Claire sneakily checked on the Bitch Herd. No response from Aifric still.

Maybe she thinks the spot-squeezing thing was gross? That I'm gross? *Maybe she's not responding cos they're all out without me?*

Claire tried to dismiss the thought before it could take hold and ruin her night.

'What's up?' Jamie had released the waiter from the craft beer agonising and was looking over, concerned.

'Oh, nothing.' Claire flipped the phone face down on the table so Jamie wouldn't see it was open to WhatsApp.

She needn't have bothered, as he immediately said, 'Bitch Herd living up to their name?'

'It's nothing.'

'Ironic names are very dangerous,' Jamie remarked.

'C'mon ...' Claire said brightly, changing tack as the waiter reappeared with their drinks. She took a sip of her mojito. 'Let's play.'

'Okay.' Jamie kicked off their favourite game: guess the relationship stage. 'Table by the window beside the monstera plant. They're together five months. She's wondering if they're going to acknowledge their six-month anniversary in March. He's ... still talking to his ex on Facebook.'

'No, no,' Claire protested. 'You're so cynical. She's fretting over next month's anniversary and HE's trying to gauge whether six months is too early to propose.'

Next Claire cleared her throat meaningfully and flicked her eyes to the table right beside them. Two men were finishing a shared starter of chicken wings. They were both attractive but shared a slightly shell-shocked look.

Claire leaned towards Jamie and dropped her voice. 'New parents out for their first night since the baby.'

One of the men took out his phone. Jamie and Claire leaned towards them slightly to try and catch what they were saying.

'I'm just having a quick look, to make sure she hasn't texted.'

The other man rolled his eyes. 'Stop it, we've only been gone an hour.'

'But what if she's having an emergency!'

'You checked five minutes ago and they were fine. Anyway, I know what you're up to. You're looking at photos, aren't you?'

'I'm not!' The guy with the phone pressed the screen to his chest.

'Oh really, you're not?! Then show me the phone, David.'

'Okay, fine.' He turned the phone around. 'You got me. But look at him. He's just divine.'

The other guy softened instantly. 'Isn't he just amazing?' They both gazed lovingly at the phone.

Claire raised a glass, as if to say, 'Am I right, or am I right?!' Just as Jamie raised his to clink, Claire spotted Aifric standing at the front of the restaurant, waiting to be seated. Beside her was Paul, who Aifric always described as a serial entrepreneur, which Claire kind of suspected was a positive way of saying he was a serial scammer.

The sight of the two of them together flooded Claire with giddy relief. Aifric and the others weren't out without her! Aifric was on a date with Paul!

Claire pulled out her phone and caught Jamie frowning.

'Stop obsessing, Claire. I don't like that they always make you feel so insecure like this. They're truly not worth it, babe. They didn't even visit you once last year—'

'Relax,' Claire interjected – she did not want to talk about last year. 'I'm just texting Aifric,' she continued. 'She and Paul are up by the doors. Maybe we could have a drink with them after dinner instead of the movie?'

'Okay.' Jamie didn't sound particularly enthused as Claire tossed off a quick text to Aifric.

Hey guess where I am?!

From her seat she could see Aifric taking out her phone and checking it. Claire looked down at the WhatsApp thread to check if it said *Aifric is typing*, but nothing.

Maybe she's just distracted, Claire reasoned. *But if we're going to go for a drink, we should arrange it sooner rather than later.*

The starters arrived: deep-fried jalapenos and mini fish tacos.

Claire pulled back from the table. 'I'm just going to the loo real quick. Start without me.'

She swiftly made her way to the back of the dining room and slipped behind a crowd of people at the bar. She could still see Aifric from here. She dialled her number – the only number she knew off by heart – and watched as Aifric pulled out her phone again and stared at the screen. But she didn't answer. Instead she turned and showed the phone to Paul, who shrugged and rolled his eyes a little. Aifric returned the phone to her bag and snapped it shut.

Claire's thoughts began to hurtle with hurt and confusion.

Maybe she's just in the middle of something with Paul.

Maybe she hates you.

Maybe she's tired. Or has PMS.

Maybe you've done something to upset her.

Maybe she has a sore throat.

Oh, c'mon, Claire, that's the stupidest one yet.

Now, Claire wished she and Jamie could leave. She didn't want to run into Aifric after that; it would look so desperate. She slunk off in the direction of the bathrooms, debating her options. They'd been having such a nice time. She hated ruining it, but seeing Aifric ignore her had soured the night irretrievably.

In the toilets, she composed a message to Jamie:

> *I'm so sorry to do this. I don't know what's happened but I feel really sick. Can we go? I can just meet you round by the side.*

When she'd sent it, she let the tears come. The usual refrain started up in her head. *Why am I so pathetic? Why am I such a loser?*

She didn't worry about Jamie seeing her crying. It made the lie more convincing; she always got teary when she wasn't well. And she *did* feel nauseous. Just not for the reason she'd told Jamie.

The next day, Lila was bent over the badge-maker, lining up her little round drawing with the plain metal disc underneath and the clear plastic cover on top. They were sitting at the kitchen island with Sonny in his highchair and the quiet chatter of Frankie orchestrating a battle with his Duplo figures in the background.

'You never told me how last night went.'

'Grand.' Claire smiled, trying to ignore the sickening stir of fresh embarrassment as she thought back to the restaurant. When she'd woken up that morning, for a moment she couldn't quite locate the reason for the niggling uneasiness she felt. It only took a second for the image of Aifric looking at her phone and showing it to Paul to assail her, and a lurch of revulsion kicked in her stomach. Revulsion at herself.

Her desperate self.

'What's wrong?' Lila was staring at her.

You can't get anything past her, Claire thought. *Is the eleven-year-old child I mind actually my best friend?*

'Nothing's wrong, sweets ... Last night was really nice and then I sort of ran into Aifric and ...'

Claire hesitated, spooning yoghurt into Sonny's chubby lips. She didn't want to detail how she'd run out after seeing Aifric ignoring her call. How to explain the complexities of adult female friendship to a little girl?

Lila put down the badge-maker, folded her arms and sighed heavily.

'Claire, I don't like Aifric for you. I get that you have this, like, historic friendship, but she doesn't treat you well. I know what I'm talking about.'

Her voice was concerned but stern and the sight of her little world-weary face made Claire smile in spite of everything.

Just then, Sonny slapped his hand down into the puddle of yoghurt he had been silently spreading on his highchair tray.

'Oh no,' Claire said, resigned, as yoghurt dripped down her face. 'I'm just going to clean him up and then we'll make smoothies.' Lila nodded as Claire hiked the baby up out of his seat and made her way out to the bathroom just off the kitchen.

'How aww ru?' Sonny babbled in her arms.

She smiled at his little attempt at adult pleasantries. Words that he'd picked up from her.

'I am not good,' she told him quietly as she sat him on the toilet seat, dampened a face cloth and began wiping yoghurt out of his strawberry-blond curls.

As she rinsed the cloth, she stared at her yoghurty face in the mirror and a memory rose up before her: she and Aifric in the exact same positions in her parents' bathroom. They were still in their itchy grey school uniforms. Aifric sat on the toilet seat, her face caked in a concoction of yoghurt and oats, while Claire had avocado mashed with honey smeared on her face. They'd both coiled their hair on top of their heads and slathered in egg whites and lemon juice, a sticky mix which was supposedly going to give them shiny locks – all beauty methods they'd picked up in *Seventeen*.

'Are we rides yet?' fourteen-year-old Aifric laughed as bits of porridgy sludge dropped off her face.

'We're definitely delicious.' Claire licked at the avocado beside her mouth. 'I need some Doritos for my stuff!'

'What we need to do is get this shite off and call Eoghan Whelan right now!' Aifric had giggled. Beauty experiments and prank-calling the hot guys in their year had been two staples of afternoons in Claire's house. Sonny yelling drew Claire back to the present moment.

'Alright, alright. Relaaax, chicky.' She soothed him and took out her phone, spotting the perfect chance to text Aifric, who had still not replied to last night's message. 'C'mere little chunk.' Claire held the phone out and squeezed in beside him so their yoghurt-smeared faces were side by side. She snapped a pic and WhatsApped it to Aifric.

Look who's re-enacting Claire and Aifric circa 2005!

The message blue-ticked while she was still looking at the phone, but there was no sign of Aifric typing.

Claire sighed.

'How aww ru?' Sonny chirped again.

'Great,' she intoned flatly, trying to push away the self-pity.

'Mess! Mess!' Sonny held up his hands, coated in Petits Filous, and she couldn't help but smile.

This is what's great about my job, she thought. *Kids are such cute, self-centred narcissists you don't even have time to dwell!*

'Okay, let's get you clean.'

Later she stood waiting for the tram listening to *Your Hot Friend* and staring at her thread with Aifric. It felt fitting that the gals were talking about relationship red flags and ghosting. It was now seven p.m., four hours since she'd sent the picture, and she was feeling increasingly nihilistic.

She wished she could give less of a shit about things, the way Amanda and Lexi did. It'd only been a week since they'd pissed off half the internet by making fun of a guy with depression and here they were talking about how to mess with a guy's head when he ghosted you.

'I know, I've been in monogamy jail for literally years now,' Lexi was laughing. 'But I swear I am still the authority on dealing with male ghosts.'

'Okay let's hear it. I think we should all cut Lexi some slack, though. The poor gal thinks she's still relevant but she's about to give us some extremely 2018 dating advice. She hasn't been in the singles trenches for fully five years.'

'Lol, shut up,' Lexi snapped. 'Right, so my tip is posting a pointed meme on your socials cos you know he's probably still lurking. I used to have a little folder on my phone with memes and GIFs to fuck with male ghosts' heads. So here's one: the image is a hot girl shrugging and the caption says: "*gets ghosted*. Me: Thank you for the free fifteen-day trial." You see, you wanna select the meme carefully. You need to strike a balance between letting them know that you fucking KNOW WHAT THEY'RE DOING and showing that you could not give a single fucking crap.'

'Yassss!' Amanda clapped her hands. 'Okay, that's our show for today, Hotties. Remember to do all the bullshit that other podcasts are always banging on about, rate, review, join the patreon, blaa blaa.'

Claire pondered the episode as the tram approached.

What we really need is friendship red flags and some kind of rules or guidelines for dealing with them, she mused as she stepped on to the mercifully quiet carriage and found a seat. *Is Aifric ghosting me? Or more like breadcrumbing, giving me just a little, enough for me to keep trailing around?*

Not for the first time, she wished she had a Lexi or an Amanda. *Aifric and I used to be that way. Didn't we?*

She took out her phone and brought up her Insta story. Her last post had been a picture of her breakfast burrito. *God I am basic.* She checked the viewers. She'd become convinced that Aifric had her on mute because she interacted with her so little on Insta now, but with a gust of relief she saw her profile there, near the top of the list of people who'd watched it.

Ella, her therapist in the clinic – *just say hospital, Claire!* – would strenuously discourage this kind of over-analytical behaviour. Unhealthy and self-harming, would probably be her take.

When did I last see her?

Ella had actually sent an email last month that Claire couldn't quite bring herself to reply to. She brought it up now.

Hi Claire,
I hope you are well and had a nice restful Christmas? Rest is still very important at this stage in your recovery. I know you said you can no longer do the Wednesday slot, but I think it's important we find a different time that works. Let me know and I will try to accommodate your schedule.
Warm regards,
Ella

Ella's concern made Claire anxious. She didn't want to need a therapist.

I'm feeling better, I should really reply even just to get her off my back.

Claire hit reply and started to type.

Hi Ella
I

... 'I' what?

I don't wanna talk about stuff? Stuff is hard? I want to just ignore stuff?

Claire sighed, abandoned the message and opened Google. She shifted in her seat, recrossing her legs, and searched for just the right thing to post to her Instagram. Lexi and Amanda were right: Insta was a great way to pass-agg people. She often saw women she followed posting memes about bitchy friends and toxic relationships. Things like graphics stating:

She's not your friend if ...
She makes you feel bad about yourself.
She never listens to your issues.
She always picks her boyfriend over you.

She didn't want anything that harsh, just something to show Aifric that she had noticed her behaviour and was hurt.

In the image search, Claire saw a picture of a little girl posing beside various snakes in the zoo, captioned: 'When you look back at old pictures of you and your past friends.'

Claire laughed grimly to herself and quickly posted it to her Insta before she could change her mind.

The tram swerved on through the streets, the February darkness punctuated by street lamps and the golden windows of pubs.

Her phone buzzed with a WhatsApp notification. *No shit,* she smiled to herself. It was Aifric replying to her message about the yoghurt facial! She felt her gloom palpably dissipate as she read Aifric's message.

Oh my god this is so us in second year! All that's missing is a plate of Bagel Bites. Fuck me, I miss them, they've disappeared off the island like. And so sorry I didn't get back last night. Paul was all 'no phones on date night'. Listen, I've been meaning to ask you, I'm going dress shopping in a couple of weeks with my mum and all the aunts are you game!? We can talk about the party favours.

Claire quickly hopped back over to Instagram and deleted the meme she'd posted. *That was a total overreaction,* she told herself as she returned to WhatsApp, and beaming, dashed off a reply to Aifric's invitation.

I am there!!!! CANNOT WAIT!

A second text from Aifric dropped in below.

Sorry just realised it's gonna be a very me-centric weekend with the dress shopping on Saturday and the brunch Nadia's organised on the Sunday LOL. XXX

Claire frowned. What brunch?

She left her thread with Aifric and spotted a new message from Nadia, who rarely texted her directly, inviting her to a 'brunch summit' the day after the dress-shopping to discuss what she was referring to as the 'Aifric Engagement Roll Out'.

Claire's mood darkened once more. There'd been zero mention of the brunch until now. *Aifric must've told Nadia to invite me like this second.* She took a breath trying to unclench her jaw. *I'm overthinking.*

A buzz from her phone signalled another message from Aifric. It was a picture of the two of them in their teens, laughing with what looked like Ready Brek smeared on their faces.

> *From the Claire and Aifric annals!!! Can't believe we've been friends for over 20 years WTF.*

Claire's mood rebounded instantly and happiness bloomed in her chest. She sent a GIF of a panda laughing. Her thoughts flickered to the half-composed email to Ella, but she didn't return to it. The robotic lady voice of the Luas announced her stop, Spencer Dock, and Claire hopped off, her steps lighter. All niggles about the belated brunch invite and therapist emails banished.

CHAPTER 9

Abi handed Lexi her coffee and they grabbed a corner table in the little basement cafe off Merrion Square in Dublin's city centre. The cafe was quiet for a Friday morning and Lexi was glad; the apology video had gone out two days before and Lexi was feeling more than a little bit exposed.

'So, how is the apology going down?'

Lexi looked uneasily at him. When he'd got back from the research trip a few days after the whole debacle and seen everything online, he'd sent her a very cold text:

I can't believe you.

He hadn't answered her calls and it was only after a few pleading texts that he'd agreed to meet her this morning.

'I haven't looked at the video, to be honest,' she admitted, blowing on her coffee. 'Jonathan will take the temperature and let me know today.'

'Why did you wait a week to make the apology?'

'Jonathan felt a slower rollout would make it look more considered, more sincere.'

'Oh, did he?'

Abi was not thawing, and after the last few days and the deluge of hate and opinion online, Lexi wasn't sure she'd be able to hold it together.

He stirred his coffee and looked across at her. 'So would it *be* more considered and sincere, Lexi? Or just *look* more considered and sincere? Is how it looks the most important thing?'

'No! Abi! We ARE sorry! So, so sorry.'

'Lexi, why the "we"? You are getting dragged into Amanda's shite non-stop. I know this isn't you.'

Lexi dropped her gaze. 'Well, I'M sorry, then. I was upset when she said it. It was never supposed to air. Then it did. What can I do? I have to stand by her. She's my best friend. And like ...' Lexi sighed heavily. 'I know how this is going to sound, but the fact is she's my business partner. It's a tricky time. There's real stuff at stake. Jonathan and I have put in an offer on the house. The Podify execs, thank god, haven't pulled the deal. They're going through with it; they just want to wait it out for a couple more weeks for things to blow over. Amanda and I just need to keep our heads down.'

'Lexi, I am seriously questioning your judgement here. I see you, you know. I see your Lexi persona and then I see you when you're yourself. You're anxious. You've completely lost touch with your other friends. You're so wrapped up in Jonathan and Amanda and now you're about to get even deeper into this whole thing. What exactly will your obligation to Podify be?'

'The Podify deal is not some life sentence,' she replied. 'We're committing to a year with them. It's a major opportunity, with major money.'

'And what if you and Amanda fall out? This whole major money opportunity is predicated on your friendship. You're putting a helluva lotta eggs in one basket, Lex. What are you going to do? Hand back the money the next time Amanda throws you under the bus?'

'She's never thrown me under the bus,' Lexi argued.

'She should have made that apology video on her own and owned her own mistakes. I find it really hard to believe that she'd have sat beside you if the situation was reversed.'

'Of course she would, she's—'

'Your best friend, yeah yeah!' Abi shook his head, frustrated. 'Lexi, I wish you would listen to me. I am practically the only person in your life who *doesn't* have a vested interest in you now. You, Amanda and Jonathan are a house of cards.'

'Abi, you're blowing this way out of proportion. Seriously. You're acting like they're plotting to screw me over. We all need each other equally. If anyone could get screwed, it's Jonathan: me and Manda could ditch him tomorrow! Well, except it wouldn't be a great idea for the mortgage.'

'You see! You fucking see!' Abi pointed at her, his rising tone attracting the attention of the barista. 'You're all tied up together and it is precarious as fuck.'

'Abi, please can you just be nice to me right now? You don't know how it feels to weather a week of people hating you.'

His face softened slightly. 'Okay, look. People don't hate you. It's just people online.'

Lexi shook her head. 'There's no difference between online and offline any more. It's all the same thing now.'

'Can I ask you something?'

'Yes,' Lexi ventured, unsure if she was going to like the question.

'Do you still enjoy this stuff? Are you and Amanda even real friends any more?'

'Yes,' Lexi cried. 'Like, of course this has pissed me off, but she's still my best friend. We have niggly things with the pod and stuff, but I love her. And she loves me. And we make it work.'

Abi gave a weary grin. 'You sound like a married couple.'

'Well …' Lexi shifted a little awkwardly. 'We're actually going into therapy together. Sort of couples' therapy. But platonic. It was something I asked that we do this year just to keep the lines of communication … well … ya know. Anyway, our first appointment is at twelve, just next door.'

'I see.' He was inscrutable.

'Don't judge,' Lexi warned. 'It's just to help us …'

'Stay professional best friends?'

'That's mean,' she said sharply. 'Look, we have an unusual friendship. We're navigating a new kind of terrain. Podcasting duos didn't exist five years ago. It's just to keep our relationship healthy. And make sure that we don't lose sight of what matters to us in all this: our friendship. And actually, I'm going to have to go if I'm to get there on time.'

She gathered her jacket and bag and leaned down to hug him.

'Thank you for coming to meet me. And I know you care, but don't worry – there's so many good things happening.'

'Maybe we should just start?' Lexi uncrossed her legs, then recrossed them in the other direction. 'It's so awkward just sitting here, isn't it?!'

'Here' was Roslyn Sullivan's therapy suite in the Marriage Mind

Magic clinic and they'd been sitting in silence for nine and a half minutes.

'Are you feeling awkward?' Roslyn smiled from her chair on the other side of the low glass coffee table, where a lavender candle flickered and a box of tissues rested.

'No, no,' Lexi protested, smiling. 'I'm not awkward. I'm just really sorry she's late.'

'Hmm.' Roslyn jotted something down in the notebook she had resting on her knees. 'Do you find yourself apologising for Amanda a lot?'

'Oh no, not really.' Lexi shook her head so vehemently she felt a twinge in her neck.

Lol, unless you count this week's large-scale public apology video which according to a text Jonathan had sent right before the session now had over 50k views and was 'playing well'. This is the kind of thing I should be telling her, I suppose.

'That's not altogether true, is it?' Roslyn prodded gently.

Lexi sighed and cleared her throat nervously. Roslyn smiled expectantly.

'Eh, no,' Lexi admitted. 'Sometimes Amanda can be a bit loose with her opinions and obviously because of the show … well … we have to maintain a united front.'

'Do you?' Roslyn raised a neat dark eyebrow. Everything about her was very neat and precise. From her helmet-like bob to her silky tailored trousers with a cream cashmere top. It must be a lot of pressure to look the part of a therapist. You had to look perfectly together at all times, as if your own life wasn't going to shit. And all that while listening to other people's boring problems. Though being one half of *Your Hot Friend* came with its own annoying sartorial demands; she had to look hot on the daily. Even at therapy, she was wearing a lilac tie-dye tracksuit with a matching crop top. Not for Roslyn's benefit but in the very likely event that she'd be accosted by Hotties at least once on her way there and back.

'I kind of do have to show a united front, yeah. Being best friends isn't just *part* of our schtick. It's the *whole* schtick.'

'Do you think that's a good thing?'

This conversation was going in the wrong direction. *We're not paying her for us to come up with answers.*

Lexi folded her arms. 'I don't know, do you not think it's a good thing?'

The door burst open at that point and Amanda strode in.

'Bébés! I am so late! I cannot even believe myself sometimes!' She flopped into the little armchair beside Lexi, dragging a hand through her long blonde hair. No actual apology, Lexi noted. Across the table, she spotted Roslyn also noting something.

'Amanda ...' Roslyn looked across at her and smiled. 'It's great to meet you and I am so glad that you've chosen to work with me. Firstly, thank you both for filling out the intake forms. I find it's very useful to get a sense of you as individuals before the first session. Though, Amanda,' she added delicately, 'I didn't actually receive yours?'

Lexi rolled her eyes. Of course not; Manda couldn't do one fucking thing without being nagged a million times.

'Ooops, right, sorry.' Amanda started digging through her bag – a bag that hadn't recently been used to ferry vomit, Lexi thought a little petulantly. 'Here it is.' She leaned across to Roslyn, unfolding a sheaf of white sheets of paper. 'Right,' Amanda sat back, 'so what the hell do we do here?'

'For our first session, I would like to get a firm handle on your relationship history to date and then if we have time we will start to catalogue the instances of "relationship distress". Then between now and our next session, I'll be able to take some time with all the information and start to work on identifying patterns in the various conflicts. And in the meantime, I'm going to give you some communication guidelines – language you both can use when addressing the difficult emotions that come up between you. I would usually also give intimacy homework but as this is a platonic relationship, I'll think of an appropriate alternative. How does all that sound?'

'Absolutely batshit,' Amanda announced, just as Lexi said, 'Great.' Lexi looked at Amanda and gave her a ratty little headshake.

'What?' Amanda yelped at her. 'Like, no offence, Roslyn, but this is totally dumb. We're not married, Lexi. We don't need counselling.'

'Even if you think it's not necessary now, Amanda, a lot of couples get counselling to preempt any problems. Also, Lexi has already expressed some issues she is experiencing in the relationship.'

'What the fuck?' Amanda rounded on Lexi. 'You were talking about me when I wasn't even here yet?'

'No.' Roslyn cut in before Lexi had to respond. 'She actually filled out her intake form.'

Now it was Lexi's turn to round on Amanda: 'Did you not even fill it out, Manda?'

'She wrote some things down alright.' Roslyn held up the crumpled first page of Amanda's form, which had 'THIS IS WANK' written in huge letters across it. 'And this.' Roslyn held up the second page, on which Amanda had scrawled a big pair of boobs.

Amanda burst out laughing. 'Where's the lie?' she crowed, as if

Roslyn wasn't sitting right there. 'Look, Lexi, she's a dark entity. She's trying to drive a wedge between us.'

Lexi sighed. *Why the hell did I think she would take this in any way seriously? She could at least be a little contrite after the week we've had.*

'Amanda, Lexi has very real issues that you need to hear. And maybe you have some of your own?'

'I don't, hon.' She exhaled with obvious impatience.

Roslyn filed Amanda's useless forms in a binder that was propped on the floor by the leg of her chair. For the first time, Amanda looked a little concerned.

She gestured towards it. 'What? Are they going to be thrown back in my face at some point?'

'They are for my records,' Roslyn answered curtly. 'Now, you two met when?'

'The year of our Lord two thousand and five,' Amanda said in a sing-song voice.

'And how did you two meet?'

'We met on the first day of secondary school,' Lexi offered up quietly.

'And how was that?' asked Roslyn without looking up from scribbling in her notebook.

'Well, it was the best day of my life,' Amanda snapped defiantly.

Roslyn immediately looked up. 'Can you speak about that a little more?'

'Becoming friends with Lexi is hands down the best thing that ever happened to me. She is the most amazing friend in the world. And look at what we've created together.' Amanda smiled over at Lexi and she couldn't help but thaw a little.

She took up the thread. 'That summer was so hard, my mum had just died and the first thing that happened when I got to the new school was these girls laughed at me because my hair was kind of shitty and knotty at the back. I was twelve years old, like. I only had my brothers and my dad, who were all totally useless. Anyway, Amanda came up and called them stupid bitches.'

'I was rad, even then!' Amanda interjected, grinning triumphantly at Roslyn.

Lexi laughed. 'You completely were. I couldn't believe that someone cool like you was actually talking to me, never mind being nice.'

'I fixed her hair,' Amanda told Roslyn. 'She did look like shit. Not like the hot ride we see before us now!'

'That's lovely.' Roslyn gave an efficient little smile and continued on. 'And how did the relationship progress?'

'Progress?' Amanda sounded scathing again. 'We hung out, Roslyn. All pretty average stuff. We kissed boys, shared dolly mixtures, held each other's hair when we were drunk.'

'Sorry, let me clarify. How was the power dynamic from then on? Was one dominant and one submissive?'

Amanda snorted and made no move to answer.

'No one was *dominating* ...' Lexi answered carefully. 'But sometimes Amanda could be kind of, ya know, forceful about stuff.'

'What? C'mon, Lexi. Don't be such a dose. What was I ever "forceful" about?'

'Just things. Your idea about what we should do and how we should look.'

'Oh my god, you're thirty years old and you're still whining about this? Grow up,' Amanda snapped. 'Nobody made you lose your virginity to Eddie Mahoney. Christ.'

'I know! I just … felt pressure … to live up to who we were trying to be.' She lowered her eyes. 'Kind of like now, to be honest.'

'Are you being this way because you and Jonathan are getting the house together?' Amanda gave her a sullen look. 'Cos I think I've been pretty good about Jonathan. It's not exactly on brand for us that you're this boring bitch who's practically married now—'

'Well,' Roslyn said firmly, raising her voice slightly. 'I think you should both pause for a breath. Let's de-escalate for a minute. There are obviously a lot of things coming up here and we are going to have plenty of time to explore them all in the coming weeks. Let's leave it there for today, shall we?'

Back outside the clinic, Amanda and Lexi didn't get a chance to say a single thing before their names rang out behind them.

'Amanda! Lexi!' A young girl was jogging towards them. 'Eeeek, I can't believe it's you!' She was very small and tanned to within an inch of her young life. She couldn't be more than sixteen. Lexi always felt weirded out when confronted with their younger listeners. No wonder mammy Facebook groups across the land were non-stop complaining about *Your Hot Friend* – she and Amanda were literally shaping the young minds of the country.

'Hey, Hottie.' Amanda blew her trademark air kisses – something she'd long perfected to get out of having to actually hug the Hotties. Lexi tried to stay a couple of feet back, but the girl rapidly closed the distance and gave her a little shy hug.

'I just love you both so much. SO MUCH. Me and my bestie are just like you guys. She will die that she missed this! DIE!'

'Will we do a piccie and we can post it on the *Your Hot Friend* account?' Lexi pulled out her phone while the girl babbled, 'Yes! Oh my god, oh my god,' over and over, so many times, it sounded like she was having a seizure.

The three of them leaned into the pic and shouted 'Hotties!' before sending the girl on her way with promises to give her and her best friend a shout out on the next episode of the pod.

The encounter with the Hottie couldn't have come at a better time, thought Lexi. The tension from the session had dispersed and Amanda, who'd looked fed up when they'd left Roslyn, now had a playful glint in her eye.

'I am not sure about yer one, bébé. Her hair didn't move ONCE! And she's trying to come between us, Lexi.'

Lexi grinned. 'Of course she isn't. She's doing her job. She's doing what we're paying her to do. You promised you'd give therapy a shot. It's future-proofing the show.'

Lexi turned her phone back on to two messages, one from Jonathan and one from Abi.

'Jonathan says the apology is going over well. So that's a relief.'

'Amazing but stop deflecting. Our *Your Hot Friend* account is paying yer one and I really resent wasting budget on that when you won't let me pay for my lip flip out of the account.'

'Ugh, I'm sick of squabbling over the money, Amanda. We need some kind of ... I dunno ... corporate structure!'

Amanda burst out laughing at this. 'You sound insane! We don't need an accounts department – we just need you to recognise that tweakments are not optional extras in 2023!'

Lexi laughed in spite of herself. 'You don't see me charging stuff like that to the company card!'

'That's because you're so gorgeous.' Amanda pulled her into a hug, pinching her cheek.

Amanda had incredible bounceback on being pissed off: her commitment to having fun was far stronger than her commitment to staying mad. It was a very endearing quality, even if it sometimes undermined Lexi's own attempts to talk more serious issues out.

'Stop sexually harassing me,' Lexi deadpanned.

'Oh, gonna go running to HR now, are you?' Amanda hooted.

Lexi grinned as she read Abi's text:

Hope therapy gave you some insights on yours and Amanda's friendship?

She smiled to herself. *It did,* she thought. They weren't perfect, but small squabbles about lip flips and weathering shitstorms online didn't take away from what they each had: a best friend.

CHAPTER 10

'He-e-e-ey, fam-a-lam!'

Every day of the three weeks since they'd brought Ted home from the hospital, Bert's cheery greeting from the hallway had been like fingernails on Joanne's soul. She glared at the living-room door, waiting for him to come in. *No doubt he'll be 'so excited to be home' or some other nonsense. Easy to get excited about it when you get to fucking leave every day.*

Since the spat at the hospital, he'd apologised profusely and been ultra-careful with his words, which was somehow pissing her off even more.

'Helloooo!' Bert's happy little head peered round the door and he bustled in, knocking over a drying rack full of tiny baby clothes. 'Sorry, sorry.' He scrambled after the drying and proceeded to stumble straight into the bouncer, where Ted was miraculously asleep for the first time in six hours. 'Sorry! Sorry, little man, didn't see you down there.'

Joanne remained impassive on the sofa, watching Bert grapple with the rack and the baby, who had roared to life and resumed his natural state: intense crying. To Joanne's worn-out mind, Bert's 'didn't see you down there' sounded like a dig.

'It's a perfectly valid place to put the bouncer,' she snapped.

'Of course.' Bert looked perplexed. 'I didn't think it wasn't.'

'Didn't you?'

Bert's eyes widened innocently. 'I really didn't. Jo ...'

He cuddled Ted to his chest and picked his way through the sea of nappies, damp laundry and cups of half-drunk tea to sit down beside her. She tried not to stiffen at the contact. She was just fed up with being touched at all times; between the baby and Bert there was never a moment without human contact. *What a weird thing to detest*, she thought. It truly goes to show that too much of any good thing is bad.

Joanne just about tolerated Bert kissing her temple before shifting away to the other side of the couch.

'So how was your day? Get up to much?' Bert was jigging the baby, which stemmed the crying somewhat.

'What are you trying to get at?'

Bert's eyebrows shot up. 'Absolutely nothing. I am literally making conversation!'

'You're looking around thinking I haven't done a tap all day.' Joanne pushed herself up off the couch, gingerly, as her c-section scar still hurt. She stomped around the room grabbing up breast pump paraphernalia and used dishes, trying not to wince with every lean and bend.

'Jo! Stop! Please sit down. I want to do that. You should be resting.'

'I'm so sick of resting. And I can't cope with the mess. I hate this. I know I'm being a bitch ...'

'No you're not!' Bert looked stricken.

'I am,' Joanne snapped. 'You've no idea of all the horrible things I think about you all day long.'

'I'm sure you don't mean it,' he offered generously. 'You're tired. It makes a person crazy.'

'I've googled "best-poison-to-murder-with-undetectable",' she announced bluntly.

'Just to be clear, would that be for me or the baby?' Bert was deadpan.

'You, of course! I love Ted!'

'Great, happy to hear it. I would advise you delete your history before committing the murder. Ted needs his mummy. You don't want to be doing fifteen to twenty while he's growing up.' Bert arranged the baby on his shoulder and rose from the couch.

'Stop acting so nice.' Joanne backed away as he came towards her.

'I'm not *acting* nice. I *am* nice.' Bert slid his arm around her waist. 'If you kill me, you'll have no one to mind Ted while you go out with the girls.'

'I'm not going out with the girls,' Joanne moped, allowing herself to be drawn into a hug with Bert and Ted. 'They keep inviting me to literally the most un-parent-friendly activities of all time. Dinner at this new tapas place that only starts serving at eleven p.m.! A weekend in Manchester! What do they fucking think I'm doing here?'

Bert led her over to the other sagging corduroy couch, which faced towards the galley kitchen just off the main room. 'You two sit here while I get dinner together.'

Joanne lay Ted across her lap and stroked his head dreamily. 'You're our velvet mouse!' she cooed. 'Even if you do scream all night and all day.'

'You just need to explain to Aoife and them that your schedule is different now that you have a baby.'

'It's like they're not even trying to understand. I shouldn't have to explain to them that I can't come to an EDM gig less than a month after major abdominal surgery with fluids streaming from my every orifice.'

Her girls' group chat had overnight become a source of misery since the post-birth haze had lifted. After their initial flurry of excitement that there was now a baby in the gang, their enthusiasm for cute pictures seemed to have faded significantly. Nobody had even *feigned* interest in the video she'd put in the group that morning.

It had been overshadowed by a video Erica put in of waking up in a randomer's house. The video opened on a close-up of Erica, full face of last night's make-up, whispering to camera: 'Girlies, I haven't the first fucking clue where I've ended up. I'm gonna turn the camera around and see if any of you know whose living room this is.'

The camera panned wide to reveal a quintessential Dublin rental populated, by the looks of things, by straight men. The curtains were drawn, giving the whole room an underground bunker vibe. A large flat-screen telly had been placed incongruously on top of a boxy, older TV. There was a beer can tower in pride of place on the mantelpiece and many, many ominous tissues, balled up and abandoned around the place.

'Any of you recognise it? I don't think anyone's here, though I guess it is like eleven a.m. on a Thursday. I suppose even people who hoard old tissues and Dutch Gold cans have somewhere to be on a weekday morning.' The video cut off.

Through some light sleuthing, the group eventually ascertained it was the house of Eugene Fitzpatrick and immediately segued into comparing notes on who'd slept with him when.

Nobody had even *mentioned* the video Joanne had shared: thirty-six seconds of Ted opening and closing his eyes VERY cutely.

'You shouldn't have to explain that you can't do gigs and late-night tapas right now, but you do.' Bert's reasonable tone grated even more when he was right. 'Why don't you invite them here?' he added.

'I suggested they come over last Sunday, but you know what they're like.' Joanne sighed. 'If it's not a full-scale booze-up, they just can't see the point.'

Ted started getting tetchy lying on his back so she scooped him up and tried to offer him the boob. But he wasn't having it.

Joanne stood to commence pacing. Pacing and leaking seemed to be the two dominant activities of her life now.

Nobody tells you, she thought at least a hundred times a day as another indignity or painful realisation hit her.

Nobody tells you how lonely you are, even though you're never alone.

Nobody tells you the lengths you will go to to get the baby to sleep – or to keep them sleeping.

Only earlier, she had strongly considered weeing herself when he'd fallen asleep on top of her on the couch. It was only the knowledge that she'd be the one cleaning it up that stopped her. She knew she'd just have to move to the loo and risk waking him up. Which is, of course, exactly what happened.

Nobody tells you how scary it is ALL THE TIME.

Nobody tells you how much you will worry about every little thing.

'I think we should have another.' Bert interrupted her machine-gun-fire thoughts. He was leaning against the doorway to the kitchen, spatula in hand, smiling dreamily.

Joanne had no words for the complete insanity that had just come out of her boyfriend's mouth.

'Don't you think?' Bert circled her to gaze at Ted's face, squished against her neck.

'What reality are you living in?' Joanne turned and stared at Bert.

'The reality where we have a beautiful family and every good thing in the world, Joanne.'

'Don't do that.' She closed her eyes. 'Don't make me feel bad for not loving every minute of this.'

'I'm not.' Bert frowned. 'You're the one making this harder, you know. By trying to do everything yourself and not seeing your friends and shutting me out.'

'I'm not shutting you out – you just don't have any clue what my life is like when you're not here. You still get to go to work and do the thing you're passionate about.'

'You could pick up some freelance design work if you're missing it; we could sort a minder for Ted.'

'I can barely pick up the dirty laundry with Ted glued to me like a beautiful limpet all day long. How am I going to "pick up" freelance work?'

'Jesus.' Bert started pulling out onions and carrots for the Bolognese. 'I cannot say anything.'

'No, to be honest you can't,' Joanne snapped. 'You have no idea what this is like. Your version of this parenthood thing is nothing like my version. You don't have someone completely dependent on you for survival.'

'You think you're the only person whose life has changed.' Bert shook his head.

Bert was a patient guy, but Joanne knew he'd only be pushed so much more before he erupted.

So why am I trying to push him?

She didn't even know exactly. Only that weeks of exhaustion and worry pulled at her and Bert was the only person within reach she could lash out at.

I've been alone all day wishing Bert was home and now that he is, all I want to do is needle at him until he explodes. It's illogical. I've never needed him more and I've never hated him more.

'I actually really want you to go out with the girls,' Bert said. 'You need to get some space. You barely leave the house all day. It's not good for you.'

'You think I'm being a bitch, don't you?' *I think I'm being a bitch.*

Bert rolled his eyes. 'Stop telling me what I'm thinking. Tomorrow is Friday. Pump some milk and go the fuck out, will you? It'll be good for you. And us!'

The next night, Joanne found herself hurrying along the drizzly streets feeling equal parts stressed, excited and anxious to be out. It was weird being away from Ted; her arms literally felt empty. But she was glad to be away from Bert. It had been nothing but clipped responses between them since the night before.

We need to get a breather.

As she made her way to Benji's Bar, giddiness started to overtake her anxiety. She'd forgotten how jazzed the city could feel when the work week was done and Friday arrived. Even in the midst of February, people were outside, hunkered under canopies, smoking and laughing.

Inside the packed bar, Joanne grabbed a Guinness and some crisps before tucking herself into a booth. She was the first one of her friends there – she'd been committed to getting out the door promptly as she knew she was on a tight schedule. Ted would have a bottle while she was out, but she knew her boobs would become a problem in a few hours' time. From her research, she'd gathered that she'd probably have three hours before needing to pump. In case she ran into issues sooner, she'd brought a little manual breast pump with her that she and Bert called the Tit Sucker and the rest of the world called a Haakaa. It might buy her some time.

Joanne watched the customers pressed against the bar, trying to shout their orders over the music. It was hard to get her head around the fact that all these people had been out here living their lives the whole time, while Joanne had been lost in the completely foreign country of motherhood. All through pregnancy, she'd been so focused on worrying about loving her new, unexpected baby, she hadn't given much thought to whether or not she would love her new, unexpected life. She felt a bit deceived. Nobody had told her that nothing would ever, ever be the same again, and nobody had told her how destabilising that would feel. Though how could anyone truly get across the magnitude of that shift?

Jesus, can we just have one night without mild existential dread, Jo? She pulled out her phone to dispel the maudlin thoughts and checked on the Fuck Keto WhatsApp group. All six of them had announced their lateness, detailing where exactly they were at on their various journeys to Benji's. Erica was only just out of the shower. Aoife was stuck in work!

Joanne checked the time. Quarter past eight. She'd already been there for twenty minutes. *They just don't get that I'm on the clock,* she thought, trying to hold her disappointment at bay while doing the breastfeeding calculations.

She'd just ordered another pint and started to crunch her way through a second bag of crisps when a message came in from Kate, proposing that since so many of them were still on the way, they should come up to the Bridge, where she was.

Why are you even fucking there, Kate? Joanne glared at the phone. The Bridge was easily forty minutes' walk away, at the opposite end of town. The point of Benji's had been that it was close to Joanne's house, so she could get the maximum amount of time out before Ted would need her, though obviously they'd all forgotten this.

A message arrived from Aoife:

Do you mind Joanne? Are you already in Benji's?

Of course I'm here, I've been here for the best part of an HOUR.

Joanne typed her reply but then deleted it. *If I get narky about this, I'll be ruining my own night,* she reasoned. *And they'll include me even less than they already are.*

All good with me. I'll jump in a cab.

A cab I can't afford.

Another hour later and at last all of Fuck Keto were crowded together around a large wooden table, taking turns ranting about life over the frenetic clatter of a trad band in the corner.

Joanne hadn't offered up a rant yet and was concentrating on drinking steadily. With the minutes ticking down till boob o'clock, at this point she kind of just wanted to get drunk and try to feel like one of them again. But as the conversation pinballed from one thing to another, she felt like she was watching from the other side of a window.

'Fitzy left poppers in his parents' house and the next time he went over, his mum had put them in a diffuser in the downstairs bathroom!'

'Did you see Jenna's new lips? She got the lip flip but it's a complete botch job. They look like a distended anu—'

'Please don't finish that sentence!'

'Primavera tickets are on sale in a matter of weeks. We need to get a gaff sorted but also somehow make sure that there isn't enough room for Debs and that fuckhead girlfriend of hers.'

Joanne got herself another martini. She didn't usually drink spirits, but it seemed like the economical choice. Why get a gin and a mixer, when she could get booze mixed with more booze?

Aoife grinned over at her. 'Jo's a thirsty bitch tonight! Being locked down with a baby that good, yeah?'

Joanne raised her glass in response and winked.

'My cousin just had a baby and has turned into a monumental bore. Literally all she talks about is baby sleep schedules and poo consistencies.' Erica wrinkled her nose. 'It is ick.'

Iseult cut in: 'I feel like women become mothers and either they fucking hate it and never stop complaining or they hate it but pretend they love it and start acting like they're in a cult. Either way, it's a fun-suck.'

They all turned to Joanne expectantly.

What the hell kind of response am I supposed to give to that?

'What?' She rolled her eyes. 'Are you waiting for me to tell you which I'm going to be? Have you not seen my new Instagram account documenting my #journey? My new handle is @TedsMummy.'

The whole table froze, apparently unsure whether or not she was joking.

'Oh. Good ... for ... you?' Aoife was visibly shaken.

'Oh my god, lol, your faces!' Joanne rolled her eyes. 'You all look like I just said I was opening a pop-up restaurant selling human-flesh carpaccio.'

They all laughed and Joanne felt a comforting glimmer of normality.

'I love you,' Aoife said sloppily into her ear. 'We miss you! C'mon, let's go to the jacks.'

'Oh! Me please?' Iseult waved over.

'You can go next,' Aoife placated her. 'Joanne's the guest of honour. Plus she's probably wrecked – she needs it more!'

Joanne's mind raced. She hadn't really thought they'd roll out the coke; they were only having a few drinks in the pub. She knew it was stupid to care, but she didn't want the whole table hearing her declining drugs: it was very un-her.

'Oh ...' She kept her tone casual. 'I'm grand actually. Coke and breastfeeding wouldn't be the best pairing.'

'No, don't worry!' Aoife smiled. 'I looked it up for you and it's all good. You just need to wait twenty-four hours afterwards before you breastfeed again. How often does Ted feed?'

'More than once a day, Aoife!' Joanne laughed but was silently willing her to drop it. She turned back to the rest of them and grinned. 'I'll be back and badder than ever in a couple of months!'

As conversation resumed, Joanne realised that not only were her boobs killing her, but she was also starting to feel very ... sloshy. Aoife presented her with another martini and she felt the sudden dreaded realisation that it wasn't a matter of if she was going to puke, but when. She had to bail out.

A goodbye could take upwards of ten minutes and she wasn't sure she'd have the time before all the Guinness, crisps, gin and vermouth decided to escape her body. She subtly gathered her bag and coat and announced she was going to the toilet, then made a break for outside and a welcome blast of chilly night air. The drizzle had stopped, but she'd still give anything to get a taxi and not have to walk all the way home. The prospect of puking somewhere along the canal felt super grim. She took a few deep gulps of air to steady her stomach and pulled up her banking app. The total wasn't amazing, but it wasn't as bad as she'd been expecting. She flagged the next taxi and was home in fifteen minutes.

In the semi-darkness of the living room, she just about got herself settled on the couch, the double breast pump enthusiastically milking her, before she spewed up the full sixty quid's worth of drinks into a bowl of popcorn that had been left on the floor from earlier. *What a fucking waste.* She hadn't even got her coat off in time.

'Well, well!' Bert appeared at the bedroom door. 'This is utterly debauched! Tits and milk and puke!'

Joanne reached awkwardly around the breast pump tubes and bottles to wipe her eyes.

'Wait.' All traces of mockery were gone from Bert's voice. 'Are you crying?'

'I'm not crying.' She was.

Joanne could hear how testy she sounded and immediately regretted it. She looked up at him, hoping he could see her remorse. 'It just wasn't what I thought it was going to be,' she explained sadly.

CHAPTER 11

Lexi sped up, wishing the spitting late February rain would ease off. Her hair was gonna look shite and today was hands down the most important day of her career so far. They were signing the Podify contracts at last.

Nearly two weeks had passed since the apology and their first therapy session. Two weeks that had been mercifully uneventful for *Your Hot Friend*. They'd done their shows and posed at various product launches and parties for bar openings. Lexi'd even ventured back to SoulFit and, after a little awkwardness, the other girls had added her to the new WhatsApp group. No one from her school friends' group had made contact, though, and Lexi didn't feel she could text any of them directly – the debacle had made her realise that she hadn't spoken to any of them one-on-one for ages. It felt like they didn't understand her and Amanda's lives and really, how could they? It was hard balancing other friends when she and Amanda were so close, their whole lives entwined. It was definitely something to bring up in one of their next sessions with Roslyn Sullivan.

Lexi's phone rang and she hit 'accept' to bring up a video call from Amanda.

'Babe, me and Jonathan are here already. We're gonna order – what do you want?' Amanda looked outrageously gorgeous on the screen: all long bleached hair tumbling and no make-up, but for a slash of berry lipstick. She also looked slightly out of place in her tiny halter top. Visible just behind her was the dining room of the Madison Hotel, full of extremely well-to-do business people and rich tourists.

'Iced latte and caesar salad. I'm two minutes away,' Lexi replied.

Five minutes later and Lexi was shaking out her hair in the enormous hotel lobby. *I should've got a taxi,* she thought, assessing herself in the huge gilt mirrors to the right of the entrance. She took off her neon yellow rain jacket and fixed her dress – a stonewash denim pinafore under which she wore a sheer white bodysuit and silver bralette. She ran her finger under her eyes to tidy her mascara and then headed into the Madison bar.

She immediately spotted Jonathan and Amanda by the windows. It felt slightly weird sometimes that Jonathan was Amanda's manager too, that he thought about Amanda nearly as much as he thought about her.

When we get everything signed with Podify, we're going to discuss a new manager for Amanda, Lexi resolved. *We need to start separating our friendship from the business.*

'Check out the Madison on a Monday! This is some major rich-people shit.' Amanda was saying this to her phone, filming herself pointing around the opulent room, where other diners were moored on overstuffed Regency furniture, tucking into drinks and platters of seafood.

Amanda turned the camera to Lexi as she neared the table, and she felt herself automatically slide into Hotties mode.

'Hey, gals.' Lexi held up her fingers in the peace sign and blew a kiss before slipping onto Jonathan's lap and draping her arms around his neck. 'This is our gimp! We let him out of the mask for the occasion.'

A woman tutted at the next table and Amanda laughed, zooming over to her briefly before Jonathan grabbed the phone out of Amanda's hands.

'Now, now. Can you two be good for one single day while we get the signatures on the contracts? And then you can bully strangers all you want. Okay, Manda?!'

Amanda pretended to pout.

'Sub is the preferred word, anyway,' Jonathan explained with practised patience. 'I'm sure you can both refrain from being offensive for two hours while we get some sweet, sweet moolah.'

A waiter appeared with their order and Lexi kissed Jonathan, then hopped over to her own chair.

'So how's the house-hunt going?' Amanda wound her pasta around her fork, barely even feigning interest in her own question.

'Actually, funny you should ask ...' Jonathan paused in his careful deployment of condiments on his burger and grinned at Lexi.

'Shut up!' she squealed.

'I won't!' Jonathan laughed. 'Our offer was accepted!'

'Oh my god! I was so sure we'd be outbid again!' Lexi couldn't believe it. She felt a sudden lightness, as though in a dream. 'This is amazing. When will we be able to move in?'

'Well, these things take a bit of time. It's looking good, though. Because the old lady died there and no one moved in, the family are keen to push the sale through quick, so their solicitor is ready to go.'

'Yay!' Amanda intoned dutifully. 'A toast to the aul wan having the courtesy to snuff it before you two came along!'

'So Lex, we'll be transferring most of your signing fee straight to the solicitor to secure the deal. Hope that's okay?' Jonathan didn't wait for Lexi's answer. 'The fact that we're paying a good chunk in cash was a big part of us getting the place. Over the next couple of months, we'll get the mortgage hijinks sorted. Don't worry – it's all in hand. We could even be in before summer, which is good going for these things!'

Lexi couldn't help but snag on Jonathan's words: 'we'll be transferring most of your signing fee'. *What is he contributing? She chewed the inside of her cheek. Don't spoil the moment, Lexi. We can talk about it later. The main thing was she was going to live in the beautiful house on Orchard Terrace!*

She flung her arms around him. 'I can't believe it!'

An hour later, up in the penthouse suite of the hotel, Podify's director of development, Mark Stuart, leaned across to shake their hands. In the middle of the room, an enormous table was laden with vitamin water, chocolate-dipped fruit and cupcakes bearing the *Your Hot Friend* logo. The rest of the Podify team hovered, dutifully applauding their arrival.

'Girls! So exciting to meet you both!' Mark boomed. 'And great to see you again, Jonathan.'

'Wow, this looks amazing.' Jonathan swept his arms across the table. 'Great for the content.'

'It is,' Mark agreed, suddenly adopting quite a formal tone. He looked to be in his late forties and wealthy in that generational wealth kind of way. He was tanned, with shiny blond hair. His parents probably owned a house in the south of France that they referred to as something obnoxious like the 'little bolthole'.

'Shall we get that all-important content out of the way first, in fact?' Mark looked expectantly at her and Amanda. They obediently pulled their phones out.

'Excellent.' Mark clicked his fingers in the direction of two younger women, both clutching tablets. 'Martha and Angie will run through all the products we need featured. We work with a host of innovative brands that you're going to love.' He fixed them both with a stern look and repeated, 'You're going to love them.'

Why does that sound vaguely threatening? Lexi caught Amanda's eye and they held each other's gaze and pursed their lips. It was their special look: it meant nothing to the casual observer but they each understood it to be a general *What the fuck?!* at whatever was going down.

Jonathan came between them and steered them over to the enormous free-standing Podify logo at the far end of the room. 'Relax and just do your thing, gals,' he said, then added in a whisper, 'Do your thing but don't spook them, okay?'

He released them and returned to Mark's side, presumably to do some laddish back-slappery if Mark's knowing chuckles were anything to go by.

Lexi unlocked her phone and started snapping pics of Amanda backing her ass up onto the 'y' of Podify.

'Get over here, Lexi,' she called.

Lexi turned the camera around to them both, hit the button to go live, and they started twerking in and around the sign.

It was definitely harder with eight or ten people in office attire silently watching on.

'Okay, Hotties!' Amanda had now started filming as well and was taking the lead, thank god. 'This is it! Pay day for ya girlies.' She swung the camera around to take in the crowd in the boardroom. 'We are selling out and gonna be CORPORATE HOES from now on!' Lexi tried not to dwell on the understandable wincing at the word 'hoe' coming from certain corners of the room. Mark looked happy enough, which was the main thing.

Lexi ended her story and pulled Amanda's camera her way. 'Nothing's gonna change, Hotties. We love you so much and we cannot wait to celebrate with you guys in a few weeks in our first live show as a Podify podcast!'

'Check out our cupcakes,' Amanda yelled, holding the little cakes in front of her boobs.

'See, we're still us!' Lexi grinned happily. 'Thank you to @CakesNBakes for making these gorgeous, sweet nibbles. We're so excited to expand our *Your Hot Friend* content and take it to the next level! We'll be doing more shows, making even more connections with you guys, our incredible community, and making—'

'Makin' more coin,' Amanda interjected.

'Shut up, Manda! I'm trying to get all emotional here.' Lexi mugged for the camera but having all these people in the room was making her more conscious of her 'Lexi persona', as Abi'd put it. She had the sensation that she'd pulled on a strange mask.

'Okay, okay, Lexi. Catch a feeling, then!' Amanda started lasciviously tonguing the icing of one of the cupcakes.

'I just wanna say to all you Hotties out there, never take your best friend for granted.' Lexi threw her arm around Amanda. 'This gal is the single greatest thing that ever happened to me and I cannot believe that we get to do this amazing thing together. I love you so much. Don't ever forget, no lad will ever know you and love you like your best friend, so treat her like the kween that she is.'

Lexi cut the live video, the room applauded and she felt the weirdness wriggling in her stomach again. Why was she feeling so nervy? It wasn't that she didn't mean what she said: she did.

You're putting a helluva lotta eggs in one basket, Lex. Abi's words came back unbidden, but she quickly banished them.

'That was beautiful, girls.' Mark started laying out contracts and pens on the table.

Amanda and Lexi quickly snapped some more pictures of the various bottles of spirits and make-up bits – gifts from the many brands that were coming on board to sponsor the show now that they were going to be on Podify. Martha and Angie shadowed them, helping them with the correct hashtags and brand names to use as they posted it all to their stories. Things were about to get way more formal and efficient with *Your Hot Friend*.

'Now!' Jonathan boomed. 'We gonna make this official?'

'Yes, yes.' Mark pulled out chairs for Lexi and Amanda. To the rest of the room, he announced, 'Perhaps we'll just have the legal team here for this bit. Thank you all for helping to give the girls a big Podify family welcome.' He waved most of the room out, leaving just Jonathan, Lexi, Amanda and the two-man legal department.

Jonathan caught Lexi's eyes and mouthed 'I love you'.

She smiled; it did feel momentous. After their latest run-in on Twitter, a few of their haters had set up an online petition to try to get sponsors to drop them. But here they were, about to make more money than they'd had in their whole lives. The deal had even been reported in the business sections of the newspapers, described as a landmark one in Irish podcasting.

'So we've made some tiny adjustments to the contracts since the last little ...' Mark cleared his throat, 'eh ... hiccup. Aaron, perhaps you could just go over these with everyone?'

Aaron leaned over his copy of the contract. 'So if everyone could turn to page fourteen, section C ... you'll see I've just added a clause about the sensitivity listener. Basically, all pre-recorded episodes will be vetted by this person – yet to be appointed, but I believe the recruitment team have some good candidates lined up.'

Lexi's stomach swooped unpleasantly. They don't trust us. She didn't blame them, but it was a disappointing realisation. *They think we're ignorant, just like everyone else, but they want our audience.*

'That is fucking bullshit.' Amanda was clearly ready to fight it.

'No, it's not,' Mark said evenly. 'It's in place to protect everyone, most of all you and Lexi. We don't want to be locked into permanent damage-control mode every time you spout off some offensive nonsense.' The love-bombing portion of the Podify deal was clearly over. Mark looked steely.

'The kamikaze nature of *Your Hot Friend* is what the Hotties love,' Amanda argued. 'Lexi? Jonathan? Anyone want to back me up?'

'Eh ...' Franky, Lexi felt relieved at the thought that it wouldn't all be down to her to keep Amanda in check any more. The prospect of having someone else helping to keep the content on the right side of the line made her realise just how much anxiety she'd been carrying around. 'I think it's fine, Amanda. It'll be good. All the Twitter spats take up so much time. They're boring. Let's just go with this.'

'I'm with Lexi and Mark here, Amanda.' Jonathan nodded.

'Fine.' Amanda sat back, folding her arms. 'But if numbers are suffering cos the content is being neutered, I don't want us to be penalised.'

'Amanda, that won't happen.' Mark's tone was soothing. 'And if it does, we have a whole content team for you girls to brainstorm with to help you keep hitting your targets.'

Ugh, targets. The pressure. This was going to be very different from the old days when it was all so free and easy.

'Speaking of targets ...' Aaron cut back in. 'We've just adjusted the figures again slightly. Page seventeen, everyone.'

Lexi flicked forward in the contract, her eyes widening at the numbers, which had leapt up from the last time they'd talked.

'We think they're eminently doable. We've been looking at reported figures for *Can He Be Zaddy*, which is the closest market equivalent, and we think we can be aiming higher.'

'Mark, *CHBZ* is in America,' Jonathan interjected. 'The market is massive; it's not a good comparison.'

'Jonathan, they're targets. Everyone relax about the numbers, okay?' Mark grinned chummily, before his smile immediately dimmed again. 'We are firm on this figure, though.' He tapped the page. 'The first pre-recorded episode to go out on Podify needs two hundred and fifty thousand downloads, minimum. We think if the LIVE launch in March goes well – and it should, you have three weeks to prepare for it – this shouldn't be too hard. We need to come out of the gate strong, to show management that they haven't backed the wrong fillies.'

Lexi was disliking Mark more by the second.

'Fillies?' she mouthed at Amanda, who immediately let out a

'neeeighhh' in an inordinately good impression of a horse, startling everyone in the room. They both collapsed into giggles and Lexi's uneasiness ebbed.

The figures would be fine. Everything would be fine. *We're in this together.*

'The launch is going to be epic,' Amanda announced confidently. 'Me and Jonathan have been brainstorming a big surprise that's going to net us LOADS of traction on the LIVE show – no one can resist a bitta harmless gossip, right?' She winked at Lexi. 'Nothing libellous – don't worry your pretty little head, Mark!'

'We're doing "One Truth, One Lie",' Jonathan explained. 'It's the perfect intro to the new iteration of *Your Hot Friend*. It's a bit like Truth or Dare but more kind of psychological. Lexi and Amanda will tell each other one truth and one lie, and they each have to guess which is which. It'll create some irresistible drama. We're aiming for this to generate lots of "viral moments" – perfect for drawing both new and long-time listeners to the first official episode, which will already be in the can and going live the next day.'

'Okay!' Mark clapped his hands together, looking delighted. 'That sounds ... *juicy AF*, as you girls would say.'

Lexi forced herself to smile gamely at him. 'It will be, Mark, it absolutely will be.' She was firm, though she actually had no idea what Amanda and Jonathan were up to. *What brainstorming have they been doing?*

She picked up the pen, thinking about the little front door that she would be painting hot pink the second they got the keys. 'Where do I sign?'

CHAPTER 12

'Claire! My goodness! How are you?'

Aifric's mum, Connie, caught Claire by both shoulders, locked eyes on her and began the dreaded head-tilt, international symbol for abject pity.

'I'm fine! Totally amazing!' Claire shuffled her shoulders to try and slip out from her grasp, but Connie only gripped harder and stared into her eyes more intensely.

'Claire, how *could* you be okay?' Her voice positively dripped with sorrow. Connie was a woman who fed off other people's troubles. Like most Irish mothers, she reported deaths and illnesses with the enthusiasm of someone listing off delicious options on a menu.

'Claire!' To her relief, Aifric emerged from behind the curtain of white taffeta that marked the transition from the front of Happy Endings Bridal Boutique to the rarefied back room, where the fairy tale really began. 'Mum, leave Claire alone!' She nudged Connie back through the gap in the partition and turned to hug Claire. 'I'm so happy you're here. Everyone's in the back.'

'They know what "happy ending" means, right?' Claire giggled.

'Shhhh, my poor mother! She's an innocent.'

Beyond the curtain, Claire was met with a slightly confusing sight. This was not the intimate gathering she had been expecting. A dozen distant relatives were leaned and perched around the all-white room. This was the odd squad of Aifric's family: she could see the two distant cousins who'd tried to become Mormons after seeing *The Book of Mormon*. There was also the second cousin once removed, who'd become radicalised on Facebook and was constantly, passionately arguing for men's rights. Aifric's closest-in-age cousin, who now went by the name Moon, was sitting cross-legged on the large white sofa. Moon was known for insisting that rubbing sprigs of lavender under your arms was as good as deodorant and for using the clumps of hair she got when she de-haired her hairbrush as tampons.

It immediately dawned on Claire what was going on. These were the people that Connie must have *insisted* Aifric invite. And she, Claire, was one of them. She tried to keep her face neutral. *No. That's paranoid, Claire.*

But why were none of the rest of the Bitch Herd here, then?

This was clearly not the real wedding-dress shopping outing but some kind of decoy one, where Aifric had invited all the dud people she felt obligated to include.

'Everyone ...' Connie clapped her hands to bring the room to attention. 'This is Claire, everybody. Aifric's oldest friend.'

Not best friend but OLDEST friend. Claire tried to smile as they all murmured greetings, but she sensed it was coming out more like a grimace.

'We're just getting started.' Aifric turned Claire around to show her the rail behind them. 'This is the shortlist. What do ya think?'

I think I didn't even make the shortlist of your friends, Aifric.

Claire looked at the dresses. They were all identical: taffeta nightmares, as though Laurence Llewelyn-Bowen's shirts had had an orgy and birthed five dresses.

'Lovely.' She shrugged, then caught herself. *I have to remind Aifric why we're friends.* She slapped a smile on her face. 'I mean GORGEOUS! They're all so different – how are you going to choose?'

'I know,' Aifric beamed, without a trace of irony.

'I brought us some bubbles!' Claire pulled the champagne, which had cost her €35, out of her tote bag.

'Oh.' Aifric looked awkward. 'It's kind of early, isn't it? And today's more of a nip in, nip out kind of dress-shop.'

Is it? Was there a bride alive who didn't want to milk every single aspect of the wedding hoopla? What kind of woman wants to be efficient about the dress?

'Where are the rest of the girls?' Claire asked, unsure if she even wanted the answer.

'Oh, I just wanted to keep this to family.' Aifric trailed her hand along the dresses. *Is she avoiding looking at me?* Claire wondered.

Suddenly Aifric turned back. 'Actually, I have a brilliant idea. Will you be like the official photographer of the try-on? And we can send some pics to the Bitch Herd ...' She held Claire's gaze meaningfully. 'So they don't feel left out.'

Claire felt a rush of relief. *Stop being so paranoid,* she admonished herself. *I'm not a dud. I'm the one she chose specifically to come.*

'Claire, come and sit with me. I'll mind you.' Connie waved to her as the shop assistant emerged from a hidden door carrying even more tulle.

Claire smiled tightly and obediently made her way over. *I don't need to be minded, sheesh.* Aifric must've told her; Claire's mum would never have brought it up at bridge. Maybe it was nice that Aifric had cared enough to tell her mother what had been going on, though she certainly hadn't seemed to care back when it was all going down. Aifric hadn't even come to see Claire in the hospital. She'd barely texted. These things made people uncomfortable, Claire knew, and she'd resolved not to hold it against Aifric, even though Jamie had been upset on her behalf.

When Aifric disappeared into the changing room with the first dress, Connie picked up Claire's hand and started patting it. Unbearable. Claire tried to pull back slightly, but Connie only tightened her grip. She was not relinquishing the hand, so Claire tried to change the subject.

'It's great to see Moon!' She nodded over to where Moon sat in the lotus position, nothing but the thin gusset of her yoga pants between her crotch and the white couch. Claire winced. *Let's hope she's not on her period.* The hairpon – as Moon called it on her Instagram – was just not the iron-clad menstrual solution she claimed it was.

'You poor thing.' Connie evidently would not be distracted. 'I see you're still not looking your best,' she added helpfully. 'Though of course you wouldn't. When did you get out?'

'Oh, a while ago now. I got home just before Halloween.'

'And how long were you in?

'Em, not for that long. Six weeks.'

'Jesus.' Connie pressed Claire's hand to her heart. 'You must've been really bad.'

'Yeah, I wasn't great.' *God, she is salivating for the details.*

Claire would be giving her nothing. This was the problem with mental illness. Either people didn't want to talk to you AT ALL about it and acted like nothing was happening, or they wanted all the gory details. It was hard to decide which was more offensive.

At that moment, Connie abruptly dropped Claire's hand, enchanted at the sight of Aifric emerging from the dressing room. 'Darling! You're gorgeous!'

Aifric twirled to reveal the back of the dress gaping open.

'Obviously it'd be in my size.' She laughed.

'Yes everything's made to measure,' the store assistant added. 'We only keep sample sizes in the shops, but bigger brides can get a good idea.'

'Can they?' Connie was up examining the dress. 'Why do you only carry elf sizes? This is ridiculous; this wouldn't fit a baby.'

The assistant stiffened. 'It's standard industry practice.'

Now Moon was on her feet and looking indignant. 'Is it standard industry practice to make women feel like their bodies aren't the "right kind"? I can't believe the patriarchy has even managed to breach this sacred female space. Men have got women acting as the patriarchy's foot soldiers, upholding misogynistic beauty standards and hating our vaginas.'

'What have vaginas got to do with anything?' The men's rights cousin was rolling her eyes. 'The "patriarchy" is an invention by feminists to portray themselves as victims and keep good men down.'

'Please stop saying vaginas in front of the dresses,' one of the Mormon-wannabe cousins pleaded.

'Claire!' Aifric spoke up firmly, silencing the squabbling. 'What do you think?'

Claire took in the full, frilly spectacle and prepared to lie. 'You're breathtaking. Let's get some piccies.' Claire slipped carefully through Moon and the Mormons and snapped Aifric from a few angles, then Aifric slipped back into the changing room to put on another. Claire returned to her seat beside Connie, who immediately reattached herself, like a misery-loving tick gorging itself.

'What were the other patients like, then? I'd say there were some characters.'

Connie's words sliced at Claire. Talking about the hospital still felt too raw and a wave of anxiety engulfed her. The doctors had said she could go home as long as she continued to take her medication and see her counsellor. The thought of Ella caused a stab of dread. It'd been six weeks since Ella emailed. *I have to reply to her. I have to go to her. It's just hard to find the time. I'll go.*

'They're not characters,' she replied stiffly. 'They're just ... people.'

'Oh, of course they are. I didn't mean anything by it. My uncle Mad Paddy was the same,' she added, as if this was somehow a redeeming statement.

Claire nodded, smiling grimly at this. At least it would entertain Jamie later.

'Here's another one.' Aifric had returned in a dress so identical to the previous one that Claire wondered if Aifric was trying to test them.

'Oh, divoooon!!!' An aunt was up and pawing at the bodice. 'I love it. LOVE IT.'

'Piccies, Claire!' Aifric didn't quite snap her fingers, but the tone wasn't far off. 'Yep, coming.' Claire dutifully captured the dress from all angles.

While Aifric changed into the next one, Claire shared a few of the pictures in the Bitch Herd chat. A flurry of OTT responses flooded in.

Stunning!
Beautiful!
Hottie!
Ridey Bridey!

Then a message from Gillian appeared, wrenching Claire out of her boredom and pitching her straight into a black hole.

Ugh, hope you're surviving that bunch!!! This is getting me so excited for the real shopping trip!

This was accompanied by a spate of champagne flute emojis, cake emojis and dancing woman emojis.

As she stared at the WhatsApp, the message disappeared as quickly as it had materialised.

The notification *This message was deleted* replaced the text.

And then below that three words that released a dam of angst in Claire:

Sorry wrong thread.

✦

'Claire! Hey!' It was the day after the wedding-dress shopping and Aifric was waving to her from outside the upmarket brunch spot they'd chosen for the wedding summit. Dylan's was probably the most expensive place in the city. Two poached eggs on toast was

€18.50; Claire had checked when they made the booking, just so she could mentally prepare and not pass away from shock while sitting at the actual table. In preparation, she'd eaten a protein bar on the walk over. There was no way she was dropping twenty quid on a glorified fry. She'd be nursing a black coffee and tap water.

'Hey, bridey!' Claire pecked Aifric on the cheek and followed her into the crowded restaurant. She'd resolved not to make a big deal of yesterday's text. She didn't want to be The Claire Problem. Seated over to the right were the rest of the Bitch Herd: Nadia, Helena and Gillian, all standing up and singing, 'Here comes the ride, here comes the ride!!!'

'Shtaaaap!' Aifric giggled as she and Claire joined them.

Gillian cleared her throat and with an air of gravitas began to speak. 'We are gathered here today to celebrate the pending incarceration of our good friend Aifric.'

'Ha, shut up!' Aifric pouted prettily. 'Let's order, I'm starving.'

Over the course of the next hour, not a single sentence NOT containing the word 'bride', 'wedding' or 'Aifric' was uttered. Even when Aifric got up to go to the toilet, she announced, 'This bride's gotta pee.' Claire nursed her coffee as the others tucked into stacks of pancakes and elaborate cocktails – the Bloody Marys came draped with what looked to be actual baby lobsters.

Even though it was a vortex of wedding talk, it was fun chatting about the various minutiae of the nuptials and Claire relaxed. It felt like old times. Then Nadia pulled up the agenda she'd drawn up for the gathering, to 'keep us on track'.

Claire could see from the agenda's running order that between *Discussion Point 17: Bridal Shower* and *Discussion Point 19: Hen*

Do they would be interrogating her about *Discussion Point 18: The Wedding Favours.*

She had some ideas and even a couple of pictures to show the gals and so wasn't concerned until Gillian pulled up a full-colour deck detailing research, costings and mood boards for *Discussion Point 3: Mr and Mrs signage,* aka the small wooden signs that would be hung above Aifric's and Paul's chairs during the wedding meal.

Oh fuck. Claire wondered if she should go to the jacks and try to pull together some more bits – copy and paste some text from a wedding blog, perhaps?

The thought was cut off by Nadia's introduction of *Discussion Point 4: The 'Pre-Hen Do' Do – Girls' Trip to Ibiza.*

'Gals, I've put together all the info here regarding the "Pre-Hen Do" Do.' Nadia distributed pink folders to everyone. 'The first bit is just a little letter from me to Aifric saying how honoured I am to have been entrusted with organising this trip.'

Claire scanned the letter, which spanned four pages, front and back, single-spaced in size twelve font. The others were cooing over the missive.

'Nads, this is so sweet.' Aifric dabbed at her eyes.

'Awww, it's nothing.' Nadia blew her a kiss, then glanced around at the rest of them. 'There's so many private jokes between me and Aifric, it'll probably be like hieroglyphics to you gals. Don't worry, you can all skip to page five. This is the itinerary for the weekend. We're checking into the hotel on May the nineteenth, which is a Friday, and then check-out is Sunday the twenty-first, so we have two nights to get our bride fucked up!'

'Yaaaasss!' Gillian raised her hands up over her head.

'Everyone needs to book their own flight, except obvi Aifric. I'm sorting that, honey.' Aifric beamed as Nadia sternly looked around at everyone else, adding: 'I'll let you each know what you owe me for Aifric's part of the trip, okay?'

Claire nodded, trying not to look nervous. Two days abroad didn't come cheap and this wasn't even the hen do itself but the *pre*-hen do. God knows what they had planned for the actual hen.

Nadia trailed her pen further down the itinerary page. 'I went to the trouble of listing the different flight times on the day, so closer to the time we can all figure out what works best, and on the following pages ...' she flicked on in the booklet, '... are transfer options.'

Claire scanned down the pages: there were no prices listed. This was going to be a feat of budgeting. She would not be checking a bag. She'd need to wear her togs and four pairs of knickers and several bras on the plane over. Maybe a sarong would do her clothes-wise.

'Okay,' Nadia continued. 'Over the page is our daily activities – they're all priced individually so I've listed the websites where you can get that info.' She said 'that info' as if it was barely relevant.

She turned the page and barrelled on: 'Each night we have a different theme for our outfits and let's just say Aifric and I want MAXIMUM EFFORT for the clothes. We need pictures for the 'gram. We have a Mean Girls night and a Pocahontas Night – headdresses mandatory!'

Gillian and Helena nodded emphatically.

Fuck. Claire thought frantically. Not only was one of the themes really inappropriate, but she would definitely need to check a bag to comply.

'Nads, this is amazing.' Aifric looked enchanted.

'Right, next page,' Nadia barked, practically high off getting to display her organisation skills. 'Accommodation is the Hotel Torre Del Mar, aka paradise. I've put some pictures here to give you all a flavour. As you can see, it is five-star luxury. All meals are included in the rate, as are the drinks and passes to three of the biggest clubs. It's pricey but sooooo worth it.'

Yet again there was no information on the money front. Despite working IN FINANCE, Nadia definitely didn't seem to give a shit about it. Claire bit her lip. She didn't want to ruin the mood, but surely the others were wondering too?

'What kind of "pricey" are we talking about?' she asked tentatively.

'Claire!' Helena rounded on her. 'We're not talking about it here!' She ran an impatient hand through her perfectly blow-dried hair, her eyes flickering over at Aifric.

Of course: it dawned on Claire now that there were no prices because they were all paying for Aifric and her 'not-even-the-actual-fucking-hen-do' do. God forbid Aifric would have to see the sordid financials.

While the others were moaning orgasmically over the hotel pics – infinity pool with actual palm trees dotted about in the water and vast marble bedrooms with sea views – Claire slid her phone onto her lap under the table and googled the hotel. Upon finding the rates, she struggled not to gasp audibly: €225 a night in May!

She bit the inside of her cheek, feeling the pressure gathering behind her eyes.

Don't react, don't react. I can figure this out.

Maybe she could get a loan. People were always getting loans off the credit union for bullshit things they didn't need.

Or I could ask the Sweeneys and pay them back out of my wages?

Her parents seemed out of the question. With kitchen rosters, labelled food and her dad sleeping in the box room, it didn't look like they were in the greatest financial shape. She and Jamie had a little saved, but she didn't want to use the money for a trip he wasn't getting to enjoy too.

'I've allocated pairs to room together.' Nadia's brusque voice punched through Claire's building anxiety. 'Everyone's got a roommate except, eh ...' For the first time all afternoon, and perhaps ever, Nadia sounded a little hesitant.

Claire looked down at the little table of names in the folder and saw immediately that the box beside hers was empty. She wasn't even surprised.

'So, Claire ...' Nadia was pretending to examine the booklet. 'Because you're not sharing, there's just a weensy little bit extra on your room – the single occupancy fee.'

It wasn't so much the fee itself as the casual tone in which Nadia delivered this information that really sparked the surge of rage in Claire's body.

'Oh, just a weensy little bit extra, is it?' she snapped, not even caring about the dismay passing over the rest of the girls' faces.

'Claire ...' Nadia sounded tense. 'No need to escalate now. We know how you can get, but it's really not a big deal.'

We know how you can get.

'If it's not a big deal, Nadia, then *you* sleep on your own and pay the single occupancy fee.'

'Well, that's not possible.' Nadia sounded stunned at the very suggestion. 'I'm in with Aifric. And Helena and Gillian are sharing.'

'It's just a fucking table on a Word doc, Nadia. You can change it.' Claire wanted to reign her upset in, but her words were escaping her grasp, hitting the others like feeble pebbles thrown by a child. 'Surely there's a trio room?'

'Look, Claire.' Helena sounded irritated. 'We all picked who to share with, alright? So that's what happened. It's so *you* to make a big deal out of it.'

'It's so *you all* to leave me out like this.'

Claire burned with humiliation, instantly regretting her outburst. She tried to calm down. She knew what Ella, the counsellor, would say: *You need to get grounded, Claire.*

Claire clenched her fists in her lap under the table, digging fingernails into flesh. It wasn't exactly the kind of grounding Ella would encourage, but the sting helped her slow her thoughts down.

'No one's leaving you out,' Gillian soothed. 'It's just an uneven number, that's all.'

No one's volunteering to switch, Claire noted unhappily. *God, I'm thirty-one and it feels like the first-year Irish college trip all over again.*

'Maybe we could take turns in the solo room?' she suggested. She knew it was tragic to be begging, but it was unfair that she'd been saddled with this.

'It's too complicated.' Nadia snapped her folder closed and the others followed suit. 'We need to get on to the next item on the agenda.'

Claire wanted to walk out, but then they'd roll their eyes and talk about her; she was sure of it. She dug her nails in harder, looking down at her whitening knuckles. When she raised her eyes, she caught Aifric looking at her.

'You could always ...' Aifric's voice faltered as Nadia's head shot up. 'You could always bring someone with you to share with.'

'But it's your "pre-hen do" do, Aifric.' Gillian looked scandalised at the idea of an interloper.

'I don't mind.' Aifric smiled magnanimously. 'If you have a friend to bring, Claire?'

Claire narrowed her eyes.

She's only saying this cos she thinks I have no other friends I can invite.

She's right.

She summoned a smile. 'That's really kind, Aifric.'

Aifric appeared to be basking in her role as benevolent queen, safe in the knowledge that Claire wouldn't take her up on her offer.

'Actually,' Claire continued. 'There's a really close friend that I'd love to bring along.' *Is there, Claire?! What are you talking about?*

'Oh?' Nadia straightened up and looked over.

'Yes!' Claire snapped. 'I do have other friends, you know.'

I absolutely don't.

'Of course you do,' Aifric said in a placating tone, shooting the others meaningful looks which Claire chose to ignore. 'Brilliant – I can't wait to meet her.'

Claire was the picture of calm for the rest of the meal, taking it on the chin when they all voted against her chocolate truffle favours idea – too messy, too predictable, too risky with allergies and dietary requirements.

Underneath her calm exterior, however, she was having a mild breakdown. Another fucking one.

Why did I say that? Now I need to make a new friend in like three months! I haven't managed to make a new friend in twenty-five years. Fuck. A woman has about as much chance of being murdered by a serial killer as she does making a new friend after thirty.

Did I mention: FUCK.

That night, Claire sat cross-legged on her bed with her laptop, grateful that Jamie was out at his boxing class and wasn't there to witness Claire spiralling.

Her problems were circling. Why had she said she had a friend? How the fuck was she supposed to pay for this not-even-the-actual-fucking-hen do? Why was there so much attendant bullshit around two people effectively signing a contract? And what the hell wedding favour was she going to make?

She was flicking between different bridal blogs, hunting for ideas. She leaned in to examine some hand-carved busts of the bride and groom. She clicked the small icon to add the picture to her Pinterest board. They'd be very labour-intensive, but at this point she was throwing anything and everything at Aifric. She scanned the rest of the ideas she'd amalgamated on her Pinterest: handmade candles, homemade jams, woven baskets, pot pourri with a signature scent.

She decided to take a break from one problem and embark on another. *For a little change of scene,* she thought wryly.

In a new tab, she started to type in the Google search: 'How to make friends' …

Google immediately swooped in with suggestions:

… in your 30s

… as a man

… as an adult

… in a new city

On seeing that 'How to make friends in your 30s' was the first suggestion, Claire brightened up. *Maybe I'm not the only sad bitch paying the single room occupancy rate? Maybe other people find it hard too?*

She clicked the first link, which promised five tips for making friends over thirty.

Tip one was 'be more receptive'. She pulled a face. *Think I've got that covered; nothing screams 'receptive' like googling how to find a friend!*

The next tip advised Claire to remember that strangers were just the friends she hadn't met yet.

Vom! She was going to pull a muscle if she kept rolling her eyes so hard.

Still, she pulled up the Notes app on her phone and started a new document, titling it: Make a Friend You Sad Bitch!

An article she'd once read about goals said that the most important thing to do when setting out to achieve an objective was to give yourself a deadline. Under the heading she typed 'D-day: May 1st'. It was a tight turnaround. In that time, Claire needed to locate a person, foster a friendship and bring said friendship to a place emotionally where they would be close enough to go on a trip together.

She read the next suggestions from the article.

- Join a club or defined community, e.g. golf club, new mothers' group, book club.
- Get to know your neighbour.
- Download apps to meet people, but invest your energy and time in taking the friendship offline.

I definitely can't become friends with a neighbour. What if it went sideways? Then we'd have to avoid each other until the end of time.

She scanned the 'defined communities' suggested: golf club, new mothers' group and book club. Golf was an obvious 'no'. If she wanted to befriend a middle-aged man, she could spend more time with her dad. Book club would be a reasonable option if she wasn't under such time pressure. Her mum's book club only met once a month. She needed to fast-track this friendship, which meant seeing the potential friend much more frequently.

Her gaze rested on 'new mothers' group'.

Mothers' groups met in the mornings: she'd seen them around the coffee shops and parks in the city. Weekday mornings when the rest of the world was at work ... and Lila and Frankie were in school...

She thought about Sonny ...

He was starting to say a few words, but 'this crazy bitch is not my mother' would be beyond him for a few years yet. He was a bit old, though. She knew these groups were largely for brand new mums. She brought up her camera roll and scrolled to her most recent picture of Sonny.

I could say he's big for his age ...

It would be extremely rude of them to quiz her – his supposed mother! – on his age.

Making friends with a new mum in the immediate area was definitely too risky, but maybe if she cast the net just a little wider, she'd be safe enough. She could lock down a new mum and then just ghost her after the trip.

This is insanity, the other side of her brain insisted. How would you keep up the pretence? Even if you conned a mum into being your friend, how would you go about asking her not to mention your supposed child to the rest of the Bitch Herd on the holiday?

Claire frowned. *I could just tell her I don't want to monopolise the holiday with baby-talk? That might work …*

The rational side of her continued pointing out the obvious flaws in the plan.

This is Dublin. Someone would recognise him!

She peered closer at the picture. He had beautiful long lashes. *Not if I said he was a she …*

CHAPTER 13

At five a.m. on the last Monday in February, in the still-dark kitchen, Joanne watched with utter defeat as four litres of water diluted with Milton cascaded onto her kitchen floor.

She burst into hot, angry tears, not even bothering to move out of the way of the lake-like puddle advancing over the lino and soaking her slippers. Her hands hung by her sides while the baby continued to sleep, snuggled against her chest in his sling. He'd woken up half an hour ago and she'd only managed to coax him back to sleep by putting him into it. She knew if she tried to lie back down, he'd wake up – his preferred sleeping positions seemed engineered to be as awkward and inconvenient for her as possible. Anyway, she knew she'd never drift off. It had made more sense to try and get ahead on the day's drudgery; she had to go to her mother's second-cousin-once-removed's wake that evening. She tried not to think about the fact that by six p.m. tonight her eyes would be burning and no doubt look like two piss-holes in the snow. And god knows what time she'd escape. Irish wakes were notoriously difficult to extricate yourself from. By the end of the night, she'd no doubt be tempted to climb into Carmel's coffin, just for the lovely little lie down.

She was due back to work in another two weeks and, even though she was struggling to imagine how she'd manage the early-morning starts, she was keen to get back to some kind of normal life.

The first job on the day's list had been to change the water in the disinfectant bucket where they soaked Ted's bottle to kill germs. Milton needed to be replaced every 24 hours. It was old-school, but they didn't have a dishwasher or a microwave to do the job so instead it was a four-litre bucket. The same four-litre bucket she'd just managed to upend while trying to lift it onto the counter without waking the baby.

The will to deal with her life was flooding out of her at the same rate as the Milton was flooding her kitchen. Dead-eyed, she pulled her dressing gown down off her shoulders, dropped it into the puddle and swished it around in a lacklustre effort to dry the floor.

'I could blame you for this,' she told the whorl of hair poking out of the sling. 'Manoeuvring a four-litre bucket while trying to keep the baby attached to you asleep is not easy.' Despite her huffy words, the little ear she could see, as delicate as a petal, brought up a smile. 'But look, the fact is you're just a squishy little helpless dote! It's your prick of a father I blame,' she added darkly.

As she refilled the bucket at the sink, taking care not to splash the baby, she calculated how many times she'd done this. Ted was six weeks now, which meant she must've changed the Milton at least forty-two times. Bert had changed the Milton zero times. And it wasn't like he didn't know – she'd bitched at him about it, but he seemed to think she was joking.

Only last weekend, she'd pointed out that if it weren't for her efforts, Ted would never have had a sterilised bottle in his entire life.

He'd shrugged amiably. 'Why does it even matter?'

'I don't fucking know, but I don't want to find out,' she'd screeched.

At the tap, she glared at the rising water line in the bucket. In direct proportion to the water filling the bucket, loathing was filling her body. It was easy for Bert to opt out. The baby hadn't come out of *his* body, dragging half *his* insides with it. The baby wasn't knitted into the very cells of *him*. He could just plod along and dismiss fears about Ted as irrational. He seemed completely immune to the love-terror that Joanne was permanently gripped by.

She carefully, carefully lifted the tub from the sink, trying to ignore her protesting lower back. Once she had it on the counter, she measured out the Milton and tipped it in. Just as the disinfectant swirled through the water, she felt another emotion swirling through her loathing. Resolve. Steely resolve.

She opened the fridge, grabbed the plastic water bottle Bert used when he worked out from the fridge, emptied it and dipped the bottle into the Milton to fill it up. 'Oh, the Milton's no big deal,' she muttered. 'You won't mind fucking drinking it, then.'

She sniffed the bottle. It didn't smell particularly strange. She screwed on the lid and put it back in the fridge. 'Berty-werty has to have his chilled water,' she mimicked petulantly. Then she sat on a kitchen stool as the sky lightened until at seven a.m. Bert appeared. He jumped when he saw her.

'Gah! You look like a serial killer there.' Then he noticed the floor. 'The fuck happened here?' he asked conversationally, stepping around her sodden dressing gown, opening the fridge and grabbing his bottle, along with – Joanne noted – a packet of rashers.

If the Milton killed him, would I care?

With the life insurance policy, he's actually worth more to me dead than alive.

Bert unscrewed the lid. It definitely wouldn't kill him, Joanne knew, it would just taste bad.

She stared in silence as he brought the bottle to his lips. He tipped his head back, still clutching the packet of rashers. She knew he was going to cook them and leave the dirty pan in the sink. She fucking knew it.

What if it is dangerous to drink it though? *I'll be the one who has to take him to hospital …*

The thought of spending hours in A&E with Bert snapped her out of her fugue state and forced her to her feet. In two steps she was across the room and slapping the rashers out of his hand.

He pulled the bottle away from his mouth. 'What the hell!?'

She took advantage of his confusion to take the bottle from him and tip it down the sink. 'I'm just so sick of the smell of rashers,' she hissed. 'I cannot take another day of it. Who has a cooked breakfast every day of the week anyway? It's a luxury no man of a six-week-old should even be *able* to have. You think I don't want to be having cooked breakfasts every day? Well, I don't get that, do I? Also you never wash the goddamn pan.'

'You could have a—'

Bert started to reply, but Joanne quickly drowned him out with an exasperated hiss of swearing – she wanted to scream but couldn't bear to wake Ted.

She finally stopped to catch her breath and Bert, keeping his eyes on her at all times, carefully stooped to retrieve the rashers.

'I'll just have … an … an egg so,' he whispered, as though trying not to rile an unpredictable animal.

Joanne was still slightly panting. Fury was great cardio.

'I'm taking Ted to the park today.'

Bert nodded cautiously.

Joanne continued. 'Then tonight is the wake.'

'I know. I have it all up here,' he said, lightly tapping the side of his head. 'Good for you to get out.'

'It's a wake, Bert. It's not me "getting out". It's familial duty.'

'But still it'll be good for you. Like I keep saying, you should try one of those mother-baby groups.'

'There's no point, I'll be back to work soon.'

'Even still, I think you need to get out more, see the outside world, see other people—'

'What's that supposed to mean?'

'Ehh … ehm …' He looked around frantically, as if searching for an answer to 'What's that supposed to mean?' that wouldn't cause her to explode further. 'I … ehh … I have to go to the loo!'

Joanne could feel a headache coming on from all the glaring. 'Fine,' she snapped. 'But do NOT take forty-five fucking minutes.'

Bert turned and fled. Joanne picked up the rashers, walked out to the yard and hurled them over the back wall.

The wake that night was uneventful except for the moment Joanne had joined the queue for what she assumed was the toilet but realised too late was actually for the corpse. When the queue spat her out beside the coffin, she hadn't a clue what to say to Carmel. Death had shrunk her to the size of a doll in the coffin.

'Well ...' Joanne had cast about for something to tell her. 'Carmel, you've finally reached your goal weight!'

'She'd have been delighted,' the woman behind Joanne had whispered, misty eyed. 'I was in Slimming World with her all these years. Sharon, our leader, is here too somewhere.

'Carmel ...' The woman had leaned down to the corpse. 'You got there! Better late than never. You're an inspiration.' Then she'd snapped a discreet pic, explaining: 'We always celebrate success stories at the meetings.'

On the train home, Joanne took out her phone to relate this ridiculous interlude to the girls when she saw a text from Aoife.

Shit's hitting the fan here.

Beneath her words was a link. Joanne nervously tapped it.

AD AGENCY YOUR STORY DECLARES INSOLVENCY, read the headline. She texted Aoife straight back.

Oh fuck, are you alright?

Aoife is typing ...

Joanne waited, anxiety boiling up inside her. She and Bert had been counting on her being back to work in two weeks' time. She made more money than Bert. They'd calculated that even though a lot of it would go on childcare, it was still the best option. She switched over to the calculator app but couldn't even think what numbers to input. The state maternity benefit was not enough to live on. Their expenses were low, but rent was high. Money was still extremely tight.

Finally Aoife's message dropped.

I actually have a job lined up. I've been looking for a while. I start in mid-March. Two weeks away. It's fairly basic but better than nothing obvs, just design stuff for She magazine.

Joanne's galloping thoughts screeched to a halt.

Since when has Aoife been looking for a job?

Why had she not mentioned it? She'd been all 'Can't wait till you're back in the office'. Joanne took a deep breath and texted Aoife back; she didn't want to assume anything.

Did you know this was coming?

Aoife is typing ...

Why would she not have told me?

Joanne stared down at the phone. But the 'why' was obvious. The economy was a shit show. She and Aoife would've been going for the exact same jobs. They had the exact same amount of experience. They'd worked for the exact same company.

Aoife is typing ...

She doesn't know what to say.

Joanne leaned her head against the train window. It was dark: all she could see was her own face, pale, her eyes just shadows.

Aoife is typing ...

At last a message appeared.

No! Of course not, I'd been thinking about it for ages.

It didn't take that long to type eleven words. She'd obviously been getting her story straight. She'd known the company was going tits up.

CHAPTER 14

'Home sweet ... cannot wait to get the hell out of here!' Jonathan swung open the apartment door.

Lexi followed him in, edging around the various bags and crates crowding the hallway. Even though it was only the 1st of March and they still had no official move-in date, they'd begun packing so that some things would be sorted before the Podify LIVE launch in two weeks' time. With her nerves building, Lexi was clinging on to some sense of order and control wherever she could, and labelling boxes and taking stuff to the charity shop was keeping her sane ... ish.

The dull March morning meant the narrow entrance to the flat was gloomy, but nothing could dampen her mood. The house sale was moving forward and starting the packing had her giddy.

In the kitchen, Jonathan was putting the kettle on to boil for coffee. She walked over and leaned into his back, sliding her arms around him.

'So, what's the plan for tonight?' Jonathan handed her a coffee.

'We're having drinks, ordering food and toasting the deal! Ebony and Paul are coming, Becca and Cassia, few other TikTokers Amanda is courting ...' Lexi listed the people

Jonathan high-fived her. 'Excellent – great networking opportunity.'

Lexi gave a self-conscious laugh. 'That's not true! They're friends! Sort of.'

'Sure, sure.' He batted a hand at her absentmindedly. 'You know what I mean. I'm gonna put up some fairy lights on the balcony. I think that'll make a really good spot for people to get shots for their socials, etc.'

'Hmm.' Lexi nodded. 'Sounds cool. Manda's coming over beforehand to do a quick record – we have a BitchSesh to do.'

BitchSesh was their weekly agony aunt video that they did exclusively for their paying listeners who subscribed to the show on Patreon for €5 a month in exchange for extra content. Hotties sent in their dilemmas and she and Amanda offered solutions with a healthy side of general snark and bitchiness. It was a very popular segment.

'Of course. I put this week's emails in the BitchSesh Slack thread.' Jonathan turned around, looking a little giddy. 'So, how do you feel about a little early housewarming present?'

'Very good! I mean we're nowhere near moving in, but ...'

'I know, but it's not exactly something I can keep under wraps. But don't worry – the landlord said he didn't mind as we're only here for a few more weeks.'

'What?!' Lexi put down her coffee and pulled him closer. 'What are you talking about?'

'Go into the office and see!' he responded gleefully.

'Oh my god, you didn't?!' She hurried down the hall and listened at the office door for a moment but heard nothing. She opened the door gently and there, nestled in the middle of the room, was a sheepskin rug. A sheepskin rug that was cradling a tiny, sleeping puppy with a big pink bow wrapped around her middle.

'Oh my god,' Lexi whispered as Jonathan appeared at her shoulder. 'She's so gorgeous. I can't believe you did this.' She closed her eyes as tears blurred her vision. Sometimes, the tears caught her off-guard, rising up when someone was kind or something nice happened. It was because mixed in with the loveliness of these occasions was a little kick of sadness. It had been building since signing the deal the week before. Happy times like these would always be bittersweet. She didn't have a mother to celebrate with or send inspo pictures of what she wanted her new kitchen to look like or agonise over paint options with.

Jonathan understood the tears. He put his arms around her and pulled her back to rest against his chest.

'She's so beautiful it kind of hurts,' Lexi breathed. 'What is she?'

'She's a teacup chihuahua! She's ten weeks old.'

Lexi crept closer and knelt down by the pup. She was the colour of sand and so small she could easily fit in Lexi's hands if she cupped them together. Her ears, which were twitching in her sleep, were incongruously big compared to the rest of her. Lexi ran her hand lightly over the puppy, who immediately shivered and opened her eyes, blinking up at Lexi. She wasn't skittish; she licked at Lexi's hand and pawed at the blanket.

'Not me passing away from the cuteness!' Lexi beamed up at Jonathan. 'Does she have a name already?'

'Nah, not really. The breeder just called her Number Four.'

'Breeder?' Lexi turned to look at him. 'You're not supposed to buy dogs, Jonathan.'

'Oh, nobody needs to know.' He waved a hand, as if to bat

her words away. 'Just tell the listeners that we got lucky with the adopting.'

'But it's not right in general.' Lexi stood. 'It's not always about optics all the time.'

Jonathan laughed, as if this was supposed to be a joke, then shrugged. 'She probably would've ended up in the dog shelter anyway. And look at her, Lexi! She's yours now. We can hardly give her back.'

Lexi turned back to the puppy, who had padded to the edge of the blanket and was putting one tentative, tiny paw on the wooden floor.

'I know, I know.' Lexi couldn't bear to dampen the moment.

Jonathan smiled and clapped his hands together. 'Names! And she needs an Insta account. What about *Your Hot Pup*?'

Lexi giggled. 'She's too young to consent! She needs to grow up out of the spotlight! Also she'd have more followers than me within like a week. Then *we'd* be working for *her*!'

She carefully crouched down again and gently scooped the dog up, lowering her nose to the soft fur under its big, slightly elfin ears. The little pup smelled yeasty and somehow comforting.

'Okay, we're going to call you Scout, after *To Kill A Mockingbird*.'

Jonathan laughed. 'That's pretentious.'

'It's not. My mum read me that book!'

'Fair enough. Okay, the puppy love-in is over – there's a lot to do today. There's a full dossier on how to care for Scout over there. She's microchipped and vaccinated. Plus I bought you one of those crazy lady buggies so you can show her around the neighbourhood later.' He pointed to the corner behind the door, where a neat little pink pram with a canopy and mesh enclosure stood.

'Fuck, that is CUTE!' Lexi, still cradling the surprisingly compliant puppy, leaned up and kissed Jonathan's soft lips, running her hand along his rough jaw. 'You think of everything.'

'I just wanted to treat you and celebrate all the big changes.' He smiled down at her. 'Right, not to go all manager mode, but you, my friend, need to work, work, work before tonight! Today's BitchSesh is sponsored by the puppy food that will be supplying Scout's every meal from now on, so you better put her on the 'gram! The brand is PuppyLove and the script for the ad is on the Spon Slack. The marketing manager said she's familiar with the format and you can riff a bit but make sure to get the three key points across – I've bolded them for ease. I'm heading to the gym. Catch you later.'

After lunch (Green Juice PM) at her desk, Lexi's phone rang and she was surprised to see it was Abi. They were back on reasonably good terms, but she'd thought he was away studying the arrival of the minke whales; from March through to November they migrated to the west coast, he'd told her. If he was back early, he could come to the party tonight!

'Lexi?' He was practically shouting over the roar of wind, confirming that he was, in fact, still away.

'What's up?'

'I just had a call from Dad's neighbour, Margaret Mahon. She told me that she hasn't seen any lights on in the house the last two nights. She knocked and stuff. I tried the phone, but—' The wind was blasting now, completely drowning Abi out.

'Abi?' Lexi's jaw clenched. No lights and no answer … Her father had to be drinking. Or worse.

'Sorry, sorry, it's loud here.' Abi was back, the roar having abated somewhat. 'I'm sure he's grand – he hates yer one and probably just didn't want to answer her – but will you swing down and check on him anyway?'

An impatient knock on the door told her Amanda had arrived.

'I—' Lexi stalled. She didn't want to say she had to work. She pulled the phone away from her ear to check the time. It was nearly three. It was a three-hour round trip.

'Lexi?'

'Sorry. Yep, I'll get it sorted and text you, okay?' The door went again. 'I've gotta go. Mind yourself.'

Lexi checked on Scout, who was padding around the office and sniffing at the large pink paper hanging from a roll overhead at the back wall – the backdrop for the BitchSesh record – then headed out to the hall and opened the door.

Lexi pulled Amanda in. 'Hang on one second; I just have a bit of Dad admin to sort. Wait here. I cannot wait for you to see what Jonathan got me!'

'Oh yeah, the dog.' Amanda grinned. 'I helped pick little number four out!'

Lexi slipped down the hall and called her dad. *Please answer*, she thought.

It rang and rang. Just as she was about to give up, he answered with a phlegmy cough. 'Lexi?'

'Dad! I'm so glad you answered. Abi told me Margaret said you weren't answering.'

'What—?' He sounded off, as though he couldn't quite get a handle on her words.

Has he been drinking? He was fine the last time we were down. Well, obviously not fine, the man lives in fucking squalor, but ...

It dawned on her then that it was nearly two months since she'd visited. *How did I let it go so long?*

'Ah, Margaret's a pain in the arse.' He coughed again. 'I'm grand, Lexi.'

'Okay.' Lexi relaxed a bit. 'Look, I'll be down really soon, okay?'

They hung up and Lexi immediately called Jonathan.

'Lex?'

'Heya, listen I just got a call from Abi. One of Dad's neighbours got on to him about Dad not answering the door. So I rang and Dad actually did pick up but ... I dunno, it's probably nothing, but it feels a little off. I've got the record to do with Amanda. Is there any way you could go down and check in on him?'

'Babe ...' Jonathan wasn't exactly rushing to oblige.

'I'm really sorry to ask. I guess I could postpone the record.'

'No, don't do that.' Jonathan was firm. 'We can't mess up the schedule with the Flowerbox ads. They got really shirty the last time when we were like an hour late with an episode. Look, I'll head down. It won't take too long.'

'Ah, thank you, thank you. Like I said, I know I'm overreacting but just in case. Love you.'

'Right, the levels are good. Can you just sit in my seat for a sec so I can check the focus?'

Lexi was setting up the record while Amanda doted on Scouty.

'I'm so happy he got her for you,' Amanda announced, scooting over to the other chair. 'You deserve all the love.'

'Did you have a gummy on the way over or something?'

Amanda laughed, returning to her own chair. 'I can be sentimental. And you do deserve all the love.'

'Okay … we are good.' Lexi hit record on the cameras; the sound was already rolling. She went to her chair, depositing a little kiss on the top of Amanda's head as she passed.

Once she was seated, they settled themselves, then Lexi clapped loudly, which would help with syncing the audio later.

'Welcome back to BitchSesh, Hotties!'

'You may notice we've got a guest bitch for this week's BitchSesh.' Lexi indicated Scouty in Amanda's lap.

'Yep, I now have competition for Lexi's heart, but I still think I'm hotter. So how does it feel, Lexi?'

'What?'

'Your fella making it offish like this. A puppy's a bigger commitment than a child, we all know that.'

Lexi laughed. 'Do we?'

'Fuck, yeah, you'll be picking up this gal's shit till you DIE. At least a kid eventually learns to wipe its own arse. A dog is a big deal.'

'On the subject of dogs,' Lexi cut in. 'One of this week's BitchSesh sponsors is PuppyLove!'

She carefully reeled off the 'key brand messages'.

Amanda looked openly bored. 'Okay, okay. Can we get on with the juice, please?!'

'Doing it.' Lexi tried to keep the irritation out of her voice as she pulled up her laptop. Then she spotted a new WhatsApp from Jonathan. 'Hang on one sec.'

All grand down here. Nothing to worry about. Heading back now. XX

'Okay,' Lexi settled herself. 'We have three dilemmas sent in by our Hotties this week. Two of them are quickfire yes or nos and one is something a bit meatier.'

Amanda straightened up and propped Scout up in her arms. 'Hit me.'

'Dear Amanda and Lexi, my boyfriend and his friend have asked me if they can have a sword fight in my mouth. Should I let them?'

'Only if your mouth's big enough, bébé. Next.'

Lexi laughed, shaking her head. 'Euphoria is ruining the kids these days. Okay, here's the next one. My fella and I have been together for three years and we've moved in together. I felt like we were probably heading towards the marriage chat so I started a Pinterest board. Nothing crazy, just casual. Anyway he found it and went mad. Which I think is kind of rich. I found his porn history last year and it was all bestiality stuff and I wasn't judgy at all, even though I'm a vegetarian AND an animal lover.'

Amanda snorted. 'Not as much of an animal lover as him, luv.'

Lexi finished reading: 'What do ye think? Is it double standards of him to be going off on me about this?'

'No, not double standards at all!' Amanda crowed, slightly startling Scout. 'Everyone watches porn. A wedding Pinterest board without the actual proposal is waaaay more fucked up than bestiality porn. Sorry to break it to you, Hottie, but he's got the upper hand here. I think vegetarian or no, you're gonna be eating a lotta pork to make this up to him.'

Lexi gently lifted Scout off Amanda's lap and pretended to shield her ears. 'Amanda!' she feigned shock. 'Not in front of the puppy. This is why people think we're uncouth!'

'I wouldn't wanna be couth,' Amanda retorted.

'Right, this one's a biggie. It's coming in from "anonymous" and they've taken great pains to protect their identity. The actual email addy has litch been created for the occasion: hottiewithaprob@gmail.com.'

Amanda laughed. 'It's like she doesn't trust us or something.'

'Dear Amanda and Lexi, Long time listener, first time contacter. I am having a really shitty time with my friends right now. Specifically one of my oldest friends (we've known each other since we were four years old). Before this year, I would've said she was my best friend. But since the start of the year, things have been extremely weird. She's really slow to respond to my texts, if she even replies at all – sometimes she just completely ignores me.

'She got engaged at New Year's and didn't ask me to be a bridesmaid, saying there were only a couple of spots. But she has asked me to make the party favours, which obviously is an honour. The rest of our group chat seems kind of quiet in general and I'm just really worried that they've all migrated to a different group without me. I feel really pathetic for how much this is upsetting me. I wasn't well for a bit last year. And I feel like everything started to change from then. None of them ever said anything to me about being in hospital and my best friend didn't visit me or anything.

'My boyfriend says they're not worth it, but they've literally been my friends since school. I didn't make any kind of college group (mainly cos I still hung out with the school girls all the time) and now I'm a childminder so I don't have co-workers. The thing that made me finally write to you was last weekend. My best friend invited me to go wedding-dress shopping, but when I got there, there was none of our friends, just lots of her aunts and cousins. I brought champagne but my bestie didn't seem to want to make a day of it at all. And then at the end, the worst bit, I texted a pic to our WhatsApp group and one of the other girls got back saying she couldn't wait for the "real" shopping trip. Then a second later she deleted the message and said, "Sorry wrong thread." My question is, do you think this is all in my head? Sometimes I can get kind of worked up over little things ... I just don't know if I'm just being needy or if she doesn't like me any more or what?'

'Oh shit, that is really fucked up.' Amanda looked upset and Lexi was relieved. Sometimes Amanda could be too cavalier with the listener dilemmas but this was one she clearly realised must be treated with care. 'Okay, firstly,' Amanda looked at the camera, 'I am so sorry this is happening to you. What your friend is doing is not good.'

Lexi nodded. 'Not good at all. Would we think there might be a bit of the Batshit Bride going on? I know, I know, it's a shitty stereotype, but we all have a friend—'

'Or twenty,' Amanda interjected.

'Yep,' Lexi agreed gravely. 'We all have friends who completely lost their minds when planning their weddings.' Lexi started fake sobbing. 'This. Is. My. Daaaaay.'

Amanda laughed. 'D'you remember the Hottie who wrote in saying her friend wanted all the blonde bridesmaids to dye their hair so that she was the only blonde in the wedding party?'

'Wait!' Lexi held her hand up. 'What about the bride who wouldn't let ANY of the bridesmaids top up their Botox or fillers for a full six months before her wedding so that only *she* looked smooth and plump of lip.'

'Sadistic.' Amanda shook her head.

'But on this front, I'm not sure that this is only shady bride shenanigans. The whole thing seems to pre-date the engagement, for starters. How shitty for her to not visit in hospital. Though ...' Lexi paused. 'It doesn't say how long she was in hospital. If it was just a couple of nights, maybe that's not too bad.'

'The no/slow text replies is crap too, but we are all guilty of being busy and self-absorbed. I've left you on read many a time,' Amanda pointed out magnanimously.

'Yeah, but it's your full-time job to be my best friend soooo ... we probably don't quite have the same concerns as these two. We're like rostered to see each other.' Lexi laughed.

'I think we can both agree,' Amanda carried on, 'that the most damning evidence here is the "Sorry wrong thread" text. It definitely supports the Hottie's hypothesis that there is indeed a breakaway side-thread that she's not on.'

'We need some solid advice that is actionable.' Lexi absent-mindedly stroked Scout's ears.

'Right.' Amanda nodded. She looked at the camera with uncharacteristic solemnity. 'To be honest, I really think you should get yourself some new friends, cos these bitches are toxic IMO. I know that's easy for us to say, but I think it's very important.'

'Maybe you could join a club of some kind?' Lexi suggested.

'Fuck,' Amanda sighed. 'It's probably easier to find a disease-free single straight man than a new best friend after thirty.'

'Keep us posted, Hottie, and remember you always have us!'

After the record, the Hottie's dilemma spun in Lexi's head for the rest of the day and on into the party, where people she hardly knew drank bubbles and snapped selfies around her. The Hottie's situation wasn't the same as hers with her schoolfriends' group. She wasn't ignoring their texts; they'd left the group after the last furore. But even if they hadn't been upset with what was said, maybe something like this would've happened anyway. Sometimes these friend groups just ran their course.

Still, my life shouldn't be all Amanda all the time. There's a lot going on in the next few weeks. After the LIVE is done and the move, I'll text Deano, explain the situation and apologise for missing the engagement party. Maybe he'd be up for a meet-up.

CHAPTER 15

Claire was sprinting through the Monday morning drop-offs – lovingly stuffing Lila and Frankie into their respective institutions so that she could get across the city in good time. In the week since brunch with the Bitch Herd and the single occupancy rate bombshell, she'd been flipflopping on her next move. She'd even written in to the *Your Hot Friend*'s BitchSesh and it was listening to their response over the weekend that had her decided.

I will not go quietly into the night. I am going to fucking make a friend and bring that friend to the Ibiza trip and show them I am not a loser.

After waving off the older two kids, she and Sonny got the tram through the city, past the financial district with its sleek anonymous buildings to the older part of Dublin where red-brick cottages were home both to families who'd been there for generations and to blow-ins, the two groups co-existing fairly happily.

It was one of those promising March days when the sun could trick you into believing that summer was practically upon you. By the time Claire was manoeuvring the pram out of the carriage, she was sweating.

Sonny's irritation at being jerked around was quite vocal. 'Ehhh, ehhh, ehhh,' he raged.

'Ssshhh,' Claire whispered. 'You're going to have to cooperate at this thing. They need to believe you're a babier baby than you are, pal. We're looking to age you down like a Hollywood actress.'

She jerked around the throng of shoppers clogging the path. She'd scoped out the route the night before and had earmarked a cafe on the way where she was going to change Sonny's quite distinctly baby *boy's* outfit for an old pink Baby-gro of Lila's she'd found the day before.

Claire bought a bag of salt and vinegar crisps from the bored girl on the till and asked where the loos were. In the bathroom, she changed Sonny, noting with a twinge of worry that he hadn't done his customary morning shite yet. She hoped there would be a place to change him at the mother-baby group away from prying, baby-crotch-examining eyes. *Relax,* she tried to calm her nerves. No one would be examining his junk.

Another five minutes' walk and she was outside the community centre on Verona Avenue. A few mothers with babies tucked into prams and slings passed her, smiling. This felt promising. *They're so welcoming! They think I'm just one of them!*

Sonny was now straining against his straps, which could be a problem. His fake age was supposed to be twelve months. Did twelve-month-olds walk? She could barely remember. They did, but kind of badly ... Sonny was pretty steady on his feet. I'll just try and keep him in the pram and if I have to unleash him, I can say he's a walking-savant.

Also, she realised, his name couldn't be Sonny. She stared down at him and adjusted the pink hairband she'd put on his little head. Sammy? A bit too gender-neutral. She needed a girlier name ... Sally? Would she have called her child Sally? she wondered. She frowned. No, too plain. But she was sure it would be best to stick to an 'S' name, just in case she forgot and accidently called him by his real one.

'Hello!' A bosomy, older woman interrupted Claire's mental name-search. 'Are you two here for the mammy-baby group? I'm Fiona, the public health nurse – I run it.' She bent down to Sonny. 'Well, hello there, missus. You're a big girl now, aren't you!' She straightened back up to give Claire a warm smile. 'What's her name?'

Shite. Claire frantically cast around her mind for something. Anything. 'Ehmm. Ssss ...' *C'mon, Claire. Something beginning with 's'*. 'Sauron!' she finally said. 'Her name's Sauron.'

Claire grimaced. Why such a weird fucking name, Claire?! As weird as the name was, it felt familiar. She'd heard it somewhere but couldn't quite place it.

'Sauron ... how unusual ...' Fiona smiled. 'All the names are so different now, aren't they? We have a little one called Hammock in the group at the moment too!'

'Oh! Hammock's nice,' Claire lied. 'My name's Claire, by the way.' She'd opted to give her real first name: one alias was more than enough to manage. Plus if this actually worked and she got a friend out of it, she had to use her real me.

'Lovely! Now *that's* a name I've heard of. Come in, come in.' She held the glass door open and led the way down a corridor with rubbery, institutional floors, its walls blanketed with posters for everything from addiction counselling to macrame classes.

Unwanted thoughts of the hospital swam into her head. They'd had classes there too – occupational therapy, it had been called. It was hard to believe that Claire had only been home four and a half months; it seemed like far more time had passed.

'Sauron will probably be the oldest of the babies,' Fiona commented as she showed Claire to the door of a large hall.

This, at least, was part of her story that she'd actually prepared. 'Yeah, she's twelve months but we were living in Kerry for the last year and I just thought this would be a good way to meet other mums in the area.'

'That's a lovely idea. It's so important for young mums to have community, and you'll be able to give some of the newbies pointers, I imagine!'

Claire didn't even have time to fret about this as Fiona brought her into the airy space, at the centre of which was a clutch of women chatting in folding chairs, jigging babies on their laps and surrounded by overstuffed nappy bags and prams.

'Girls!' Fiona boomed over the din. 'This is Claire and Sauron, they're new to Dublin!' She gave Claire a little push towards the group before disappearing back out the door.

'Hiya!' A dark-haired woman waved Claire over to the island of mothers. 'Claire, is it? And … Sauron?'

'Yep.' Claire nodded.

'I'm Lola,' she said. 'And this is Hammock.'

Claire smiled carefully, focusing on not betraying any reaction to the baby's name. A woman who introduced herself as Roisin took over the introductions and went around the rest of the circle.

'This is Isabel's mummy, Emma.'

'This is Freddy's mummy, Barbara.' And so on.

Now that she was here, confronted with the reality of these women, the absurdity of this scheme was suddenly hitting her. *What am I doing here? I can't make a friend here and bring her to Ibiza.*

Claire continued to smile calmly as her thoughts raced.

I should leave. No, maybe that would look even more suspicious. I should stay for the group and then run.

'Jesus, babies are such wankers, aren't they?'

This pronouncement alerted the group to a new arrival, a short girl with blonde hair clipped back behind her ears. 'Seriously,' she continued, 'they're so conniving. It's like they find the one tiny thing that's giving us just a modicum of pleasure and then they shit all over it.' She pulled down the stretchy wrap on her front to expose the top of a little head, furred with gingery hair. 'This morning I brought home a coffee from the fancy place, as a little treat for me. But could I have that?' she asked the little head. 'Could I have that little soupcon of pleasure? Noooo. The little – admittedly gorgeous – prick did a piss the second I took his nappy off and you know the boy ones have serious range.' She looked around at them. 'That's right,' she snapped. 'The wee arced up and went directly into my cup. Directly. Into. My. Cup.' She concluded this enraged anecdote by plonking herself into a chair.

'Oh, Joanne!' Roisin looked slightly scandalised at this little speech, as though the new girl, evidently called Joanne, had just broken some unwritten contract. 'But motherhood ... it's still just so rewarding, isn't it?'

'You're deluded.' Joanne scowled. '*Ted's* the best thing ever.' She nodded at the lump. 'But the day-to-day is a bit of a slog. Also I've developed a deep, borderline psychotic loathing for my boyfriend which is also taking up a lot of my energy.'

Her gaze shifted to Claire suddenly and Claire tensed. She'd managed to come this far without having to speak. Having woken up the the lunacy of her plan, she just wanted to run down the clock and get out of there.

Joanne was looking at Sonny now. 'That yours?' she asked.

'Hmm-hmm,' Claire nodded.

'She looks a fair bit older. Does it get any better?' Despite her blunt tone, a pleading look had entered Joanne's tired eyes.

'Yeah!' Claire did, at least, know this for certain. She'd witnessed Norah in the dead-behind-the-eyes era. It did pass. 'It gets easier.'

'Does she sleep?' a mother with a similarly desperate expression asked.

'Yeah. She's settled down a good bit now.'

'Don't worry, gals,' Roisin cut in, clearly unhappy that Claire was being mined for expertise. 'My Harriet sleeps through the night, has done since she was six weeks old. You'll all get there.' She turned to Claire. 'How old is Sauron anyway?'

'She's twelve months.' Claire jigged the pram a bit to subdue Sonny's mutterings of dissent at being confined. 'I've just moved back to Dublin and wanted to get to know some mums around here—'

'Wait! Hang on!' Joanne barged back into the conversation. 'Are we all going to just ignore the elephant in the room here?'

Claire tensed. *Oh god, what?*

'You named your baby Sauron!'

'Yes,' she ventured tentatively. *Why WAS it so familiar?!* she wondered again.

'So you're one of those *Lord of the Rings* fanatics?'

Shit, that was it! Sauron was some *Lord of the Rings* character –

though she'd no idea what type of character. *Shit, shit, shit.* She'd probably heard Lila talking about her. She was just going to have to roll with this.

She gave a tight little nod. 'Yes, I love *Lord of the Rings*.'

'Okay, okay. No offence but fan or not, it is off the wall to call your baby after an evil disembodied flaming eye.'

Noooo, Claire wailed internally. *Sauron is a villain. And an eye.*

Say something, Claire! she urged herself.

'Well, that woman's baby is called Hammock!' she said, pointing at Lola to take the heat off herself.

Oh god, not that, Claire!

Lola instinctively held her baby closer. 'I don't have to defend my son's name to you people. It has meaning for us.'

'What? Was he conceived in a hammock or something?' Joanne deadpanned.

'Yes, as a matter of fact,' said Lola.

'Okay, wow! Fuck!' Joanne exclaimed. 'Sex in a hammock is no small undertaking. 'Fuck, yeah! You should commemorate that!'

'This is not appropriate subject matter for around the babies,' Roisin announced, waving her hands as if to dispel any lingering odour of the unseemly conversation.

'What's the problem? They're barely sentient.' Joanne rolled her eyes. 'Plus the only reason they're all here is cos we rode someone.'

'Okay! Okay!' Roisin gave a zipped-up little laugh. 'Of course I'm down for a little TMI girl-talk as much as the next person, but I usually need a couple of wines before I'm ready for S-E-X chat,' she said delicately.

Joanne stared at her in disbelief. 'Hon, I shit myself in a labour room full of strangers this year. TMI does not apply to me any more. I'm guessing it doesn't apply to any of us. We've all had babies dragged out of us one way or another in the last few months. Or we've had babies grating the nips off us.' She was in full TEDTalk mode. 'Now. This woman ...' she swept a hand over to Lola, 'got railed in a hammock and that cannot be easy to do. This achievement should be recognised and she deserves to be commended.'

'It must've been murder on your back?' one mousy woman asked Lola quietly.

'Oh, no,' Lola shook her head. 'I was on top.'

'Was it tied to a tree or what?' asked another worn-out-looking woman.

'No, we have a stand. We got it from IKEA. It's fab.' This led the conversation down the inevitable IKEA avenue and after another twenty minutes of chat, Claire felt she could make her escape. It was nearly time to collect Frankie and put this batshit scheme behind her. Also a noxious odour was coming off Sonny in waves that would have been sure to hit the others soon enough.

She said her goodbyes and made her way to the bathroom, where she was relieved to see the changing table was off in a corner. If anyone came in while she was changing Sonny, she could fairly easily block him from view. This was good, as just as she'd lain him out and got his little pink baby suit undone, Joanne and Ted came in behind her.

'It's shite o'clock.' Joanne laughed.

'Yes!' Claire shifted to make sure Sonny's little penis would be hidden. *Relax, Claire, it's the size of a cashew nut!* She doubted Joanne would actually notice it even if she was looking directly at it.

Joanne leaned against the sinks, waiting for the table. 'How'd you find your first meet-up?'

'Good.' Claire pulled the wipes out of the nappy bag. 'They're very …' Claire searched for a word, 'nice?'

Joanne snorted. 'Yeah, nice,' she echoed.

'Nothing worse than nice!' Claire giggled, knowing it didn't matter what she said: she wouldn't be coming back.

'Thank you!' Joanne grinned. 'I thought they might have converted you already!'

'Nah.' Claire grinned back. 'I'm kind of allergic to that whole "too blessed to be stressed" thing.'

'Thank god. You know, I've been praying for someone sound to join this group. None of my friends have done the baby thing yet, so they don't really get why I'm not out every weekend any more. Do you want to get coffee or something sometime? I'll give you my number …' Joanne pulled her phone out of the baby sling.

'Eh—' Claire couldn't believe it. One morning in and she was getting a number. Pity she could literally never see this woman again. 'Sure,' she agreed. She figured refusing to take it would seem odd. It was so annoying: Joanne seemed like actual friend material. *If only we'd met when I wasn't lying about having a baby.*

Keeping one hand on Sonny's tummy, Claire took out her phone and typed as Joanne called out her mobile number.

'Cool, I have you now.' Claire smiled.

'Call me and then I'll have you,' Joanne said.

Claire paused. 'Oh … I … eh …' Claire searched for some reason to not comply, but her mind was blank. 'O-kay.' She hit the call button and Joanne beamed down at her buzzing phone.

'That's great, Claire. We should deffo meet up. I was supposed to go back to work next week but the whole fucking company just crashed and burned so more maternity leave for me I guess.' She looked morose.

'Fuck, I'm so sorry. That's awful.' Claire turned back to Sonny so she could finish his nappy. She pulled down the front flap, forgetting that Sonny was liable to send up a fountain of wee the second his nappy was off. Typically, this was a particularly high arc. Behind her, she could hear Joanne gasp.

'Oh shit, that's some range.' Joanne paused, then added slowly, 'I didn't actually realise girls did that too.'

Claire scrambled to answer. 'Yeah, it's mad! They do!' She laughed lightly, trying to stop the urine from flowing right off the changing table.

Joanne hurried over to help her and before Claire could cover Sonny's penis, Joanne's eyes landed on it.

'What the—' Joanne stopped trying to mop up the pee, her eyes pinballing between Claire's face and Sonny's penis. 'Is that a ... Is she a ...'

'I have to go.' Claire zipped up Sonny's suit without even putting on a fresh nappy, bundled him back into his buggy and charged out.

She kept her head down as she rushed through the throng of mums leaving the hall. She ignored their waves, practically throwing herself and the pram out the door to the street. She didn't particularly think that Joanne would give chase and demand answers, but equally there was no telling what a bored new mum would do for a bit of distraction.

A couple of blocks away at the tram station, Claire sat stress-eating the crisps she'd bought earlier and willing the tram to come.

Her WhatsApp pinged. To Claire's horror, it was a message from Joanne.

Okay. So just to clarify ... you just pretended your 'son' was your 'daughter'???!!! Should I be taking this to the authorities? Or has motherhood just got you this exhausted!? Cos TBH I can kind of relate!

Claire tapped out of the message. She felt like such a loser.

This is the dumbest thing I have ever, ever done.

Well, maybe not the dumbest.

She winced, thinking of the grey Sunday last September when everything had felt so hopeless. Shame crept over her as images assailed her. The stony-faced coastguard grabbing her roughly. People on the pier watching. Then at the hospital, the foil blanket, Marian white-faced and scared. Her dad crying quietly. Then the blank days and the blank weeks and the blank months that followed.

Summoning all her resolve, she wrenched herself back from that awful ledge of her mind.

I am well; I am doing better; I am on track with my meds. This was just a stupid idea. I will think of another way to make a friend.

CHAPTER 16

The crowds streaming into the Liberty Theatre on a damp Thursday night were all of one single demographic: girls in their twenties with short skirts and shorter tops, holding hands with their friends and giving the finger to passing motorists who were catcalling them from rolled-down windows.

Lexi was watching from her dressing-room window directly above the main entrance. The atmosphere was amazing. Only twenty minutes to go. She loved their live shows. They'd never made her nervous, even as the audiences grew from modest crowds of 100 or 150 in the early years to actual thousands.

Tonight they'd be performing for 3,000 people in-person and another maybe 20,000 on the livestream. And that was still only a fraction of their overall audience. This was also the most important show they'd ever done. Podify were expecting huge eyes on this. It was vital tonight went well: their first episode on the new network was going out tomorrow and they needed to hit 250k listeners. They'd recorded it earlier and scheduled it so that they could drink their faces off tonight and take the day off tomorrow. Lexi was fretting about the listener figures, but Amanda insisted she had something spicy for the games part of the show that would definitely have everyone tuning in tomorrow. Lexi just hoped it was legal and not too offensive.

Lexi checked her outfit. It was always hot under the stage lights, so clothes-wise, even in the middle of March, less was always more. Tonight she was wearing high-top Reebok runners and an oversized black hoodie as an extremely short dress.

She pulled up FaceTime on her phone and selected Abi from her contacts. As much as she'd wanted him to come to the show, he'd arrived back from his research trip just in time to babysit his new puppy-niece. A couple of rings and his weathered, teddy-bear face filled the screen of her phone.

'You've barely been gone an hour and you're already checking up on me?' He grinned.

'I have severe separation anxiety,' Lexi wailed. 'Where is she? My baby!'

Abi obediently disappeared and Scouty's big brown eyes appeared, her tongue immediately lapping at the screen.

'You're so beautiful, I could cry,' she told the pup. 'Is she being good?'

'She pissed in Jonathan's loafers so I'd go with ... yeah?' Abi's voice came from somewhere behind the dog.

'She has it in for those loafers. She's dead right, they're disgusting. I have to go in a sec, but will you just make sure to put her white noise machine on at bedtime? She needs the reassurance.'

'I will.' Abi was back looking at her. 'You know, I couldn't help but notice that she appears to sleep in a small cot attached to the side of your bed ...'

'Shut up, don't judge,' Lexi laughed. 'You won't understand until you have a baby of your own. I have to go! Wish me luck – biggest moment of my career and all that. You'll watch, right?'

'Of course, me and Scout will be cheering you on. Please just try to give me a signal when you're about to say something gross about your sex life. The *Your Hot Friend* content is not family-friendly.'

'Well, aren't I lucky that you're the only one in the family who gives a shit, then?!' Lexi laughed then had a familiar pang of guilt; even though Jonathan had checked on her dad a couple of weeks ago, she still hadn't made it home.

'Ah now, Dad cares. In his way.' Abi shifted a bit to bring Scout back into shot. 'Say "Good luck, Mama!"' He waved the dog's paw and ended the call just as Amanda and Jonathan ploughed through the dressing-room door.

'Five minutes, Lexi.' Jonathan was using his manager voice, as if she was the one holding them up.

'You look so hot, Lexi!' Amanda squealed. She looked gorgeous herself, in a silver sequin playsuit and chunky, neon-green Chelsea boots.

Amanda leaned into the mirror and reapplied her red lipstick, using her actual lips as only the faintest guide. 'Well?' she pouted at Lexi.

'They're getting more insane every time you apply.'

'Girls!' Jonathan clapped his hands. 'Downstairs. Showtime. Now. The Hotties are getting restless.'

As they clattered down the back stairs, Lexi could hear the chanting: 'Hotties! Hotties! Hotties!'

Lexi and Amanda took their places on the stage. There was also a lot of stamping and general screeching coming from beyond the musty velvet curtain.

'I love them so much,' Lexi shouted to Amanda, who was shimmying her mic up under her playsuit while the sound guy blushed a deep crimson.

'Lex-ay, Lex-ay, Lex-ay ...' The Hotties were now singing her name to the tune of 'Olé Olé Olé'. She took the mic the sound guy was proffering, attached it near her mouth, fed the wire down her hoodie and clipped the little pack to the band of her bra.

Now they were doing Nicki Minaj's 'Anaconda' but with 'Amanda'.

'Okay, places, places.' Jonathan and the stage manager with the headset ushered them to two high chairs on either side of a high table laden with colourful cocktails.

'The questions are all picked out and printed on the cards.' Jonathan indicated the little stack on each chair. 'You're here.' He steered Lexi to the left side and took Amanda's hand to lead her to the right.

'Ready?' the stage manager called, now back at the side of the stage.

Jonathan turned to Lexi: 'Ready?'

She nodded.

'Ready?' he asked Amanda, who smiled and, after a beat, nodded.

Lexi felt a sudden wriggle of nerves. Did a funny look just pass between Jonathan and Amanda?

Jonathan hurried away, giving the stage manager the thumbs-up.

Lexi opened her mouth to ask Amanda if something was going

on, but just at that moment the curtain started to rise and the chanting of the Hotties reached a peak.

Twenty minutes in and the show was a hit. The vibe in the room was electric and Lexi could see on the monitors down in front of them that there were at least 30,000 people tuning into the livestream. This stream, with audience reactions and comments scrolling underneath, was also being projected behind them and on screens to the right and left of the stage.

'Okay!' Amanda held her arms aloft in an attempt to quell the screaming and laughing rising from the audience. 'So we're gonna do a quickfire round of Ask Us Anything before we do our little game of One Truth, One Lie.'

Lexi picked up her cue cards. 'I have some questions here that were sent into the *Your Hot Friend* inbox. So first up is: "When did you realise *Your Hot Friend* was going to be such a hit?"'

Amanda doubled over, laughing. 'Are we a hit?' She smirked at the audience, who erupted in cheers again.

'Okay, okay.' Lexi grinned, exasperated. 'Please don't get them riled up again, ye're all like bitches in heat tonight! Okay, to answer this question, my first time thinking we were on to something was when the gals on *Can He Be Zaddy* talked about us on their podcast. That was like a "whoa, pinch me" moment. I was like … "Is this becoming a thing?!" What about you, Manda?'

'Mine was our very first solicitor's letter threatening action!'

The crowd howled in appreciation but Lexi tensed. Libel laws in Ireland were a bollocks and they'd flown too close to the sun on several occasions. Lexi shuddered, remembering the whole debacle with Mr Fleming.

Amanda was taking out her phone. 'I actually have one of my fave solicitor's letters as my screensaver!'

'No!' Lexi needed to steer her away from this subject asap.

'Yes!' Amanda shouted. 'Lexi, you gotta hear this one – it's a trip down memory lane for us.'

'Stop! You're giving me anxiety.' Lexi was trying to sound amused while also trying to scream 'STOP!' at Amanda using just her eyes.

'Read it! Read it! Read it!' The crowd were gagging for the tea.

Lexi waved her hands at the baying crowd. 'It's boring.'

'Okay, okay. Hotties, I wish I could read it, but we can't afford another scrap with a former maths teacher who cannot be named for legal reasons.' She winked at the crowd. 'Actually this is totally triggering even me.' She adopted a sincere, troubled tone. 'To this day, every time I close my eyes, I can still see his quadratic equations bobbing up and do—'

'OKAY!' Lexi roared across her. 'Please stop!' She turned to the audience with a pleading look. 'Hotties, unless one of you is a trained solicitor who will handle all our libellous slander pro bono … PLEASE STOP encouraging her!' She laughed.

'We should've got Jonathan to re-train before he became our manager,' Amanda said dolefully. 'Though, actually …' She brightened up and produced her next card with a flourish. 'This does relate to our next Ask Us Anything … this Hottie wants to know if it's ever weird that our manager is also Lexi's boyfriend!'

'It's probably weirder for me,' Lexi giggled. 'Who else has a boyfriend who knows her best friend's dress size?!'

'I need that info for wardrobe!' Jonathan shouted over from the side of the stage.

'Yeah, yeah,' Lexi called back, delighted they'd moved away from the knotty lawsuit threats. 'But to answer this listener's question, it's actually amazing that I get to work with my two favourite people in the world and it's truly never been tricky at all.'

'Next Ask Us Anything is, "You never seem to fight on the podcast. Are there rows behind the scenes that none of us ever see?"'

Lexi paused to think. It was always important to balance relatable with aspirational. The Hotties needed to envy them but also to see themselves in them. 'We don't really fight,' she said slowly. 'Sometimes we scrap a bit!'

'Yeah, but only over like little things. Whose merch designs we're gonna do, borrowing clothes, who's hotter,' Amanda chirped happily.

Lexi's mind flashed on Roslyn Sullivan's reasonable face – if the Hotties knew they were in couples therapy, they would lap that goss up. Though they still hadn't managed to get back in since their first session. Things had been so crazy with the Podify launch.

'Okay, time for One Truth, One Lie, bébés,' Amanda happily breezed on, and Lexi gave herself a little mental shake to refocus.

Amanda picked up the next cue card. 'Right, first up we have the most embarrassing moment of all time. Lexi?! So we each have to come up with a true story and a made-up story and the other has to guess which is which.'

'Okay ...' Lexi pretended to think. They'd prepped their stories in advance, though they hadn't told each other of course! 'It's actually so hard to think of a single thing about my life that Amanda doesn't already know,' she told the audience.

'Okay.' She sat up straighter and turned around to face Amanda. 'When I was like eighteen and away with my dad and brothers, I saw Louis Tomlinson in an ice-cream shop in Brighton. He was behind me in the queue. So I was all like, "Be chill, be casual, Lexi!" I paid the girl at the counter and made my way back outside. And that's when I realised I didn't have the actual ice-cream cone. I'd forgotten it. So I went back in and said it to the girl and she was like, "No hon, I gave it to you." And I was like, "Eh, you didn't, I don't have it." And then.' Lexi paused and looked round the audience for effect. 'Then, gals, Louis FUCKING Tomlinson tapped me on the shoulder and told me I'd put the ice cream cone IN MY BAG cos, remember, I was SO chill, so casual!'

Amanda cackled. 'That has to be the lie.' She wiped her eyes. 'There's no WAY you wouldn't have told me that!'

'Wait.' Lexi held up a hand. 'You need to hear the other option.'

'Go on,' Amanda urged her as the audience quietened down again.

'So, the year I was twenty-two, I was at the Love Music Festival and I'd spent all afternoon trying to hold my place in the very front of the main stage for My Chemical Romance—'

'Is being at an MCR gig the embarrassing bit?!' Amanda cut in and Lexi laughed.

'I know, I know. Look, the lengths I was willing to go to for MCR were sad. Case in point. With about two hours to go, I was desperate for a piss. Desperate. Now, everyone was absolutely packed in and covered in sweat and beer and I just thought … what's one more fluid?!'

The room erupted in gales of laughter.

'Okay, the truth is …' Amanda paused for effect. 'You deliberately pissed yourself in the middle of a crowd for My Chemical Romance?'

'Is that your final answer?' Lexi grinned.

Amanda paused for a minute. 'Hmm, so hard to decide. Both are plausible, both are very YOU things to happen …'

'We've got some guesses coming in from the gang on the livestream.' Lexi peered at the monitor. '@BaileyS thinks it's the ice-cream in the handbag, but pretty much everyone else is guessing I pissed myself … GALS!' She looked at the audience imploringly. 'Is this what ye think of me?!'

'Fuck, yes, that's what they think of you!' Amanda shouted. 'And it's what I think too. You soiled yourself to be close to Gerard Way! That's the truth here.'

Lexi paused to eke out the tension, then took a breath and lowered her head in shame. 'I did.'

The auditorium howled and Lexi threw back some of her throat-burning tequila cocktail.

'Uh-oh, it's all kicking off in the comments.' Amanda was looking at the monitor. 'Lot of in-fighting among the MCR stans about who was the hot one. You're getting a lot of judgement here for being a basic and fancying Gerard.'

'I liked Frank too,' Lexi defended herself, giggling. 'Okay, enough about me, thank you. Your turn, Manda!'

She extracted the next card from the stack. 'This one says: "What's the worst thing you've ever done to a friend?"' She shot a pretend-nervous look at the audience. 'Uh-oh, I can only assume that this is going to be about me. I think I'm the main friend Amanda has!' She winked and stuck out her tongue.

'Okay, this stuff is pretty heavy,' Amanda began, clearly hamming things up for the audience, who'd gone completely silent.

They fucking love any whiff of dirt, Lexi thought gleefully. *This whole show couldn't have gone better. The MCR story is bound to go viral; MCR Twitter is a major force in the world. Podify are gonna be creaming themselves over the figures.*

'Right: One Truth, One Lie,' Lexi repeated, pulling a pretend terrified face for the livestream camera. 'What's the worst thing you've ever done to a friend?'

'So in 2014 you got a pixie haircut and I told you you looked like Gwyneth Paltrow.' She turned to the audience. 'This is back when "You look like Gwyneth Paltrow" would've been a compliment. Younger Hotties might not know that she wasn't always a complete dose. Anyway ...' Amanda turned back to Lexi and picked up her hand, holding it with an earnest, very un-Amanda look on her face. 'I told you you looked like Gwyneth, but actually you looked like ... Ellen DeGeneres.'

'Oooooooh,' the crowd collectively winced.

'I cannot believe you,' Lexi breathed, trying to sound mortally wounded. 'That is so cruel. You let me think it was working for me! That is the worst thing you've ever done.'

Amanda hung her head, then bounced upright again. 'Or is it?!' She wiggled her brows.

'Okay, let's hear the other one then.' Lexi sat back, amused.

Amanda arranged herself, tugging at the bottom of her playsuit.

Lexi frowned. *Does she actually look nervous?*

She looked across to Jonathan, who seemed to be deep in conversation with the stage manager.

'Lexi ...' Amanda took a deep breath.

The audience were the quietest they had been all night, gazing up at them expectantly. Even the comments on the screens had ceased.

'Back when you and Jonathan were first seeing each other, BUT,' she rushed to add, 'before you were like *official* official ... Me and Jonathan ...' She took a breath. 'We hooked up.'

The three thousand people in the Liberty Theatre were completely silent, but Lexi knew what Amanda was doing. She burst out laughing.

'Manda! Shut up, lol! You're supposed to make both stories sound convincing!' She smiled at the audience, who began to titter nervously.

Amanda remained silent and the laughing died away.

Lexi froze. Disbelief engulfed her.

This isn't happening ... She was struggling to compute. Her brain felt sluggish. *What the fuck is Amanda playing at, pretending she's serious? She's not serious.*

Icy dread spread through her chest.

The silence continued and Lexi's eyes veered to the monitor, where the comments had resumed and were now feverishly scrolling under her own stunned face.

@ElliKnits: Is this a stunt?

@OwenParsons: Whaaaaaat IS HAPPENING???

@YourHotMess: More clickbait bullshit. Their whole world is a sham.

@ImeldaPsychology: I'm a clinical psychologist and I can see from their body language that this is FAKE.

Lexi's dread was giving way to rising panic. Her insides churned; the tequila was not helping things. She needed to get this under control.

It's not true, just calm down. She pulled on a smile. *This is fine. This is fine. Amanda is just trolling. Of course she is; that's what she does.*

'You fucking troll!' Lexi grinned at Amanda and silently pleaded with her. *Whatever this is, STOP IT.*

'Lexi, I'm not messing with you. I figured it was time to just say it. It wasn't any big thing. Like I said, it was before you and Jonathan were serious. It's a *historic* hook-up so, you know, nothing to get mad about, but I figured as we're here being honest with each other ...'

'I ... eh ...' Lexi blinked rapidly a few times. *Do not cry up here.* She was completely paralysed. Could she even get herself down from this stool? She pictured stage hands coming out and lifting her offstage.

The silence in the room was slowly being overtaken by an angry buzzing. Hotties were swarming in each other's ears over what they were witnessing.

The comments scrolling on the monitors and the big screens were ramping up.

@YourHotMess: Looks like Amanda's finally turned on her ... what did Lexi expect?!

@LindyF: They're as toxic as each other.

@LeslieAnn: Guys this is so sad to watch.

@Sams_tea: Guess Lexi will finally realise what it's like to be on the other side of Amanda's hateful shit.

@KatieH: Where the fuck is Jonathan right now??? #shittinghimself

@Gloria: No way! He's the Svengali, he's in on it for sure.

Lexi looked to where Jonathan stood. He mimed for her to smile and then made the 'wrap it up' signal and Lexi felt a thud of shame. He's not even embarrassed. Or concerned.

He's the Svengali. He's in on it for sure.

'Lexi? We're okay, yeah?' Amanda waved a hand in front of Lexi's face. 'The statute of limitations on a historic hook-up is like a few years, right?! You'd only been seeing each other for a few weeks. I didn't know it would last!'

Lexi knew there was only one way she would make it off the stage with any kind of dignity. Be the cool girl. Be chill.

'Oh yah ... babes!' She tried not to falter as she pulled her long hair up off her neck and tossed it back, hoping she was giving nonchalance. 'Of course, we all know that the retro ride doesn't count!'

The mood in the theatre seemed to be swinging back around with every word Lexi uttered. Shock was being replaced by a palpable relief. They could all start having fun again. No one was hurt. Lexi wasn't gonna wreck the buzz by having *feelings*.

'There's actually a formula for the vintage ride,' Lexi continued riffing, feeling numb.

Just play the game, Lexi.

'The formula states that if you sleep with your friend's new fella ... once the relationship lasts longer in years than the number of weeks they'd been together when the hook-up took place, it's off the books, doesn't count any more. So ...' Lexi forced herself to grin over at Amanda, as if all this was hilarious. 'How long had me and Jonathan been seeing each other when ... ya know ... ?'

'Oh, only like three weeks.' Amanda was nodding vigorously, evidently relieved that Lexi was apparently fine with being publicly humiliated for an audience of literally thousands. At the other end of the stage, Jonathan was nodding too.

Again the commenter's words rose up before her: *He's the Svengali, he's in on it for sure.*

What the fuck had they been thinking?

'So three weeks means that once me and Jonathan had celebrated our three-year anniversary the slate would've been scrubbed clean. Yay!' Lexi finished flatly.

'Okay, so ...' Amanda rushed to pick up the thread. 'This has been the most amazing night ever! Lexi and I just appreciate all of you Hotties so, so much. You let us do our dream job every single day and we looooove you. We are so happy that we will be bringing *Your Hot Friend* to the next level at our new network Podify! So don't forget to like and subscribe to all our content. And if you've got any clips from tonight's show that you feel like sharing, go right ahead and don't forget to tag @YourHotFriend and @Podify on all the socials! Whoop whoop!'

Amanda stood and reached over to Lexi. Lexi slid off her stool and mutely took her friend's hand. She smiled stiffly into the blinding stage lights, glad that she couldn't really make out the faces in the crowd.

It was a weird sensation, living a moment and being so certain that it would soon be making its way across the internet in the form of a million pithy memes.

Amanda leaned forward to bow and Lexi obediently followed suit. Her mind was blank. The roar of the crowd was loud, yet somehow muted in her ears. Time had slowed to a crawl. The curtain started to lower and Lexi felt a strange sense of inevitability about it all. Of course Amanda would eventually do something like this to her. She had never been averse to *saying* shitty things. Why wouldn't that eventually extend to *doing* shitty things.

Why did I think I'd be immune?

As the bottom of the curtain touched down on the stage floor, shutting the last gap where light was pouring in, Lexi pulled her hand out of Amanda's.

In the sudden gloom, they stared at one another.

'You're pissed off?' Amanda spoke softly.

Lexi unclipped her mic and started to walk away. Amanda grabbed her hand back, pulling her own mic off.

'Don't be mad! That score with Jonathan was nothing, and don't you see? We've got a viral moment for the AGES in the can now. We're securing our position at Podify and we'll hit that listenership target on tomorrow's episode no problem! Which means bonuses!'

Lexi felt sick.

'That was perfect.' Jonathan appeared beside them, two hands up for high-fives.

Amanda hesitated in returning the high-five and Lexi slapped his arms down.

'What the fuck did you think you were doing?'

Jonathan ducked away from her hands. 'What's wrong? We were getting our big moment. And we NAILED IT.' He raised his hands again.

'Stop trying to high-five,' Lexi snapped. 'Why did "our big moment" have to be the worst moment of my life? Why didn't you tell me?'

'Lexi.' Amanda moved to give her a hug, which Lexi expertly blocked. 'We didn't tell you cos it had to be authentic.'

'I'm talking about you two sleeping with each other, not about the show, though that was the most fucked-up thing ever.'

'It was so long ago; it meant absolutely nothing,' Jonathan explained calmly. 'We were just brainstorming over the last few weeks and we thought hey, maybe it would come in handy for leveraging some views. Creating hype, yanno?'

'WEEKS?' Lexi's mind reeled. 'You've known you were going to humiliate me for weeks?' She tore off her mic and put it on the table.

'C'mon, Lexi!' Amanda tried again to pull her into a hug, but Lexi backed away.

Amanda was emphatic: 'I did it for us! EVERYONE will be talking about it! The buzz is gonna be incredible. But we have to come out united or else the whole narrative will be ruined. We need to get photographs at the afterparty for socials.'

Lexi turned and walked off the stage. Amanda and Jonathan were calling her name but they sounded distant, as though she was under water.

Why did I make them my whole life?

She passed the stage manager and the sound guy, who both averted their eyes. Keeping her head down, she walked straight to the side door of the theatre. She pulled her hood up and stepped into the lane. Deserted, thank god. She headed away from the theatre, down one backstreet and then another.

Abi was calling her phone. She pressed accept, but when she tried to speak, she found that all she could do was cry.

Abi was talking. He was taking charge. He was collecting her things. She was to get a taxi and meet him outside her and Jonathan's apartment. They were going home to Hereford.

All the way through his authoritative run-down of the plan, calls were coming in. Amanda calling. Jonathan calling. Amanda calling. Jonathan calling.

'Get in a taxi, Lex,' Abi told her.

Somehow she managed to obey his instructions and found one. However, as soon as she was settled in the back seat, she realised numbly that she had left her bag with her wallet and house keys in the dressing room. The dressing room where no doubt Amanda and Jonathan were now discussing her.

Amanda calling. Jonathan calling. Amanda calling. Jonathan calling.

'Where are we going, luv?'

Lexi hesitated. 'Ehm, just hang on one sec.'

Amanda calling. Jonathan calling. Amanda calling. Jonathan calling.

An image of them together flashed into her mind and the feeling of humiliation filled her like bilge water.

How is this happening?

Suddenly, the things that had seemed so positive just that morning were crowding in on her, choking the air from her body. The house she'd just bought with Jonathan, tying them together. The six-figure deal she'd just signed, locking her into podcasting about her life for the next year. Her most important friendship – her only fucking friendship – exploited for a business.

How could they do this to me? For five years, they kept it secret. Did they discuss it when I wasn't around? Did he think about her when he was with me?

The taxi driver was still waiting for an answer.

The sight of her internet coach Aine's name flashing on her phone stopped her whirring head. Aine would have a plan. She'd have been watching the show, as she always did – part of her approach was to stay up-to-the-minute with Lexi's life as it played out online. That way she could make informed predictions about how Lexi's posts and videos would land with the audience and make tweaks accordingly.

'Hang on one sec,' she told the driver as she answered the call.

'Lexi!' Aine's voice came through loud and clear. 'I'm so sorry. It's desperate. Just desperate.' She paused awkwardly and then having expended exactly three seconds on words of sympathy, immediately moved on to the game plan.

'We're looking at a classic Level Eleven Crisis rollout with a few tweaks.' She was off.

Lexi glanced up at the driver and mouthed 'One sec' while Aine zipped on through the plan.

'I'm going to take over your TikTok and Twitter accounts so

that we can maintain business as usual over there and you don't have to contend with your mentions, which we both know are going to be a fucking mess. We need to get a video of you and Amanda at the afterparty looking totally unruffled up asap, so you need to get over there. Maybe include Jonathan? If you can stomach it.'

'Aine,' Lexi cut in. 'I ... I don't think I can do that.'

'Lexi, honey. We've got to shape the narrative. The whole internet is already gagged over this. You don't want to be a figure of pity, do you? Cos pity doesn't sell, believe me. You go in there, do a boomerang with Amanda, and get back out. This way Podify don't get completely spooked. They'll be jizzing their pants over the figures on this, but if they think there's unrest in the *Your Hot Friend* camp, they could get very nervous. I'll liaise with Jonathan tomorrow and we'll get this show back on the road.'

'But Aine, why would I want this show back on the road?'

'I dunno, hon. Several hundred k seems like a pretty good reason. You've signed a contract? How about to save face? To keep doing what you have to admit is a pretty cushy job?'

'I can't imagine ever speaking to them again, never mind broadcasting it.'

'Look, don't decide right now. Let me and Jonathan figure out some options. Get to the club, quick photo op, and then go to ground. I'll stick up the odd Insta post, but nothing controversial – we're just buying ourselves time until we get a sense of what your narrative is, okay?'

'Okay.' Lexi hung up and leaned forward to the driver, who was messing on his phone. 'Sorry about that. We're going to the Lizard

Lounge and if you could just wait outside, I'll be in and out in two minutes and then we're going out to Dún Laoghaire.'

She sat back and texted Abi:

I have to make a quick detour to the afterparty. Aine is insisting I look like I'm totally chill and having fun on Insta. I'm going in for literally ten seconds to get a shot and then I'm heading straight to you.

Lexi pushed through the heaving crowd at the Lizard Lounge, and as she moved deeper into the club she could sense the intrigued and pitying faces she was leaving in her wake. Finally she got to the curtained-off area right at the back, where Amanda surely was.

'Lexi!' It was Marcus St James, one of Amanda's buddies, sloshing champagne and pretending to bow down before her. 'Oh my god, you're an icon, you took that humiliation like a true pro. My god, it was so degrading.'

'Lexi!' Amanda materialised. 'Where did you go? You were ignoring our calls.' She lowered her voice and glanced back to the large table, where Jonathan and a throng of Podify execs were backslapping with enthusiasm bordering on mania. 'We were worried you wouldn't come,' she added, and Lexi tried not to wince at the 'we'. 'I brought your bag and stuff.'

Amanda grabbed a flute from the table and thrust it at Lexi. 'We have to toast. You're not actually that upset, are you? It literally couldn't have gone better – you saw the figures on that livestream!'

'I saw the figures, Amanda!' Lexi gritted her teeth. 'And all I could think was: all those people are going "poor Lexi, what a sad bitch that she didn't see that coming".'

'Don't worry.' Amanda waved her phone. 'Most of the hot takes are saying you were in on it and that we're like the devil for being so cynical and calculating. Lol, have they never watched reality TV? We're not making fucking documentaries here.'

'Brilliant, so I'm also being blamed for my own degradation.'

Lexi could see Jonathan was now looking over at her. *Is he concerned for me or for how this will go down with the Podify people if they see I'm not playing ball?*

She held his gaze. *I live with this person. We have a dog. We're about to have a house.*

His eyes cut away and he turned to Mark, who was holding his glass up for a toast.

'Don't be so sensitive, Lexi. I thought you could take this.' Amanda actually had the nerve to look derisive, and Lexi could feel her hurt start to harden into rage. How many times had she had to stand up for Amanda in past years?

'It's not *sensitive* to not want to be the one left in the dark while you two plot behind my back.'

'Lexi, the Hotties ate it up – the Podify cash is in hand. You should be thanking me. We'll have total creative control over the pod now; the execs won't be annoying us about "problematic" jokes or whatever.' Amanda rolled her eyes.

Lexi regarded her friend. *How did we land here?*

'Amanda, I'm not doing the podcast any more. How the fuck did you think I would?'

'Oh c'mon, Lexi.' Amanda was dismissive. 'What are we … breaking up!?'

'Yeah.' Lexi looked at the floor. 'I think we are.'

She crossed her arms. 'Don't be an idiot. We've been friends for ever.'

'That's no reason to stay together,' Lexi responded flatly.

'Lexi, we've just signed a million-euro contract. Who's going to get the podcast feed?'

Lexi laughed grimly. 'Wow – it took you less than a minute to move on to the logistics.'

'Fuck off, Lexi. There's money at stake here.'

'Yep, guess there is.'

They glared at each other.

'I can't believe you want to throw everything we have away.' Amanda knocked back the last of her drink just as Jonathan made his way over.

'Lexi, Manda.' He leaned in to speak to them quietly and Lexi felt another punch of hurt at him using Amanda's nickname. 'Can you gals look a little less like you're tearing strips off each other right now? The whole of Podify are over there and they love the views, but we don't want them to think something's wrong.'

Lexi felt a veil of misery draw down around her. 'Something *is* wrong, Jonathan. How could you do this to me?'

Amanda shifted uncomfortably, folding and refolding her arms, while Jonathan put his arm around Lexi.

'Lexi …' She allowed him to pull her closer. 'We did it for the views, babes. Nothing personal. I honestly didn't think you'd care. You're the one I live with, for god's sake! You're the one I've just bought a house with. If I'd wanted to be with Amanda, I could've been with Amanda. Obviously.'

'This is too fucked up.' She pressed her lips together, shaking her head as she slipped out of Jonathan's grasp and backed away . 'I feel ... so ... stupid.'

She examined them both: they felt alien to her. She thought of teenage Amanda, fixing Lexi's dodgy make-up or helping her put her dad to bed when he'd passed out in his chair in the living room. She thought of Jonathan, giving her Scouty. Of the million small ways he always helped her.

How could those people have done this? Am I being too sensitive?

She flashed on the conversations they must have had when she wasn't there. The planning behind her back.

'Don't feel stupid.' Jonathan looked stricken. 'Lexi, it was so long ago. Seriously, it meant nothing.'

'The fuck is not the problem, Jonathan. You guys don't seem to get it. The fuck IS history. You two lying about it and going behind my back and dragging it out for everyone to see, however ... That is the fucking problem.' Lexi raked her hands through her hair and fixed her hoodie. 'Aine says I have to get a few shots of this "afterparty" for socials. So let's go.' She looked sullenly at Amanda. 'Then,' she continued, 'I want a trial separation. From both of you.'

CHAPTER 17

'O. M. G. Hold the FUCKING PHONE!' From the couch beside her, Bert leapt to his feet, still staring at his laptop, clutching his face in shock.

Joanne was torn. Obviously she wanted to know what thrilling thing was happening, but she also didn't want to break her eleven-hour run of silent treatment over an unsteeped porridge pot.

It's probably just sport, she thought. *I am not asking him. Not worth it. But if he wakes up Ted, I will claw his stupid little eyes out—*

'Fucking HELL, no WAY!' He was back sitting again but watching the screen through his fingers. 'Oh god, oh god. Oh no, no, NO!'

'Bert!' Joanne yanked his huge wireless headphones off his head so he could hear her. 'You're gonna wake up Ted if you don't shut up. What is wrong?'

'Sorry. Sorry, babes, but this shit is wild.' He pointed to the screen, where two girls were perched on stools, wearing barely any clothes and chatting to each other. Comments were scrolling on the sidebar. It was obviously a recording of a live feed.

'It's *Your Hot Friend*. You literally won't believe what I just witnessed.'

'Oh my god.' Joanne rolled her eyes. 'I thought something actually important was happening, but it's just your little podcast besties.'

'It's 2023,' Bert replied calmly. 'It's completely normal to have deep and rewarding relationships with the hosts of your favourite podcast.'

'Who don't even know you exist!'

'Actually they gave me a shout-out on the show one time cos I'm their only cishet male listener, appara.'

'Very happy for you. But seriously, stop shouting. You don't realise how loud you're being with these on.' She handed back his headphones.

'Don't you wanna know what just happened? Well about an hour ago – this is a replay. This is on par with the storming of the Capitol Building!!! Or at least that time the dog got onto the pitch at Croke Park in 2004.'

'Stunning player, as I recall,' Joanne said. 'That Jack Russell got two possessions.'

'Anyway, Jo. This was unbelievable ...'

It took less than five minutes for Bert to bring her up to speed, especially as the internet was already awash with TikTok breakdowns of the heart-stopping moment one of the hosts announced she'd slept with the other's boyfriend.

'The whole of TikTok thinks they're body-language experts,' Bert remarked.

'Oh my god, this is brutal,' Joanne moaned. 'Why the actual fuck would they do this to that poor girl?'

She was shocked at how upsetting she was finding it: best friend betrayal was hitting way too close to the bone. In the two weeks since Aoife had told her about Your Story's collapse and her new gig with *She* magazine, they hadn't spoken.

'Why'd they do this to Lexi?' Bert looked perplexed. 'She has to have been in on it?' He was now examining a slow-motion playback that one TikToker had made.

'That woman ...' Joanne pointed at the laptop, 'is in on NOTHING. She looks devastated.'

'Ah no.' Bert pulled out his phone and flicked over to Instagram. 'See? There's Lexi and that's Amanda, the blonde one.'

He turned the phone to Joanne. Lexi was posing with a cocktail in a dark club, with Amanda sticking her tongue out in the background. 'They're totally fine. It's all a spoof to get all eyes on them with their new deal. Apparently, they've just become the highest-paid podcasters in Ireland.' Bert ambled into the kitchen and put the kettle on.

'That can't be that hard!' Joanne quipped, continuing to watch Bert's Instagram. In the next story, a rowdy Amanda was putting her arms around Lexi and kissing her cheek.

Joanne put the phone down on the coffee table. 'I wish I even had a friend *left* to fuck my boyfriend.'

'Aww, Jo. It'll come right with them. They'll cop on. They just don't have a fuckin' clue what having a baby is like.'

'I don't even care about that. You know it's not that.' Joanne glared down at her lap. 'She could've told me.'

'Of course she could've.' Bert leaned against the kitchen door frame, his arms crossed. 'You know why she didn't, though.'

'You're just trying to make me feel better.'

'I'm not, Jo. She is jealous of you and your talent. She always has been, and she knew if she was competing with you for jobs, she just wouldn't get them.' Bert came over, pulling Joanne into a hug. 'It's a shitty, shitty thing she did.'

'This would have been the end of my first week back to work, you know ...'

'I know,' Bert murmured into her hair. 'Look, don't stress. You will get a job and we have the pay-out. Three months' wages will keep us going for a bit. Meanwhile, why don't you see if there's any courses or something that you'd like to do?'

'Any courses?' Joanne pulled away. 'Bert, I am looking after your baby round the fucking clock.'

'I know. I just thought, you know, as an outlet or something.'

She narrowed her eyes at him.

He's just trying to be nice ... she reminded herself.

She nearly felt sorry for him. These days, post-baby Bert could bring her a large McDonald's chicken nuggets meal with a Smarties McFlurry and she'd still want to slap it out of his hand.

'I don't want an outlet, Bert. I want four full-time nannies, rostered back to fucking back, twenty-four-fucking-seven, okay?'

CHAPTER 18

From her prone position on her childhood bed, tangled in slightly fetid sheets, Lexi cast her eyes about for something to put on her Instagram. After the first twenty-four hours, Aine had given Lexi back the account and told her to post frequently and innocuously.

It had now been over two hours since her last story and she knew if her silence continued, they'd all start reading into it. The takes online since Thursday night had been rolling in continuously. It was now Saturday afternoon and the Google alerts for *Your Hot Friend* had not stopped pinging. When the episode they'd pre-recorded went live on Friday morning, it shot to the top of the charts, just as Amanda had predicted. Lexi couldn't bear to think of everyone listening to her stupid, dumb little quips, all uttered without any idea of what was about to happen.

Aine was checking in regularly. She'd had an emergency meeting the day before with Jonathan and Podify, to iron out the arrangements for Amanda and Lexi to share the podcast. They were billing it as a temporary separation. Podify were grudgingly happy to proceed, as long as the audience numbers remained robust. The drama suited them for now, but Lexi knew they'd expect some kind of reunion at some point. She was trying not to think about it.

Lexi lifted her phone up to frame a couple of angles of her childhood bedroom, but it was grim: the image of the brown curtains closed, holding the late-afternoon sun at bay, was a bit too Nan Goldin. She trained the phone on her feet and snapped a pic. *Maybe a moody filter and a quote?* She shook her head. It's giving depressed-girl-on-Tumblr-in-the-mid-2000s. She definitely didn't need ANYONE reading 'depressed' from her posts.

A soft knock on her door didn't even nudge her to move. It could only be one of two people: her dad or her brother. They'd both been tiptoeing around her since she had taken up residence in her bed.

She had left the *Your Hot Friend* afterparty the minute she'd taken some pictures inside the club. Since then, she had racked up a stunning 156 missed calls from Amanda and Jonathan. More were from Amanda than Jonathan, it had to be noted.

The shy little knock came again.

'Come IN,' she snapped, not lifting her head from the pillow. For some reason, the tentative rapping was more irritating than just a normal knock. Which was, of course, not fair.

'Lexi?' Her dad peered into the gloom, holding a cup of coffee. 'Love ... ?' *He couldn't look more awkward,* she thought peevishly, and then felt bad.

He's trying. He has no idea what is actually happening here.

Abi had tried to explain their sudden appearance in the early hours of Friday morning, but they'd been too exhausted to get into the whole fiasco.

'Yeah, Dad.' She struggled up to sitting, stuffing her phone under her pillow.

'Lexi ...' He shuffled forward, attempting to both smile and avoid looking directly at her at the same time. A feat of awkwardness: it wasn't how he behaved around her brothers. It had been like this since her mum died. He hadn't been cut out to be Dad to a teenage girl. Even once she'd grown up and was no longer running around, sneaking out at night and generally putting the heart across him, he'd remained diffident. 'I only have the instant,' he said, apologetically. 'If I'd known you were coming I would've got your stuff in ...'

'Yeah, sorry.'

Lexi knew she didn't sound sorry, but today of all days she fucking wished she had a mother. A mother would press her on why the hell she'd shown up crying in the middle of the night. A mother would have sage wisdom and real-life examples of times when friends let us down. And she wouldn't be proffering horrible instant coffee. Mothers knew that tea or wine were the appropriate crisis drinks. God. Though since her mother had been dead for more of Lexi's life than she had been alive, Lexi had to admit she didn't know if her mother really would have been any use in this situation.

Ironically, Amanda was the person she was actually missing even more right now. Amanda would be cheering her up and athletically bitching about whoever had screwed her over. Had she not been the one doing the screwing, in every sense of the word.

'Will you be staying here now?'

'I don't know, Dad.'

A thrust of grief caught her off-guard and she burst into tears. The question had immediately brought up thoughts of their gorgeous new home. The home she would never live in now.

How're we going to get out of that? What the fuck is happening? How did everything crumble to fucking dust in the space of one night?

'Jesus,' he said. 'I'll get Abi.' He hurried back through the bedroom door, shouting for his son in a voice amplified by rising horror. 'Abi? Abi? She's ... she's upset.'

Lexi closed her eyes and let her head sink back against the pink satin headboard, trying not to remember all the times she and Amanda had sat up in this exact position, ringing boys from school, the year her dad had got the cordless house phone.

How could Amanda do this?

Somehow the cavalier way she'd revealed the betrayal far outweighed the actual betrayal itself. It *had* been years ago. It didn't *need* to be a major deal. If they hadn't chosen to haul her up in front of thousands of people and offload it on her like it was no more than a juicy plot twist, it wouldn't have been so bad.

'Lexi!' Abi appeared, trailed by their dad. 'It'll be okay. It's okay,' he intoned soothingly, giving her a hug.

'What's going on?' Their dad looked from one to the other. 'Is it Jonathan? Or the new house?'

'Yes.' Abi spoke in a measured voice, but she felt him tense. 'It's Amanda, Dad. And Jonathan. They did this really messed-up thing.'

How do you explain to your dad – who still laments the end of Teletext – what being humiliated live on the internet even means?

'We were doing a live show of the podcast to launch the new deal ...' Lexi started.

'Okay ... This is the deal with Polygamist?'

Abi snorted.

'Podify,' Lexi corrected. 'And we were supposed to be playing this game in front of a live audience and loads of people watching online—'

'But hang on ...' His brow furrowed. 'You said the pod ... pod ... podshow was like being on the radio?'

Abi took over. 'It is, but they video it. That way they can stream it live online as well. It's all about diversifying, engaging the audience across all platforms.'

'I see. Ahh ...' He shook his head, as though to clear the confusing thoughts crowding in. 'Will I get us chipper for dinner?' He'd obviously hit capacity on how much techy babble he could take on board.

'Chips would be nice.' Lexi tried to smile.

The next day, Lexi and Abi drove back to her apartment in Dublin in the overheated Saab.

After three nights down home, Lexi had reached her limit for spending time at her dad's. Incredibly, facing Jonathan was now somehow the lesser of two evils. Plus, Lexi knew that the only way out of her horrible ocean of anxiety was to take some kind of action. What that would be she still didn't know; she was hoping that standing in front of him would give her some clarity.

'Will I come in with you?' Abi asked.

Lexi stared at her hands. 'It's okay. My stuff is mostly packed up, cos of the move, but Jonathan might ... well ... yanno, we might talk for a bit. Can you maybe take a little walk or something?'

'Sure.' Abi gave a tense nod. 'But when you say "talk" you mean tell him to fuck himself, yeah?'

'It's not that easy, Abi. What about the house and—'

'You can stay with me as long as you need, you know that. The guys are totally cool with it.'

'But Abi, he's—'

'He's a shit, Lexi. You know that time you asked him to go check on Dad when I was out west? He didn't do it. I asked Dad.'

A bolt of shock hit Lexi.

'Are you serious?' She shook her head, trying to remember what Jonathan had said. 'But he texted that afternoon saying everything was fine, that Dad was grand'.

'Well,' Abi shrugged. 'He's an asshole. I guess at least he's consistent with his assholery.'

Anger rose in Lexi's chest but then the guilt rapidly overtook it.

'I should've gone myself, Abi. I'm so sorry. I was recording with Amanda. I chose the fucking podcast over Dad.' She pressed her fingertips to her eyes. She didn't want to look like she'd been crying when she faced Jonathan.

'Look,' Abi sighed. 'You trusted him when he said he'd go. And Dad is okay.' He pulled her into a hug. 'I'm gonna get a coffee, you text me when you're done.'

'Thank you.' She pulled back and looked at him. 'Thanks for everything, Abi. You were right about everything, I guess. I hate that.' She grinned blearily.

'Yeah.' Abi nodded. 'Obviously your life falling apart slightly undercuts the triumph for me. Slightly.'

She laughed as they got out of the car. 'I won't be long,' she promised, waving Abi off, and then headed into the building.

Her key in the lock immediately prompted the skitter-skitter of paws in the hall. She opened the door and scooped up the pup, burying her face in Scouty's fur.

'I missed you!'

Why did she always smell like toast and wet jumper? And why was that so nice?

'I missed you too, babe.' Jonathan appeared at the other end of the hallway. 'Oh.' He stopped upon seeing the dog in her arms. 'Right, you meant her. Gotcha.'

He shuffled forward with his arms outstretched.

'Absolutely not.' Lexi drew back.

'Right.' He pulled back. 'Aine said you still aren't taking it well.'

'What kind of dead-inside sociopath WOULD take this well, Jonathan?' Lexi scowled. 'Oh, wait, probably you and Amanda, right? Cos this is just business. Just CONTENT. Never mind that I'm humiliated. Never mind that I am your girlfriend, not just your client. Never mind that we just bought a HOUSE together. All this time, you and Amanda were planning this behind my back. You were sitting on the couch beside me every night knowing you were about to do this to me.' Lexi put Scouty down and walked through to the bedroom, where she pulled the suitcase out from under the bed and started stuffing in clothes. Jonathan followed her.

'We couldn't tell you, Lexi. Audiences are so savvy these days. They can spot engineered drama a mile off.'

'Thank you.' Lexi zipped up the case and pushed past him back out to the kitchen-living.

'You're welcome.' Jonathan followed her. 'I'm glad you're getting it.'

'I'm saying thank you for making my decision easier.' She pulled out a box marked 'Lexi Books Etc'. 'There's no getting past this, Jonathan. You're a fucking prick.'

'Lexi, please, c'mon. We finally got the house sorted – we're about to move in! Our lease here ends in two weeks. The sheer admin involved in breaking up right now …'

Lexi laughed bitterly and pulled the suitcase and her box out to the front door.

'I meant trying to do all that admin while grieving our relationship.'

Lexi rolled her eyes.

'We can rent it for a while. Or you can live there. Whatever.' Exhaustion engulfed her like a dense wave. 'We'll work it out, but right now all I want is to get my stuff and get the fuck away from you.'

She texted Abi.

Ready when you are.

Abi got back immediately with a thumbs-up.

'Lexi …' From Jonathan's pleading tone, she wondered if something resembling an apology was coming.

He spread his hands wide, imploringly. 'You can't leave.'

Even through her hurt, the fearful part of her agreed. *I can't do this.* Amanda and Jonathan WERE her life. She swallowed back the ache that was rising in her throat.

'Lexi, please just wait. Just think for a minute. The podcast is fucking huge – you can't just chuck it all away. This shared custody of the show is bollocks. Messing with an established format rarely works. We'll lose the Hotties' loyalty. There's a billion other interview podcasts out there, but they don't generate the same engagement, the same communities. The magic is you and Amanda together. Your friendship and your dynamic. And look, let's be real for a minute on a purely numbers basis ... Amanda's better than you. She's more dynamic. She's fearless and it makes her more compelling. If you're doing every second show, it's gonna be real obvious, real fast who the star is. I know it's hard to hear that, but I just don't want you getting hurt.'

'Okay.' Lexi pushed by him to grab another box labelled 'Lexi Hair & Make Up'. 'Scouty!' she called, bending to snap on her dog leash. 'Best girl,' she whispered, stalling so that she could keep her tears in check. Then she straightened up. 'Jonathan. Thank you for being such a massive douche. Truly, you've made this decision so fucking easy. Aine will be in touch to arrange collecting the rest of my stuff. We'll keep paying the mortgage fifty-fifty until you organise a tenant.'

She pulled open the door and to her immense relief found Abi waiting outside. He hurried forward and grabbed the two boxes, pausing briefly to say, 'Fucking prick,' to Jonathan and then continued on, over to the lift.

Lexi took the suitcase and led Scouty out the door, yanking it closed behind her.

CHAPTER 19

Hi Claire. Sorry for yet another Voicy, I know we haven't SEEN each other in like FOREVER ...

A month! Claire thought. *Aifric, it's been more than a month.*

Claire was sitting on the living-room floor, flicking back through her diary to find the last in-person meet-up she had marked. *Aha!* The Bitch Herd brunch at the end of February. It was annotated: 'Nadia dominated. Single-room occupancy bullshit.' It was now the end of March.

But – and I know this is going to sound so cringe and clichéd – but the life of a bride is just go, go, go!

Claire hastily turned down the volume.

She had to be quiet, as it was four a.m. She'd woken up in the dark and her mind had slammed straight into fifth gear, parsing Aifric's latest communication. With her thoughts racing, she'd known she wouldn't get back to sleep. She had a prescription for sleeping pills, but they made her groggy. At least today was Friday, so work – in four hours' time – would be fairly chill. So she'd started sorting out the chaos of her craft box and now she was listening again to Aifric's Voicy from last night.

> So, update! I have finally found my D.O.D., aka dress of dreams. But seriously, you didn't miss out much on the dress hunt. I had poor Nadia and Gillian TORTURED. I had to ply them with bubbles just to get them through the fifty fucking shops we went to LOL.

The image of the three of them gave Claire a pang. She shook it off. Picking up her notebook again, her hands flew over the pages, flicking forward and tallying up the number of purple hearts she'd input. These corresponded to voices and texts from Aifric. There were a fair few throughout March, at least. It was nice that they were bonding over the wedding favours.

> So anyway: Favours. Time is ticking on and I'd really like to get this boxed off – if you know what I mean.

Aifric hadn't been sold on the homemade herbal tea in hand-sewn teabags embroidered with Aifric's and Paul's initials that Claire had made last week for the wedding favours – though Aifric had said she needed to see a few together to make the call. Claire had done eighteen. They'd not made the cut. So now she was trying out little crochet keyrings – hearts and flowers.

> Really looking forward to the next prototypes. I think we just need to make sure it's nothing too cutesie. No hearts or flowers – we don't want PREDICTABLE. Okay, see you soon darl.

Three hours later and Claire was getting on the tram to work. Despite the lack of sleep, she was feeling okay. Grand, even. They'd told her at the hospital that she needed to watch this: if she was getting elated it could be a bad sign. But she was totally on top of her meds again. She could admit that she'd been a bit ropey mental health-wise a few weeks ago – the mother-baby group was definitely not her sanest hour. She cringed every time she remembered that girl Joanne's baffled face. The text message she'd sent was still haunting Claire's WhatsApp, obviously Claire hadn't replied. For about a week she'd fretted that police were going to show up at her door. It had been a crazy thing to do but she'd caught herself before it escalated, hadn't she? Not like last year ...

Claire put in her headphones and started to flick back through her wedding favours research while the latest *Your Hot Friend* loaded.

'Hey, Hotties!'

Lexi's voice chirped in Claire's ears and she immediately tensed. She wanted the best for Lexi and supporting her meant listening to her solo episodes, but they were, it was undeniable, increasingly cringe.

It had been just over two weeks since the *Your Hot Friend* live meltdown and the *YHF* friend-world was still in shambles. For several days, no one knew what was happening. Would the show end? Would they patch things up? Conspiracy theories were flying: some thought the whole fiasco and its extended fallout was a hoax, a cynical bid for more attention while they cemented their place on the new network. The appearance of official 'feud merch' on the *Your Hot Friend* website did seem to support some of this; though, as many in the forums pointed out, it was also completely on brand for Amanda and Lexi to be capitalising on the very real demise of a twenty-year friendship.

When the solo episodes began, it rapidly became apparent that Lexi had indeed been blindsided live on the internet and the Hotties had dutifully picked sides: Team Amanda and Team Lexi.

Claire had duly bought a Team Lexi tee and tote bag. With the whole future of the podcast up in the air, she felt compelled to – this might be going towards Lexi's retirement fund. Lexi's supporters seemed to be in the majority: of course they were; if Amanda and Jonathan did bang and Lexi didn't know until the live show, then it was an open and shut case of mega-scale betrayal. Unfortunately, the quite sensible Lexi supporters tended not to be as outspoken as the Amanda stans. Most of that camp were of the opinion that Lexi was a buzz wrecker for having feelings. Feelings that were now getting in the way of their weekly content.

Amanda immediately brought on her celebri-bestie Marcus St James to co-host her episodes, but Lexi's plans still seemed TBC. So far, Amanda's episodes had been raucous and raunchy and were constantly at the top of the charts. Lexi's not so much. Her first two episodes were about her new dog and moving in with her brother, who she'd dragged on for the occasion. The dynamic was simply not there and the reviews had been damning.

@Sarah487 Ugh the Lexi eps are unlistenable. No one wants to hear about deworming the dog, babes.

@MadBitch88 Oh my god TRADGE that Amanda is straight to the top of the charts with Marcus while it turns out Lexi's litch had zero friends apart from Amanda the whole time.

@eilers_still_with_it Your Desperate Friend more like.

Claire gave the newest episode her best shot, but it was just so obvious that Lexi was struggling and it made for bleak listening. Maybe she really *didn't* have anyone to bring on the podcast.

When she got to the Sweeneys', the morning chaos was in full swing. Norah was in the family bathroom trying to finish her make-up while Sonny yelled from the bath beside her. That's what everyone in the family did with him when he needed to be contained: stuck him in the empty tub.

'It really is perfect for him,' Claire remarked, joining them. 'He's like a spider – he just slips down the sides when he tries to escape.'

Frankie was crouched up on the sink doing his own make-up, while Lila stood at the door narrating every single thought as it entered her head. Claire honestly had no idea how the Sweeneys not only tolerated the constant maelstrom but appeared to even enjoy it. Claire loved the kids, but she also loved leaving them and going home.

'Hey, Claire!' Norah shouted over her children, smiling at her in the mirror. 'Guess what I have?'

'What?'

'Some juicy, delicious, succulent gossip.' Norah was grinning madly and elaborately licking her lips – their secret shorthand for gossip.

'Amazing.' Claire smiled as she hauled Sonny up out of the bath.

'You go trap these kids under something heavy and we can have a quick dissect before you've to leave for drop-offs.'

The 'something heavy' in question was iPads for Lila and Frankie and a small high-sided ball pit that Sonny adored.

'Minding a toddler is just moving them from colourful prison to colourful prison, isn't it?' Claire giggled.

'Right.'

Norah poured them two coffees. With her connections in the entertainment world, her gossip was always good. Claire leaned forward on the kitchen island.

'I think you're gonna like this one A LOT! I know you're more into grass-fed local gossip and this is as local as it gets and SO bizarre. So guess what job came across my agent's desk this week? A very discreet casting call is being run in the next fortnight for a VERRRRY unusual prospect.'

'Claire!' Lila called over without peeling her eyes from the bizarre corner of YouTube she'd stumbled into. 'I think we need to look at constructing a Doomsday bunker ...'

'Norah, we've about two minutes left before I actually have to start supervising your children.'

'Right! Sorry!' She gulped down a bit of her coffee. 'So apparently there's an influencer in Dublin who needs a new best friend.' Norah raised her brows at the lunacy of her own announcement. 'Like a best friend who is going to be ON THE PAYROLL!'

'Shut up!'

Could it be Lexi? Claire immediately wondered. *Lexi wouldn't resort to this, would she? Who the fuck would?*

'I know.' Norah was shaking her head. 'I mean, at first, I was like this is the sickest, weirdest thing. But then, as Roxanne – you remember my agent – as she said, there's a bloody million celeb

PR couples in the world, so what's the difference here? And I guess lots of friendships come with different agendas these days.'

'It's so sad, though,' Claire mused. 'And so are PR relationships. I was traumatised when I found out it wasn't true love with Tom Hiddleston and Taylor Swift. They shouldn't be allowed to toy with us like that!'

'Roxanne put me forward but the casting director says they need an unknown and that I was outside the age range.'

'Shame.' Claire was attempting to appear invested in the chat but her mind was spinning.

A fake friend. For Lexi. It's too sad, she thought before flashing on the document called 'Operation Friend Escalation Schedule' in her Notes app and the fake baby debacle. Queasy shame stirred in the pit of her stomach. *God, I'm pathetic.*

'Get this, they said the right person would have to be willing to fabricate a "backstory". A BACKSTORY!'

How is this real life? Claire wondered as Norah elegantly drifted among her children, depositing little goodbye kisses and murmurs of love.

The day passed without much hassle. After school, she bribed the kids with every sweet known to man so that she could deep-dive on Lexi and find out if anyone on the internet had caught wind of any rumours about auditions for a 'friend'. It appeared not.

I need a friend. And she needs a friend.

How can you get an audition? she wondered

Around four p.m., Claire decided to text Norah.

Hey I was wondering if you would mind me trying out for the friend audition thing? It sounds kind of fun?! Obviously I'd only do it if it didn't interfere with work.

Norah got back with her agent's email and a winky face.

Even with Norah's blessing Claire agonised about sending Roxanne an email. *I probably wouldn't have a hope of getting it.*

And what if it all worked out and she went from being someone forced to pay the single room occupancy fee to someone suddenly having not just any friend but a bona fide celebrity one? It might arouse suspicions among the Bitch Herd.

Though it's not like they ever ask me anything about my life.

The thoughts swirled and pursued her all the way home on the tram and even into bed that night, despite Jamie's best efforts to start something.

'I'm sorry.' She kissed Jamie's neck. 'My head's just not in the game.'

'I can tell,' Jamie replied gently. 'Are you doing okay?'

Claire frowned. 'Yes, why?' Sometimes she worried that Jamie could hear the cacophony in her head.

'You seem a little edgy. What time were you up at this morning?'

'Only a bit before you.'

'Right.' Jamie seemed to be selecting his words with care. 'It's just … well …' He got up out of the bed and riffled through the drawer in his bedside locker, pulling out a handful of the abandoned tea bags. 'What are these, Claire?'

'Oh, they're nothing. An aborted wedding favour idea!'

'There're tons of them. I found them in the bin. These must've taken ages.'

'No, no. Sure you know how fast I sew.'

'Aifric ...' Jamie looked troubled. 'She can't just expect—'

'No! Aifric doesn't know about them.' Jamie didn't need any more ammunition about Aifric and the Bitch Herd. 'I just changed my mind about them. C'mon back to bed.'

Jamie hesitated. 'I really don't want you taking on too much, Claire. You know it's not good.'

'I swear, I am totally good. You know I love this stuff.'

After Jamie fell asleep, Claire's thoughts gained pace.

Maybe it isn't even Lexi auditioning for a friend?

Maybe I should make signature Aifric-and-Paul-infused gin in little individual bottles?

Maybe it's totally believable that I have a friend the Bitch Herd don't know about? I am a thirty-one-year-old woman.

What about handmade soaps? In the shape of their initials?

I could just email Norah's agent. She mightn't even reply.

Are soaps vegan-friendly? Must check. No doubt Nadia or Gillian will kick off.

Then and there, Claire got out her phone – she needed to take action, if only to shut her brain up. She dashed off an email to Roxanne, explaining that she was a young, unknown actress who'd heard about an unusual opportunity. She hit send and then, riding her wave of decisiveness, she googled 'vegan soap recipe' and ordered the recommended product – lye – along with the protective gloves and goggles that she'd need.

Done and done.

The next day, Roxanne emailed her back with a time and date for the auditions and a detailed non-disclosure agreement.

CHAPTER 20

Joanne was on the couch, struggling to type on her laptop while Ted was waging some kind of hand-to-hand combat with her right boob. In the pictures on Insta breastfeeding always looked so serene, they never showed how much manhandling even tiny babies could do.

It was the first Friday evening in April and Bert was at the restaurant. She would have been back to work three weeks by now and even with her redundancy package they'd had to postpone getting full-time childcare for Ted. On one hand, this was a good thing, as she got to spend more time with him, but on the other hand, Joanne now felt the road map out of this motherhood vortex had somehow disappeared. She adored Ted, of course, but work had always been important to her. She'd no idea when she'd be back to some kind of steady gig. Despite Bert's optimism, there really wasn't much out there.

He'd had one good idea though. He'd been lapping up the spectacle of his favourite podcast imploding, and a couple of weeks back he'd encouraged Joanne to pitch a line of 'frenemy feud merch' to the podcast manager, Jonathan. Incredibly, he'd gone for it.

'There's really no end to the weirdness of people,' she told Ted now as she typed up the invoice.

The ping of her phone alerted her to a text from Bert:

I've picked up an extra shift this evening so I won't be home till late. Sorry. Remember, it all helps towards getting the car before the summer tho! Then we can maybe get away for a week. XXX

'Fab,' Joanne told the baby. 'Another night of *Catfish* and chilling on our own, for fuck's sake.'

I probably need a hobby, she thought despondently as she flicked on her favourite reality show. The *Catfish* team were confronting a woman who'd posed as a seven-year-old boy on the internet.

'There's really no end to the weirdness of people,' she repeated.

Her thoughts fell back to the strange encounter with the girl at the mother-baby group four weeks before. *What the hell was happening there?* she mused.

Joanne had kept meaning to follow up, but between cuddling Ted and glaring at Bert, time had really got away from her.

She glanced again at the TV, where the not-a-seven-year-old-boy woman was now crying. *Maybe I should have done something about that whole thing?* she wondered. Beyond telling Bert, who had found it bizarre, though not particularly disturbing.

Joanne picked up her phone and typed 'why would you pretend your baby is a girl?' into the Google search bar. The first result that came back was a Reddit thread titled 'Why would someone pretend to have a child?'.

It wasn't exactly what she was after, but she clicked it anyway, out of curiosity. The reasons given ranged from mental illness to attempts to get attention or money. One suggestion caught Joanne's eye.

The poster had typed:

> Anyone remember the story of the nanny who pretended the kid she babysat for was hers? She set up a GoFundMe saying that she needed money for the kid's surgery. She pretended that this baby, Blake, was a girl called Suzie!!! Wild.

Joanne felt a stab of anxiety. Could it be something like this? She googled the story and read with mounting unease about an American woman who had used photographs of the child she minded to raise over $10,000 for a false medical procedure. Joanne felt sick. 'This is beyond fucked up,' she informed Ted, who was still feeding in a mildly aggro way.

She swapped him over to the other side and went to GoFundMe's website. For the next forty minutes, she searched as many pages of Dublin fundraising campaigns as she could. She was in tears by the end of it. And had donated thirty euros she absolutely didn't have to spare to three different campaigns.

People just have such difficult, heartbreaking lives. If that girl is fucking with people in this way I am going to absolutely murder her.

Joanne put Ted into the sling and went into the kitchen to decide what to eat for dinner. She was tempted to get a takeaway but couldn't really justify the money. She contented herself with cheese and crackers and ate while waiting for the kettle to boil.

As she stood there, she copied the link to the American nanny story and went into the WhatsApp thread she had started with the baby group girl that day. She re-read her message, which was blue-ticked but had been ignored:

Okay. So just to clarify ... you just pretended your 'son' was your 'daughter'???!!! Should I be taking this to the authorities? Or has motherhood just got you this exhausted!? Cos TBH I can kind of relate!

On reflection the message she'd written was a bit too jovial, but then at the time she hadn't given much thought to the darker implications of what she'd seen.

She pasted the link to the American nanny news article and then added below:

If this is what you're up to I will fucking find you because I have literally never heard of anything so fucked up and I'm the first to admit that I am a pretty shitty person so if I think it's bad ... it is SERIOUSLY bad.

She pressed send. If Claire had blocked her number, she would have no way of knowing. The message would never blue-tick and the lead would go cold. If the girl had any sense, she'd have probably got rid of the phone.

She made her tea and went back to GoFundMe while it brewed, searching for 'Claire', 'Sauron' and 'Dublin', but she got no matches. The girl surely wouldn't have been that stupid, but it was worth a try. Joanne went back to WhatsApp and enlarged Claire's profile pic, but it was just a generic beach shot.

Joanne returned to the couch. Her next Google search was 'what do I do if I think a child is in danger' but before she'd even finished typing, a message dropped in from none other than 'Claire'.

'Oh my god.' She scrambled to open it.

I swear it was NOTHING like this. I SWEAR ON MY LIFE. Please can you just leave me alone, it was a stupid mistake.

She frowned. At least the girl was answering. And Joanne could see at the top of the screen that she was still typing.

A further message dropped in.

Look, I am a nanny. That is true and Sonny (Sauron's real name) is a little boy I mind. But I would NEVER do anything like that GoFundMe thing and I would never put him in harm's way. What I did was so stupid and wrong but I swear there was nothing bad going on and I am NOT trying to get money out of anyone.

Joanne was intrigued. This was truly the most fascinating thing to have happened in months. 'Aside from your birth, obviously,' she informed the now-dozing Ted.

Why were you pretending he was your baby? And a girl?

There was a protracted pause before Claire's next message appeared.

I can't tell you that.

Another gap … then she added:

It's embarrassing. I've just been having a hard time lately and that seemed like a good idea but obviously it absolutely wasn't and I swear I'll never do it again. Please, please don't tell anyone. I love my job. But yeah ... like I said, I was having a bit of a crap time.

This made Joanne pause unexpectedly. She hadn't anticipated feeling sorry for 'Claire'.

What's your real name?

My name is Claire. For real.

Joanne nearly laughed at this.

Not exactly a criminal mastermind then are you? Unless you're double bluffing me.

I can prove it.

Joanne jolted upright as her phone buzzed with a video call. Claire was obviously really eager to make sure Joanne didn't think she was still lying. Joanne swiped the flashing button to answer.

'Hi.' Claire looked mortified.

'Hi,' Joanne replied.

'See …' Claire held up a driver's licence to the camera, showing her picture and the name Claire Sheehy.

'Okay. Claire Sheehy. So why did you do it?'

Claire looked away from the camera. 'I really can't tell you. But I swear it's nothing … *evil*.'

'But you get that I don't feel like I can just drop it? You're nannying for someone who has no idea you do this.'

'I only did it that one time.' Claire glanced around nervously.

'Yeah, but you were caught, so who knows how many more times you were planning?'

'It was such a stupid plan.' Claire was looking desperate. 'Sometimes I just get so focused on an idea that my logic gets kind of skewy. But you have to know I wasn't doing anything dangerous. Please don't report me. Like I said, I feel like my job is all I have. I feel like I'm losing my friends. I love my boyfriend, but it's not the same as having a gang.'

Joanne paused at this, surprised to find she had something in common with this girl.

'I know how that can feel,' she said quietly.

'Really?' Claire looked doubtful. 'But you seemed so sure of yourself.'

'I guess, but I have no idea what I'm doing. And I'm the first of my friends to have a baby so they don't get what I'm doing either. I feel like all I do is worry and leak. I don't have a whole lot to talk about with them. Like, they couldn't care less about my baby not taking a shit for like ten days.'

'Oh, poor little guy.' Claire frowned. 'Have you tried prune juice with a teeny tiny bit of brown sugar? Everywhere online says water and sugar, but prune juice is better. It worked amazing when Sonny used to go on shite strike.'

'Okay … I'll try that.' Joanne grinned. 'Any other insights?'

'It's definitely normal for everything to feel crazy.' Claire smiled. 'Norah, the woman I mind for, had that for definite. She told me she was crazy anxious after having her first. She didn't have any mum-friends, didn't know anyone.'

'Okay.' Joanne fixed Claire with a look. 'This is comforting, but I still need to know why you crashed a mother-baby group before I can make a call on whether or not I should contact your boss.'

She watched Claire swallow. 'I thought it might be a good way to try and make friends.'

'Really?' Joanne was utterly perplexed.

'I know, I sound insane. I just didn't know what else to do. I can show you my sad bitch list of different ways I was gonna try and meet people and make them my friend in time for this trip I'm going on in May. I called it Operation Friend Escalation.'

'Ha! No need to show me. I believe you – it's just too weird a thing to make up!'

Claire winced. 'Yup.'

'So how's the friend plan going now?'

'I have sort of a plan ...'

'Please tell me,' Joanne pleaded. 'Save me from another boring night alone in this house!'

After a bit of wheedling and then blackmail, Claire relented and told Joanne her convoluted tale: the aptly named Bitch Herd, a head-wrecking wedding, a supplementary single occupancy fee and a 'friend audition' for an anonymous Irish celebrity.

When Claire had finished, Joanne roared with laughter. 'I'm sorry,' she gasped. 'I'm not laughing AT you. Or well, I am. I just was not expecting your Plan B to be even crazier than the Plan A.'

Claire laughed grimly. 'You don't understand, I cannot show up solo to this girl's holiday. I am so sick of being the dud one in the group.'

'You're not the dud one in the group. No offence, but your friends sound horrif. Those hand-sewn teabags must've taken ages and they sounded really nice.'

'Do you think you'd like to still get coffee some day?' Claire asked shyly. 'We could go early while Frankie and Lila are in Montessori and school. You could bring Ted and I could bring Sonny.'

'Not Sauron?!' Joanne grinned.

'You know, I feel like there're parts of Dublin where that name would totally fly.'

'Fucking right,' Joanne agreed. 'South County Dublin for sure. But yeah, we should have coffee. Though if you're thinking of grooming me to be your plus one on this Ibiza trip, I'm afraid there's no way I can swing it.'

'Oh,' Claire said lightly. 'That's … I mean … of course …'

'It's not that I wouldn't want to,' Joanne rushed to reassure her. 'I actually just …' She hesitated.

Is it weird to talk about money with someone you barely know? Is there anything not weird about this turn of events?!

'It's just that money's so tight since Ted was born and I'm not working.'

'I totally understand.' Claire smiled. 'Let's pick a day! If we do next Tuesday morning, I can tell you all about the auditions, they're the day before!'

'Brilliant, can't wait.'

CHAPTER 21

'Okay, take this left. It looks like a dead end, but it'll bring us round to the back of the building.' As Aine gave the taxi driver directions, Lexi pulled at her hood to cover the left side of her face.

It was seven o'clock on a Monday morning. The sun had risen half an hour ago and, driving down the quays, the April day was looking promising: clear and dry. The auditions wouldn't be starting for another two hours, but Aine was adamant that they arrive early, to avoid exposing Lexi's identity. She was extremely edgy about Lexi being spotted and photographed on her way into the theatre space where the friend try-outs were being held.

'We've taken every possible measure,' Aine had reassured Lexi when collecting her from her dingy house-share. Lexi, Abi and Scouty were now sharing a bunk bed in a grotty room in Inchicore; not a single inch of it was appropriate for Lexi to post on social media.

She'd been there for three weeks but had yet to meet any of the nine other housemates, as they were on tour: they were all in a Slipknot tribute band, called Slip'not. One whole wall in the living room was given over to their collection of mildly sinister masks, which managed to be both ghoulish and kind of funny, given that they were of significantly lower quality than the real band's masks, made out of things like spray-painted hoover hoses and Fairy Liquid bottles painted black.

To look at her Insta, anyone would think Lexi was still living the life of glam internet girlie, but behind the scenes, it was shambolic. The Podify deal was on extremely shaky ground since they'd split custody of the show and the execs had put a hold on the next instalment of their payout. Now their deal had been renegotiated: as long as the figures of the new show format continued to hit the agreed targets over the next three months, Lexi and Amanda would each get their money and the show would continue to air. Lexi had been hoping that the figures would remain strong enough to make this temporary arrangement a permanent solution.

The big, HUGE problem was that Amanda's episodes with Marcus St James were killing it and Lexi's solo efforts were not. Hence this humiliating plan of engineering a best friend, to match the rapport she'd had with Amanda.

'You can stop here,' Aine announced as they drew level with a large steel door. She pulled out her phone, dialled and then said simply, 'Outside, now.'

A moment later the door swung open and a young guy nodded at Aine as she paid the driver.

Lexi pulled her hood right down over her face and followed Aine into the building. A series of dark, narrow corridors eventually led them to a door marked 'Rehearsal Space'. Here was where the candidates would be brought in less than two hours, though they would come in through the normal front entrance.

Abi had scoffed at this level of secrecy, until Lexi showed him some of the forums dedicated to her and Amanda, where people frequently posted pictures of them out and about doing completely innocuous things. It had always delighted Amanda and weirded Lexi out. She genuinely didn't mind when the Hotties came up to her on the street, but the thought of them taking pictures without her knowledge or permission had really got under her skin over the years.

Lexi tried to focus her thoughts on the fake-a-friend scheme. The payment structure was a bit of a tricky issue. All she could initially offer the 'friend' was a profit share of the episodes they appeared on, with a bonus once the two of them had managed to get the figures back up to match Amanda's. It wasn't the most attractive proposition ever. It was going to be hard enough to find someone suitable, and then she'd have to sell them on the financials. Unless they had something of their own that they wanted to use the podcast to leverage, though Lexi really couldn't see what would be in it for them. Aine was still only around because Lexi had paid her a year's retainer at the beginning of March, before the shit hit the fan.

'Here we are.' Aine spun round in the centre of a large, mostly bare room with wooden floorboards and a high ceiling. The light from two huge sash windows fell on a couple of folding chairs, a large folding screen and a trestle table where Aine was already laying out bottled water, snacks and paperwork. Each of the actors had been prepped to sign immediately if they got the role. They'd also been told to keep the afternoon clear, with a view to starting the gig right away. Preparing for the role was going to be an intensive process, they were told.

'Great.' Lexi nodded. The room smelled of dust and cigarettes. How the hell had it come to this?

'Right!' Aine was bustling around. 'You'll be here behind

the screen.' Aine showed Lexi a chair with a small folding table beside it. 'Here's the little peephole you can watch through. I'll be out front dealing with the candidates, of course. If at any point you have some input or a question for them, just write it on one of these.' She placed a stack of cards and a marker on the table. 'And slide it under the screen to me. If I don't see the card or you haven't heard me pick it up, give two knocks on the table to alert me. Sound okay?'

'Sounds deranged – like this whole thing, really.'

'Lexi, this is way more normal than you think.' Aine gave her a reassuring pat on the shoulder.

Why couldn't me and Aine be friends? Lexi suddenly wondered. *We do know each other. We've never actually gone out for drinks or anything, but …*

'When I was working in LA, people were being auditioned for all kinds of stuff. I know of one publicist who did a casting call for a fake EX-girlfriend. His client had such a bad reputation that they had to INVENT a previous girlfriend, so that there was at least one woman from his past who wasn't saying he was a dick!'

'Wow.' Lexi nodded. 'That does make me feel better. Kind of! But you know … I was just thinking about how funny it is that we've never got a drink together or anything! I've known you for years … maybe you and I could—'

'Okay!' Aine neatly hopped back and whipped out her tablet. 'Let's not muddy the professional waters here. I'm pretty full up on the friend front. Plus you couldn't suddenly trot out your internet coach on the podcast and pretend we were already best friends. That'd be *too* sad, even for … well, you know.' She snapped her mouth shut.

'Of course.' Lexi drew her lips into what she hoped looked like a not too pathetic smile.

Jesus, Aine's on the payroll already and even she's not willing to do this.

'So.' Aine was scanning the iPad. 'It's a very small pool we've got to choose from because it was just too risky to cast the net too wide. I didn't want to approach anyone other than my most trusted contacts. We have four girls across two different agencies. They know discretion is tantamount; they've all signed non-disclosure agreements. I've taken further measures in that their call times are thirty minutes apart, to reduce the risk of them seeing each other and knowing who else has gone for the role ...'

Three hours later, Lexi was stationed behind the screen, drinking the coffee Aine had ordered. They were waiting on the last candidate. The previous three had been far from ideal.

The first girl had claimed in her bio that she had a playing age of between twenty-five and thirty-five. On her arrival, it immediately became clear that this was an out-and-out lie. She was too young – Lexi'd never be able to invent a history with a twenty-year-old.

The second candidate, on the other hand, was too old and had a hard edge to her.

'Do you enjoy podcasts?' Aine had asked.

'I'll enjoy whatever the fuck I'm being paid to enjoy if I get the gig,' she returned curtly.

It wasn't that Lexi had thought she would truly be friends with whatever person they hired ... but she had definitely been hoping for something a little bit less transactional.

She'd slipped a note out to Aine:

She's too mean, she'd deffo think I was a loser for needing to hire a friend.

'We're looking for a slightly more collaborative approach,' Aine had said, prompting nothing more than a scoff and a door slam from the actress.

The third candidate had seemed promising until Aine asked about previous experience. The girl had enthusiastically rattled through a long list of TV and theatre she'd done.

'Oh, I'm so sorry,' Aine had said, cutting across her. 'This is unfortunate: I'd said to your agent that we specifically want an unknown. We really can't have anyone who's had a lot of coverage online, for example. We need a blank slate.'

Now the last possibility was on her way in and Lexi was feeling desperate.

Maybe this proves that this idea was STUPID ...

Aine appeared beside her with a nut bar and a banana and started to detail all the reasons why Lexi shouldn't lose hope.

'Keep the faith,' Aine implored. 'I think this next one's actually very promising. I looked her up online and she has a private Instagram with about thirty followers. No TikTok profile. She basically doesn't exist. Which is actually so hard to find these days! With all the others, we'd have had to do so much work on re-imagining their online presence to seamlessly work a long-standing friendship into their narrative.'

Lexi chewed morosely through Aine's pep talk.

'The agent says that she's new on the books and hasn't been in a single thing. I'm not surprised – her aesthetic is a little grannycore – but if she seems okay, that is definitely something we can work on. She's not Amanda-hot, but she's not ugly either. That could even play better with listeners, inject a bit of relatability!'

Aine's phone buzzed, alerting them both to the arrival of the last girl.

'Okay!' Aine jumped up, clapping her hands and clattering out of the room. 'Let's keep the energy going.'

Lexi debated escaping. After listening to the first three auditions, she didn't think she'd ever be ready to admit to someone that she needed to pay them to be her friend. NDA or not, their friends and other halves would know all about the pathetic podcaster paying for a pretend friend. With no skin in the game herself, surely the girl would eventually blab it somewhere? Lexi could serve all the solicitor's letters she wanted; it wouldn't matter, because everyone would already know the truth.

Just as she was about to write a new card for Aine saying they should forget the whole thing, the door opened. Lexi paused, listening as Aine brought the girl into the centre of the space.

'It's Claire, isn't it?'

'Yep, I'm Claire. Claire Sheehy.'

'Excellent. Hello, Claire Sheehy. So we have a bit of a different type of role that we're auditioning for today. Basically, it's not acting as such. It's more of a lifestyle thing. This is something you'd have to be willing to jump into feet first. Really immerse yourself. Sort of like method acting, as it were.'

'Sure, I'm cool with that.'

Through the peephole, Lexi studied Claire with interest. She looked nervous but determined.

Aine cleared her throat. 'So I notice that you have a very spartan Instagram account. Not many pics up. Would you say you're not very social?'

'Well …' Claire tugged at the dark denim pinafore she was wearing. 'I suppose I don't post a lot. I use Insta more to look at other people I follow. I am social, but …' She paused, looking uncertain.

'Yessss?'

'I'm social but I suppose … ehm … I'm finding myself … a bit, sort of … em … out of the loop with my friends.'

Interesting, Lexi thought, adjusting her position to get a better view.

'Tell me more about that.'

'I suppose … I don't know if other people get this but, now that we're older, I just feel really distant from them. Like a lot of it is probably because all of us are doing such different things now. We had so much more in common when we were in school and now it's just …' She bit her lip and Lexi could see she was trying not to let her upset show. 'It's just really started to feel like it's them over there and me over here, you know?'

'That's interesting, Claire. Do you know what a showmance is?'

'Yeah, when two celebs are put together for clout or whatever.'

'Well, this role is for something similar, only it's a platonic showmance … Would that be something that would be of interest?'

'Yeah.' Claire looked nervous but eager. 'I feel like I'm always on the periphery of my friends, like an afterthought. We're going away on a "pre-hen do" do and I have to pay a single room occupancy charge because they all paired up to share rooms. I suppose this would be a particularly good gig for me, because if I got it, it wouldn't just be about money. I kind of want them to realise that they're not my only friends. That I'm worthwhile.'

Lexi grabbed the marker and notecards.

She's perfect!

She slipped the note out under the screen.

On the other side, she could hear Aine pause to look at it. 'Give me a moment,' Aine told Claire.

Aine appeared round the back of the screen and leaned down to Lexi's ear to whisper. 'Do you not think she sounds a bit desperate?'

'She sounds the same level of desperate that I am,' Lexi hissed back. Aine gave a shrug that seemed to say, *Yeah, you're both pretty pathetic alright.*

'I think it's ideal,' Lexi continued. 'She wants something out of this as well. She won't judge.'

Aine was nodding. 'If she wants to impress her friends it's in her interest to not blab about the true nature of the relationship.'

'Exactly!'

'Shall we deliver the good news together? Or will I do a *Love Is Blind*-style pull the screen back?'

'I'll just walk around, thanks.' Lexi grinned and stood.

Aine skipped ahead of her, obviously committed to something of a big reveal. 'So, Claire! Are you ready to meet your new best friend?!'

Claire raised her eyebrows and smiled. 'I got it?!'

Lexi walked out from behind the screen, feeling stupid but also strangely excited. 'You got it!' She gave a shaky laugh, aware that she now sounded like the nervous one.

'Oh my god!' Claire whooped and then quickly reigned her excitement back in. 'I'm so happy.' She grinned. 'This is gonna be really good. I promise. I can't believe I got it.'

'You don't even know the full extent of what "it" is yet!' Lexi hoped her cheeks weren't burning with the embarrassment she was feeling.

'Well, I'm a really big fan of the podcast ...' Claire glanced nervously at Lexi. 'So I know what happened – which was so fucking shitty, by the way! And, so, I'm pretty sure I know what we're doing here. I'm your new podwife, yah?'

'You are.' Lexi nodded, silently wondering if Claire being a fan was a good or a bad thing.

Claire was looking confidently at her now. 'I know this'll sound creepy, but I think it's really good that I know you so well already. And I know the podcast! I've been listening since day one – I think this is going to be great.'

'It is,' Aine agreed in a firm voice. 'As long as we all put in the groundwork. Faking a years-long, devoted friendship is no small feat.'

Aine checked her watch. 'It's not quite twelve. Claire, you mentioned before that you need to get back to work in a couple of hours? I propose we get straight into the game plan then take a quick break for lunch. We'll order in – I don't want you two seen together until everything is in place. We'll be soft-launching the fauxship on socials from this Saturday. I know it's a tight turnaround but we are aiming for you to join Lexi on *Your Hot Friend* from next record, which is next week. Wednesday the nineteenth, we'll kick off at seven p.m. That works for you, Claire? We can work around your hours if needs be and of course, all going well, you'll be compensated. Right, let's get settled with our packs. I've compiled a lot of the backstory already. We just need to slot in some particulars of your life, Claire. To give it the ring of truth.'

Aine marched over to the trestle table, cleared some space and started to lay out three large folders. Two had 'Aine' and 'Lexi' written across the front. The third simply said 'TBC'. 'We can fix that now,' Aine muttered as she wrote 'Claire' on a new sticker and stuck it on the front.

Lexi caught Claire's eye and grinned. Claire returned a rueful little smile.

Aine pulled an iPhone from her bag. 'It's the latest model,' she informed them.

Lexi frowned. 'Do we have the budget for that?'

'We do,' Aine replied firmly. 'It's a really essential piece of kit, Lexi. Claire needs to have top-level content on her new Instagram.' To Claire, she said: 'I'll be walking you through that, don't worry.'

'But …' Claire looked from Lexi to Aine. 'I have literally no followers. There're about twelve posts on my account.'

'That's better than if you had followers.' Aine pulled out chairs for Lexi and Claire. 'Over the next few days, I'll be building your account from the ground up. I'll do up some posts, incorporating pics from you and your life and then lots of pictures of you and Lexi to show that you've been best friends forevs. On that, I need you to supply me with pictures from every decade of your life, Claire. I want a really good selection of dates and locations, okay? Holidays, birthday parties, old embarrassing outfits. Oh yes!' Aine cut across herself again. 'I'm sorry, I know I'm going at like a mile-a-minute, but we need to brainstorm a new aesthetic, Claire.'

'Oh. I—'

Lexi rushed to reassure Claire. 'Nothing drastic, we promise.' She smiled. 'You don't have to start dressing like Amanda. But just a little more fashion-focused, more directional.'

'Any questions now, before we sign you up?' Aine was handing Claire a pen.

The girl tucked back her auburn hair and chewed her lip. 'Well, a big part of this for me is this girls trip I have in May that I kind of said I was bringing a friend to … I just want to make sure that's something we could agree on? It's in Ibiza.'

Lexi nodded slowly. A girls trip with randomers sounded hellish. Although if Claire had skin in the game and needed this fauxship to work as much as Lexi did then that could only be a good thing. This weird little set-up needed to be watertight after all.

'Consider it done.'

CHAPTER 22

Claire left the audition elated. Niggling prongs of anxiety were threatening to penetrate the bubble of excitement, but there was no way she was going to ruin this moment with thoughts of practicalities.

Jamie will not think this is a good idea.

People will ask questions.

Aifric and the rest of the Bitch Herd will totally notice and be suspicious.

Claire gave a mental shrug. *Fuck off, brain.*

Spotting a taxi, she waved and threw herself into the back seat. After giving the Sweeneys' address, she settled in to admire the city from this unusual vantage point; taxis were not normally a part of her life, she'd swung the morning off by promising she'd head straight back up to the kids as soon as she could.

Next Claire texted Joanne, who was the only person apart from Norah who knew the full picture of what she was doing.

> *I got it!!! You're looking at the new bestie of Irish podcasting's It Girlie, Lexi Maloney! Obviously you're taking this to the grave. I'm technically breaching my NDA right now! I feel so fancy having an NDA!*

Joanne replied immediately:

I dunno what to say about this ... Psychotic? Amazing? Whatever makes you happy, I guess!

I'll give you the blow-by-blow at coffee tomorrow. We still on for that?

Claire paused before hitting send. Maybe Joanne was just being nice cos she felt sorry for her? She started to mentally scroll back through all the things she'd said to Joanne in the last week. *Joanne probably thinks this is the most pathetic thing ever.*

Another message from Joanne dropped in.

I am gagging for all the details!!! You have to give me the full rundown at coffee tomorrow!!!

Claire beamed. *I have to stop being such a bitch to myself*, she thought as the taxi pulled over at the top of the lane to the Sweeneys'.

Is that even possible?

Probably, if I'd kept up going to the counsellor.

Claire paid the driver and thanked him. All the while her mind stayed on the small matter that she was doing exactly what they told everyone not to do: she was taking her meds but ignoring all the other work of dealing with her issues.

But trying to not be mad was hard. It was a full-time job doing all the things they tell you to do: going to the therapist and meditating and drinking enough water and going for stupid walks. How was she supposed to fit it all in?

'Claire! Claire! Where've you been?' From just up the lane, Lila burst forth, gate-crashing Claire's thoughts. She gathered Lila into a hug and was grateful to turn away from the grim concerns knotted in her mind.

That night Claire handed Jamie his bag of chips and geared herself up to tell him her news. The chips were a ploy she hoped would keep him from paying too much attention to what she was about to impart.

'So I have a bit of news.'

'Oooooh! Norah gossip?' Jamie grabbed the vinegar from the table and began topping up the chips.

'Sadly not Norah gossip but still fun.' Claire was determined to keep this announcement light. 'So I've been kind of getting friendly with that girl from *Your Hot Friend*! Chatting on Insta and stuff.'

'Oh?' Jamie looked up.

'Mmm.' Claire rooted in her bag for a chip. 'It turns out that we've met before. When we were a bit younger.'

'Really?' He frowned. 'And you never realised? That's weird.'

'Well, it's not really.' *Casual, Claire, keep it casual.* 'She's pretty different now. And, I guess, you don't really know what it's like on Insta with some of these girls. Between the filters and the filler, I didn't recognise her. They're all complete catfishes on there!'

'God.' Jamie winced. 'I don't think I'll ever get the attraction of it. It's so fucked up.' He glanced over. 'Sorry, I know you like it …'

'There're pockets of fun. Anyway … You remember the whole thing about her break-up with her podcast partner?'

'Yep. Dystopian, as I recall!'

Jesus, if he thinks that's dystopian, imagine he knew about the friend audition.

Claire had resolved to disclose none of the truth about how she'd got the gig or anything about the changes to her social media presence. Jamie and his crowd were not very active on Insta. Claire had already changed her settings to hide her account from any of Jamie's circle. She very much doubted they'd notice. Lying to Jamie ignited an uneasiness that reminded her of last year when she'd started to feel … not herself. She'd devoted a lot of energy to hiding what she was going through from him.

'So, anyway …' Claire focused on her chips again. 'Lexi's suggested that I come on the show and be her new co-host!'

'What?' He looked stunned.

'Yeah!' Claire replied brightly. Then held up a chip. 'By the way, oh my god, how good are these?!' *Deflect, deflect, deflect.* This was stressful.

'Yeah, they're great,' Jamie replied absentmindedly. 'But … Is this not a bit bizarre? Does she not have any real-world friends to co-host? No offence, like, but …'

'We've become friends!' Claire argued.

'Sorry! Sure, sure.' Jamie looked troubled.

'Why do you think it's such a bad idea? It's something fun! I'll make a bit of money and I can do it on top of my normal job.'

'Is this anything to do with the Bitch Herd?'

Claire immediately shook her head, but Jamie carried on.

'I have to be honest: I've been worried. Some of all that is feeling a bit familiar. The obsessive behaviour, the lists, the hyper-focus …'

'This has nothing to do with that. I was in a bad place last year, yes. But that was serious stuff. I thought I was …' Claire dropped her voice. 'Look, whatever, it was worse.'

'Claire. The last time you got sick started off with innocuous things too … The exercising. The buying stuff. All the voice notes.'

'Everyone sends crazy long voice notes! They're a blight on our generation!'

'I got one that was forty-three minutes, Claire. And I thought I was listening to it on double speed until I realised that you were actually manic.' He looked at her, speaking slowly and deliberately. 'And, as we both know, you spiralled.'

She turned away from him, trying to take a deep breath without him seeing that she was a little gaspy. But Jamie knew all her tells; it was very inconvenient sometimes.

Claire still found it impossible to revisit the events of last September. It was too raw. Her mind had gone darker than she'd ever thought possible. They'd had a heavy summer drinking and partying. She'd taken a pill at a festival and things in her head seemed to spiral from there.

She now knew how it felt to find the ground beneath give way, to have reality itself start to slip. She knew the terrible horror of sliding closer and closer to a precipice and being no longer in control. Her thoughts, her body, her actions – none of them had felt like her own.

With effort, she pulled herself back to the present and realised Jamie was slowly and gently rubbing her back.

'You're safe, you're safe,' he intoned.

Claire gathered herself, ready to put on the show. 'I know I am,' she replied, keeping her voice calm. 'I'm really good, Jamie! I swear. I know better now. I know what I'm like now … when I get that way. *And this is not that, I promise.* I'm excited. I want to do this thing.'

'Won't it be very exposing?'

Claire stiffened. 'What's that supposed to mean?'

'Just that you'll be on show. You show me all the stuff people post online about that girl Lexi. I don't want you to be scrutinised like that. People will find out about your personal life.'

'Like what about my personal life? Are you saying people will find out I'm mental? That I was in the bin last year?' Claire allowed a shard of anger to enter her voice. It was manipulative – Claire knew that this was not what Jamie was getting at – but she felt certain she could leverage what he'd just said.

'No!' He grabbed her shoulders. 'Seriously …' He was emphatic. 'I love you and I don't want strangers being dickheads about you. You know I don't think there's anything to be ashamed about for having mental health stuff. You got sick and you got well and I think you're amazing. And I think your friends were fucking shitty about it,' he added. 'I think your parents could've been better about it too, but I swear I am not saying that you shouldn't do something you want to do because you are – WERE – sick.'

'Thank you.' Claire pulled him close and kissed him.

She felt bad. She'd absolutely backed him into saying exactly what she wanted him to say. But fuck it; it was a means to an end.

'Yum, chip grease!' she murmured with her eyes still closed. Then she opened them and pulled back slightly from Jamie. 'I'm really excited about this, you know,' she said. 'It'll be good for me!'

She carefully chose to ignore the strain hovering at the edges of his smile.

The next morning, in the sunny park, Claire found herself arguing many of the same points with a similarly uncertain Joanne. Of course it was minus the whole 'you sure you're not careering into a manic episode' aspect. Claire would not be disclosing that to her, ever.

'Would everything not just be easier if you skip the Ibiza trip, say you're tied up working and ditch this whole charade?' Joanne asked, vigorously rocking Ted's pram and thwarting Sonny's valiant attempts to play with its filthy wheels.

'But I want to do this,' Claire insisted as she pulled out the binder Aine had given her. 'It's about more than Ibiza and the single occupancy fee. I've always loved *Your Hot Friend* and now I get to be a part of it. It's a podcast fan's dream! Like being pulled out of the crowd at a gig and getting to play onstage with the band.'

'Is it? I feel like to be a podcaster, you kind of have to be inherently insufferable! And you're not!

'Podcasters are not insufferable!' Claire flicked open the binder.

'Of course they are. Who thinks their thoughts are so important that they simply MUST be heard by everyone???'

Claire chose to ignore this in favour of flipping through childhood pictures of Lexi. Each page had additional text detailing where and when the pictures were taken, along with anecdotes from the trip. There were the usual beach snaps and visits to the zoo – even Disneyland Paris. In these photos, young Lexi hugged a woman with the same wide-set eyes and full lips as her. They wore matching Minnie Mouse ears.

'This is her mum.' Claire turned the folder round to Joanne. The accompanying paragraph, clearly written by Aine, gave a dispassionate rundown of Lexi's mother's illness and death. 'I knew she'd died, but I didn't realise how young Lexi was when it happened. That's so sad.'

Joanne nodded, gently nudging Sonny away from the wheel with her foot. 'Is he alright to be doing that?'

'He's very hardy.' Claire laughed, but picked him up anyway and presented him with a digestive biscuit.

'So what's the next plan of action?' Joanne asked wearily.

'Aine is sending over this whole timeline of me and Lexi's friendship for us to bone up on. She's created a massive back catalogue of images of us when we were kids growing up.'

Joanne pursed her lips. 'I can see what you're doing there, you know. Trying to spin this into something that sounds halfway normal. She's photoshopping you into each other's lives.' She shook her head but couldn't help laughing.

'Sure, that's one way to put it,' Claire replied breezily, grateful that Joanne seemed more entertained than weirded out. 'Aine's thought of everything. She's rebuilding my Insta with loads of these pics and tagging Lexi and then putting little comments underneath from Lexi's account.'

'Lunacy.' Joanne snorted. 'I'm glued to this. Will I get to meet her?'

'Sure, at some point, I guess.' Claire couldn't picture an odder trio than her, Lexi and Joanne, but if she got to know Lexi better it could be nice.

'Thank god. I need to talk to more people who are not that fuckface I'm living with. I'm pitching for a big design commission this Thursday and if I get it I will actually be able to meet some people and do something!'

'I will cross everything for you. Will Bert be minding Ted? How is Bert?'

'Fuckface? He's grand.' Joanne rocked the pram even more aggressively. 'He's actually better than grand. He's truly never been better. Meanwhile I am getting the life drained out of me by his hell-spawn. And Bert does this thing now where, when he sneezes, he doesn't even make the TINIEST effort to suppress it any more. Just sneezes freely. As loud as he fucking likes. I can't even remember what I ever liked about the guy.'

'Right.' Claire was at a loss. 'That's awful,' she said vaguely.

'It is, Claire,' Joanne insisted. 'If I blink too fucking loud the baby wakes up, but god forbid Bert compromise his sneeze satisfaction one tiny little bit to allow for the fact that we have a child now!'

'Yes, of course. So inconsiderate,' Claire said soothingly. 'But like, you guys are alright yeah? Relationship-wise?'

Joanne made a *pfft* sound. 'I dunno. Probably. To be honest, with the cost of living the way it is, we can't really afford NOT to be, know what I mean?'

'That's nice.' Claire smiled and they both cracked up.

'That's love in the late capitalist age, baby!' Joanne shook her head. 'So what's the game plan with Aifric and the rest of the Bitch Herd? Aren't they going to notice that you suddenly have a lifelong best friend they've never heard a word about?'

Claire had been turning this very issue over in her own mind and had decided to call on a branch of her family that had served her well in her teens: the distant cousins in Wexford contingent. Back in the early two thousands, her Wexford cousins had made frequent appearances in fictitious anecdotes from her life. Whenever her friends talked about the mad nights drinking they'd been on, Claire, desperate to seem just as worldly, would claim she'd done similar things with her cousins when she'd been down in Wexford.

'Well, the Bitch Herd would've heard me mention my Wexford cousins a fair bit over the years,' she told Joanne. 'So I'm just going to say I always knew Lexi through them. They don't really know *Your Hot Friend*; it wouldn't be their scene. Plus ...' Claire messed with Sonny's wispy curls. 'They barely read my texts or listen to my Voicys as it is, so I doubt they'll commit to listening to a whole podcast episode. Anyway, I'm gonna soft-launch me and Lexi to them at the Crafternoon we're doing next week.'

'And a Crafternoon is ...'

'What it sounds like: an afternoon of crafting,' Claire replied firmly. 'We're all getting together to make bunting and do an emotional check-in for Aifric. Brides can get really stressed.'

'I truly can't imagine what she's going through right now,' Joanne deadpanned. 'Planning a party with the help of literally everyone in your life, on a budget that's the equivalent of a down payment on a house.' She shook her head with reverence. 'It's unimaginable. How do brides do it?'

CHAPTER 23

Two days later a message on Joanne's phone alerted her to Aoife's arrival on a bright mid-April morning. They were meeting early as it was Thursday and Aoife needed to be in her office by nine thirty. Her new job was doing layout for *SHE* magazine and Joanne had to admit a very mean, bitter part of her was glad when she'd heard the details – it sounded like a snake pit of office politics.

I'm outside. Didn't want to ring in case Ted's asleep.

It was considerate, Joanne noted, pulling on her dressing gown and creeping out of the bedroom, where Ted was indeed snoring softly. Who knew three-month-olds snored? The cuteness!

It had been six weeks since the bombshell of Your Story's crumbling and in that time, she and Aoife hadn't spoken – unless you counted participating in a mutual WhatsApp group, which Joanne didn't.

She knew this morning was Aoife's bid to patch things up. She had forwarded Joanne an email at the start of the week for a big commission she'd heard about, suggesting that Joanne pitch for it.

Then she'd proposed coming over to brainstorm, like they used to at work. Aoife had even offered to look over the pitch deck, which Joanne was grateful for: she'd put most of it together during night feeds and in the mornings barely had any memory of the work she'd done.

The commission was a big deal: creating a huge and bold design to revamp one of the city's only skate parks. It was a designer's dream, as the scope for interpretation and creativity was huge. Joanne's meeting with the panel – made up of city councillors and members of the local skate group – was that afternoon. Bert had been reminded a million times to come home straight from work so that he could take the baby an hour beforehand while Joanne got her head in the game.

'Hey.' Joanne eased the front door open and beckoned Aoife in.

'Heya.' Aoife went in for an awkward hug and Joanne felt herself softening already. She'd railed about Aoife a fair bit over the last few weeks, but she was touched at the effort she was making.

In the kitchen, she started making coffee.

'So.' Aoife sat down between two towering stacks of laundry on the couch. 'Bert at work?'

'Yes! He's on the early shift, which worked out perfectly. I've got the Zoom at three, but he'll be back at two and I can psych myself up and run over notes and stuff.'

'Amazing!' Aoife smiled. 'Look … Jo, I … I really …'

Joanne focused on spooning out the coffee, not sure she even had the energy to get into apologies, or explanations – whichever Aoife was about to offer.

'We should get started,' she announced abruptly.

Sometimes, with friends, the fight just wasn't worth having. People cooled off and things went back to normal and the resentments could then lie peaceful and dormant, till the next time someone did or said something annoying. It was the natural way of things.

Aoife nodded and pulled out her laptop, accepting Joanne's proffered mug. Joanne pulled over a kitchen chair and brought the pitch deck up. The next hour flew by as they refined the pitch; Joanne was feeling a growing confidence and excitement. *This is my thing: being creative is more than a job to me!* She couldn't wait to meet the clients and sell them her vision, one she felt pretty confident they would go for. It wasn't just a colourful mural; it would be a project the local community could be a part of creating.

'Okay.' She checked the time. 'I have to get Ted up or he'll be like the Antichrist this afternoon. Will you have one more coffee for the road?'

'Yes please!' Aoife got to her feet. 'I'll stick the kettle on.'

When Joanne returned with a very snoozy, pliable Ted, she found Aoife helpfully putting away the dishes.

'Ah don't, you're too good,' Joanne protested. 'Here, get a Ted cuddle in, he is SO cute when he's just awake.' She placed the baby in Aoife's arms.

'Ah, the little babser,' Aoife cooed, then fixed Joanne with an inscrutable look. 'So, Joanne, I have to ask … Why is there a message scratched onto the underside of one of your pans? It looks demonic.'

Joanne laughed. 'It's not demonic. It's practical.'

'Riiight … Not really explaining anything there, are you?' Aoife grinned.

'Okay, okay.' Joanne retrieved the pan from the drawer and

flipped it over to where she'd etched an aggressive missive with a compass several weeks ago:

> Bert, if you are reading this, it means that you have finally, for once in your stupid, fucking, godforsaken life deigned to wash a fucking pan after using it. Congratulations, you absolute fuck.

'There is an explanation,' Joanne said mildly. 'The man will not wash a pan. He'll do the *dishes* – cos they're easy – but he appears to not consider pots and pans a part of the dishwashing activity.'

'Yes … ?' Aoife continued to cuddle the baby.

'So I have been waging an incredible, completely one-sided, silent war with Bert and he's yet to notice. I'm calling it the PAN-demic. Basically, I realised that I was constantly, ROUND THE CLOCK washing greasy rasher pans despite never eating rashers myself. All his. And no part of him ever seemed to question the fact that he leaves his crusted, greasy rasher pans on the stove and when he comes back to make more rashers a few hours later, the pan is washed and dried and waiting for him in the press. What does he think is happening?'

'Okay.' Aoife was grinning now.

'So, I carved this note as a test, but of course he's never seen it because he doesn't ever wash the goddamn pans. Since then I've abandoned subtlety and now any time I find a rasher pan idling on the stove I just fuck it over the back wall into the overgrown lot.'

'But what about when he goes to make rashers and can't find a pan?'

'He's so far bought four replacement pans and I've had to fuck them all over the back wall as well.'

'Okay.' Aoife laughed. 'You have to nail this pitch. I'm sensing *Shining* levels of cabin fever here.'

After lunch, Joanne showered while Ted complained at her from the bouncer on the floor of the bathroom. Then she blow-dried her hair while pumping enough milk for Bert to give him while she was on the call. It could still be very hit or miss whether Ted would have the bottle, but Bert would just have to make it work.

Next she started her make-up, noting with dismay that it was after two already. She was trying to run through openers for the panel while operating the bouncer with her foot and trying in vain to apply eyeliner.

At half two, she began ringing Bert. Over and over. Where is he? She fended off tears of frustration as the phone continued to ring. She tried texting him:

Where are you? This thing starts in half an hour!

Then she started trying her mum, even though there was no way Emer could get over from Skerries in time.

At five to three, Joanne, utterly resigned, sat in front of her laptop and waited for the meeting to start. Ted was lying in his bouncer under the desk where she'd set up his baby gym; at three months old he was finally taking an interest in some of his toys.

Please just give me half an hour, she silently pleaded.

Onscreen, several windows opened up and suddenly the panel were there smiling and waving at her.

The first twenty minutes of the meeting went perfectly, but then Ted started to protest from under the desk. Joanne was careful not to break eye contact as she began rhythmically tapping the bouncer while nodding along to what Marie, the local councillor, was saying.

'We absolutely adore your community-focused approach, Joanne. Can you tell us about any projects you've undertaken before that were like this one?'

'Sure, of course.' Joanne beamed, then realised she was tapping the baby's chair so hard it was bouncing between the floor and the desk. *Chill, Joanne.* She slowed the rocking. *Feck, what did yer woman ask? Previous community stuff ... yeah, yeah.*

'I did eh ... a thing ... a project in college ...' Ted was starting to cry under the table and Joanne tried to maintain eye contact as she searched with her foot for a soother to placate him. 'It ... the project was very ... em ... good.' At last her toes closed around the dummy and she expertly shoved it in his mouth. The crying stopped, but Joanne now couldn't get her big toe back out of the little handle. *FFS!*

'Can you give us more on that?' Marie asked patiently.

'Yes, sorry, of course.' Joanne smiled. She just needed to sit perfectly still and keep her leg elevated so that she didn't accidentally pull the soother back out. 'I actually included a link to the finished piece. It was a sort of interactive installation. It's on slide three.'

While each of the panellists was looking for the link, she took the opportunity to dive under the desk, free her toe and secure the soother.

A couple of minutes later, as the panel praised her work, Ted spat the dummy out and began howling. It had been a mistake to let him see her boobs: she'd effectively dangled a roast dinner in front of him and then whipped it away. She scrambled to mute herself. Mercifully, none of the panel seemed to have heard. There was nothing else for it: she was going to have to give him a boob if she was to have any hope of finishing this interview.

She tilted her camera up so that only her head and shoulders were visible, then swiftly ducked and grabbed the baby. She had him up and latched within seconds and returned her attention to the meeting. Now all three panellists were looking at her expectantly and she realised they must've asked a question.

She unmuted, thinking fast: 'That's a really good question. Do you think you could maybe elaborate?'

Marie frowned slightly. 'Well, it seems pretty self-explanatory. Does the timeline fit your schedule?'

Joanne was suddenly aware that Ted was slurping and sucking at quite a volume. 'Eh—'

'I'm sorry, Joanne,' Marie interrupted. 'There seems to be some sound on your end. Is someone … eating soup beside you?' She wrinkled her nose.

'Sorry, no … it's the eh …'

At that moment, Ted pulled off her boob and unleashed an enormous slosh of milky vomit, some of which she could see from the screen had made it up into her hair. This prompted confused looks all round and Joanne felt her energy for subterfuge waning. 'Look, I'm sorry,' she sighed. 'I have to go.' She debated blaming the childcare situation but was worried that might hurt her chances even more than this dire performance had. 'I hope you'll consider me for the project.' She smiled as warm vomit spread over her bare stomach and into her lap. 'I would just so love the opportunity.'

Their rejection email came before Bert even appeared. He'd taken on a second shift on the fly and clearly hadn't seen her messages.

'I forgot, Jo— I am so, so sorry. I can't believe I did this. What can I do to make it up to you?' He looked tortured.

Joanne rolled her eyes. 'Just do the fucking things you say you'll do, Bert. It's pretty basic stuff. You know what? It's actually mad that the patriarchy's been so successful, given men can be so fuckin' helpless.'

'Please, Jo ...'

But his pleading was only making her blood boil even more. 'Bert, I could have coupled up with a disembodied erect penis and it would have been more helpful than you.'

CHAPTER 24

Lexi woke up on Saturday morning feeling like she was at the bottom of a well. In the month since her life had imploded, she'd grown accustomed to this sensation each morning. It was strange and lonely going from sleeping beside Jonathan to lying in a narrow bunk bed. At night, even while thoughts of Jonathan and Amanda assailed her, she still caught herself missing him. Cognitive dissonance, she told herself. He'd done the worst thing imaginable, she was hurt and furious but you couldn't just turn off love, even as much as you wanted to.

She contemplated her current view: the underside of the top bunk. Visible through steel bars and mesh above her was the stained and haunted mattress of her brother. Was sharing a bunk with your brother as an adult creepy? Yes.

The bed above her creaked ominously and then an even more ominous noise assaulted her – Abi farted and Lexi knew then and there that she didn't have time to be bogged down in a funk. *I need to get my life back on track by any means possible, if only to escape Abi.* She extended one long, bronzed leg up to the mattress above and gave a vicious kick.

'Fuck off,' Abi grunted.

Lexi swung herself up out of bed and stepped into her sheepskin slippers. She gazed around the room: it was all peeling eighties wallpaper and disturbing stains on the carpet, walls and ceiling. She hadn't even wanted to unpack her bags: the thought of her clothes so much as touching anything in this house gave her the icks, but she knew she needed to settle in and make the best of it for the time being: she and Jonathan were still waiting on final signed contracts to come through for the house in Orchard Terrace before they could make any decision on it.

They'd agreed to share custody of Scouty for the time being. Lexi hadn't wanted that, but knew it was the most practical option – she was, after all, a working mum. Jonathan had her this morning. Luckily she didn't have to see him, as Abi was taking care of the handovers for her.

Lexi got out her phone and started a list of what she needed to get to make a corner of this hell-pit Instagramable. Sponcon didn't stop for anyone and it had been difficult these last weeks trying to make her life look less grim on the 'gram. She needed to improve the aesthetic radically, especially as *Your Hot Friend* had a couple of new sponsors who needed to be impressed.

A gentle tap on the door interrupted her.

'Eh, come in?' She tried not to sound overly welcoming – she needed to get on with her day. She assumed this was a member of Slip'not: the band had returned, noisily, at about three in the morning. She was pretty sure she had no interest in meeting any of them, but she had to play nice, seeing as they were letting her stay.

'Hi.' A sheet of greasy dark hair swung round the door before the owner even came into view.

Lexi, suddenly self-conscious in her vest top, folded her arms across her breasts. She didn't want to be wank fodder for some random metal-loving incel.

'Hi,' she replied curtly as the rest of the Greasy Hair Curtain Boy stepped a little way into the room.

'Lexi! Welcome to our home.' He smiled and Lexi was wrongfooted by his cuteness. 'And your home too now! I'm Shay, the drummer, and I curate the biscuit tin. We all have little jobs, see. We're so happy to have you.' He had surprisingly sweet eyes: wide and long-lashed and smudged with eyeliner. His lips were full and he had a slight overlap in his front teeth that was so adorable it was almost painful.

'It's great to be here.' Lexi was surprised by this warm and surprisingly respectable greeting. She'd assumed anyone in a Slipknot tribute band would be ... well ... weird. 'And great work on the biscuits. I love the pink wafers.'

'Hey, Shay, how was the tour?' Accompanying these groggy, disembodied words, Abi's arm crept out from under his duvet and extended down from the top bunk to bestow a fist bump.

Greasy Hair Curtain Boy aka Shay reached up to bump him: 'I know you're probably still finding your feet, Lexi, and I'm not sure how much Abi's said, but just wanted to let you know we do family dinner on Sundays at five p.m. Nothing mad fancy, just a lovely roast – we take turns doing it. It's me tomorrow!'

'That sounds nice.' She smiled, wishing she was wearing a scrap of make-up.

'Great.' Shay grinned. 'Okay, I've to get down to practice. Everyone's contact numbers are on the chart on the fridge; add yours too when you get a chance.'

He was edging down the hall now, towards the muted thump that had just started to drift up from the basement. Lexi stepped into the doorway to watch him go.

'Have a great day! Hopefully see you at dinner tomorrow. If not before.' He turned and threw up an arm to give a goofy little wave as he descended the stairs.

Lexi slid back into the room. She felt a bit ruffled by the encounter but in a kind of pleasant way. Though why? She was definitely not looking for anything. And he was so not her type.

He also seemed to barely notice me.

Lexi was used to having a tangible effect on men. It was, she admitted, pretty arrogant to think this, but facts were facts. But that boy hadn't broken eye contact even for a second to check out her body. He'd seemed more interested in getting to band practice. She tried not to be miffed.

He isn't that good-looking, she decided. *He's kind of short. Well, not short, but he's probably not taller than me. I could never wear heels.*

She grinned at this line of thinking. *You absolute narcissist – he hardly looked at you! He was just being nice.*

At that moment, Abi rolled clumsily down out of the bunk and began his morning routine of scratching every inch of his body.

This fauxship on the podcast had better work. Living with my brother cannot become a thing!

Later that morning, Lexi was having brunch with Claire outside a cafe in the middle of the revamped Docklands, and was giving her the full ins and outs of her living woes.

'So, I love my brother Abi, but I need to be living in a separate building from him STAT!' Lexi grimaced. 'Even just a separate room would do.' She munched on a sweet potato fry – one positive of the whole life-implosion was she no longer had to drink juices instead of eating meals.

'I can't even imagine.' Claire was giving her a sympathetic wince. 'I'm an only child.'

Saturday crowds were milling; Lexi had already been accosted for pictures with Hotties four times.

Another one approached now, launching straight into a tearful account of how *Your Hot Friend* had got her through some really tough times.

'I went up two full jeans sizes, Lexi,' she said through sobs. 'From a six to a ten. It was like literally a trauma. But you gals pulled me back from the brink. I stopped eating breakfast and lunch for a few months like Amanda suggested and I am back to myself!'

Lexi could tell Claire was horrified. As was she herself. Lexi couldn't specifically recall Amanda recommending an eating disorder on the podcast, but you couldn't rule ANYTHING out with her former bestie.

'Please don't do that.' She pulled the girl into a hug. 'Seriously, that's really not good.'

After the girl left, Lexi tried to shake her unease. She was starting to feel more and more unsettled by what she'd been a part of.

'Are the Hotties always like that?' Claire whispered after another girl had come up, stood in front of Lexi and shouted 'I love you, seriously I LOVE YOU!' over and over for three solid minutes.

'Ehm …' Lexi didn't want to say yes because she'd sound like a wanker and she was afraid it would put Claire off to find out that something similar might be in store for her. 'Just ... like ... some of them,' she replied. 'It's the whole parasocial relationship thing ...'

'What's that?'

'It's hard to explain ... Hang on.' Lexi picked up her phone and searched for a definition. '"Parasocial interaction refers to a kind of psychological relationship experienced by an audience in their mediated encounters with performers on online platforms".' She paused, biting her lip. 'Kind of ironic that I have all these people who think they're really close to me and meanwhile I've had to hire a best friend.'

'Well ...' Claire tapped on her phone, looking for something, then turned it around to show Lexi. 'We're not the only ones struggling with the "new friends in your thirties" thing. I've been compiling loads of data around it. This is fully a thing.'

Lexi took the proffered phone to examine the document.

'This thing is twenty-nine pages long.'

Claire blinked and looked away. 'I know,' she said lightly. 'It's a big fact, I've been having trouble sleeping. I get this way sometimes. These are all testimonials, it's really interesting.' She tapped the phone. 'So many women in their thirties saying they're starting to re-evaluate their friends or they're losing touch with them and having to use apps like Bumble BFF to meet people. Take my friend group. I'm seeing them for this Bridal Crafternoon on Tuesday for Aifric's wedding and it'll be the first time I'm seeing them in weeks.'

'Yeah, as me and Amanda were getting bigger, I lost touch with a lot of people,' Lexi said quietly. 'I kept meaning to text some of my old school friends. Then after things blew up with Amanda, I felt like I couldn't. It'd look really bad, like I was just coming crawling back ya kno? Anyway …' She made a concerted effort to brighten up. 'Let's get posting about our girlies' brunch. Shall we?'

She snapped a picture of Claire holding up her bellini and posted it to her story:

Brunch with this babe – lots of scheming and dreaming …

'So,' Claire started to speak and Lexi could see she looked a bit nervous.

'Yeah?' Lexi coaxed her.

'Well, remember I mentioned that I have this trip coming up in May with my girlfriends. It's just two nights … Are you still up for it? … I don't want them to think that I don't have any other friends I can ask.'

'Of course! Sounds fun and great for Insta content.'

'Amazing, thank you!' Claire beamed as she reposted Lexi's story to her own newly revamped account and added her own caption:

She's an oldy but a goody – nobody knows you like the OGs!

'OK! Soft launch is underway!' Lexi smiled, raising her own glass.

'Whoop!' Claire grinned. 'Let's go get this weird friend montage nailed!'

A couple of hours later, Lexi and Claire were still trying to pack in as much besties' content for socials as possible. To her surprise, Lexi was having fun, doing stupid poses with the clothes in her favourite vintage store and stopping for ice-creams and even a couple more cocktails along the way. Naturally that was when Abi's text bombshelled in:

Dad's been on. He seems to have had a fall. He's okay but we should go down to him, Lex. Where are you? I can collect you. I'll take your car.

'Shite,' she muttered, interrupting Claire's slightly tipsy rendition of 'I Feel Pretty' as she pranced around RetroRedux in a battered old mechanic's jumpsuit that said 'John'.

'What's wrong?' Claire asked.

'It's my dad.' Lexi sighed, sending a pin to Abi so he could see the street they were on. 'He lives on his own and he's a bit ... I dunno ... helpless?' She shrugged. 'The rest of my brothers very wisely left the country. Abi's back now, which is good, cos it means it's not all completely on me any more ... Abi says Dad fell and we've to go down to him in Hereford, so we'll have to cut this short.'

'Is he okay?'

'Yeah, Abi says Dad's grand, but we still better check on him. This is so fucking annoying. I'm supposed to be meeting Jonathan and Amanda tomorrow morning to discuss how to work some of the advertising now with the shared podcast. Sorry,' she rushed to add, 'that sounds awful. I just don't love going back there. To my house like. It's just not a nice place to be for me.'

'I get that.' Claire gave Lexi's arm a gentle pet. 'My parents' house is kind of hell at the moment. I've been avoiding them both a lot because they're separated but neither of them can afford to move out so they're locked in together. My mum sends me Voicys about the singles scene in Shanganagh and my dad just seems really fucking sad. And I know this sounds bad, but I can't help it: I just find it easier to avoid him altogether. Like I don't have a thing to say to a middle-aged man who's hating life.'

'Exactly!' Lexi nodded. 'Sorry for your troubles and all, but I'm just so glad I'm not the only one. My dad drinks a bit,' she added, watching for any hint of disdain or judgement in Claire's face.

'That's so tough, Lexi.' Claire had pushed up the sleeves of her jumpsuit, looking exactly like a mechanic assessing a particularly fucked-up car engine.

'This has been really fun,' Lexi ventured tentatively.

'It has …' Claire replied, sounding equally tentative.

'Why does this feel like the end of a *date* date?' Lexi grinned.

'Well, it was a date of sorts!'

'Are you feeling okay for Wednesday evening? Aine's doing up a bit of a script as it's the first recording and … you know … we hardly know each other. Lol.'

'Surc,' Claire grinned. 'I'll see you then. Good luck with your dad.'

When Lexi and Abi reached their dad's house, the curtains of the front windows were drawn.

'Why's he got them closed? It's only four o'clock,' Lexi muttered at the back of Abi's head as they shuffled down the side passage of the house to the back door.

Abi knocked but didn't wait for an answer and they carried on into the house. Inside, everything seemed to be choked in a strange haze. Lexi felt an immediate kick of fear. Something was very off. While Abi veered left into the kitchen, Lexi hurried on down the narrow hallway to the living room, which glowed with light from the

TV. The air inside the house seemed to be singed with a chemical odour, but there was no smoke or heat anywhere, thank god. She could see the back of her dad flopped slightly sideways in his chair and she rushed to rouse him.

'Dad! DAD! Are you okay?'

He stirred a little.

'What is that smell?' Lexi's eyes were stinging and tearing up slightly. She peered into his face. He looked grey and his mouth was slack, but his eyes were open now.

'Lexi. You're ... here ...' Each of his words faltered, as though finding them was very taxing. Lexi frowned. She couldn't smell alcohol, but that could just be because the other odour was so overpowering. She checked him over and thankfully he didn't seem to have any scratches or bruises.

'Dad!' Abi appeared at the living-room door holding a frying pan with a tea towel and Lexi pulled the neck of her jumper up over her face as the smell intensified.

'Abi ...' Her dad propped himself up awkwardly to turn and look at his son. 'Thank you for ... I'm sorry for texting you like that. I shouldn't have ... I ... I think I'm fine.'

'You left this pan on the stove, Dad.' Abi was clearly trying to keep his anger from seeping into his words. 'It is hotter than the fucking sun. Another few minutes and I think it would've caught fire.'

Lexi stepped back from her dad's chair and scanned the room suspiciously. There were no cans or other tell-tale signs. But that didn't necessarily mean anything.

She scowled. Her reserves of fucks to give about her dad's drinking had long ago started to dwindle.

'Why are the curtains closed, Dad?' She knew she sounded harsh, but she wasn't in the mood to play pretend with him or with Abi.

'My eyes were ... just ... feeling a ... I had a ... a ... headache.'

She peered at his face. He looked unfocused but not drunk as such.

Her dad's particular brand of drinking had never been of the chaotic alcoholic variety. Lexi almost wished it had, because that was something you could confront someone with. That led to behaviours you could present as evidence as to why the person's drinking was hurting themselves and others. The deeply hidden, private drowning that drinkers like her dad did was harder to bring out into the light. He never made a scene. He didn't lash out or say terrible things. He barely even drank in front of them. He cracked his cans alone in his chair and, in that way, made himself as unreachable and untouchable as any volatile person mired in addiction.

'Let's get dinner together,' Lexi said to Abi, keeping her eyes trained on her dad. 'Do you have any food in?' she asked him, making a monumental effort to gild her words with a little kindness.

He lifted his arm gingerly and gestured out towards the kitchen. 'Soup?' he suggested.

'You need more than soup. I'll go to the shop.' Lexi headed for the hallway, relieved to have a reason to leave.

She made a quick stop in the kitchen to assess what needed to be bought. Abi came in behind her.

'That was weird.' He spoke quietly, opening the window to try and get the fumes from the pan to dissipate.

'Was it? He's clearly been drinking.' Lexi poked through the cupboard. 'Ugh, the shit he eats.' She held up a can of roast chicken. 'I didn't even know you could still get food this disgusting.'

'He seems so ...'

'Sloshed?' Lexi rolled her eyes.

'You think it's just that?'

'When's it ever been anything else?' She shrugged.

She grabbed two shopping bags from under the sink. 'I'm gonna just do a simple pasta, okay? I'll get Dad some fruit and bits for breakfast too, but I'm not staying the night, Abi. I can't. I need to be back for my meeting with Jonathan and Amanda in the morning. I don't want to go straight from here wearing today's clothes and with crusty make-up, looking like a loser.'

After dinner, during which their dad seemed to be a bit more with it, Abi and Lexi headed back to Dublin. The mood of the grim house clung to them. Only once they were each tucked into their respective bunks did Lexi bring up their dad again.

'You probably think I'm being really hard on him, Abi, but it's been lonely the last few years with you away studying. And when I go there, I get so down. I've tried to get him to help himself. I'm not even talking about the drinking. I know at seventy he'll hardly change that, but I tried getting him out of the house. Golf club, movie club. I paid for us to learn bridge together. Bridge! He didn't want to know, so I'm sorry that I am tired of it all, but I have to work on keeping myself happy too you know. I'm not being selfish. A lot has just happened and I'm just trying to keep my head above water, okay?'

'Lexi,' Abi spoke quietly. 'I haven't said a single thing about you being selfish. But there's probably a reason YOU'RE thinking it.'

'Fuck off, Abi.'

'Goodnight, Lexi.'

In the morning, Lexi tried to put aside her worries, as she dithered over what to wear. She wanted to look casually amazing. She pulled joggers and jeans out of her bags and ignored Abi moaning from his bed.

'What time is it?' he whined.

'It's after ten.'

'It's a Sunday, Lex. It's my god-given right to have a lie in.'

'Right.' Lexi gathered together her knickers, a plaid shirt, grey joggers and pink knitted bralette and headed out to the shared bathroom to get dressed. The loo had a strangely haunted vibe, with one of those mini carpets that hugged the bottom of the toilet – a piss sponge basically.

She dressed and did her make-up, trying to ignore the gloom spreading inside her. She smiled at her reflection and then burst into tears. She did not want to see Amanda and Jonathan.

She glared at herself in the mirror. *This will fuck your make-up. You can't show up looking like you've been crying. You can't be this pathetic.*

She held the rim of the sink, staring down and watching the tears drop into the bowl. She hadn't seen Jonathan in the flesh since she'd collected her bags from their house and she hadn't seen Amanda since the night of the show. Seeing them now, after her first solo episodes had bombed, was going to be excruciating. She continued to grip the sink and tried to concentrate on calming her breathing.

When the tightness across her chest began to loosen, she looked up to assess whether or not her make-up had survived the tears. She blotted her damp eyelashes, taking care not to smudge her mascara everywhere. Then she dabbed some more concealer around her eyes and blotted her red lipstick. Finally, she pulled a brush through her hair and stepped into her runners.

'They're the ones who should be nervous,' she announced to the empty room. 'They're the pricks here.'

'They are,' came a muffled, consoling reply from the other side of the door.

'The fuck—'

Lexi pulled open the door to find none other than Shay and a different greasy hair curtain boy. Greasy Hair Curtain Boy II, as it were.

Shay was smiling at her, his big eyes crinkling and lovely, while his friend looked like his eyes were about to pop out of his head, cartoon-style, at the sight of Lexi's bralette.

'Sorry, didn't mean to interrupt, just wanted to show my support. So who are these pricks?' Shay asked. 'I hate them,' he added vehemently, still grinning.

'Oh, just ...' Lexi stalled, wondering briefly if lying was the way to go. Then, taking a breath, she realised she couldn't be bothered making something up. 'It's my ex-manager, who's also my ex-boyfriend, and my ex-best friend, both of whom I still sort of have to work with.'

'Jaysus, a nightmare.' He shook his head sympathetically. 'We used to have a lot of in-fighting in the band. Creative differences and all. We actually had to do a lot of work on ourselves. Though now it's really paid off.'

'Right.' Lexi pulled on her red flannel shirt, moving out into the hall. 'We actually tried couples' therapy. My friend and I ... but ...

it was probably too little too late …' She shrugged. 'I'm meeting them right now, because we still have to run a business together.' She rolled her eyes.

Shay's friend finally tore his eyes from her boobs and spoke. 'Now? It's a Sunday.'

'Sponcon never rests.' Lexi sighed.

'Ah, so you do a bit of influencing as well as the podcasts?' Shay twinkled at her. 'I googled you!' he added brightly.

His earnestness seemed so completely at odds with his grungy black tee-shirt, which declared in dripping-blood font 'THE BEAST IS RISEN'. And that wasn't even getting INTO his Slipknot tribute-band persona which appeared from the mask he wore onstage to be an amalgamation of Miss Piggy and Our Lady. Yes, she'd googled him too.

'We do sponsored content on the podcast and then tie-ins on our own socials. We've got a couple of new brands coming on board.' Lexi tried to sound pleased about this, but her dread at seeing Jonathan and Amanda was overshadowing any optimism at the thought of new income.

'Those two are absolute dicks,' Shay said quietly. 'I read about what they did.' He leaned a little closer to her. 'Good times are coming, you'll see.'

Lexi tried not to show the effect his proximity was having on her.

Oh my god, what is going on? I am actually nervous here.

He is short. He has spots.

She cringed slightly at these deeply shallow thoughts. He did have a rash of acne along his jaw, but like everything else that she and Amanda would have deemed a flaw – his teeth, his hair – it just seemed to work for him. It was him she realised, his essence.

He just has Cute Boy Energy.

Lexi stepped around the two of them, towards the top of the stairs. 'I need to go,' she explained.

'Good luck.' Shay gave her a goofy thumbs-up. 'We'll see you at dinner yeah?'

'Uh huh …' Lexi nodded, pretty sure she would be in no mood to have dinner with nine bizarre strangers later, but no need to tell him that. 'See you then.'

Jonathan and Amanda were exactly on time to the meeting in Dublin's excruciatingly chic Bridge Cafe. Lexi resented seeing them so publicly, but knew it was a necessary evil.

'We need to give them grist for the Rants.ie mill. You two haven't been spotted in public in a month,' Jonathan had reasoned when they arranged it. 'And with me there, they'll be beside themselves speculating about what's going on. It'll be a great bump for this week's figures.'

He wasn't wrong. The Rants.ie *YourHotFriend* forum was awash with hate, cruel comments and hilariously off-base gossip about Lexi and Amanda, but every time an episode got posted there – invariably one of the controversial ones – the figures soared.

Now, across from Lexi, Jonathan was trying unsuccessfully to lift his paleo toast to his mouth before it crumbled into a trail mix. The Bridge brunch menu was wanky in the extreme: you couldn't find a dish without an activated nut or a cauliflower sausage for love nor money.

He swallowed a few crumbs of his dusty bread. 'It's particularly good to have you two out and about today,' he said. 'It's a Lexi episode week and the stats will be on the floor.'

'Jonathan!' Amanda glared. 'That's fucking mean.' She turned to

Lexi. 'Lex's just trying to find her feet, aren't you?' She tried to pat Lexi's shoulder.

Lexi leaned out of reach and seethed as she forked a green matcha pancake into her mouth.

'It's just facts.' Jonathan spread his hands and shrugged. 'She knows she's bombing. It's not like the listeners are tiptoeing around it.'

'We could get back together, Lexi?' Amanda ventured.

Lexi felt a twinge of temptation. In so many ways, it would be so easy to go back to how things were. Luckily Amanda's characteristically unsentimental next words pulled Lexi back from the brink of considering it:

'Anytime you want to get over yourself, I'm ready.'

'I'm over everything,' Lexi snapped. 'I've got a new co-host – one of my old friends.'

Amanda snorted. 'An old friend that I haven't met? You don't have one of those, bébé.'

Lexi ignored this, stabbing at her pancake again.

Jonathan cut in. 'Ah yes, I saw you debuting her on your Insta yesterday. Great feelgood content, if a bit tame.'

Lexi crossed her arms. 'I don't need your "feedback" on my content any more.'

'Yes, content!' Jonathan said brightly, pretending she hadn't spoken. 'Let's get down to it. We've two deals on the table. They're both in the wellness realm, so they have money to spend! One is an exciting new food intake monitoring system called the Trauma Diet: it's a psychology-based approach that harnesses a client's trauma and puts it to good use to aid their pursuit of weight loss! And the other is a treatment that is having something of a resurgence in LA:

Trepanning. Last big in the sixteen hundreds. Loads of tanning salons and beauty clinics will be rolling it out in the coming weeks.'

After they'd finished up finessing the scripts for the new ads, they parted ways. Amanda had seemed subdued after Lexi brought up Claire, and when Lexi turned to walk towards the quays to catch a cab back to the house, she found to her surprise that Amanda had come after her.

'Lexi,' she called, breathless from jogging.

'What?' Lexi was wary.

'Have you really got this new girl? Claire?' She must have watched Lexi's stories in the bathroom at the cafe.

'Yeah,' Lexi nodded, wondering if Amanda was jealous or just suspicious about this out-of-the-blue friend. Or perhaps a bit of both.

'And like … where's she from? You've literally never, ever mentioned her in our twenty years of friendship.' Amanda actually sounded more hurt than sceptical.

'I met her through my cousins in Wexford. I've known her since we were kids.' Lexi pulled up a picture of her and Claire aged eight, eating ice creams at the seaside. Aine's photoshopping skills were pretty lit. The original image of Claire didn't have an ice cream and Aine had put one in to give more veracity to the image. She really was going above and beyond with the whole thing.

Amanda looked at the picture dolefully. 'I guess … I just don't ever remember you mentioning her.'

'Well, you wouldn't, would you?' Lexi shot back. 'Your self-involvement knows no bounds.'

'Maybe people in glass houses, Lexi …' Amanda's sadness flared into anger. 'All you've been wanking on about since New Year's is your house and your puppy. It's been so tedious. I've been carrying *Your Hot Friend* for the last couple of years since your life became so goddamn boring.'

'Alright, Manda, byeeee.'

Lexi started to walk again, but Amanda was refusing to be shaken off.

'Then you insist on dragging the arse out of this victim thing,' she hissed, just behind Lexi. 'This girl … Claire … whatever. She's not me. You need me.'

Lexi whipped around and was about to unleash when she noticed Jonathan with his phone up just across the street. She froze.

'Why are you stopping?' he called. 'This is great stuff. Keep going. They'll eat this up on Rants.ie.'

The bizarreness of the situation jolted Lexi out of her paralysis and hit her with a strange revelation. They'd chronicled their friendship and co-modified and packaged it for the consumption of others and now they were doing the same with their break-up.

'I'm going,' she said plainly. 'I'm done. I'm having dinner with some new friends.'

Back at the house, Lexi was disappointed to find that the chairs on both sides of Shay were taken.

This is so weird, she thought. *I am having a full-blown secondary-school-style crush.*

She slipped in beside another guy, who waved at her but kept his big Bluetooth headphones on, his head bobbing rhythmically.

Lexi tried to look occupied, fixing her knife and fork while sneaking another look in Shay's direction.

Shay stood and started bringing in dishes piled with crispy roast potatoes and plates of meat, along with a big nut roast for the vegetarians, of which there were many, Lexi noted.

While everyone passed salads and veg around, Shay cleared his throat.

'Gang, big welcome for Abi's sis Lexi, the newest member of our motley family.'

Everyone applauded and whooped in unison.

'I won't go round the table and introduce everyone in one go, cos that might be a bit overwhelming, but we have a chart.' He pointed to the wall behind Lexi where, she spotted for the first time, there was something of a Slip'not family tree, showing photos of everyone along with their name, age and the date they'd joined the band. In the bottom right, she and Abi had been added under the heading Honorary Members. Shay, she spotted, was twenty-seven, which was not obscenely young for her ... only three years!

'So, you'll get everyone's names gradually, don't worry!'

'And then to be extra confusing, you've to learn all our stage names,' a red-haired lad down beside Abi piped up. 'I'm Eamon, by the way, and my alter ego is Beelzebop! Like Satan, but a Satan who likes a bop.'

Lexi nodded gamely. 'O ... kaaay!'

'So quick bit of emotional housekeeping.' Shay was now reading from his phone while eating a roast potato like an apple with his other hand. 'A few people have confided that they've been feeling a little bit burnt out after all the gigs in the last few weeks. And I am totally feeling that too. I think a bit of self-care and compassion should be on everyone's Time To Give A Fuck About Me list this week, okay?'

Around the table, everyone was nodding in response to this baffling statement.

'You are so right,' one of them piped up. 'My hydration has gone out the window and I'm not meditating – I can really feel the impact in my body. We all need to prioritise our wellbeing.' He looked at the others around the table meaningfully.

'Absolutely, Steve.' Shay fist-bumped him. 'Now, moving on. Lexi, we usually all agree to read an article or listen to a podcast episode during the week so that we can discuss and kind of unpack it at dinner! Nothing super serious, just something to keep us engaged and challenging the culture we're consuming. We take turns picking. So this week we had Hellmouth's choice.' Shay pointed at a tiny, nervy looking guy at the head of the table. 'Eckhart Tolle in conversation with Brené Brown.' Shay sat down. 'Well, what did we all think?'

'I loved their discussion about vulnerability,' Hellmouth announced.

A broad guy with wasps tattooed to his forehead and straggly bleached hair down to his waist chipped in. 'Did you not think that Eckhart's breakdown of emotional labour was overly simplified, no doubt informed by his lived experience as a cis white man?' Lexi checked the chart: the guy's band name was Screaming Foetus.

Not having a single clue who or what Eckhart Tolle was, Lexi didn't contribute to the discussion. After her tumultuous weekend, she was grateful she could just sit and listen and enjoy the food.

As the band swapped points and insights on everything from 'emotional granularity' to Brené's hair, Lexi couldn't help but think of Jonathan and Amanda. They would scoff at the level of earnestness in this room. They'd scoff at every single aspect of this situation. She thought back to earlier, in the street, when she had looked from Jonathan to Amanda and felt disorientated. The two people who'd supposedly been closest to her were like strangers now. Two deeply cynical strangers.

She felt like she was coming out of a long, strange dream. For so many years with Amanda, she'd never questioned things. She just went along with her, because ... well ... she always had. Now, sitting in this slightly gross house filled with lads who in the past she too would have filed under 'slightly gross', Lexi suddenly felt unexpectedly lighter.

With Claire, she could make a fresh start. She could build herself back up. It wasn't the 'easy' route but maybe it was the right one.

Her phone buzzed in her bag by her feet.

As Lexi read the words, she could hear Amanda's voice in her head.

> *Bébé. We know we made a bad call, right? J and I. We're assholes. Seriously, I know that. But please don't write us off. I miss you so bad. Marcus St James is a fucking nightmare, he's no craic. I cannot stand the thought of you doing* YHF *with some blow-in bestie, even if you have known her forever. Please just promise me this is temporary. I'll go back to therapy, I'll do whatever it takes—*

There was more to the message, but Lexi clicked the phone to black. She didn't want to read Amanda's words and be persuaded. She needed to get out from under her and find out who she really was without Amanda.

CHAPTER 25

On the Tuesday after brunch with Lexi, Claire was making her way to the Crafternoon Tea which was taking place on a boat. It was Claire's idea of hell. A party on a boat was not a party but a hostage situation. Nadia was obviously keen to be as extra as possible about every one of her bridesmaid duties. It wouldn't have been enough to simply host an afternoon tea at someone's house and do a bit of macrame. The Crafternoon Tea at Sea was also about to become the most expensive two hours of Claire's life. They'd all had to Revolut €100 for the tea, cakes and tiny sandwiches. The craft material costs would be forwarded onto them separately.

About five hundred yards from the boat, Claire abandoned her Maps app, having spotted the sign for the event – a giant teacup. Ahead of her she could see a few of her friends walking together.

They probably all arranged to meet beforehand, she thought darkly.

A buzz from her new phone drew her back from the precipice of being pre-emptively pissed off. It was Lexi, tagging her in a picture of the two of them on her Instagram.

> Can't wait for my record with this one, my new podwife, tomorrow night!!! Keep an eye on the @YourHotFriend feed to catch the episode the second it drops!

Claire reshared the story with a fluttering heart emoji and hurried on to catch up with the girls.

'Hey!' she called.

Nadia whipped around, a beat passing before she cranked up a smile. 'Hi, Claire.' She turned and strode on.

Claire hurried to fall into step with them.

'How's life?' Helena asked.

'All good.' Claire smiled, mentally steeling herself for the rollout of Operation Lexi's Been My BFF For Years. They must have seen her Instagram over the last few days. She'd never posted so much in one weekend before. Even after she'd left Lexi on Saturday, she'd still had things to put up on Insta, following the schedule Aine had made: a bit of chat about recording her first podcast; a reel about her coffee routine yesterday morning. Really banal stuff but already her Insta was getting a bit of traction, thanks to Lexi resharing and commenting on everything.

'I am crazy busy.' Helena fanned herself dramatically. 'So happy to have an excuse to get off work a bit early for this.'

'Yeah,' Claire echoed, wondering if Helena was deliberately not asking her about her news.

They arrived at the gangplank, where a young guy in a neatly pressed naval uniform waved them aboard the gleaming boat.

Claire followed Nadia and Helena down a narrow set of wooden steps and marvelled again at the sheer lunacy of this marriage of crafting, afternoon tea and the high seas.

Below deck looked like a Pinterest factory. Most of the Bitch Herd and Aifric's cousins were there already, gluing beads to doilies and doing other baffling activities.

'Helena, you sit here,' Nadia barked, indicating a chair beside her own. 'Claire, you're over there.' She pointed to the darkest corner, basically the bowels of the cabin. 'Glue guns are one between two so no hogging. Every work station has the directions laid out and in terms of output we have strict targets so I recommend you get your heads down. No prosecco will be popped for another hour, until Aifric gets here.'

Claire took her seat beside Gillian, settling herself at her work station and examining the picture of the origami swan garland she'd been tasked with making. The aesthetic in the picture was firmly 'Rustic Backyard Wedding'. The bride and groom were standing under an arch strewn with fairy lights and the swan garland. A small wooden sign hung just above their heads. It said 'Soulmates'.

'What are you making?' Gillian leaned over. 'Ah, the garland. Ugh, I'm so glad I dodged that one. It looks soooo complicated. But you are the craft queen! All I have to do is cut out four hundred of these.' She held up a shiny foil gold star. I can't believe Nadia is withholding the alcohol, though. Like this is exploitation. We're down here in the hold of a ship, in steerage, doing manual labour. The least she could do is fill us with booze.'

'Why isn't she?' Claire made a tentative start on the first paper swan, consulting the steps with each new fold of the paper.

'She wants the bulk of the work done before Aifric gets here. She says the bride has enough stress going on and that if she comes here and sees there's still loads to do, she won't enjoy the crafternoon.

Nadia says we all have to hit our KPIs by four thirty and then we can just do a bit of show crafting when Aifric's here.'

Claire held up her first finished swan. 'This is cute.' She looked back down at her assignment sheet. 'I just have three hundred and seventy-nine more to do.'

Now the crafternoon on the high seas made perfect sense. If Nadia had thrown the party at a location they could have escaped from, they would inevitably have made a break for it, sometime around the first hundred metres of bunting. At sea they were trapped. Like the tagline for the seminal Phillip Noyce thriller, *Dead Calm*: 'In the middle of nowhere there is nowhere to hide'.

An hour later, Aifric's arrival lifted the hostages' spirits somewhat. She floated among the ranks, doling out kisses and compliments, and Claire straightened up her work station, trying not to look too eager as Aifric wafted over, trailed by Nadia.

'Claire!' Aifric peered into Claire's corner, where the table was piled with stiff-winged paper swans. 'These look gorgeous. Isn't Nadia amazing to have put all this together?!'

Nadia closed her eyes and smiled beatifically to receive the praise.

'Nadia's been up on deck for the last hour on TikTok!' Gillian huffed, nursing the warren of paper cuts on her left hand.

Aifric chose to ignore this outburst. 'It all looks lovely. And I'm so happy that Claire could even make it,' she added in a tone that, while friendly, seemed to carry a definite edge.

Claire faltered for a minute. She'd felt deflated that none of them had commented on her Insta stories with Lexi and had been wondering if maybe they hadn't seen them after all.

'Do you mean with the new podcast ... ?'

'Yes, obviously!' Aifric's demeanour was bright, but there was something off, the slight clang of a minor note in her tone.

'But I would never have not made it!' Claire insisted. 'And Lexi and I aren't recording our first episode till tomorrow night.'

'Oh, "Lexi" is it?!' Again her jolly delivery betrayed a certain irritation.

'Yeah, Lexi ... that *is* her name.'

What is wrong with her? Claire thought.

'I never knew you knew her,' Aifric said.

'Oh, yeah ...' Claire had rehearsed this moment for days and was ready to sound casual and convincing. 'Well, when we were younger, she was friends with a few of my Wexford cousins. And then we recently got back in touch through Insta ...'

'You've never mentioned knowing her though,' Aifric remarked blandly, though her eyes narrowed slightly.

'Well, none of you guys really follow the show, so why would I? Anyway, you know the way it is, we all have different sets of friends ... work friends ... college friends ...' Claire waved her hand casually towards the rest of the Bitch Herd, in the manner she'd been perfecting over the course of Sunday and Monday. She'd actually eschewed practising in the mirror in favour of doing it in front of her phone camera. That way she'd been able to watch back many different takes, with a variety of different gestures and emphasis. And she'd been able to send them to Joanne for comment.

'Unhinged', was Joanne's feedback.

'*We* all have different friends.' Aifric indicated herself, Nadia and the rest of the room. 'But, no offence Claire, you never have.'

Well, that fucking stings.

'I have,' Claire insisted, trying not to sound childish. 'And it's Lexi,' she said firmly. 'Oh! And I have another friend called Joanne,' she added. She immediately regretted the afterthought, because it did sound a bit juvenile, but whatever ... An exciting realisation was striking her: *Aifric is jealous! She's jealous of me and my other best friend!*

Claire was delighted. Though the 'delightedness' was slightly tempered by the niggling fear that all of this over-analysing was actually just fundamentally pathetic anyway.

Jesus, the bitch in my head is relentless, she moaned silently. Then she mentally noted the phrase as potentially good for tomorrow's record. Aine had told her to collect some anecdotes and 'takes' for the show and Claire had immediately set up a Notes app page for it. So far it was a paltry list, devoid, Claire was sure, of anything remotely interesting or entertaining:

Anyone else get a contact high from seeing other people run for and catch a bus?

Nobody talks about Loop De Loops any more. I love them. But are they Loop De Loops or Loop The Loops?

Why do we still not acknowledge that installing/changing the batteries on smoke detectors is the most annoying life activity of all time and should be rewarded with a Nobel prize?

'It just seems crazy that you've had this friendship we've never heard anything about.'

Aifric was now fiddling with one of Gillian's stars, to Gillian's visible consternation. She looked exhausted. She had exactly

400 and if something were to happen to one, she was liable to riot.

Aifric looked up at Claire again. 'And you always listened to that podcast ...'

'I did, but—'

'Claire!' Nadia cut in, putting a protective arm around Aifric. 'I just don't think now is the time for this argument.'

'I'm not having an argument. We're chatting.' Claire was flummoxed. She'd wanted Aifric to take notice but she didn't want her to be angry. Claire looked at Gillian, who just shrugged, and Aifric, whose eyes were averted.

'If you say so, Claire,' Nadia said shortly. 'Now, you both need to pack up your crafts – CAREFULLY! – and stow them with the rest.' She flicked her head towards the boxes that were neatly stacked at the back of the cabin. She then steered Aifric back to the steps and up and out to the deck, where the sun was making a tentative appearance and drinks were at last being poured.

Claire couldn't help but feel this whole plan was backfiring slightly. She'd wanted to show them that she wasn't a loser. She hadn't counted on it making anyone angry.

Why does Aifric care? She barely replies to my texts; she never invites me anywhere; she didn't make me a bridesmaid; she rejected my handsewn fucking teabags.

Though, as Joanne had pointed out, teabag favours at a wedding did bring to mind unfortunate tea-bagging references potentially not in keeping with the beauty and gravitas of the event.

Claire could feel her mind start to pinball from thought to thought, as if the ideas and words weren't quite hers.

Slow down, Claire ...

Then suddenly the words were out and raining down on Gillian, driven by a force she wasn't in control of.

'What's-that-all-about? What-could-I-possibly-have-done?'

The speedy feeling of her voice was horribly familiar, a bit like a wave gathering inside her: unnerving and unstoppable. She shook her head and tried to do the thing Ella had told her to do when she needed to feel grounded and stop the overwhelm.

Name three things you can see:

The paper swans, the glue guns—

But more thoughts cut across. *Why is this happening? I'm on top of my meds. I am ... am I? I should leave before I say anything weird. Wait, did I say that bit out loud just there?*

The gathering wave paused for a second. Claire stole a glance at Gillian, who appeared to be shrugging in answer to her previous question, 'What could I possibly have done?'

That's good, that's fine. I'm not babbling. Out loud at least. But I have to go right now.

Fuck.

I am on a boat.

The mounting wave resumed its unrelenting rise. The wave always made her feel like she was suffocating from within. It made her feel unsafe in her own body. As it rose and became denser and denser, the space for her to breathe and think and be rational seemed to close down. In past moments of mania, she'd found it impossible to control or stop the mounting pressure of the peaking wave. And that made her panic more. It was a vicious cycle.

For reasons she'd never identified, the cascade of words that inevitably followed gave her some relief: the word-deluge felt a bit like a release valve. But it was very fucking inconvenient when your release valve was so obvious, loud and weird. Also, she knew by now that her friends didn't deal well with a slightly hyper, babbling Claire.

I have to be calm. We are having proseccos and toasting Aifric.

Ignoring Gillian, she spotted a toilet off the cabin. She hauled herself in and slammed the door shut.

She pulled out her phone and started recording a quiet, frenzied Voicy to Joanne.

'I'm stuck on this boat and I am starting to not feel good. At all. I'm in the jacks so it's fine right now, no one can hear me, but I have to go out and be normal. But Aifric is actually really miffed about the Lexi thing and I wasn't expecting that. I don't know what the fuck I'm going to do right now. I'm in a toilet – did I say that? But I have to get back out there and I feel like I'm just PENT UP. I need to run off and jump in the sea or something. But subtly, know what I mean? Ugh. I know I sound insane. I need one of my special Uncrazy Yourself Fast pills but they're at home. Ugh, why is this happening? I feel like I'm just maybe not *manic* manic, but just feeling a bit stressed about Aifric, yanno? And I probably haven't been sleeping great. Anyway. Okay. I'm going to delete this, thanks for listening. Byeeee.'

Claire looked at the little paper plane symbol beside her audio message. Even despite the tweaky speedy gaspy feeling, she grinned at the idea of sending it. Imagine! Joanne would completely panic. She didn't even know that Claire was on medication. Claire hit the little bin icon to delete it. Despite the claustrophobic little loo, which now that she was taking it in had the same shape, size and feel of a coffin, she was feeling a bit better. She was, she noticed, involuntarily doing the mental counting that could sometimes wind her back down a bit.

One, two, three, four, five ...

She pushed out the door to the now completely deserted cabin and counted her way up on deck.

I can't get off the boat but that is totally fine. I don't need to. Just go and smile and we'll be home later and we can have a herbal tea and an Uncrazy Yourself Fast pill and be grand.

Up on deck, she hovered at the edges of conversations and smiled vaguely at the jokes being batted back and forth.

Small sandwiches are the perfect food for when you're feeling a bit manic, she thought brightly to herself. *A teeny bite goes down quick.*

You sound mental, the bitch voice said.

Nadia clapped her hands and made a tearful speech about Aifric that appeared to include several veiled allusions to some kind of treachery that Claire couldn't fathom.

'There is NOTHING more important right now than celebrating you and your happiness and achievements. At least to most of us, anyway ...'

Later, when they'd finally docked and said goodbye in the fading light, Claire had been surprised by Nadia catching up with her a little way down the quays.

'Claire! CLAIRE! We need to talk.'

In the last hour Claire had been feeling better, a bit more level, but apparently the universe hated her today. She turned around and with what she hoped was a decent impression of a smile said, 'Yep?'

'What do you think you're doing, Claire?'

'I'm … going home?'

'Don't be funny,' Nadia spat. 'You know what I'm talking about. All this Lexi-this, Lexi-that and the podcast stuff.'

'Oh-kaaaay. But I barely mentioned it.'

'Me and the girls all agree that it is not on.'

'What exactly is not on? Me having another friend?' Claire couldn't believe they were all taking it so badly.

Maybe I've been too sensitive all this time – imagining that they weren't including me.

'Ugh, not that.' Nadia rolled her eyes. 'The podcast. Announcing it all over socials. We all agree that it is BEYOND selfish to be having "big news" during someone else's engagement.'

Claire didn't know which batshit part of this to jump on, but the phrase 'we all agree' sliced deeper than the accusation of selfishness. 'Who's "we all"?' She looked at her feet. 'The bridesmaid's group chat, I suppose?'

'It's been raised there, yes,' Nadia agreed primly.

They talk about me behind my back. And not in a good way.

Claire clenched her jaw at this confirmation of the fear she'd held for so long. She was glad that with the advancing dusk, Nadia probably couldn't properly see her fighting tears. Claire took a steadying breath, trying to ignore a circling thought:

If they routinely make you feel like this, why do you stick around?

'Nadia, I wasn't trying to take the attention away from Aifric's wedding. I honestly wasn't thinking about it in those terms. But like …' Claire paused to select her words carefully. 'People can't help having life events at the same time as a friend's engagement. That's ludicrous.'

'Wow.' Nadia folded her arms. 'Now you're calling Aifric's feelings ludicrous. Minimising her experience. Wow. Wow. Wow.'

As Claire opened her mouth to argue strenuously against this characterisation, her phone rang. Both of them started at the jarring sound.

'What kind of deviant is phoning me!?' Claire muttered and Nadia even dropped her bullshit momentarily to watch Claire take her phone out.

Dad was flashing on the screen.

'What the hell?' Claire glanced up at Nadia. 'He *never* calls me.'

'Shit,' Nadia muttered, spotting the name. 'Could it be serious?'

Claire hit accept and brought the phone to her ear. 'Dad?'

'Claire?'

'Are you okay? What's wrong? Did you mean to call me?'

'I ... eh ... I did.' He sounded uncertain himself. 'How are you?'

Claire covered the phone to whisper to Nadia: 'He's asking how I am ...'

Nadia made a wincy face.

Claire spoke into the phone. 'I'm grand, Dad. But why are you ringing?'

'Well ... your mother's out. Again. And I just thought I'd check in with my little Claire-Bear.'

'I see.' Claire couldn't help but be weirded out: the man had never rung her before. Literally never.

'So ...' Claire had no idea what to say to her dad on the phone. She couldn't imagine anyone knew what to say to any dad on the phone. Dads and phones were like fish and lipstick – they had no business even being in the same sentence together.

'Can I maybe call you back—' she began, at the exact same time that her dad was saying, 'Actually I'll just talk to you when I see you.'

'Brilliant,' he said.

'Oh, great,' said Claire, laughing nervously at how obviously relieved they both were.

She hung up and struggled for a moment to remember why Nadia was standing in front of her. The call from her dad had at least dispelled the tension somewhat.

'How's he doing?' Nadia asked.

'He seems kind of lost.' Claire started to walk towards the street where her bus went from. 'He's probably lonely, but I don't know what to say to him about any of it.'

Unexpectedly, Nadia nodded at this. 'It's really hard at the beginning, but one of the best things that came out of my parents' separation was that I kind of got to know my dad for the first time.'

'Right.' Claire remembered the year Nadia's parents split up. Nadia had gone on a mercifully fairly mild teenage rampage of vodka and shoplifting – a rampage that thankfully abated after a few months. Claire had never felt close enough to her to ask her much about it. 'Do they get on better now?' she ventured.

'Ah, kind of.' Nadia rolled her eyes. 'Anyway, it'll settle down, you'll see.' She hesitated. 'Look, Claire. No one cares that much about your podcast. I'm just letting you know that "big news" needs to be handled differently when you have an engaged friend. It's not a big ask, Claire. It's just about being sensitive to how you boast on socials, okay?'

CHAPTER 26

'I'm sorry, what?!'

Joanne was walking Claire to the studio for her inaugural recording of *Your Hot Friend*.

'It is crazy, right?' Claire was still riddled with edgy anxiety, despite having doubled up on her medication: she'd found her pill organiser when she got home last night and realised she had missed a few days. 'Or maybe I am being insensitive?'

'Are you being insensitive for just LIVING and putting up a pic or two on Insta about it? Absolutely not.'

Joanne was using the buggy to plough through the evening rush-hour pedestrian traffic that was clogging the paths around Elmfield Square. The recording studio was just up ahead, in a large warehouse covered in a brightly painted mural. Claire was massively grateful that Joanne had offered to walk her there when she finished at the Sweeneys', as Joanne's committed stream of ranting was helping her to ignore her mounting panic about how the record would go.

'Like, what is she suggesting people do?' Joanne railed. 'Just put their entire lives on hiatus while their friend is engaged?'

'No ... but ... I think she just means it's kind of not on. You know the way, like how it's poor form to get pregnant if you're a bridesmaid.'

'Is that a rule? I've never heard that.'

'It's not a rule; it's more like an accepted wisdom,' Claire informed her confidently. 'So that you're not detracting from the bride during her engagement.'

'Okay, that is outrageous. They can't honestly expect you to downplay your LIFE!'

Claire shrugged. 'I guess I just know these girls. I know what they're like.'

'It's pure madness to me.' Joanne stooped to pull a plastic bag from the bottom of the pram and produced a small, shallow non-stick frying pan coated in whitish congealed fat and scabs of black burnt flakes. She looked around, scouting for a bin. 'Mind this.' She thrust the pram at Claire.

Claire rocked the baby gently, watching with interest as Joanne tried to jam the pan into several bins, all with too-small openings.

'What is your mother doing?' she muttered at the baby.

Joanne at last came to a post box with a large mouth-like drawer for depositing letters and successfully dumped the pan in before storming back over, scowling, head high, as if challenging anyone to question what she'd just done in broad daylight.

'What the fuck, Jo? There could be CCTV. Now you've made us accessories.'

'Lol.' Joanne took the pram back and continued up the cobbles to the warehouse. 'I'm sorry, okay? As you know, I was throwing Bert's unwashed rasher pans over the back wall but I've had to stop, cos I'm afraid it'll attract attention. And rats.'

Claire didn't bother pointing out that there were considerably more witnesses out here than in Joanne's yard. Her mind was already racing away from her, to the room somewhere inside that building where she would be making her debut on *Your Hot Friend*.

'I can't believe I'm doing this.' She pulled on her lower lip. After the unexpected dressing-down from Nadia, she'd had a night of agonising whether or not it was actually the right course of action. She'd wanted Aifric to be a little jealous, not angry. But she also had to acknowledge she wanted to do this for more than just the purpose of showing her friends she had a life. She wanted to see if she'd be any good at it. She wanted to see if she and Lexi could become friends and if this opportunity would take her somewhere.

'Claire!' Aine materialised at the door to the building. She rushed forward to embrace Claire and then turned to Joanne. 'Who are you?' She narrowed her eyes, glaring from Claire to Joanne and back.

She thinks I've blabbed – which I have – but still! How dare she!

'This is my friend, Jo. She's just dropping me off.' Claire gave Joanne a squeeze in farewell, attempting to communicate to Aine through the medium of hugging that Joanne was a person who could a) be trusted and b) didn't know anything anyway. It was quite a lot to put on a hug, but Claire felt confident she'd succeeded somewhat.

'Good luck!' Joanne waved and turned to head back towards her end of town. 'Coffee Friday? Can't wait to hear the show.'

Upstairs in the little sound-proofed booth, the air felt still and expectant. Or maybe Claire was projecting. *She* felt expectant, though far from still. Even through the slight fug from the medication, her head still felt speedy and verging on unmanageable.

It's the unknown of it all, she told herself. *It's nerves. I just need to get started; I'll feel better once this first episode is done.*

Aine was bustling in and around her, arranging water and scripts in front of the two microphones. Then, standing off to one side and using what looked like a curtain cord, she lowered a vivid pink backdrop behind the chairs. '*Your Hot Friend*' glittered in diamante across it.

'The iconic OG backdrop!' Claire beamed, taking a seat. 'I haven't seen them use it in for ever.'

'Well, with the split, locations for recording are still very up in the air. As you know, in the pandemic they were using their own houses for a while. But given the state of Lexi's new place ...' Aine made a 'yikes' face. 'And I assume from how you dress, yours wouldn't be much better, so we're here for the time being.'

'Hey, gals!' Lexi stood in the doorway with iced coffees.

'Hi!' Claire didn't know whether to do kisses or just wave. It was odd being so formal when they were going to be BFFs on mic for the next sixty minutes. She hadn't really heard from Lexi since the weekend, aside from a kiss-blowing emoji response to a text she had sent asking after Lexi's dad. They'd had a genuinely fun time on Saturday – or at least Claire thought they had – but in the days since, she had been lightly agonising over certain dumb things she'd said, jokes that hadn't landed. *Do other people gets these angsty hangovers after socialising with people?* She couldn't even *think* about that awkward moment at the end when she'd misjudged the vibe and gone in for a goodbye hug that she was now pretty certain Lexi hadn't wanted ...

Ironically, an unexpected hug from Lexi just then shut down the beginnings of this spiral and Claire laughed involuntarily.

'What's so funny?' Lexi slipped into her chair and sipped her coffee.

'Oh just the bitch in my head was being a cunt. I was ...' Claire fussed with the straw of her coffee. 'Never mind ... How are you?'

'I'm grand. Bit of drama with my dad. Nothing serious.' Lexi gave a defeated little shrug. 'Getting used to living in a house full of shower-resistant boys again. Worrying about money and what the fuck I'm going to be when I grow up. It's all very nostalgic, actually. This was my life from age thirteen to twenty-three!'

'There should be a different word for nostalgia when it's like bad nostalgia,' Claire mused.

'I think that's called trauma.' Lexi grinned wryly.

'Oof, yeah,' Claire nodded. 'To be honest, I was having similar with my friends yesterday.'

'Oh yeah? How did the crafternoon go—'

'Girls.' Aine's bored voice emerged from the gloom behind the camera. 'Save it for the pod. Can I just get levels on each of your mics? Count to ten, Lexi.'

What did 'Save it for the pod' mean? Claire looked down at the script in front of her. The first section was titled 'Intro/general catch-up', followed by the instruction 'Tone: loose and conversational/free-wheeling'.

The second section was called 'Origins Story'. Here was actually some typed-up dialogue, beginning with Lexi saying, 'So we probably should give the Hotties our whole meet-cute story.' And Claire responding, 'Just please, no mention of the ridiculous outfit I was wearing.'

Claire grimaced. The script sounded kind of naff.

'Claire? When you're ready …' Aine nudged her to begin counting.

'One, two, three …'

'That's great, gals. I'm gonna hit record. And we'll just do our best. It's not going to be like the Amanda days …'

She was apparently only speaking to Lexi at this point. Claire couldn't but feel indignant. *I'm right here.*

'We'll probably have to do quite a lot of stop-starting,' Aine continued. 'I'll do what I can to make things punchier and tighter in the edit, but look, let's just give it a try …'

Later, Claire wondered if Aine's defeatist, lacklustre demeanour had been a premeditated strategy to elicit a good performance from Claire.

Whether by design or by accident, it worked spectacularly well. From the moment Aine hit record, Claire was in a flow. Having listened to *Your Hot Friend* for so many years, she had an innate sense of what would play well off Lexi. She didn't try to emulate Amanda; she knew no dynamic could be aped in that way. But she knew Lexi's humour. She found the same stuff funny – of course she did, she'd liked the podcast all these years.

'Okay, Hotties.' Lexi took the lead. 'Welcome to another episode of *Your Hot Friend: Lexi edition*! Wait, what am I saying? It's *Your Hot Friend*: *Lexi AND CLAIRE edition*! That's right: there's a new Hottie in town, though she's not new to me! Here is Claire Sheehy, my Ride or Die since forever.' Lexi clapped.

Claire waited for Lexi's applause to trail off, then deadpanned: 'A single person clapping is quite possibly the saddest sound in the world.' In the moment, it seemed like a pretty good opener to introduce her podcast persona. Not that she had much of a plan for her podcast persona, except that she just wanted to come across as less neurotic than her usual self, if that was at all possible.

She couldn't have predicted the meme-ability of that completely throwaway remark.

At home that night over chickpea curry, she gave Jamie a tentatively positive report of the podcast and he'd been somewhat encouraging.

He obviously still had reservations, though, because later, in bed, after they'd turned out the light, his voice found her in the darkness. 'Just please don't latch on to this, Claire, in a ... you know ... obsessive way.'

The plea was quiet, but it still succeeded in prodding a fear coiled in Claire's chest. Would the podcast be too much for her? *It won't. It won't,* she thought adamantly.

'Please stop worrying.' Claire turned to Jamie and ran her arm up under his tee-shirt, pulling him closer. 'It'll be a bit of fun. A nice distraction. NOT,' she added, 'an obsession.'

After the episode aired the next day, quote tweets, reshares and memes of the 'clapping' line completely overwhelmed the internet for some hours. People repackaged 'A single person clapping is quite possibly the saddest sound in the world,' using pictures of solo people applauding and pairing them with lines detailing low-grade achievements:

Me at work: Writing one single email.

Me: Ticks one solitary thing of my silly little to-do list.

Me: Finally taking a shower after two weeks of debilitating depression.

And tagged in every meme was *Your Hot Friend*'s socials and even Claire's Insta account.

She was buzzed. By ten a.m., she'd gained two thousand new followers. She recorded and deleted three separate Voicys for Jamie, who was at work. But in each one, she'd sounded a bit hyper, so instead she wrote a text:

Looks like Lexi and Claire are a hit!

Jamie had responded with a doubled-handed high-five emoji.

Lexi said she was thrilled with the response to the episode and even Aine could admit it had surpassed expectations. The figures climbed steadily throughout the day as word spread on social media and no doubt pinged from WhatsApp group to WhatsApp group that the new co-host of *Your Hot Friend* was an interesting change of pace. The Hotties were flocking to the Insta, quoting their favourite stories and anecdotes from the episode.

@heather_irv: Oh my god @KateG you have to listen to the story of their first cigarette!!! They smoked actual grass wrapped in toilet paper just like us!!!

@FionnualaMalone: I am sorry but the story about how the school uniform tights were so consistently rank and smelly that Claire put the little tree air fresheners in her shoes like insoles was so brilliant. She's so neurotic, I love her.

Following the success of the first episode with Claire going live, Lexi decided to treat herself to a night of slobbing around. When you were a professional 'hot girl' it truly was such a relief to just lean into being a minger on your night off. She listened to *Can He Be Zaddy* as she got into her fleecy pyjamas and then did a highly involved skin care routine reserved only for nights when she knew she wouldn't have to be on Insta – it involved aggressive tackling of blemishes and usually left her face a livid, decidedly unattractive red. Next she did her hair oil treatment and rounded it all off by applying dots of Sudocrem to the couple of spots she had – no doubt from the stress of her recent life-shitstorm.

In the mirror she plucked a few stray hairs from her brows, before pulling out her headphones and grabbing her laptop. She ordered a large pepperoni pizza from the local place, lamenting the fact that she'd have to go downstairs when the delivery person got there.

I should've held off on the uglifying till after I got the pizza, she thought ruefully.

She had the room to herself as Abi was out with friends but she wasn't sure she had the house to herself; she'd heard faint sounds of the TV earlier. Why did she care if any of the lads saw her? I see them when they're sweaty messes after practice.

Though Shay always looked very cute in a dishevelled way after a few hours pounding on the drums ...

She got on with plucking her brows until her phone went; it was the delivery driver saying he was outside.

'I'll be right there,' she told him.

She stood and took another look at her raw red face and quickly wiped away the Sudocrem just in case.

I'll just dash down. Shay's probably not even there ...

In the hall, she eased the front door open as soundlessly as possible – someone was definitely in the TV room but unfortunately when the driver openly recoiled at the sight of her, she couldn't help but laugh. She tried to stifle it but then when the driver asked in a worried voice: 'Are you okay, miss?' she lost it completely and was overtaken by a fit of giggles.

'I'm fine, I'm fine.' She tried to compose herself. 'Thanks a mil.' Taking the pizza, she shut the door carefully and was just starting up the stairs when a voice behind her stopped her.

'Lexi?'

Shite. She didn't need to turn around to know it was of course Shay. *The universe must hate me,* she thought darkly.

'Yeah?' She turned a little but tried to keep the full extent of her face from view, ironically with her own greasy hair curtain. 'Hey. Just having a quiet one.'

'Wanna come in and watch *The Hills: New Beginnings* with me? I have a shit ton of sweets in here! And beers. The other lads are out.'

Lexi wavered. She did want to hang out with him. They hadn't really been alone together. *I could go upstairs and change? But I don't want to look like I'm trying too hard.*

As she wavered, Shay came towards her and took her hand. 'Come on! We live in the same house but we hardly know each other. Let's hang out.'

Lexi allowed him to lead her into the living room, where he had the TV paused on Spencer Pratt's face.

'Do you wanna watch this or a movie?' He settled himself back on the couch and Lexi sat down beside him. *Thank god I got rid of the Sudocrem,* she thought with relief – although her appearance hadn't seemed to register with Shay when he looked at her. He was just smiling in his cute-boy way.

'This is cool.' Lexi passed him a slice of pizza and they munched and watched in silence for a few minutes.

'So,' Shay handed her a can of IPA. 'The first show with your new host went amazing!'

'Yes!' Lexi was shocked. 'Did you listen to it?'

'Yeah, of course,' he grinned. 'Your dynamic is perfect, great chemistry.'

'Yeah, Claire was brilliant, she really hit the ground running. She used to listen when it was me and my old host ...' she trailed off, wishing she hadn't brought it up.

'What happened there was fucked up,' he said with an endearing fierceness. 'I can't believe someone could do that to you, Lexi.' Hearing him say her name was somehow intimate and she found herself desperately wishing she didn't look so shiny and red right then. She also couldn't help wishing this was more than just a casual night in.

CHAPTER 27

On Friday morning Joanne sat in the park, unloading her morning misery on a very patient Claire, who was gasping, seething and generally validating her in all the right places. Even though the pitch meeting was over a week ago she was still raging with Bert.

'I know I've been on one about this but I just know if Bert had showed up and taken Ted like he was supposed to I could have focused more. Bert is all "oh I wanna be supportive" but then lets me down the very first time I ask him to do something.'

Claire wasn't quite joining in with Joanne in calling Bert 'a fucking living nightmare who should be put down', but Joanne could respect that. Going in too hard on friends' other halves could be dicey. Almost invariably, the couple patched things up and then the fact that you'd called the other half a bag of dicks was filed away for future reference.

'I feel like I can kind of relate to how you're feeling.' Claire was giving Ted his bottle – Joanne was amazed he was accepting it, he was still firmly a boob man. 'You've both experienced this big thing together.' She indicated Ted, content in her arms. 'But ye've come at it from completely opposite ends, know what I mean?'

'Yeah ...'

'Like it feels like you should be even closer right now, which makes the fact that you're not even harder to swallow.'

'That's smart.' And, Joanne had to admit, quite sensible – Claire had nailed something she herself had been trying to work out for weeks. Joanne picked up Sonny's beloved tennis ball and started a game of fetch.

'Me and Jamie had something similar last year and I'm still not sure we're really back to normal.'

Her face sagged ever so slightly and Joanne wondered if she should probe further, but before she could, Claire spoke again. 'You should have called me. I can always take Ted. Even if I'm at work. Norah would understand – she's really sound.'

'Thank you. And I am so sorry – I'm being so self-centred and boring!' She grinned at Claire. 'What about the response to yesterday – it's incredible!'

'Ah, thank you!' Claire looked thrilled. 'And thank you for the text yesterday! I can't believe you listened straight away – you're the best! Like literally the best – not one of the Bitch Herd have mentioned a thing. Nothing!'

Joanne grimaced. *They sound horrendous. Why does she persist with them?*

Though, in a way, maybe it wasn't that different with her and the girls ... Her mother said that friendships come back, but Joanne wasn't feeling overly optimistic. She was actually going out with them all that night but was feeling a bit meh about it. She'd known Claire less than a month and already felt Claire knew more about her day-to-day than any of her old friends.

She was pretty sure Claire felt the same.

The one part of Claire's fake friend podcast plan which didn't seem like a terrible idea was that hopefully Claire would gain confidence from the whole thing and finally jettison the other bitches for good.

'You were fantastic.' Joanne threw the tennis ball again and watched Sonny totter after it. 'Like such a natural,' she continued. 'And so funny. I couldn't get over it. Not in an offensive way – I know you're funny obviously – I wasn't surprised or anything. Just surprised that right out of the gate you seemed in your element.'

'I know! I kind of felt that. I was mega-nervous going in, but the second Aine hit "record" I got over it. It's mad how you almost forget about the mics and the audience. You're just cocooned away, just chatting.'

Joanne flashed on the desperate gaffes Claire had told her about from Amanda, the previous host. 'Yeah, but don't forget completely.'

'Don't worry, I won't.' Claire grinned and a little giddy flush spread across her cheeks.

'What?' Joanne demanded. 'What are you smiling at?'

'Nothing!' Claire laughed. 'Okay, something,' she added, giggling. 'You know how people review podcasts?'

'I guess. You know I'm not a podcast person. Audiobooks all the way.'

Claire rolled her eyes. 'They are practically the same thing. Anyway, people review podcasts on iTunes and loads of people have already put reviews up of my episode and they are amazing.' Claire beamed, her eyes glistening slightly with emotion, and Joanne felt a ripple of unease.

'That's great.' Joanne took care to keep her tone even. 'But is it a good idea to read them? You don't want them getting in your head.'

'Don't worry, I know!' Claire replied. 'I promise it was one little peek. I will not be going back for more, but I just wanted to get a general vibe and the vibe is high!'

'Oh my god, Joanne! Your nanny friend was hilarious on that podcast!' That night Erica was passing out the shots that she'd decided to kick the dinner off with.

Joanne accepted her sambuca and immediately flashed back to her pump 'n' dump puking episode the last time she'd been out with them. She hoped to god they actually got around to ordering tonight – in the old days there'd been many a night that the 'dinner' part of 'let's go for dinner' just never happened.

'Yeah, she's fab.' Joanne knocked back her drink. 'She's been saving my sanity the last month. Bert would be dead by now if I hadn't had her to vent to.'

Joanne spotted an awkward look between Erica and Aoife. *They think I'm guilt-tripping them.* Not wanting to alienate them, she quickly added, 'She's saving my sanity cos she's around like – we have the same kind of schedule. We bring the babies to the park.'

'This is the baby she pretended to have so that she could become your friend?' Aoife said.

'Well, yes and no.' Joanne rushed to defend Claire. She massively regretted texting this to their group chat. It'd been a nugget of interest from her otherwise monotonous new life as a mother, and how was she to have known that she and Claire would actually become friends? Or for that matter that Claire would be on the way to becoming a micro-celebrity just weeks later?

I need some kind of cover so Aoife or the rest don't spread it around.

'It turned out,' she continued, 'that it was a bit of a joke between Claire and her boss. Totally random.' She shrugged, knowing full well that this was not remotely a satisfactory reason for baby-faking, and quickly leapt into relating the near-murder of Bert that morning to distract them.

'I was supposed to be having a lie-in. My first in forever. And then at seven fifteen ... SEVEN FIFTEEN ... he arrived in with Ted, insisting that he was refusing the bottle and that he ... and I quote ... "only wanted his mummy". The absolute knob-jockey.'

'Prick,' Kate spat.

'What a wanker!' Aoife joined in.

'Jesus, Jo. Aoife's right.' Erica was venomous. 'How fucking useless can he be? Like the thing with guys like Bert is that ... yanno ... they're not that good-looking, so the whole point of them is that they should be super grateful to you for being with them at all. And that extends to doing shit around the house and parenting your fucking baby!'

OOF! They weren't supposed to tear him down SO readily. A bit of sympathy and some light outrage on her behalf would have been enough.

Bringing this up was a mistake, Joanne realised. Claire had been a lot more understanding; the gals, on the other hand, were going for the absolute jugular. She searched for something to say to redeem Bert in their eyes.

'Well, he's adjusting too, I guess.' Joanne could see they were unconvinced by this.

'You should leave him, Jo. Seriously,' Erica announced confidently. 'You deserve better than this half-assed effort.

Joanne couldn't decide if she was going to laugh or cry at this. 'It's not that easy. He's not just my boyfriend any more. We have a kid together. I need him to parent half my baby!' She tried to laugh as she stared down at the menu.

Over dinner, Joanne stayed quiet but was silently boiling at the injustice that this night out was being wasted with her feeling like shit. Her annoyance swung from herself to the girls to Bert – which she knew was irrational. *Bert's not even HERE and he's wrecking my buzz.*

And then suddenly Bert WAS there. The waiter had just taken the main course plates when Joanne spotted off to her left what she thought for a minute was a mirage. A deeply unwelcome mirage: Bert looking helpless, with the car seat swinging down at his side, in which Ted sat scrunched, red-faced and bawling.

Joanne shook her head in utter disbelief.

'I'm sorry, Jo,' he appealed to her once he'd arrived at the table. He was visibly sweating and having to raise his trembling voice over the crying. All the girls stared up at him. 'I think he ...' Bert raised the baby seat to indicate Ted. 'I think he needs you. I just couldn't get him to sleep. I'm sorry.'

Joanne found she couldn't respond to this, so incandescent was her rage. *How does he even have the balls to show up here right now?* she wondered.

Deciding that silence was always more terrifying than an outburst, she stood without a single word and walked past Bert and through the door of the restaurant. He hurried out after her. In the car on the way home he babbled apologies for fifteen minutes straight. Still she said nothing. Once they arrived at the house, Joanne took Ted and without a word went into the bedroom to nurse him, locking the door behind her.

CHAPTER 28

'Hey, Hotties!' It was the first Friday night in May and Lexi sat crossed-legged on the floor of her bedroom, talking into her phone. 'If you haven't caught up with me and Claire's latest episode yet you have GOT to get on it. It features an epic story of Claire being kicked by an irate sheep and a comprehensive list of our Irish celebrity crushes!'

Frantic ringing of the doorbell interrupted Lexi's spiel and she ended the Insta story on a slightly abrupt note to go and answer.

The ringing and knocking continued as she reached the door and started to fumble with the array of locks that Screaming Foetus had insisted on ever since his guitar was stolen.

'I'm opening it, I'm opening it,' Lexi yelped over the cacophony. 'Who is it?'

'It's Abi,' came her brother's voice, roaring directly through the letterbox.

'Well, can you calm down?' Lexi hissed, turning another key, and trying not to sound too irritated – he was helping her out, after all.

Abi was still doing all the Scouty handovers for her, as she had zero desire to see Jonathan, who'd dropped her a text each time a new episode with Claire landed. Podify insisted that there were still two episodes a week just as *Your Hot Friend* always had. So the latest episode with Claire was actually their fourth together and as Jonathan's most recent text said, they were 'gelling well'. Lexi'd managed to resist replying to his messages. It had been a struggle. She still got a bite of humiliation when she thought of the night of the live show, but she also couldn't entirely erase five years of history. Even with Shay in her sights, she was still occasionally capable of drifting into nostalgic reveries about her and Jonathan.

'Lexi! Let me in!' Abi blasted through the letterbox. Scouty was also starting up.

'I am, hang on! The more you shout, the more you're distracting me. Where are your keys?'

'I don't know, I'm addled. Jonathan followed me back here.'

Lexi stopped dead. 'He what?'

'He was trying to get me to tell him where we're living and when I wouldn't, he tailed me! He's parking right now.'

'Christ.' Lexi peered out the grubby little window to the side of the front door. Jonathan was staring directly at the house while doing an unbelievably shit job of parallel parking out front. She felt a pang of satisfaction; *he's trying to fight for me*. She wrenched herself back from the thought. I don't want him. Or Amanda, she reminded herself as, at last, she got the door open and Abi and Scouty tumbled in. Lexi rammed the door closed and turned round with her back to it, as if that might keep Jonathan at bay.

But do I want to see him?

Abi, appearing to read her mind, aimed a finger at her. 'Do not let him in. Seriously, Lexi, he's scum. When I got to the flat, I found him doing sponcon with Scouty. He had put a Rolex around her little paw and when it kept falling off, he started trying to put it on her little neck. Messed-up.'

'Oh my god.' Lexi knelt to cuddle the pup. 'Joint custody is so hard. This must be how Mohamed Hadid felt when Yolanda was pushing Bella and Gigi in front of the cameras all the time.'

Behind Lexi, the door started up once again. It was Jonathan.

'Lexi, I know you're there. Please talk to me. I know you're getting my messages.'

'You know I'm getting them and you know I am choosing to ignore them, so I'm not sure why you think it's a good idea to come here.'

'I just miss you so much,' came Jonathan's plaintive reply.

Lexi wavered for a moment, then was jolted by a loud slam on the door. Jonathan had thrown himself against it.

'Lexi, seriously, let me in! There's some unsavoury types coming. They look like goths. Oh my god ...' His voice was rising hysterically. 'They're coming up the path!'

'Lol,' Abi snorted. 'It's the lads. Better let them in.' He moved past Lexi and Scouty and opened the door. Jonathan, who had apparently been crouching and cowering on the other side, fell into the hall.

The whole of Slip'not stepped neatly over him, barely glancing his way. They'd been 'reconnecting' at an ayahuasca ceremony. In the nearly two months that she'd now been living there, they'd become like extra brothers. Well, not all of them. She was definitely not having brotherly feelings towards Shay. But she wasn't sure what genre of feelings he was having towards her: brotherly, friendly or ... bonery?! They'd stayed up several nights watching movies and drinking beers, which was very nice. Now, as he passed her, he found her eyes and mouthed 'You okay?', nodding his head back towards Jonathan, who was still curled on the floor, dodging the band's heavy boots.

Lexi smiled and rolled her eyes to reassure him.

When Slip'not were gone, Abi picked up Scouty, looking at Lexi with an exasperated sigh. 'I suppose you're going to hear him out then.' He stalked into the kitchen after the band, who were now squabbling over who was on tea duty and what biscuits to have.

'Lexi!' Jonathan pulled himself up to standing. He lowered his voice. 'Who are they? Are you okay? You can't stay here, Lexi. This place …' He looked around, apparently unable to find a word bad enough to describe it, then ran a hand through his hair. 'I want a tetanus shot just standing in this hallway. And Scouty can't live like this. There's probably asbestos!'

'It's perfectly fine, Jonathan.'

'Why don't you move to the new house?' He took a steadying breath. 'The sale's nearly through. We don't have to put it straight back on the market. I'll keep paying my half of the mortgage.'

Lexi's resolve tripped a little at this, but then he added, 'It does not look good to the Hotties that you're here in this grotty shithole with this coven of losers. Not very aspirational.'

Anger flared in her. 'Just leave, Jonathan.'

'Please, Lexi. I wanted to come and tell you to your face how impressed I am with your episodes! Claire was a stroke of genius. Where've you been keeping her? You guys have an amazing rapport.' He lowered his voice. 'It's much better than Amanda and Marcus St James. Early feedback from focus groups indicates that they're just a shade TOO bitchy – it's such a tricky balance.' He shook his head and pressed his lips together, as if to say *You can't please 'em all.* 'I'm sure Aine's told you that yours and Claire's episodes have been performing really well. It's a kind of cosier vibe. So, well done.' He patted her shoulder, leaving his hand to linger as he added, 'I'm so proud of you for clawing it back.'

Lexi picked up the lingering hand and moved it off her body. 'You don't get to be proud of me,' she spat, aware her voice was climbing into a much higher register than she wanted. She wanted to stay cool and collected, but she was struggling in the face of Jonathan being, well, Jonathan. The hum of the lads in the kitchen had dropped away, she noticed. They could obviously hear. Then Scouty trotted out to her, in what Lexi figured was a show of solidarity. Shay appeared right after the dog and picked her up.

'Sorry, sorry,' he muttered, cradling Scouty. 'Best she doesn't see this.'

He had started to back away when Jonathan thundered, 'What's that supposed to mean?'

'Eh …' Shay looked uncomfortable but continued quietly. 'My parents got divorced when I was a kid and they had joint custody too. And, well, I just hated seeing them arguing at handover. I was only five, but it's really stayed with me.'

'How dare you judge us!' Jonathan glowered. 'You don't know our relationship; you don't know us.'

'I know Lexi,' Shay countered.

'Oh, you do?' Jonathan looked at her. 'What is he? Your rebound?'

'Just go, Jonathan. Please. Leave us alone.'

'Oh, leave "us" alone, is it?'

'I meant me and Scout,' Lexi sighed, glancing at Shay. His expression was inscrutable.

'You trying to move in on my girlfriend? And my dog? Trying to play stepdad, is it?'

'You sound insane, man.' Shay was clearly trying not to laugh. 'I just live here.'

Lexi frowned. *He laughed that easily.*

'You should go, though,' Shay said, handing Scouty back through the kitchen door, where a pair of heavily tattooed, disembodied arms reached out and lovingly received her.

The whole of Slip'not were obviously listening and keeping abreast of the situation, no doubt ready to come to her rescue should she need.

'I'm not doing—'

Whatever Jonathan was 'not doing' was cut off by the blare of Lexi's phone. She pulled it out and saw that it was her dad.

'Abi,' she called. 'It's Dad – will you ... ?' She trailed off as Abi made his way from the kitchen back into the standoff. She handed over the phone and he answered, speaking quietly as he headed up the stairs.

Lexi opened the front door. 'Jonathan ... I'm exhausted. Please.' She indicated the front path.

'Lexi!' Abi's tone snapped her out of her exasperation and she turned to find him halfway down the stairs. 'It's Dad – he's gone to hospital. He collapsed down in the butcher's.'

A sickening queasiness flooded her and she staggered slightly as the weight of his words hit her.

'Dad collapsed? Has he been drinking? Did you talk to him?'

'No, just the nurse – she got your number from his phone. We've got to go.' He stomped down the rest of the stairs and forcibly shifted Jonathan back out the front door. 'Time for you to fuck off.'

'But … I should … should I come?' Jonathan looked at Lexi questioningly.

'So that you can continue to piss me off while I'm in a crisis?'

'Okay, okay.' He held his hands up. 'I'll take Scouty back while you're gone.'

'No,' Lexi snapped. 'Shay will mind her.' She turned around to Shay to whisper, 'Can you?' and he nodded without hesitation. Even through the terrible smog of fear descending, she felt a flicker of gratitude.

In the next moment, Abi was rushing her down the path towards her car.

'I'll drive,' he said.

'I don't have anything,' she protested. 'What if we're there for days?'

'What if we don't have days?' Abi moved to the driver's side while Lexi's heart seized at this. *He's right.* She plunged after him and into the car.

As Abi started the engine, Shay appeared at her window. 'I'll get some stuff together if you need?'

Even in her panicked state, Lexi knew she couldn't have that. 'Don't!' she yelped. His first encounter with her underwear was not going to be the grotty ones she rotated day to day.

Why are you thinking about underwear encounters right now?! her brain screamed. *And with a guy who may have no interest?*

Afraid she'd sounded weird, she added, 'I'll ask Claire to come over and get stuff if I need. But thanks.'

Without thinking, she put her hand up to the window. Shay lifted Scouty's paw to meet it on the other side. Lexi gave them a watery smile and Abi slammed the car into gear.

After the tensest hour and a half of her life, they reached the hospital. Lexi had spent most of the journey receiving an update from Flo, her dad's nurse, and in turn updating their other brothers.

Flo had told her that it was a suspected stroke. Possibly even the second one he'd suffered, the first being significantly milder – so much so it may have gone unnoticed. At the hospital, they parked in the underground carpark and hurried to the lifts.

'We should've noticed how off he was that time a few weeks ago,' Abi said, stony-faced.

'I thought he'd been drinking.' Lexi stabbed at the button to call the lift as guilt closed around her chest like a vice. 'Though,' she swallowed with difficulty, 'I know that's not a reason to not care.' She closed her eyes and shook her head. 'I should've been paying more attention.'

In a private room on the third floor of the building, her dad lay grey and unmoving.

Flo was as warm in person as she'd been on the phone. 'I promise it looks worse than it is,' she said, patting Abi's back. The granite expression he'd had in the car had cracked and he was now shaking with silent tears.

'He'd seemed off,' Lexi told her. 'But we haven't been down to see him in weeks.' She chewed the side of her finger. 'I thought he'd been a bit drunk and just not admitting it.' She didn't realise she was crying as well until Flo pulled her into a hug.

'I know your mum isn't with us any more,' Flo whispered. 'I

remember her. She was a lovely soul.'

Lexi's shoulders immediately locked at the unexpected mention of her mum. She disengaged from the hug and focused decisively on her dad's chest, which was rising and falling, seeming to keep time with the little chirps of machinery attached to his body.

'In the next couple of days, we'll know a bit more about his condition. But the good thing is he's not unconscious right now. He's just sleeping. He was conscious on arrival, too, though obviously disorientated.'

Flo left shortly after and Abi collapsed into a chair. Lexi paced, unsure of what to do.

She felt so at sea that when Amanda suddenly appeared at the door, she was immediately overcome with relief: relief that wasn't even polluted with any of the anger or hurt of recent weeks.

She rushed to Amanda and sank into her outstretched arms.

'I can't believe you're here,' Lexi said, buried in Amanda's shoulder and breathing her smell, as familiar to her as her own childhood bedroom.

'Are you okay that I am?' Amanda asked cautiously.

'Yes, I think I am,' Lexi replied. 'I think … Anyway, let's just park everything for a minute. I'm too fucking scared to be without you right now.'

'Aw, babe, it'll be okay,' Amanda intoned gently.

'I don't even know what I should be doing.'

'Talk to him,' Amanda said. 'It's good for you and for him. Tell him you're here. I'll bring you tea from the canteen.'

Lexi obeyed, taking the seat on the other side to Abi. Abi had barely seemed to notice Amanda's arrival, or else he was too upset to care.

'Dad …' She threaded her fingers through his. 'It's Lexi. I'm here.'

Please don't leave me.

Claire received Lexi's message about her dad first thing on Saturday morning and, eager to help, had immediately enlisted Jamie to drive her so she could bring clothes down to her friend.

Shay, a guy Lexi had mentioned a few times, had let her in; she'd packed a bag and then they'd driven straight to Lexi's dad's house. Lexi had told her where the spare key was hidden under a rock in the garden.

In the car, Claire had found it difficult to keep her hands off her phone. She and Jamie were listening to a podcast about plane crashes – large-scale disasters were one of their shared passions – but her Instagram notifications were buzzing every couple of seconds with likes and comments off the back of the latest episode.

'It's driving me crazy,' Jamie had eventually said. 'Don't you think you should turn them off? It can't be good for you, seeing all the comments and stuff. You'll start obsessing.'

'I'm sorry!' Claire turned her phone to silent but kept the notifications on – she was enjoying the praise too much, it was intoxicating. Seriously, whoever said external validation wasn't important clearly wasn't getting the good stuff.

> Claire's the funniest thing to happen to the internet since Wagatha Christie SRSLY.

Is Claire my best friend? Yes! Does she know it? No. #parasocialrelationship

I love Claire and Lexi, their friendship is so pure. You can tell they've been friends forever.

The itch to check the phone every time it buzzed had made the car journey seem twice as long, but at last she was standing in Lexi's living room. It was not what she'd been expecting.

The whole house was a shock. It was gloomy. Dim rooms contained worn furniture. The carpets were nearly bald in places and, while Claire was the last person to judge (during her low period, she'd skipped showers for days and days), the place was filthy. Proper stained walls, and sticky surfaces.

Jamie came in from the car and looked around. 'I guess her dad's been struggling,' he offered soberly.

'Yeah,' Claire echoed. Claire had resolved to make herself useful while she waited for Lexi to come back. She was staying over and would then head back on the bus tomorrow, ready for work on Monday. She'd find the cleaning stuff and start in the living room.

'Are you sure you're okay with me going straight back?' Jamie asked her for possibly the tenth time that morning. 'I can skip the match with the lads.'

'No, don't worry. I'll be fine. I'll be back tomorrow. Thank you for driving me.' Claire kissed him and he made his way back out to the car.

After waving him off, Claire took a moment to do a quick check of the updates on her phone.

When she next looked up, somehow an entire hour had passed.

Shite, she frowned. *Okay, just five more minutes and then I'll start cleaning.*

Another hour flowed by, as she liked comments and updated a secret new doc in her Notes app. The title of it was 'Self-Esteem – Any Goddamn Way I Can Get It'. She'd already pasted over at least fifty glowing bits of feedback and the feeling she got every time she opened it and scanned the list was one of potent pride. To paraphrase the words of yer one, Sally Field: 'They like me! They really like me!'

She'd been so giddy that last Wednesday, as they'd shopped for clothes for Claire's upcoming Ibiza trip – less than two weeks away now – Joanne had actually had to ask Claire to tone down her happiness in her presence.

'Even just for a couple of hours!' Joanne had pleaded. 'It's hard to be around happy people even when things *aren't* going to shit in your own life!'

Finally, at lunchtime, after eating the sandwich she'd brought, Claire got down to the cleaning in earnest. Lexi texted soon after to say that her dad was stable and that she and Amanda would be home at six with dinner.

Amanda? Claire frowned. *Well, I guess they're long-time friends ... And when things like this happen, maybe you just have to put differences aside ...*

That evening, when Lexi and Amanda appeared, Claire was wiping down the counter in the kitchen. The whole house smelled of Cif and wood polish.

She heard Lexi before she saw her.

'Oh. My. God.'

Lexi rounded the corner, her hands covering her mouth. 'This is wild, Claire!' She rushed over to Claire and threw her arms around her. 'I can't believe you did all this. You are the best.'

Claire laughed nervously, suddenly conscious that she probably smelled from the cleaning cardio and that she was about to meet Amanda for the first time ever.

The side door slammed, heralding Amanda's arrival, and a moment later she was standing in the doorway, two huge pizza boxes in her hands and a prickly-looking smile on her face.

'Hi, Claire,' she said, then plonked herself down on one of the newly unstickied chairs, obviously trying to broadcast how comfortable she was in Lexi's childhood home.

'This is like a slumber party,' Lexi said, appearing not to notice the edge now palpable in the room. 'An anxious one. Though they're saying Dad's definitely not as serious as they thought,' she added, pulling glasses from the cupboards and admiring how pristine they were. 'Claire, this is amazing what you've done. Seriously, thank you.'

Through dinner and a movie – Amanda insisted on *Don't Tell Mom the Babysitter's Dead*, which had apparently been a tradition since their teens – Claire tried not to feel out of things. Her rising angst was telling her that Amanda was deliberately bringing up a continuous stream of things she didn't know about: kids they'd grown up with and trips they'd taken. Another part of her was trying to quash these fears. *Lexi and Amanda are on the outs, even though they appear to have come to some sort of détente for the moment.*

At bedtime, Amanda and Claire shared the room that used to belong to Lexi's older brothers. Claire took the bottom bunk and Amanda the top – which felt pretty apt. After Lexi reiterated for the twentieth time how happy she was that they were here, she shut the door.

In the bunk above, Amanda was on her phone. Claire wished she'd brought hers in, but after several nights of lying awake devouring everything the internet had to say about her and the podcast, she'd realised she had to stop sleeping with it. One night, she'd been awake scrolling and searching her name on Twitter until five a.m. And she only noticed the time because a message had dropped in from Joanne.

I see you're online and I swear to god if you've been up all night again feverishly reading comments, I will rip that phone away from you. You're obsessed.

'So ...' Amanda said. 'How're you getting on with all that hate, Claire? It must be so hard for you ... I know you're not used to it, and you're really sensitive.'

Claire mentally stumbled at the word 'hate'. *What does she mean, 'hate'? And why does everyone say the word 'sensitive' like it's a bad thing? Better to be sensitive than a sociopath.*

She sensed she was wading into dangerous waters, but she couldn't resist. 'What hate?' she asked.

'Oh,' Amanda said airily. 'The reviews, of course! Jesus, they've been particularly harsh on you! It's a good thing, though,' she rushed to add. 'Bit of controversy. People way prefer hating people online than liking them. It'll be good for the pod.'

'I haven't seen anything like this.' Claire kept her tone even. 'Feedback's been really nice.'

Stellar, in fact, she wanted to add.

'Oh, well, the comments on socials are usually less vitriolic. You have to go to Reddit and Rants and the iTunes reviews where people are anonymous to get a real idea of what people are saying. And I'm afraid where you're concerned, it's not looking good.'

Claire could hear the smile in Amanda's voice. She felt sick. *I will not be reading them,* she vowed. 'Aine sends us the iTunes reviews every week,' she returned blandly.

'Claire! You're *such* an innocent. Aine's cherry-picking the good ones and leaving the rest out. She doesn't want to spook you and have the quality of the show decline even more.'

Claire said nothing to this, but her mind was sprinting from one horrible thought to another.

They hate me.

Lexi's going to ditch me.

The listeners know I'm a loser.

The Bitch Herd have probably seen the reviews and are laughing behind my back.

When Claire was certain Amanda was asleep, she slid out of her bed and crept back to the living room, where her phone was charging.

It was three thirty-five a.m.

Fuck. I need to get my sleeping on track. The doctors warned me about how important it is …

She pushed the thought from her head and opened up Reddit and found the *Your Hot Friend* thread.

If the first one is good, I'll know Amanda is fucking with me ...

The first one was not good.

> Claire = Absolute HeadMelt.

Or the second.

> That tights story. Just wash your fucking clothes, you scummy bitch.

Or the third.

> I get such a desperate vibe off her.

Claire sat down on the worn carpet and let the thoughts of strangers wash over her, consuming her.

When she finally managed to tear herself away and get back into bed more than an hour later, the words played like a movie on the back of her eyelids.

Pathetic. Weird. Total ick. So thirsty. Can't stand her voice. Have you seen a picture of her? Clothes are crap.

CHAPTER 29

The crack-of-dawn flight from Dublin to Ibiza was only just under three hours, but Claire was still utterly exhausted when they touched down into a bright, blue-sky day on the island. It was Friday the nineteenth of May and temperatures were already hitting the thirties. Claire's sixth episode of *Your Hot Friend* had come out the day before and on the plane, stuck in her seat for so long, the compulsion to check her notifications every five minutes had been overwhelming, dwarfing all her other thoughts and making it impossible to focus on anything Lexi was saying.

'Claire!' Lexi whispered urgently, waving her hand in front of Claire's face and startling her out of another spiral down the iTunes reviews hole that was permanently open for business in her head. 'Which one's Aifric again?' She was scanning the tops of the heads in the three rows in front of them.

'Middle of the first,' Claire muttered.

'Okay, right.' Lexi nodded. 'I'm never going to keep this straight, am I?'

During the taxi ride to the hotel, everyone grew chattier as they emerged one by one from the sleepy, early-morning travel fug.

'It is so cool to have you here,' Aifric enthused to Lexi. 'Claire told us about your dad; I'm so happy he's feeling better. By the way, we have to get a selfie at some point! Though maybe when I don't look like total shit.'

'Oh my god, you do not look like shit,' everyone crowed.

'You have never ever looked better!' Helena added, which elicited an instant glare from Nadia.

'What are you talking about, Helena?' she thundered. 'Aifric always looks this good.'

Lexi caught Claire's eye and raised her eyebrows.

Claire had filled Lexi in on all the minutiae of the Bitch Herd: the various machinations and mild, long-standing grudges between the girls. She didn't add that they had all been at least one thousand percent warmer towards her since she'd asked if she could bring Lexi to share her room. Or, indeed, since Claire's own star was on the rise. She'd apparently been forgiven for having a life. She'd noticed how every message she put in the group chat was now acknowledged by absolutely everyone. Crying laughing emojis followed even her weakest jokes and any question, no matter how banal, was pored over and given weighty consideration by all.

All her planning had worked beautifully. It was brilliant. Unless she thought too deeply about it; then her happiness could quickly become riddled with doubts. She fretted that the only reason her friends were taking an interest was Lexi. And then, once her mood was nosediving, her brain could always be counted on to layer on even more misery: the fucking iTunes reviews and the Reddit forum. She wished she'd never spoken to Amanda, who'd known full well what toxic little seeds she was sowing when she'd brought them up. Now Claire was spending more time reading the scathing comments than she was sleeping, eating and breathing combined.

When the taxi arrived at the resort, their imposing accommodation stood out among all the other sprawling white buildings that boasted pools and sea views. Palm trees flanked the sweeping marble entrance of the hotel, adorned with large gold letters announcing Hotel Torre Del Mar. It all screamed five-star luxury. As did the painfully stylish guests, drifting in and out in what Claire learned from Helena's awed whispers were Pucci sun dresses and Miu Miu sandals.

'Everyone's so rich,' Claire said to Lexi as they made their way out of the scalding midday sun to the cool marble oasis that was the lobby. 'My tramp stamp is really gonna lower the tone!'

Lexi giggled and Claire caught Aifric looking over at them. And that was the thing: every time the shitty reviews or snarky people on Reddit made fun of her and killed her vibe, Aifric or one of the others would text her to meet up, or a Hottie would stop her on the street and ask for a photo. Claire was now completely hamstrung between loving and hating the attention.

'You have to take the bad with the good,' had been Lexi's advice when Claire told her she'd gone rogue from Aine's updates and trawled the internet on her own. Though Claire was happy to note that Lexi had definitely not been impressed when she learned Amanda had told Claire about the reviews.

Claire had asked, in what she hoped were casual tones, if Amanda and Lexi had got together since the weekend Lexi's dad went to hospital. Seemingly not, though Lexi said they'd texted a little bit.

In the lobby, Nadia fielded the entire check-in and then handed out everyone's room keys, along with a copy of the weekend's itinerary.

'Girls!' In full head-girl mode, she clapped her hands together to get their full attention. 'We're eating lunch on the terrace at two, so everyone go to your rooms, have a little disco nap, freshen up and then we'll reconvene.'

'Ugh, I can never nap,' Claire muttered to Lexi. 'I don't think my brain has an off switch.'

Though she gave no sign that she'd heard Claire, Nadia immediately added, 'The nap is compulsory, by the way. I don't want anyone bailing out early on our *Pocahontas* night tonight.'

'*Pocahontas* night!' Lexi whispered to Claire, wincing. 'I'd assumed you were joking!!!'

Claire snorted. 'I wish I was. You don't know what they're capable of. Believe me it could've been worse.'

Lexi giggled quietly, which in turn sparked a fit of giggling in Claire.

Nadia glared at them but then, presumably remembering just who Lexi was, conjured up a lukewarm smile, waiting for them to compose themselves.

'Sorry, sorry!' Claire held up an apologetic hand.

'Aifric, why don't you go on up and settle in? We just have one last bit of boring logistics to cover.'

Claire steeled herself. No doubt Nadia was about to hit them with the bill. The money from the podcast and sharing the hotel room with Lexi was a massive help, but terrifyingly, this trip wasn't even the hen but the PRE-hen. This wedding wouldn't be finished bleeding her dry for months yet.

'So ...' Nadia drew them closer around her. 'This is really important. And you can't let on to Aifric that we're doing this, but I think while we are here with her, out of solidarity, we should all stick to the same pre-wedding diet she's on. I think it's really important we support her on this. Understandably, she's really worried about falling off the wagon and I think watching us splurge would just be too painful for her.'

Claire sensed Lexi looking at her – she could practically hear her thinking, *Is this for real?*

Claire turned to her and gave a very slight shrug. *Fuck's sake! Who comes to paradise, very EXPENSIVE paradise, and goes on a diet?* Claire thought mutinously as Nadia started distributing meal plans.

'It's nothing extreme. We're all just going to avoid sugar, carbs and high-sugar vegetables, and stay under the listed calorie cap per day. And the good news is that alcohol is exempt! So drink as much as you want as long as all mixers are diet. And it goes without saying absolutely no beer or cider, obviously. Or snacks in the rooms.' She concluded this little bombshell of a speech with a big smile and then bustled off to the lifts.

Lunch had been a tense affair as no one was really sure of what to order or how to calculate calories and the stress of it was nearly too much. After they'd all reluctantly declined to see the dessert menu, they'd gone out to the pool to sunbathe and, as Lexi suggested, 'Try and sleep to pass the five-hour wait till dinner time when we can eat again.'

Back in the room before dinner, Claire was adjusting her headdress in the mirror while, beside her, Lexi was trying to make hers look more boho and less culturally insensitive.

'The bride thing truly is bananas,' Claire remarked. 'The shit she has us doing.' She shook her head. 'I'm starving, like …'

'Yeah,' Lexi agreed. She looked like she was about to say something else when Claire's phone buzzed.

It was a text from Joanne.

Did you arrive safe? Where are you again? Just googled 'hating my boyfriend since baby' and according to the internet I am NOT ALONE in this.

'Poor Joanne.' Claire pasted the hotel's website into the chat. 'It feels almost cruel to show her this ...' She hit send.

'Her head's wrecked from her boyfriend and none of her friends have any kids,' Claire continued, 'so they just do not seem to be getting what life's like right now for her.'

'The three of us should go on a night out,' Lexi suggested.

'Yes! That'd be deadly. You'd like her. She's very ... blunt.'

'Yeah, I kinda gathered that when she pitched "feud merch" to Jonathan ... And look, she wasn't wrong – it sold well for us. It's so funny that she's your friend.'

Lexi, Claire spotted, was looking at her own phone and smiling slightly.

'Ooohhh, that's a Shay smile,' Claire teased her.

Lexi held up the phone to display a picture of Shay and Scouty in the park. 'I asked Abi to mind her but he says since this morning Shay is fighting him on it every step of the way. He wants to do all the walkies. And it's really helpful, to be honest, it frees Abi up to go down to Dad.'

'How is your dad doing?'

'So much better, thank god. He'll hopefully be home from hospital next week. It's such a relief. Abi and I are gonna start taking turns staying with him a bit more. I feel bad when I think about how cold I've been. I thought he was drinking but like, that's even more of a reason for me to have been spending time with him. I was just really focusing on the wrong things …' She pressed her lips together and smiled weakly. 'I'm learning, I guess.' In her hand her phone lit up.

'Ugh, Jonathan.' She made a face at the phone. 'He's complaining that I've started texting Amanda but have ignored his messages.'

'So, are you texting Amanda a lot?' Claire fiddled with her moccasins trying not to sound too edgy.

'Just a little bit. I'm still hurt, but with my dad and everything, it's just reminded me of how close we've always been. And …' Lexi spoke carefully, 'I know what she can be like … and I hate that she told you about the reviews. I've had tons of them, so has Amanda. Every podcast does. I just hate that they've got into your head when you're genuinely so good at the show.'

'Don't worry! Nothing has got into my head.'

Claire flashed on the now pages-long document of snark about her that she'd compiled on her phone. She hated reading it all, yet it was also so bizarrely moreish; she couldn't stop.

Lexi looked down at her phone again. 'It's seven, we better get down to dinner.' She sighed. 'I cannot fucking imagine what the other guests are going to make of all this.' She indicated their outfits with dismay.

'So how're the wedding preparations going?' Lexi asked as Claire chugged her vodka-soda, trying to fill up on liquids before their meagre dinners arrived.

'Everything's good,' Aifric replied, sounding strained. 'I guess I hadn't expected it to be so stressful. Even with all of your amazing help, it feels like a full-time job on top of my full-time job. There's still so much to do … the flowers, the doves, the seating chart.'

'I hear the seating chart is an emotional and logistical *minefield*,' Gillian remarked.

'Is that supposed to be helpful?' Helena laughed, inciting a swift glare from Nadia, who immediately put a protective hand over Aifric's.

'It's no laughing matter, Helena,' Nadia sniped. She turned to Aifric. 'At least your parents aren't spilt up,' she said, consolingly. 'That really complicates things. When Jeanne got married – my older sister,' she added, to fill Lexi in, 'we had to add a small marquee to the side of the main tent to annex Dad's new wife and the PT mum cheated with. Mum and Dad had a literal contract drawn up about who could attend which parts of the event.'

'That's intense.' Lexi smiled sympathetically.

Aifric sighed. 'I just thought Paul would want to be more involved.'

'I know …' Nadia looked at a loss as to how to cheer her up.

'He won't even write his own vows. He doesn't get why we don't just use the normal ones. And then he actually suggested that I just write his for him.' She shook her head as a large plate of micro-herbs and a single sliced tomato was placed in front of her.

Around them, deliciously charred meat and dishes of creamy pasta were being delivered to other tables. Deflated and hungry, Claire stared out at the pinky orange sunset and the darkening sea beyond the wall of glass that ran the length of one whole side of the dining room. What was the point of being in paradise if you couldn't even have a chip? If the micro-food had been saving her money, she might have accepted it, but the resort was all-inclusive, so she couldn't even hold on to that for comfort.

At the other end of the table, Gillian was trying to put a positive spin on Paul's apathy. 'The guys' vows are always so blaa anyway; it's probably better to just have the usual script.'

At that moment, an idea sparked in Claire. She clapped her hands with glee. '*We* should write his vows for you, Aifric. Who better to script your future husband's love than the people who know you best? No one need know!'

Claire looked at the dubious faces of her friends.

They have no imagination – it's a genius idea.

'But I kind of want him to come up with stuff himself ...' Aifric replied a little sadly.

'But Aifric, we've known you longer than Paul,' Claire pushed. She couldn't understand why none of them were getting behind what was clearly the perfect solution.

'Yeah, but he's the one she's marrying, Claire.' Helena looked down the table, apparently baffled. 'Not you.'

'This reminds me of when Aifric started going out with Dave Sullivan and Claire was all jealous and constantly trying to crash their dates!' Gillian laughed – a little sloshily, Claire noted. All this vodka with barely any mixer was a lot, especially on empty stomachs. 'Like, possessive much!' Gillian finished archly.

Claire noticed Lexi frowning slightly at this.

She doesn't get our dynamic, Claire thought defensively. *It's always hard being parachuted into a group who've known each other for ever.*

'I didn't mean it'd just be me writing it.' Claire was aware she was getting a little louder, her words rising and spilling a little. The dense wave was gathering inside her.

Stop it, Claire.

She tried to stamp it down. The marble everywhere was doing her no favours acoustics-wise. She tried to bring a little lightness into her voice to show she wasn't bothered. 'I said we'd all do it. That's all.' She picked at the label of the wine bottle and the conversation moved on to the next debate: To veil or not to veil.

By dessert – eight raspberries with a tiny thread of chocolate sauce drizzled round the plates – everyone was a bit slurry. Claire could see Gillian and Helena swaying a little as they returned from the bathroom.

'Gals ...' Helena leaned in, whispering gleefully as she took her seat. 'There is a woman in reception going absolutely batshit! It's hilarious. She's trying to come in here to the dining room, but only guests are allowed. She says her friends are already here.'

'Seriously, she seems crazy,' Gillian chimed in. 'Like fully drag-her-off-to-the-looney-bin wacko.'

Claire stiffened as Gillian proceeded to pull a 'crazy person' face.

'Gillian,' Nadia hissed, then flicked her eyes to Claire. For all Nadia's pain-in-the-hole ways, Claire was grateful for this bit of empathy. Claire hoped Lexi hadn't noticed anything, but then Gillian clapped her hands over her face, apparently mortified. 'Oh fuck, Claire!' she bellowed through parted fingers. 'I am so sorry. I didn't mean to—'

'Gillian!' Claire cut across her with no idea what to even say. She just knew she had to stop Gillian before she said anything more in front of Lexi. Lexi was looking at her with concern and Claire was starting to feel sick. The steamed cod, spinach puree and al dente green beans were all roiling in her stomach on a tide of vodka sodas.

Swallowing hard and smiling even harder, Claire resolutely changed the subject, trying to shut down her anxiety. 'Wonder who the girl's friends are?' She could hear her words – she sounded bright at least, if a little brittle – but she felt at a strange remove. Like she was acting in a play.

I feel weird.

I'm fine, I'm fine, I'm fine. The refrain spun in her head. *Be normal.*

'Hate to be them right now!' she added for good measure.

The clatter and crash of several chairs being upended at the far end of the room came as a welcome distraction ... until she saw who was at the epicentre of the destruction.

'There she is! My friend! I'm staying with her!' Joanne was pointing, while yelling in the face of a stern-looking manager. 'Claire! Claire!' she waved, while also attempting to shake off the concierges who were trying to restrain her.

'Claire! You know her?' Helena looked appalled and thrilled in equal measure.

'Well, "know her" is a stretch ... we've only been friends for a couple of months,' Claire said. Then, spotting Lexi looking over, she immediately backtracked, feeling guilty. 'But we are really good friends.'

She stood up and, all too aware that Lexi and the Bitch Herd were watching her, along with every other person in the place, she made her way across the room. The men flanking Joanne stepped back.

'Joanne, what the hell are you doing here? Oh my god, is that Ted in there?' Claire spied the bulge of the baby under Joanne's flowy beach cover-up.

'Claire! I know this'll sound crazy but ...' Joanne's eyes were darting. 'I left Bert.'

'No!'

'Yes. Maybe just for the weekend, I don't know yet. I guess I just want to give him a fucking wake-up call.'

'But how did you even get here? You said before that you couldn't afford to come.'

'I said "Fuck everything" and spent this week's child allowance on it.'

'Where're your bags?' Claire checked the floor for any sign of luggage. 'And where're your SHOES, Jo? You were wearing shoes at some point, yes?'

'I threw them at an old man in the airport taxi queue.' She looked defiant. 'And I stand by that action.'

'What's your room number, madam?' the stern manager asked Joanne, managing to make every word sound as though it had been marinated in disgust. 'Do you have a booking?'

'No,' Joanne replied. 'Can I get one?' she asked helplessly.

He consulted his tablet for a few minutes, then shook his head. 'Unfortunately, we're fully booked.' He looked at Joanne, taking in the dishevelled look, the wild-eyed expression and the baby strapped to her front. Then he turned to Claire. 'We can provide a camp bed for your room. If that works.' Claire smiled in relief until he added, 'We do have an additional guest occupancy fee of three hundred and twenty-five euros. I'll add it to your bill.'

Shite.

Joanne winced. 'I'm sorry, Claire. I'll get you back, I promise.'

Great, so I'm paying? Claire gritted her teeth.

'I'll get that bed set up.' The manager clickety-clacked in his shiny shoes out of the dining room and back over the marble to the reception.

'Can I borrow some clothes?' Joanne asked. 'I left in a hurry. I didn't want Bert to see me leaving for "a walk in the park" lugging a suitcase, yanno?'

'Jo-ANNE!' Claire stopped dead. 'He doesn't know you're here?'

Joanne shrugged. 'He might by now. He's called a few times.' She held up her phone, displaying seventeen missed calls.

'But you took Ted. This might be a crime, Joanne! Is it kidnap?'

Claire's mind reeled from one bad thing to the next. *I'm an accessory to child-theft. My friends nearly blurted out that I was a mad bitch for a stretch last year. I'm down another three hundred quid. I'm starving and now I've to share a hotel room with a baby. And what'll Lexi make of all this?*

Claire tried to hide her frenzied thoughts as she led Joanne and Ted back to the table.

'So, gals, this is Joanne! She's absconded from her marriage!'

Joanne beamed around at everyone.

She's more manic than I am. Claire felt the urge to laugh, but then her amusement withered. It was the first time she'd named the agitation that had undeniably been gaining pace in the last weeks.

'We're not actually married.' Joanne pulled a chair from another table over. 'Thank god, cos I fucking hate the guy. Marriage is for dumb bitches who don't even bother to google the success rate before signing their futures away.'

'Well, here is the lucky bride-to-be, Aifric.' Claire smiled apologetically at her friend. 'Aifric, this is Joanne.'

'What are you all wearing?' Joanne looked perplexed. 'Is that a warbonnet?' she asked Lexi.

'They said it was mandatory,' Lexi hissed.

'It's a theme night,' Nadia snapped, rising from her chair. 'Now if you don't mind, you're both detracting from Aifric.'

'Nadia!' Aifric also stood, though she stumbled tipsily, slightly knocking into her chair. She turned to Lexi. 'We're delighted to have you here – it's so fun.' She swung round to Joanne. 'And I suppose you – a person I've never met before – are a lovely surprise,' she concluded magnanimously, though the look she shot at Claire made it clear she was more than a little miffed.

In bed that night, Claire tossed and turned, kicking off the sheet, then pulling it back up. She flipped the pillow to the cooler side, then folded it around her head, trying to block out the surprisingly loud snuffles of the baby. Unfortunately the pillow couldn't block out her hurtling mind. The prevailing thought ricocheting around was the fervent wish to make it up to Aifric.

Then the perfect idea swung into focus.

She took out her phone. It was four-thirty a.m.

Fuck, I haven't been to sleep at all.

Her therapist Ella had warned her about the sleep, reminding her how important it was for her recovery. *No need to worry about it,* she told herself. *I'm in control right now which is the main thing.* She knew things were perfectly manageable. Aside from some of the anxiety, this was quite possibly the best she'd felt in months.

She started to type on her phone, but even with the light turned right down, she was afraid it was still too bright and would disturb the others. She crept out of the room and went down to the ground floor of the hotel. The whole place was dark. The sole receptionist on duty gave her a curious nod and Claire hurried on to the shadowy dining room. The sun wouldn't rise for another couple of hours but the sky was beginning to lighten. Buzzed about her idea, she set to work typing.

CHAPTER 30

'You're up early.' Lexi had just come back from her run on the beach and was passing the dining room when she noticed Claire, hunched over a table. She turned towards her, pinching her tank top to pull it slightly away from her sweaty body. 'It's already boiling out there,' she said as she reached the table. Claire was feverishly typing on her phone. 'What are you doing?'

'It's for Aifric ... well, Paul, I suppose! I wrote the vows to surprise her! And as a sort of apology for Joanne gatecrashing.'

Lexi was confused. 'But Aifric didn't seem to want that, though?'

'She said that, but it's nice, she'll like it.'

Lexi studied Claire. Her eyes were gleaming. She looked strange. Not unhappy: the very opposite, in fact. She looked very happy. Super happy. And why was that so unnerving?

'What time is it anyway?' Claire was looking around, as if she was only just noticing the clatter of the cooks in the kitchen and the sun's rays advancing across the cool tiled floor. Claire stood and Lexi noticed she was still in her pyjamas.

'It's seven a.m.,' Lexi told her.

'Cool, cool.' Claire appeared to gather herself. 'I'm going to read this to her today over breakfast,' she announced brightly.

Lexi followed Claire, wondering at her own rising unease. There was that odd moment of awkwardness at the table last night when Gillian made the remark about the crazy woman …

'Is Joanne up?' They were now at the lifts and Claire was repeatedly stabbing the button in an agitated fashion.

'She was feeding the baby when I left.' Lexi watched Claire's right hand: she was tapping her thumb against each fingertip in turn, over and over. The lift arrived and as it ascended so did Lexi's anxiety. How was Claire so amped up at seven in the morning? Had she slept at all? And how had she not picked up on the vibe about the vows at dinner last night?

When they got to their room, they found Joanne had finally answered one of Bert's calls.

'He's crying,' she told them matter-of-factly, without muting the call or even trying to cover the phone.

'Oh course I'm crying,' Bert's tiny voice protested. 'I love you. I was terrified yesterday.'

Claire quickly put on a sundress while Lexi took Ted from Joanne and motioned that they were going back down for breakfast. Joanne nodded and waved them off. Bert's sobs were still audible as they closed the door.

'Jesus. That's all very real, isn't it?' Lexi felt a flash of relief that she only had to co-parent a dog with someone else.

'Yeah,' Claire agreed as they made their way back down the hall. 'I find it hard to tell if this is a Bert and Joanne problem or a new parents in general problem.'

'Didn't you say she'd googled it and there's tons of women hating their partners after having babies? Like shouldn't she be taking that as a sign?'

'Hmm.'

Lexi could see Claire was reading through her wedding vows again. She had a very bad feeling about Claire's plan. Their whole group felt very toxic and Lexi could easily picture Claire's friends mocking her for this effort. Lexi wasn't sure what this would do to Claire, who was starting to seem more fragile by the second.

The rest of the group arrived in groggy dribs and drabs, moaning about the heat and leaping on the vodka oranges that were gamely being supplied by waiters. One girl, who Lexi was pretty sure was called Gillian, skipped the orange juice and simply dropped a Berocca directly into the vodka.

Joanne didn't appear at all, but Lexi was happy to busy herself entertaining Ted; she didn't have a whole lot to say to these girls after all.

'Okay! Gals!' Claire got up, clutching her phone and smiling. 'I have a little surprise for our bride, Aifric.' Lexi was struck again by how different this version of Claire was from the person she knew.

Everyone around the table was looking up expectantly. Lexi tensed as Claire started speaking again.

'Aifric, I am so happy to be marrying you today ...'

'Ehhh ... Whattt?!' Helena yelped.

'When we first met, I knew you were the one ... because not only are you so beautiful and smart and kind, but you're also no stranger to mooning complete strangers on a night out, as your school friends can attest to!'

'Oh, Jesus.' Helena giggled, fanning herself.

'Just like everyone who ever meets Aifric, I was instantly caught up in her charisma. Simply put, she has a light within her that illuminates a room.'

Lexi looked up to the head of the table to see what kind of reception the vows were getting from Aifric and Nadia.

Nadia looked unimpressed, while Aifric was cringing. From the look she was giving Nadia, it seemed like she was embarrassed for Claire, not herself.

After another couple of lines Aifric seemed unable to take any more. 'Claire! Can you just stop?' she interrupted. 'This is fully weird now.'

Lexi felt helpless. She should say something, but she didn't feel it was her place.

'I'm not weird,' Claire said hotly.

'No one said you WERE weird, Claire.' Nadia was impatient. 'She said you were BEING weird.'

She's not wrong, Lexi thought, feeling bad for being disloyal. These girls just brought out a different Claire: she was obviously insecure around them. Plus all the travelling and the booze was probably affecting her.

'This is a good idea,' Claire argued, talking fast. 'You said it yourself. Paul wouldn't know what to say. I know what will work.'

She's barely slept either. Lexi thought again of the strange exchange the night before, when Gillian had called Joanne crazy. 'Like fully drag-her-off-to-the-looney-bin wacko,' she had said. And then she'd apologised to Claire …

Ted was starting to squawk a little. Lexi started to jig him gently, although she really hadn't a clue what to do with him.

'Let me,' Claire said, leaning over to take the baby. With practised hands, she lay him over her shoulder. He quietened down and his silence seemed to highlight that no one had spoken in several minutes.

The baby started sucking his fist. Claire looked down at him with very un-Claire detachment.

'He's hungry.' Her voice was still a little frantic but quieter now. 'I'll take him back up and Joanne can feed him.'

Lexi watched Claire make her way through the other tables with her head down, hunched protectively over Ted. She scanned the rest of the girls at the table. Aifric and Nadia were conferring quietly. Helena was chewing her bottom lip and staring outside, while Gillian was fussing with her napkin and straightening the cutlery in front of her.

'Shouldn't someone go after her?' Lexi said. Only Nadia and Aifric even looked her way.

Aifric exhaled heavily.

Nadia sighed and leaned forward to rest her arms on the table. 'Look, Lexi. This'll probably come across as a bit harsh, but there's really no point. Claire gets like this and it's really impossible to know what to do for her.'

'Gets like what?' Lexi knew she sounded testy but she didn't care. She turned to face Aifric. 'She was trying to do something nice for you.'

'Aifric said she didn't want it,' Nadia intervened. 'But that's how Claire gets. You should know, you've known her for years as well.'

This gave Lexi a jolt; she'd completely forgotten their cover story. She needed to stay on track.

Nadia shook her head. 'She gets hyper or something. She locks onto stuff.' She turned to Aifric. 'Tell her about all the wedding favours.'

Aifric looked edgy. 'Well, she's trying to be sweet. I know she is. But the wedding favours thing is all too much. She's been making and remaking stuff. Teabags and these cute little keyrings. And any of them would've been perfect, but she keeps scrapping them and moving on to something else.'

Lexi raised a brow. 'I'm sorry, but are you complaining about her trying to handmake your wedding favours?'

'Not complaining!' Aifric sat up. 'Worried, Lexi. Have you seriously never noticed? She has these episodes and then she crashes. And I dunno, it's so fucking hard to know how to help her. She never wants to talk about ...'

Aifric stopped speaking and looked down at her lap. Lexi noticed that all the other girls were looking uneasy.

'About what?' Lexi still wasn't warming to these girls, but some of what they were describing was ringing true.

'You really don't know?' Aifric held her gaze. 'About last September? About ... ?' Aifric bowed her head and Lexi realised that she was crying.

'It's not your fault.' Nadia leaned close to her. 'It's not anyone's fault.'

Aifric looked up, her face a mask of misery. 'Maybe it wasn't then, but I'm not sure we've been handling it right since.'

'Well, it's hard, Aifric.' Gillian was defensive. 'There's no right way to act when your friend ... does that.'

Lexi felt the different elements drawing together before her. Claire's shifts in mood. Gillian's reference to the 'loony bin'. Even just the fact that Claire had wanted in on Lexi's entire loopy plan in the first place suggested there was something else going on.

'Did she hurt herself?' Lexi asked softly.

For a moment none of them spoke. Nadia closed her eyes. Helena ran a nervous hand through her hair. Gillian resumed her fiddling and pressed her lips together.

Aifric whispered: 'She went missing.'

Nadia took up the thread. 'Jamie realised. They found her in time and took her to hospital. When she was out of the woods, they transferred her to St Paul's, a psychiatric hospital, and she stayed there for a good while.'

Helena spoke up. 'To be honest, we still don't know a lot about it all. She didn't tell any of us the details; I think she didn't want us to know she was in there. And you know the way … we wouldn't all be in touch constantly. We all have our own lives.'

'Afterwards, it was impossible to know what to say,' Gillian offered. 'The few times we brought it up, she was the one to shut it down, so we figured best leave it. And then in a weird way it's easy to almost forget it happened.'

'Now I get the feeling that she thinks we didn't care, which isn't true,' Aifric insisted. 'Look, I know this will sound bad, but we were kind of afraid of her coming here in case anything happened and … well …' She gave a helpless shrug.

Lexi stood up. 'I'm gonna go up,' she said. 'I'll see you all at lunch, I guess.'

Lexi left the dining room, but instead of turning right for the lifts she turned left, walking straight out the front entrance of the hotel and into the blinding day. If what they were saying was true, this was deeply troubling. It was irresponsible not to take action and Lexi didn't want to allow anything to exacerbate things if Claire was in a fragile state. She knew what she needed to do. She felt shitty about it, but she wasn't sure there was much of a choice.

It was as much to protect Claire as it was to protect the show. It was, she knew, shallow to be concerned about the show right now, but it had to be done. Maybe things with Claire would calm down and they could resume in a couple of weeks.

Aine answered on the third ring and Lexi brought her up to speed.

'I think we just need to give Claire a bit of time,' Lexi explained. 'Like, I don't really know the extent of this thing. Her friends weren't much help and, you know, she'll probably get a bit of sleep and feel way better. But can you explain to Jonathan and Amanda? No details – just that we may need them to cover our next couple of episodes?'

Aine was as efficient and practical as ever, which was reassuring. After they hung up, Lexi ducked back into the shaded refuge of the lobby and tried not to think of the extremely tough conversation she needed to have with Claire. Not here. Not yet. They'd get through tonight and talk when they got home.

Lexi was glad she could take this one thing off Claire's plate if she was feeling a bit stressed. She worried, though, that Claire would hear 'hiatus' and think Lexi was kicking her off the show.

Reading those comments and being parachuted into online fame had obviously not been good for her. Lexi tried to soothe her mounting guilt as she made her way to the lifts.

How was I supposed to know?

She seemed grand, and clever and fun.

A little neurotic, but that played well with the audience.

How did I miss this?

Lexi stepped into the lift. She knew the answer, of course.

I was too busy pretending we were best friends and obsessing over what the Hotties would think of her to notice.

Lexi felt a kick of shame. Claire had been a good friend to her – bringing down her things and cleaning her dad's house from top to bottom. Meanwhile, Lexi hadn't even noticed that Claire was not doing well. To Lexi, it had all been transactional. All about trying to save face and show Amanda and Jonathan that she didn't need them.

She vowed now to look after Claire, whatever that might entail.

She swiped the room key and was immediately met with a strong, spiky blast of lemon.

CHAPTER 31

Claire sat on the now very cramped floor of the bedroom, trying to ignore Joanne's seemingly endless call with Bert. Her headphones were at least taking the edge off some of the cacophony. She was listening to the latest episode of the podcast. A one-star review had said that there was a story Claire told that was most definitely made up and Claire was hellbent on finding the clip. *I never say anything made up*, she railed silently as she squeezed the fifteenth lemon over a large jug. She had spent a large part of the past week grating fresh turmeric and had sustained several tiny nicks on her knuckles in the process, nicks that were now searing with the acidity of the fruit. All worth it. She couldn't wait to show Aifric the favours: handmade lemon and turmeric soaps in the shape of their initials: A&P.

She'd made the silicone moulds from a home kit. The main problem had been timing: homemade soaps needed four weeks to 'cure' before they could be used, so she needed to make ninety soaps a week for the next three weeks to hit her target of 270 A&P soaps. This week she was twenty-four shy and she was desperate to crank out a few more. She'd made sure to bring everything she'd need. Of course she hadn't counted on the fact that she and Lexi would wind up sharing the room with Joanne and a baby. Sodium hydroxide, aka lye, was a key ingredient of soap and not exactly human-friendly. It was also not allowed on planes, but she'd decanted it into a few shampoo bottles and hadn't had any issues at security. Plus she had protective goggles, gloves and a mask to handle the stuff.

'Claire!' Lexi was suddenly there in the doorway, behind her. 'Are you making … lemonade?'

'No, no, I'm just doing a few bits of wedding favour admin. Do you need the loo? Cos I'll be in there for a bit.' Claire stood and carefully took the jug of lemon juice into the bathroom, where she'd laid out all the different components of the soap.

Lexi followed her in and looked around. 'It's like a little soap production line, isn't it?'

Claire winked.

Still on the phone, Joanne gave an exasperated howl. 'You shouldn't need me to tell you that it's annoying tripping over your giant canoe shoes every few minutes. Our house is about five fucking square foot – I can't move without falling over them.'

Claire hopped up and went back into the room, mouthing 'sorry' at Joanne as she retrieved the just-boiled kettle, slipped back into the bathroom and shut the door to mute whatever Joanne's next cutting jab might be.

'I'm doing it in here because making soap around a baby … not a good idea!' Claire grinned broadly and then dialled it back a little. Lexi was looking undeniably concerned and Claire didn't want to spook her. She didn't know about the targets. 'Jo's deep into the Bert saga.'

Claire plugged up the sink and poured in the boiling water, then placed a steel bowl of olive oil in the sink to heat it.

'It's so handy that there's a kettle in the room,' Claire prattled. She was all too aware that Lexi had potentially seen too much down in the restaurant. 'Here,' she handed Lexi a mask. 'Safety first – lye can be quite corrosive.'

Next, using a small scale, she measured out a few grams of the lye crystals and dissolved them in the lemon juice. 'Now …' She picked up the sugar thermometer, sliding it carefully into the lye mix first and then into the oil. We just need them to be close in temperature,' she said brightly, swilling the oil so the hot water would heat it evenly. Another temperature check and they were ready to mix. She lifted the bowl of oil down beside the lemon mix on the floor.

Claire was acutely aware of Lexi watching her.

She's probably thinking that soap-making while on a Not Hen Weekend is a bit unusual, but I can hardly abandon it mid-batch. The soaps won't make themselves.

The fact was that this – making soaps on the hotel bathroom floor – was more relaxing to Claire than lying by a pool any day. Lying still was her nightmare scenario. Who wanted to just lie down and be smothered by the weight of their thoughts and worries? Keeping busy, busy, busy was the only way to outrun herself.

'So Lexi, you might want to step out.' She picked up the battery-operated stick blender she'd brought with her.

'What's that for?' Lexi sounded wary.

Thoughts rushed at Claire like a train approaching.

She thinks you're a weirdo. A pathetic weirdo. Everyone does.

Claire blinked and tried to calm her mind. 'To blend the oil and lye mix.'

The words came from her, but the thought that they weren't her own came up from somewhere dark within. Fear clutched at her. It was the familiar feeling of reality receding.

I'm calm, calm, calm, calm.

Ella had always told her never to say 'Don't panic' or 'Calm down' because they were negative phrases. Just to say she was calm.

I'm calm, I'm calm, I'm calm.

Claire stared at the stick blender, unable to remember if she'd answered Lexi's question.

'It's to mix the stuff, the oil and lye together ...'

'Yeah.' Lexi nodded.

Claire pulled her focus away from her fear, back to the soap mix. She donned her gloves and goggles, not bothering with the mask.

I'm already high, the fumes won't make me any higher.

She giggled a little, then caught a glimpse of herself in the mirror, tittering on the floor of a toilet in a stupid purple beach dress with her fake lifelong best friend looking on.

What if it's all fake? The idea rose like a ghost. *What if nothing's real? What if you're not real?*

The ghost idea whispered again and Claire jerked her head to her right, where it had come from. Nothing was there, but the Claire in the mirror didn't seem to move in time with her.

What if it's all fake? What if nothing's real? What if you're not real?

Claire gathered herself. *Stop this. I am real, of course I'm real. This floor is real. I can smell the lemon and Lexi's coconut shampoo. I can hear Joanne roasting Bert.*

She started to blend the soap mix and the machine's whirr was almost soothing, drowning out as it did the rest of the relentless whirring inside her. Once it was thick enough, she sprinkled the hand-grated turmeric. The methodical task was helping to bring her back down again.

'These are going to be so nice,' Lexi said, looking at the moulds arranged uniformly on the floor. She sounded oddly formal.

'Thank you.' Claire felt herself tangibly loosen: the manic spiralling up was winding back down. 'Wanna help me pour?'

'Sure.' She put on the gloves Claire passed her and held the funnel as instructed.

They poured out sixteen separate A&P soaps and then stood and admired their work.

'These are lovely, Claire.' Lexi hugged her. 'Aifric will be really happy.'

Claire cleared away the materials and then listened at the door. Joanne and Bert had moved on to money.

She turned back to Lexi. 'Maybe we just live in here now?'

Lexi looked around at the soaps. 'They smell like the soaps all my aunties used to get me for Christmas as a teenager.'

'True,' Claire nodded. 'Such a crushing present. It was like, "Here, you're at the most awkward stage of your life. You have a beard of spots and I don't know how else to tell you this, but you reek as well".'

Lexi laughed.

'Wait, we should save this for the pod.' Claire grinned. 'I feel like our every conversation should be recorded, just in case!'

'Well …' Lexi looked unhappy. 'That's kind of where it all went wrong with me and Amanda, Claire. It was like our friendship didn't exist except for the pod. I don't want that to happen to us.'

Claire felt a bounce of joy at this. They'd only been playing at being best friends for such a short while, but Lexi really had started to feel like a real friend.

Just then the bathroom door was wrenched open and Joanne ordered them out.

'Sorry, sorry.' Claire assumed she needed the loo. 'Just be careful of the soaps. They're setting—'

'On the bed, you two,' Joanne barked. 'Sit there and listen to what this absolute tit of a man just said to me.' She held the phone out to them.

Claire and Lexi sat frozen at the end of Claire's bed.

'Joanne …' Bert's reasonable tone came from the phone. 'I'm not telling your friends our business—'

'He said … HE SAID …' Joanne was nearing a falsetto pitch. 'That I have just spent hundreds on my little – and I QUOTE! – tantrum. My flying off to Ibiza without telling anyone is apparently "irresponsible" and "SELFISH". "SELFISH", girlos.'

She pulled the phone back to hiss at it. 'I should be charging you RENT for the nine months your child spent in my body. And I should be suing you for loss of income since your fucking no-show to babysit your own goddamn child cost me a job.'

'Please come home, Jo. I love you and I miss you.'

'That is just so typical of you to say,' Joanne shouted. 'Stop being so nice. I just spent all our money to go to Ibiza for like a day.'

'Jo, please. There's no one like you. I'll make it up to you. I'll build a small shed to store all my big canoe shoes. I'll stop using your towel—'

'Wait. What the fuck? You're using my towels?' Joanne turned to Claire and Lexi. 'After a shower, he dries his undercarriage so thoroughly it resembles a medical procedure.'

'It's to avoid chafe,' Bert cried plaintively as Joanne ended the call.

'He's a nightmare. He does the towel-drying in the kitchen, like. The same room where we cook and eat.' She shivered. 'He also uses the coconut oil we cook with to slather all over his beard. AND he double-dips.'

'Horrific.' Claire grimaced. 'I have no words, Jo ...'

'Look, I know I'm not leaving him. I need the manpower to raise Ted. I've made my bed and now I have to lie in it, even though it contains all thirty feet of Bert's loose scrotum skin ... Hey!' She looked towards the bathroom. 'What is that smell?'

'It's my soap project. Just figured I'd get a few done while we're here!' Claire spotted a look pass between Lexi and Joanne and was seized by defensiveness. 'Hey ...' She pointed at Joanne. 'You just ran away from home at twenty-eight years old. Making soaps in a hotel bathroom is the least of it.'

She hopped up off the bed. 'I'm just going to check on them; might be able to get another batch out this afternoon.'

She bustled back into the bathroom, relieved to be away from them for a few minutes. That's something no one ever tells you about being mental: it's such hard work trying to seem Not Mental in front of other people.

Anyway, I'm not mental. I am calm, I am calm, I am calm. Everything's real, nothing looks weird. Calm, calm, calm.

CHAPTER 32

Once Claire was back in the bathroom, Lexi hustled a perplexed-looking Joanne out onto the little terrace adjoining their bedroom. She needed to tell her what the others had said.

'What is it?' I need to put Ted down for his sleep.

'Joanne, we have to talk about Claire ...'

'Claire? Why?'

'You don't think it's at all odd that she has some kind of wholesome Mormon-housewife-meets-*Breaking-Bad* situation going on in the bathroom?'

'Well ...' Joanne frowned. 'She's really into her crafting.'

Lexi pushed on: 'At breakfast she seemed really off. You weren't there. She's been off since we got here yesterday.'

'Okay.' Joanne was at last focused. 'I totally know what you're saying, but Lexi, it's these girls – the Bitch Herd – they have her on edge the whole time. I know I've only known Claire a bit longer than you, but believe me, these girls are kinda shit. Yer one Aifric is taking the absolute piss with these favours—'

Lexi cut across her. 'But that's the thing. I talked to them this morning and they have a totally different take. They say that it's Claire getting manic about the favours.'

'Okay ... I think every single person involved here is waaaaay too invested in these party favours.' Joanne laughed, but Lexi cut her off again.

'It's not about the favours, it's about Claire being overly obsessed with them. She brought lye in her carry-on. I'm pretty sure it's not even legal to travel with something like that—'

'What's lye?'

'It's a corrosive chemical.' Lexi's frustration was growing by the second. 'I think we need to get Claire home. Aifric and them were saying there was an incident last year. Claire had some kind of episode. I know something's wrong. She's barely slept. We need to get in touch with Jamie. I think we need to get flights booked.'

At last, Joanne seemed to be metabolising the information. 'Shit, poor Claire. Okay. What will we do? What'll we say is happening? If she thinks we're trying to bundle her off ...'

'Yeah ...' Lexi pondered. 'If I say it's my dad I'm pretty sure she'll come.'

Joanne nodded.

Lexi steered Joanne back into the room and, keeping her voice low, told her to book flights for that evening. 'Better get Claire a check-in bag for her soaps.' Then she gave Joanne her card, having gleaned from their very public row that she and Bert didn't have much cash. 'I'm gonna get Jamie's contact details from Aifric and have him meet us at the airport.'

Down by the pool, Aifric, Nadia, Gillian and Helena were on the cocktails. Lexi had the strong urge to give them each a slap, or at the very least push them off their loungers.

'Gals. I don't think Claire's doing great,' she said bluntly. 'Me and Joanne think we should get her home.'

'Oh …' Aifric was the first to react, looking dismayed but, Lexi could see, also awkward.

She thinks I'm going to try and rope them in. As if they'd be any fucking use.

Then Lexi felt bad for her catty thoughts: she didn't know the first thing about what had gone on last year. She didn't know what it would be like to have a friend go missing, disappear into hospital and come out different. She thought about Amanda for a moment. Lexi had been cautiously replying to her texts but still keeping her at arm's length, even though she'd come to be with her when her dad was in hospital. Amanda was such a robust person, but maybe they were the very ones who would one day collapse.

Lexi refocused. This was about Claire.

The girls on the loungers seemed to be conferring. Lexi spoke up to make herself heard.

'I need Jamie's number. I want to make sure he's there when we land.'

'Oh-kay.' The girls simultaneously reached for their phones and started to scroll, flicking nervous glances among themselves. One by one they each shook their heads.

'So sorry, don't have it.'

'It used to be on my old phone.'

'Well, what's his last name?' Lexi tried not to sound so tetchy.

'It's … ehhh … is it MacCabe? McLaren?'

'Look, never mind.' Lexi turned to leave. She was nearly at the door that led back into the reception when she realised Aifric had come after her.

'I know how this looks, Lexi. I have felt so bad about Claire. I wanted to be a good friend to her, but everything last year … scared me. I didn't want to say the wrong thing and then because I didn't want to say the wrong thing, I just kept not saying anything at all. And I get it … that's worse. And then … I dunno … I feel like this whole engagement thing has weirdly exacerbated things. I didn't ask her to be a bridesmaid. Because I was afraid it was too much for her. And I asked her to come to my family dress-shopping day, cos she is like family and I knew the others wouldn't have come. But I think she took it the wrong way. I feel so fucking bad, like you have no idea. We …' Aifric averted her eyes. 'We started a side WhatsApp group because we all felt like how can you post frivolous bullshit in a group chat with your friend who's just tried to kill themselves?'

'Look, Aifric.' Lexi checked the time on her phone impatiently. 'I don't know you at all. But I know this: I am not the person you should be saying all this to.'

Lexi hurried back inside and placed a call to her room from reception.

Joanne answered on the first ring.

'How's it all going?' Lexi asked urgently.

'Great,' Joanne replied tightly. 'Claire's just boxing up some of the moulds.'

'Okay, yes or no answers,' Lexi instructed. 'Did you get the seven thirty flight booked?'

'Yes.'

'Have you told Claire?'

'No.'

'Okay, no probs. I'll be right up. Let me handle the excuses.'

Lexi asked the lady at reception to arrange their taxi. Then she found a quiet corner and texted Aine:

I presume we have Claire's home address? Can you send it to me please? Asap-urgent.

Next, she called Abi but the phone rang and rang with no answer. She bit her lip. She had Shay's number. He'd been so good about helping with Scouty ...

Shay answered after a few rings. He was shouting over the thump and thud of Slip'not practice.

'Hang on, Lexi, hang on. Just going outside.'

In a matter of minutes she explained what she needed.

He didn't hesitate. 'I'm in, of course I am. Text me the address when you have it and I'll get down there. I'll wait for this guy ... Jamie? Don't worry about a thing. And your friend, Claire? She'll be okay. Just hold her and reassure her. Tell her you know how it feels.'

'But I don't,' Lexi whispered. Being in damage control for the last hour had helped her not to feel fully how afraid she was for Claire. How scared she was that she and *Your Hot Friend* had somehow caused this.

'You do, Lex.' Shay was quiet but firm. 'What about when your mum died? You felt alone, right? Cut off from everyone. The world felt alien and you were scared that nothing would ever feel right again? That's what Claire's got. At least a bit. And the best thing, the only thing, that we can do is tell her she's not alone and we've got her and we know better days are coming. Just keep her safe and be her friend.'

'Thank you, Shay. I ...' Lexi wished he was here with her, but even just his calm voice more than a thousand miles away was soothing. 'Shay, I ... You're such a good person. A good friend.'

'Of course, my pal. Now send me the address the second you have it.'

When she hung up, she was relieved to see Aine had replied. She immediately forwarded the address to Shay.

Upstairs, Lexi found Joanne playing with Ted, who was flushed from his nap and full of giggles.

Claire, meanwhile, was bouncing back and forth from the bathroom to her boxes of soaps, muttering: 'I might get another batch done, if I could get some more lemons.'

'Claire?' Lexi tried to intercept her, but Claire managed to slide past and back into the bathroom.

'I wonder if the kitchen staff would cough up a few lemons?' she mused. 'I only need like fifteen.'

Joanne shrugged helplessly from the bed as she settled Ted gently over her arm to feed. 'She's been *hyper*,' she mouthed.

Joanne doesn't even have to whisper, Lexi thought, her anxiety spiking. *Claire seems barely aware that we're here.*

'Claire, you can't make more soaps,' Lexi pleaded. 'We won't get them home.'

Through the bathroom door, Lexi spotted Claire looking at herself in the mirror.

'I could ship them.'

She saw Claire take in her own reflection and Lexi felt a sudden terrible dread.

We're in a foreign country. My friend needs help. I don't know what to do. And there's a fucking baby here.

'Claire, Claire? Please listen to me.'

Claire came back out of the bathroom. Lexi finally had her attention: the edge in her voice must have broken through to her.

'What's wrong?' Claire's eyes appeared to clear momentarily.

'Look, I'm so sorry, but I think we need to cut this trip short. My dad is really not doing too well.' Lexi subtly crossed her fingers; she did not like calling on her dad's precarious health for an excuse but could think of nothing else. 'I really need you with me, Claire. I'm so scared for him.'

'Shit.' To Lexi's relief, Claire appeared to focus. 'Is Abi with him?'

'Yeah, but I need to go, please. I've booked our flights. The taxi will be here in forty minutes.'

'Okay, okay.' Claire's lucidity appeared to retreat once more. Her eyes were beginning to dart again and her head was occasionally swerving over her shoulder, as though she could hear or see something they couldn't. 'But what about Aifric?' she said. 'This whole weekend is—'

'I told Aifric,' Lexi interjected. 'She totally understands. She knows I need you right now.' The lies were disturbing to Lexi. How would Claire feel if she found out it had been a ruse ... ?

Lexi pushed off the guilt. She was too worried about the flight. Claire could barely stand still to focus on what Lexi was telling her: how would she last three hours in the confined cabin of a plane?

'Claire?' Joanne had finished feeding and was speaking gently. 'Let's get your stuff packed. These soaps look gorge, by the way. Amazing job.'

After some stilted goodbyes to Aifric and the other girls, they were at last in the taxi hurtling across the island. As they made the turn for the airport, Lexi got Shay's text saying he and Jamie were together and that Jamie would be at the airport when the plane landed late that night.

Relief flooded Lexi, though she could see Shay was still typing:

Jamie is beside himself. He's crying and extremely panicked. He told me some stuff about Claire and I think he wants to talk to you. He doesn't want you to leave Claire alone, even for a minute. I explained about Claire's friend, Joanne, being there. So will you ring when you get a moment away from the others? Claire's parents will also be there when you land. Don't worry, Lex, you can handle this.

Lexi dashed off a response to say they were nearly at the airport and looked over at Joanne. Thankfully, Claire was in the front passenger seat, talking to the driver. A lot. Her words were spilling out on top of one another and Lexi started to have the very real worry that she might not be allowed to board the plane. She was doing a very convincing impression of someone very high on drugs.

Lexi passed her phone across the baby seat where Ted dozed, so that Joanne could read the text from Shay. She rubbed her forehead tensely.

Lexi took the phone back and typed out a text for Joanne to read:

Can you handle checking in and I'll call Jamie?

Joanne read the message and gave an apprehensive nod.

CHAPTER 33

Claire couldn't understand why Joanne was insisting on doing everything at the check-in desk.

'Here, let me take Ted, at least – he's sweating in the sling, Jo.'

Claire carefully disentangled the baby from the stretchy fabric and started to bounce him. She was feeling a little bouncy herself.

Am I up to speed with my meds? I am, I am.

She shifted the baby to her hip and rummaged in her little crossbody bag where her passport and phone were. The pill sorter was right there and it confirmed that she had indeed taken her Saturday dose.

There! I can remember shit. I am self-caring the shit out of myself right now. Of course I'm up to speed.

And speed was the word: she was feeling relentlessly speedy. It was annoying not to be getting a start on a new batch of soaps while she was feeling so energised. She thought of the plane ride ahead and felt a swoop of panic. All that sitting still.

'Maybe I'm a little too up,' she wondered.

'What?' Joanne looked up from weighing the check-in bag.

Shit! Claire hadn't meant to say that aloud.

'Nothing,' she blurted. 'I didn't say anything, nothing important like.' The words were coming out fast, tripping over one another, and Claire could see from Joanne's face that she was concerned. She changed the subject. 'Where's Lexi?'

Slow the fuck down. Calm. Calm. Calm. Claire tapped her fingertips against the pad of her thumb as she carefully and deliberately thought each word, not even hearing Joanne's answer.

'This is done.' Joanne heaved Lexi's suitcase back off the scale. 'I'll take Ted – could you carry this to the bag drop?' She pointed to the desk just across the concourse.

Claire started to pull the bag through the crowd, trying to ignore the tumorous unease growing inside her. The people looked strange, as though they were far away: small and unreal, like figures in a doll's house. The clang and chatter of the busy airport was fading in and out, as though something was messing with the volume dial in her head.

A voice close to her ear said, 'Claire!' and she spun around. No one was there. She looked left and right but the strangers were going about their business, ignoring her. Maybe ignoring her a little too much, like they were trying to *pretend* not to see her.

She threw off the weird thought, turning to look back through the path she'd cut from Joanne and Ted. Lexi had returned from the loos; she could see her deep in conversation with Joanne.

They're talking about me.

No they're not.

It's you, Claire. The voice was scathing. *What's there to talk about?*

Claire shook her head and regrouped. She became aware again of the bag's handle in her hand and turned to take the last few steps to the conveyor belt that sucked the luggage back into the hidden part of the building.

Her mind seized on the word 'hidden'.

Hidden things, hidden watching, hidden places. It really is the most hideous word: Hidden. Hidden. There is a hidden place inside me.

The thoughts didn't feel like her own. The thoughts rose from the hidden place like a fatal vapour and spread through her. They came from an interloper. They felt dangerous.

'Claire!'

She didn't look up. She didn't want to look up and find there was no one there again.

'Claire?'

Another voice, and a hand slipping into hers. Claire looked up and took in Joanne's questioning face.

'Are you okay?' Joanne sounded too serious, completely unlike herself. 'We have to go through security now.'

Lexi joined them and Claire felt as though a look, or maybe a hidden message wrapped in a look, had passed between them.

'I'm not going through.' She pulled her hand away from Joanne's. 'I don't have anything to hide.'

'No, of course not. It's just ... you know ... not optional!' Joanne laughed tentatively and Claire felt the strange shroud of dread from moments before dissipating.

'Sorry.' She raised a smile for them. 'What am I like?' She pretended to giggle.

What am I like? she repeated silently.

What am I like? What am I like?

It's happening again. It's not. It's not.

It's happening again. I'll never be free of this.

She focused on keeping step with Joanne and Lexi. Her looping thoughts marched relentlessly along with her.

They have to be noticing how weird I'm being. I cannot let them see this.

Security mercifully passed without incident, but as they waited at the gate to board their plane, Claire felt as though she was just barely keeping a lid on herself. Around her, the uncanny doll's house reality had returned. The people were moving mechanically. Their features looked both too perfect and utterly strange. Stupid, boring, normal things felt hellish all of a sudden. Reality was rippling and Claire wasn't sure she could trust this world with its sinister people and hidden places.

Claire tapped her fingertips as the line moved forward. Lexi and Joanne were speaking to her gently, but Claire couldn't separate the words from the roar in her head. The mouth of the airport gate yawned before them and Claire fought the urge to run.

I can't stay in this airport with its doll people and the hidden places.

You are the hidden place.

The idea shimmered, and her resolve to be normal shattered.

'Shut up,' she cried.

Then suddenly she felt her whole body enveloped in warmth.

'Claire, it's okay. It's okay.'

She looked up to see a face as familiar as her own. Aifric.

Behind her friend, she could see Joanne and Lexi and the rest of the Bitch Herd conferring. They were suddenly there. Why?

An irate man behind Claire accused them of skipping the queue.

'Jaysus,' Joanne snapped at him. 'The plane's not going anywhere until we're all on. Have a word with yourself, will you? I've a colicky baby here and I swear to god one more word out of you and I will make it my business to sit beside you and have this baby scream into your sad prick face for the next three hours.'

Claire laughed, in spite of the weirdness of suddenly everyone being there. Why were they leaving early too? She had the impression of being flanked by her friends as the queue moved forward and they presented their boarding cards. Joanne handed Claire's over for her.

Claire was carried along the tide of passengers and her head, so nightmarish just seconds before, felt clear and calm. Better than calm; she felt buoyed. The Bitch Herd must have decided to leave because she was.

On the plane, Claire took her seat between Lexi and Aifric.

She smiled at Aifric. 'So, what are you guys doing here?'

'Oh, we'd had our fun and we, yanno ...' Aifric replied. 'We wanted to come home all together.'

Claire nodded emphatically. 'It's actually so great you're here. I took a ton of shots of the new wedding favours. I actually got some done while we were on the trip.'

As the cabin crew walked down the aisle, checking the overhead bins were secure, Claire took out her phone and brought up her camera roll to show Aifric.

'Madam?' A flight attendant interrupted her. 'Please switch your phone off during take-off.'

'I'm litch showing my friend a couple of pictures,' Claire answered hotly.

'She will, she will,' Lexi piped up beside her.

'I will not.' Claire spoke louder. 'It's on AIRPLANE MODE. This guy's just on a power trip!'

'Excuse me?' The guy was glowering at her now, but Claire was feeling more than able for him.

'I said you're just throwing your weight around for no fucking reason.'

'Claire!' Lexi looked shocked. 'The guy's just trying to do his job. Leave it.'

Claire switched her phone off. 'Unbelievable. You can't do anything these days. It's such a kind of nanny state vibe. Lol – says me, a nanny!'

She knew she was talking a lot again but she couldn't seem to staunch the flow of words. 'I actually can't wait to get home to Lila and Frankie and Sonny. That's the thing about all your jobs,' she told Aifric. 'You might think they're like grown-up proper jobs, but the rewards of working with kids ... I can't even explain it. Though now that the soap-making is going so well, I should really be thinking about scaling up. They cost next to nothing to make: the mark-up would be amazing.'

When the seatbelt light pinged off, Joanne, who was directly behind Claire, spotted her squeezing past Lexi out into the aisle and striding up to the front of the plane, clutching her backpack.

Joanne leaned forward and hissed through the gap in the seats, taking care not to squish Ted who was sitting in her lap wearing a seatbelt extender. 'Where does she think she's going?'

'I have no fucking idea, but the mood she's in, I wouldn't be surprised if she isn't trying to take over flying the damn thing.' Lexi looked shattered, understandably. Claire had been talking non-stop since they'd taken their seats. She'd also been bizarrely tetchy with a perfectly nice flight attendant.

'I've never seen her like this.' Joanne shifted in her seat to try and see where Claire had gone.

'Shit, she's fully up there pestering yer man again.' Joanne unbuckled herself and Ted and handed the baby to Helena, even though she could count the number of words she'd said to this woman so far on this cursed trip. 'Mind him,' she instructed, standing up. 'If he kicks off, give him your tit. He won't know the difference – he's a man, not very discerning.'

Joanne stopped at Lexi's elbow and crouched down to whisper to Lexi and Aifric, who Joanne had to give props to for showing up, albeit at the last minute. From everything she'd witnessed that day, she could see there was more to the Bitch Herd than just out and out cuntiness. Though there were definitely very real degrees of it.

'I think we should go explain to the flight attendants about Claire,' Joanne told Lexi. 'And I'll kind of shadow her. Like Jamie said, make sure she's not alone.'

'But what do we tell them?' Lexi looked distraught. 'That she's what … agitated? A bit unwell?'

Joanne sighed, flummoxed.

What the hell should we say? That she's talking like she's on speed? That she's full of ideas to get into soap-making full-time?

At that moment, Aifric looked across, twisting her hands in her lap. 'Tell them she's bipolar,' she said. 'Tell them she's having a mild manic episode.' She paused. 'Tell them she's never hurt anyone while manic, but that she needs to be … kept safe.'

'This is mild?' Lexi gestured up the aisle to where Claire was now pacing up and down outside the loo.

Aifric's eyes were filled with tears. 'You don't understand. This isn't the bad bit. It's what comes next that's bad ... the crash after the high. That's when she's most in danger.'

Claire was now addressing the door of the bathroom in a loud singsong.

'Come out, come out, whoever you are!!!'

'Oh Christ.' Lexi undid her belt and joined Joanne in the aisle. 'How long is left in this flight?'

Aifric consulted her phone. 'At least two and a half hours. Maybe the flight staff might have a sedative?' She too began to slide out from her seat. 'We'll all go. Lexi, you stick with Claire.' Aifric pointed towards the front of the plane. 'Joanne and I will try and explain to the cabin crew at the back so that Claire doesn't hear. We don't want her getting more worked up; it wouldn't—'

Just then the sound of Claire's shrill, indignant voice rang out over the din of the cabin: 'I am not harassing anyone. This passenger was abusing the facilities and going way over her allotted time.'

'Jesus,' Joanne muttered, giving Lexi a push in the small of her back. She watched as Lexi hurried forward, dodging the elbows and outstretched legs of other passengers. But Claire ducked out of sight into the toilet and the folding door closed behind her just as Lexi reached it. As the male flight attendant watched on sternly, Lexi began knocking frantically on the door.

Joanne turned to go to the back of the plane, only to find the drinks trolley was now making its slow trudge towards them.

'Feck,' Aifric muttered beside her.

'C'mon.' Joanne pulled her up to the front of the cabin. 'May as well start by explaining to this guy: he looks on the verge of exploding.'

By the time they got there, pushing around other passengers who were by now ambling towards the loos themselves, Claire had opened the door to Lexi. By some miracle they both fitted in there with the door locked behind them.

Joanne reached the flight attendant first. She read his badge and then gasped out his name. 'Stephan! … My friend and I have to talk to you urgently.'

'I'm sorry, miss, I have a situation here.'

'We know. It's about that,' Joanne pleaded. 'Our friend, the one with the red hair—'

'The one who was just screaming at me?' He was unimpressed. 'I have to tell you that being disruptive and under the influence on a plane is a punishable offence. If this continues, we may have to re-route and have her removed.'

'No, please, listen,' Joanne implored him. 'She's not on anything. She's sick.'

Aifric jumped in. 'It's not her fault. She's bipolar and she's having a manic episode. Do you know what that is?'

'I do.' Stephan took them both in, presumably in an attempt to assess the veracity of their story.

'She's never hurt anyone when she's had mania,' Aifric continued. Joanne could see that she was on the verge of tears. 'And her partner and parents will be at Dublin airport when we arrive, but we have to get her there. Please don't re-route. It'll make things worse.'

Beyond the toilet door, Joanne could hear Lexi pleading with Claire: 'You can't make them here. They wouldn't set and you don't have that stuff … the lye … or whatever.'

Joanne steeled herself. 'Go back to your seat,' she told Aifric. 'Check on Ted, will you?' She noted the three passengers lined up behind them, waiting to use the toilet.

Ugh, fuck. And I'd been worried that taking a flight with a baby was gonna be the hard bit.

'Look ...' She turned back to Stephan. 'You guys must have some kind of sedative on board – something? Anything? For these kinds of situations ...'

Stephan shook his head. 'I'm sorry. We can't give so much as a paracetamol to a passenger. It's a strict policy.'

More of Claire's strident words could be heard from inside the toilet cubicle. 'If you didn't want to help, Lexi, then why are you even in here? Let me get on with it.'

Lexi's reply was too quiet to catch the words but the placatory tone was obvious.

Joanne felt as though they were all being pulled towards disaster. 'If you can't sedate people, what would you normally do?' she asked Stephan.

He pulled open one of the many metal drawers behind him and lifted out a fistful of cable ties. 'We restrain people,' he said, apologetically.

Joanne's panic surged. *Oh god, we can't do that to her.*

As though he'd heard her thoughts, Stephan put them back and shut the drawer.

'Hey! Excuse me,' a woman in the toilet queue piped up. 'I wasn't listening in, but I couldn't help but ...' She shrugged, a little sheepishly. 'I have some medication from my doctor – I'm a nervous flyer. Would that help at all?'

'I think it would ...' Joanne was hopeful but nervous. She

definitely didn't want to do anything that might make Claire worse.

Seeing her hesitate, Stephan picked up the in-flight comms phone. 'Hello, this is your cabin crew here with a request. There is absolutely no need to be alarmed, but could there possibly be a doctor on board who could help with a small query? If so, please can you make your way to the front of the plane?'

'Thank you,' Joanne said.

Stephan smiled for the first time. 'Don't worry. We'll get her home.'

'I'll head down to the other loos,' one of the men queuing said. 'Good luck with your friend.'

'I'll get my medication,' the nervous flyer said, following him.

Joanne scanned the cabin to see if any doctor was coming their way. Miraculously, a tall man was making his way forward from the back of the plane.

'Hello, ehm … you rang? I'm William.' He was about forty, with a very capable, reassuring vibe.

Joanne quickly explained the situation and the offer of medication the woman had made.

'So would that work?' she asked desperately.

'Sure … It'd be beneficial to subdue some of her symptoms.' William pondered. 'I'm loath to advise, given I haven't taken her history, or indeed even seen her …'

'Look, no one's gonna sue you.' Joanne tried to keep her testiness in check. 'We just need to get her … I dunno … home? Out of the fucking toilet?'

Banging from inside the toilet interrupted the debate.

Joanne made a snap decision. 'Look, doctor, don't stress. I'm making the call. She needs to calm down fast.' She turned to Stephan. 'I take it you can open this door from the outside, right?'

'Yes.' He nodded.

'Here you go.' The nervous flyer was back with a small blue pill bottle. 'I usually take two.'

'Okay.' Joanne shook out two tiny white pills. 'Stephan, will you open the door?'

She stepped aside as he lifted the small sign that read 'Lavatory' and twisted a catch.

Lexi tumbled straight out. Claire was visible just beyond, sitting on the toilet lid and juicing a lemon into a small container. It was such an unexpected sight that Joanne nearly laughed, though one look at Lexi's ashen face made clear that twenty minutes in a confined space with a manic Claire had not been a good experience.

'Miss,' Stephan spoke in a calm and measured voice, 'I'm going to have to ask you to leave the lavatory now and refrain from ... juicing fruit.'

Claire stood abruptly, spilling the juice but seeming not to care in the slightest. 'I'm actually really sick of you, to be honest,' she said, still holding half a lemon.

'Claire ...' Lexi sounded exhausted, but Claire just batted her off and crossed the tiny distance between her and Stephan.

Joanne felt like she was watching a possession. Claire's movements were jerky and she didn't even sound like herself.

'I should be reporting you for harassing a passenger,' she said, her face flinching strangely.

Joanne had to do something. The fact that they were moving at 500 miles an hour, 32,000 feet above the earth, was making this whole situation feel even more volatile.

Joanne stood in front of Claire, blocking Stephan. 'Claire, can you please take these?' She held out the pills. 'They'll make you feel better.'

'Nope!' Claire swiped Joanne's hand away cheerily. 'I feel fucking amazing. You have no idea! If only this guy …' she leaned round to Stephan, 'would stop wrecking my head.'

Joanne dropped to the floor to find the pills. *Hell. That was fucking stupid,* she thought, retrieving them.

Unfortunately, at that exact moment, Claire took another step towards Stephan and threw the half-squeezed lemon at his head.

Joanne jumped up and put her arms around Claire, just as Lexi did at the exact same time. They hugged her tightly as she writhed and raged and Stephan pulled out the cable ties.

'I'm sorry, girls. I don't have a choice.' With the help of Dr William, they restrained Claire's hands and feet and sat her in a vacant row at the front of the plane. Claire was shouting 'This is bullshit' over and over, and Lexi had started to cry.

Joanne swallowed back her grief at seeing Claire so tormented. 'Lexi,' she whispered urgently. 'Hold her mouth open.'

Claire barely seemed to be listening to them: she just made guttural noises as Lexi prised her jaw down.

Joanne dropped the pills in and then they both held Claire's head, ensuring she couldn't spit them back out.

When they were sure that she'd swallowed, they both sat back, panting.

Claire still pulling against the cable ties. 'I was just trying to get ahead on some of my soap bits. It's not a crime to bring a lemon on a flight; I did fucking check, you know. And these hurt …' She held up her wrists. 'They're digging into my skin.'

Joanne looked around the plane. She'd never been on a flight that seemed so silent. Nobody was talking to their seatmates. In the moment, Joanne hadn't thought about it, but they must have made quite a spectacle. Mercifully, Claire seemed at last to be running out of steam somewhat.

'I have to go check on Ted.' Joanne made her way back to her seat, suddenly aware that she'd been gone for ages. Ted was awake but seemed happy being cooed at by Helena and Gillian. Nadia and Aifric both looked like they'd been crying.

'How is she doing?' Aifric asked quietly.

'It's bad.' Joanne shook her head. 'They had to restrain her.'

Nadia closed her eyes. 'I feel so shit – I was such a bitch to her a few weeks ago, at the crafternoon. How did I not see this coming? She'd been talking on and on about the podcast and I just thought it was taking over Aifric's day, you know?'

'Right.' Joanne wasn't in the mood to console any of these girls. 'Look … Stephan, the flight attendant, has arranged for me, Lexi and Claire to be escorted to Arrivals. He's not filing a report or anything; it's just to get her home faster. Can you guys collect her suitcase? Drop it off to her later?'

They both nodded emphatically and Joanne returned to her original seat to gather up her things and bring Ted up to the front row, where Claire was now sedated.

Lexi was rubbing Claire's arms and softly whispering in her ear. 'You're safe, Claire, we've got you. You're safe, we love you.'

It sounded like a spell she was trying to cast. Claire barely seemed to be hearing her, but Lexi's murmurs were soothing to Joanne, at least, as the plane began to descend and she tried to digest the strange events of the last few hours.

When the plane landed, Claire's cable ties were cut and Lexi, Claire, Joanne and Ted were led off the plane before all the other passengers. Joanne cradled Ted close and debated how to get home: between their panicked departure and the tense wait at the airport in Ibiza, she hadn't even managed to text Bert to say they were coming back.

Bert. Suddenly she craved seeing him with every ounce of her being. Solid, reassuring Bert. All she wanted was to be home and folded safely in his arms.

After passport control, a small cart sped them through the airport and they were delivered to the arrival gate in under fifteen minutes. There they were greeted by a motley crew of friends and loved ones, many of whom Joanne only recognised from Lexi's and Claire's descriptions. There, unmistakably, was Shay, in a black tee-shirt boasting a skull, with snakes coming out of the eye sockets. He had Lexi's tiny dog, Scout, on a leash. Jamie, Joanne recognised from pictures Claire had shown her. He looked distraught as he came forward to take Claire's hands. Even muted by the pills, Claire shook Jamie off. Next, an older man and woman who could only be Claire's parents hurried to her, and Claire retreated a little.

'Why are you all here?' Claire's words, though sluggish, carried an accusatory tone. She turned to Joanne and Lexi, eyes narrowing. 'Is this your doing?'

'No!' Lexi yelped. 'They're all just meeting us off the plane, that's all.'

'Well ... why is SHE here, then?' Claire pointed at a girl who Joanne now realised was none other than Amanda, Lexi's ex-best friend.

Why IS she here? Joanne wondered.

Claire rounded on Lexi. 'You're trying to ditch me.'

'I'm not, Claire. I swear. I think you just need to rest, okay? Go with Jamie and your folks. We'll talk later.'

'I fucking know what you're doing.' Claire's words were strangled. Her rage seemed to be fighting the narcotic restraints and Joanne fought back tears. It was so, so heart-breaking to see her like this.

Jamie and her parents formed a protective cocoon around Claire and headed for the taxi rank just outside the exit.

'What IS Amanda doing here?' Joanne shot at Lexi. 'Did you seriously think that would be a good idea?'

'I have no clue why or how she is here,' Lexi replied quietly, as Shay came over with Scout straining against her leash. Amanda continued to hang back, Joanne noted.

'Hello, my darling.' Lexi knelt and buried her face in the dog's fur while Joanne introduced herself to Shay.

'I'm Joanne.' She tried to smile through her tears.

'I figured.' He smiled back kindly. 'You guys have really been in it.' Shay knelt down to Lexi and rubbed her arms. 'You did good, pal.' He looked back up at Joanne. 'You both did.' Then he stood and peeked in at Ted, nestled in the sling. 'And this little guy! He's gorgeous. Congratulations!' He twinkled at Joanne. 'You're brave, taking a baby on a hen do.'

'Jesus.' Joanne rolled her eyes. 'It wasn't actually even the hen-do; it was some kind of pre-hen do! Nightmare. Anyway, Ted's a pretty good baby.'

'Yah.' Shay nodded. 'Bert's been telling me.'

'Bert?' Joanne was flummoxed. 'How'd you know Bert?'

'I just met him!' Shay replied brightly. 'He's gone for snacks. Says breastfeeding makes women really hungry.'

'Jo! Jo!' Just then Bert appeared, standing a head taller than everyone else in Arrivals and cradling about fifteen different snack options, many of which he proceeded to drop as he jogged towards her. 'Oh my god, oh my god.' He pulled her into a one-armed hug, crushing bananas, nut bars and packets of Monster Munch between them. 'I am so happy you're here. You must be exhausted. Hang on, I got you a trolley.'

Bert was frantic: he flung the various snacks at Shay and veered off to a waiting trolley that he had padded with several jackets and cushions from their house.

'Sit down, sit.'

'You brought cushions from home?' Joanne laughed. 'But how did you know I was coming?' She looked from Bert to Shay. 'Did you ...? How would you ...?'

'Actually ...' Amanda came forward and spoke for the first time. 'I contacted Bert. Aine had been in touch to rejig the record schedule so I knew a little of what was going on over there and, well, Aine had mentioned about you and the baby – I figured you'd need him here. And Bert is one of our longest-running patrons, so I just had to search our records to find his email. So yeah ... it might be a breach of GDPR ... I don't really know ...'

'And you came?' Lexi was looking at Amanda, her face impassive.

'I just wanted to make sure you were alright.' Amanda was solemn. 'I did not want to make Claire feel worse or paranoid, I swear.'

Lexi sighed. 'I don't think anything could make her feel worse, to be honest.'

CHAPTER 34

For a few painless seconds when she woke up, the morning after arriving back from Ibiza, Claire didn't remember anything. Then, in a great frenzied rush, shattered, disjointed memories assailed her and her whole body, from her heart to her fingertips, flooded with dread.

Reading vows at the table. Pouring the soaps. Squeezing lemons. A man looking at her. Lexi pleading with her in a tiny room. Some of the fragments, on the face of it, seemed benign. Bouncing the baby. Laughing. But every different shred of memory had the same taint of shame. And what about the gaps between the memories? What had she done? What had she said?

It was disorientating to find that she was in her own bed. How? She gazed around the room. No Jamie beside her. The curtains were drawn against the morning sun. What day was it? Her mind moved like molasses. It was Sunday. They had come back from Ibiza early. Why?

Me?

The dread inside swelled.

Me.

It was me.

She slid her hands under the pillows to search out her phone, but her wrists protested. The skin, she realised, was tender.

She slowly raised her arms to examine the livid red lines circling her wrists where the skin had torn. The cable ties. They'd tied her up.

Correction: They'd had to tie her up. The knowledge thudded in her chest. Dread ran in her veins, filling every cell and organ and cavity of her. Then she felt herself sink and sink and sink as more shame poured over her.

It had happened again. An episode.

It's been less than a year. Why, why, why? she intoned silently.

Why had it happened again? She'd been taking her meds.

This will never leave me. I will never outrun it. I will never be right.

They had said it themselves at the hospital last year. Bipolar can't be cured but it can be managed. As if that was somehow supposed to be comforting.

What did I say? What did I do? What must Lexi and Joanne and all of them think?

Oddly those thoughts, though disturbing, didn't seem urgent. Not any more.

Oh great! I've entered the Nothing Matters Now stage of the cycle.

Claire felt like she had last September. Vacant. Like a passive observer. Just tired of life and ready to leave it behind. If it wasn't so devastating, she mused, it'd almost be impressive how quickly depression could ransack you. One day life seemed full, packed full of possibilities and ideas, ideas, ideas and energy, energy, energy. And the next it was as bare and desolate as a beach at low tide.

'Claire?' Jamie's voice was far away. 'Are you awake? We need to talk. We need to make a plan.'

I made a plan, Claire answered silently.

She'd made it on that unremarkable Tuesday last September. She hadn't filled her pockets with heavy stones. And she hadn't jumped in; she hadn't wanted to be dramatic. She had walked in from the beach. She had walked in in her heaviest boots.

In the weeks before that, life had been intoxicating. She had felt drunk on her own sense of invincibility. She'd abandoned virtually everything else in her life in favour of running. She'd fallen into a fervour of running: logging the kilometres in an app that began to feel like a master she was serving. Jamie had complained about it. He'd wanted to eat dinner together and watch TV, but Claire had an unbearable speediness as though her mind and her blood and everything in her body was racing all the time. Only running seemed to subdue her.

Claire had begun to run at night. She ran in dark parks and down dodgy streets. She felt at home in the night, deliberately seeking out places with few streetlamps.

In the daytime, she'd bounded through the hours. She crocheted six jumpers in a matter of weeks. She began ambitious projects with Lila and Frankie – she wanted to do a mural on the ceiling of their bedroom. Claire had felt the exhilarating feeling of flying that comes when riding a galloping horse.

When Jamie tentatively began to question if Claire was taking too much on, Claire had lashed out with a venom that surprised even herself.

She'd begun to talk and talk and talk. It hadn't mattered that no one was picking up the phone; she'd talked endlessly into Voicys.

Some she'd sent, some she hadn't; she could barely remember. Any time Aifric or one of the girls did reply, Claire had felt frustrated with their sluggish responses. Why didn't they understand the urgency of the crochet charity project she wanted to get off the ground? All they'd wanted to say to her was that she was maybe taking on too much, getting ahead of herself.

Then, one day, as Claire spiralled up and up while walking to the Sweeneys' house, thinking about how she would start her very own Montessori in the autumn, Norah had rung her and suggested that instead of coming to work, Claire should meet her for coffee. It had actually seemed reasonable to Claire: she'd figured Norah would want to invest in the Montessori, neglecting to remember that Norah didn't know anything about it. Over that coffee, Norah had asked Claire to take a break from work.

Claire could barely remember much of the next four days: only what she'd been told later. She'd rampaged through her life, it seemed. Sending bridge-burning messages to her friends. Screaming at Jamie that she hated him. Anyone who had tried to get her to stop or calm down was an enemy. And then, enemies had seemed to be everywhere, and as she slept less and less the thoughts had begun to veer into strange terrain. Benign things had seemed nightmarish. And then her thoughts seemed to telescope into a despairing myopia and there seemed to be only one escape from the roar of her head

Bipolar is such a little fucker, she thought now. *It slams you up and slams you down.*

Now came more scattershot memories of the last few days in Ibiza. *Every one of those girls must hate me.* Amanda had been at the airport. Lexi would get back with her; of course she would. *I should feel sad but instead I feel so blank and why is that worse?*

The key in the bedroom door turned. Jamie had locked her in the night before, Claire realised. Of course he had: he'd probably been afraid that Claire would do something.

'Claire?' Jamie stood at the door. 'How are you?' He quickly shook his head. 'Stupid question.' He took a breath and with tears welling, tried again. 'Are you okay?'

'Yeah.' Claire wanted him to go. 'I'm feeling better.' She tried to push a little life into the words. 'More myself,' she added.

'That's really good.' Jamie heaved in a shaky breath. 'Your mum and dad are on their way back. They were here last night, but you mightn't remember ...'

'Yeah ...' Claire said vaguely. She remembered their hushed conversation. A row, really. Probably blaming each other for how she'd turned out.

I'm the reason they're miserable ... I'm the reason they broke up.

She gazed at Jamie.

I'm the reason he's miserable ... I'm a burden.

'I'm going to make you toast.' Jamie concentrated on the floor, choosing his words like a person picking their way across stones on a beach.

'Yeah ...' Claire replied.

The thought floated to the surface of her ocean: *Weird to think I'll never eat again. Weird to not care.*

'The hospital says you can come to the admissions office from twelve today.'

Weird that Jamie is making plans; I'm never going to see noon again.

'It's really lucky that they have a bed.' Jamie tried to smile, but despite the effort he still looked desolate.

'Not a lot of crazies in May,' Claire murmured.

Weird that this might be the last thing I say to him.

'I'm gonna get you toast. And sausages.'

'Mmmmm.'

Claire pushed herself upright and swung her legs off the bed. She was happy to see that someone, Jamie probably, had put a glass of water on her bedside locker last night. So thoughtful of him. And helpful. Though that would torture him later.

Can't think about that. It's a shitty, shitty thing, but it has to be done. I can't do this any more. I want to be normal. But this will never go away.

It can be managed, they'd said. But the medication hadn't worked. And talking – the bit that she'd done – hadn't worked.

She dug around under her bed for her laptop and her box of soap supplies.

Jamie will have the toast ready soon, but sausages take longer. Good.

Weird how normal killing yourself can feel when you finally get down to it.

She opened Google and typed her question.

Claire had googled methods enough times to know that the first search result was always a local charity website urging you to 'reach out'.

After a bit of a scroll, she found her answer. She already had the weighing scales ready to go. No need for her gloves or protective goggles this time!

Those fucking wedding favours are doing me a favour now.

She took down the glass of water and slowly stirred in the substance.

'Claire?' Jamie knocked and Claire quickly popped the laptop and soap kit under the bed. When Jamie looked around the door, she was simply holding a glass of water.

I could drink this down while he watches me and he wouldn't realise.

The cruelty of the thought penetrated the terrible emptiness and for a split second, grief leaked in.

Poor Jamie. He fell in love with the wrong person.

'Will you come and eat? Then we should pack your bag. Your parents are going to drive you – they're on their way back here now. I'd like to say goodbye here if that's okay.' His entire face looked raw from crying. Jamie had done the intake last time, when Claire had resisted it. 'It's all going to be okay.'

'Yeah …' Claire held the glass, hyperaware of the sliver of matter between her fingers and the liquid.

'I've just had a text from Joanne. Some of the others want to see you off too,' Jamie added.

'What do you mean?'

'Joanne and Lexi, Claire. That's okay, right? They really want to see you.'

'Oh … I … really?' Another stab of grief pierced the blankness.

They still want to see me …

No they don't. They feel guilty. They feel obliged to be nice.

'Come and eat, Claire.'

Jamie came around the side of the bed. Claire quickly put the glass back on the bedside table and allowed him to pull her close.

'Claire, I love you so much. We all do. It's going to be okay.'

CHAPTER 35

The morning after getting back from Ibiza, Lexi stared out the window of the kitchen, trying not to break down. She swallowed back the sobs, but the tears were coming anyway.

The night before, she'd been touched to discover that Screaming Foetus had driven Shay and Scouty to the airport. And now he was at the stove frying up eggs for them all. Amanda had wound up crashing on the couch. They hadn't talked much, but Lexi was glad she was there.

Now Amanda joined Lexi at the kitchen table, followed by a rumpled-looking Shay.

'Lexi, darlin'?'

Screaming Foetus came over to her, obviously noticing her attempts to stem her tears. 'Let it all out. You don't need to pretend with us. You must be exhausted. You're probably in shock.'

'I …' Lexi heaved out a sob. 'I'm sorry. I just …'

Beside her, Amanda slid her arm around Lexi, waiting for her to say what she needed to say.

'On the plane, I was in the toilet with Claire for a really long time and … I've just never seen anything like that.' Lexi folded herself against Amanda. 'She was talking so fast that it barely seemed like words. And every now and then she'd stop and it felt like she was looking at something that wasn't there. Oh fuck ...' Lexi buried her face into Amanda's shoulder. 'A couple of times I realised she wasn't even speaking to me but herself ... in the mirror. It was the scariest thing I've ever seen.'

The others were silent, giving her space to vent. Amanda rubbed Lexi's back. On Lexi's other side, Shay found her hand and held on tightly.

'Imagine ...' Lexi looked up at them. 'It was so scary to watch. Imagine how it must feel to experience it. To have your mind turn on you like that.'

Amanda nodded. 'Poor Claire.'

Lexi looked at her curiously. There wasn't a trace of the cynical note so often present in Amanda's words.

'Before I got on the plane, Jamie and I spoke and he told me that Claire tried to end her life last September. She walked into the sea off Whitesands beach. It was a really quiet morning – grey and cold with no one around. If it hadn't been for this weird current that took her some of the way down towards the harbour ... She was spotted by a man walking on the pier and he called for help. She was way out – he only saw her because he'd been bird-watching and had binoculars.'

'Fuck,' breathed Shay.

'Jamie's still convinced it's his fault. That he should've seen it coming. But he said Claire had seemed to be in really good form. Frantic, but good!'

'That's the bitch that is bipolar,' Screaming Foetus said heavily, putting slices of bread in the toaster. 'You can look the best you've ever fucking been, you can feel the best you've ever been, and then suddenly you're in freefall. I have it too.' He paused. 'It's gonna be okay, Lexi. Claire will get better and better at managing it. And the more people around you who know you have it, the safer you are. Now you and Joanne know. And we know. And we'll all help her. When the time is right, I'd be happy to talk to her about it. I'm the poster boy for bipolar! Dubious brag, I know!'

'He is!' Shay said proudly. 'Six hundred and twenty-four days since his last hospitalisation.' They both laughed.

Lexi could not imagine ever laughing with Claire about this.

'Listen.' Shay turned back to her. 'What's the plan? I can order a taxi? Unfortunately Abi took your car down to your dad's. He didn't think you'd be back so soon.'

'I want to go to Claire's, but Jamie's just texted to say Claire doesn't want us to come. He says she's totally crashed. They're bringing her into the hospital she stayed in before. I don't know what to do. Abi texted to say Dad's coming home from hospital and I really need to help.' Her WhatsApp buzzed. 'Joanne's just texted. She says she's going to see Claire off regardless.'

'Okay.' Screaming Foetus spoke up. 'My advice? As a certified Mad Bastard myself … is go to her, Lexi. Claire mightn't even remember everything that's gone on yet. But she will try to isolate right now and she needs to know that you're there for her no matter what.'

'I can go down to your dad's, Lex, and then you come when you can,' Shay said. 'I'll take Scout with me.'

'Yeah.' Amanda nodded. 'I'll go with Shay – I can drive us.'

'You really don't have to … It's too much.'

'Lexi, please let me do this for you,' Amanda implored.

'Okay,' Shay said, seeing Lexi's uncertainty, took charge. 'That's sorted. We drop Lexi to Claire's before they take her to the hospital, then me, Amanda and Scout will go down to your dad and you follow when you can. Okay?'

'Okay. Thank you.' Lexi wished she had the energy to express her full gratitude to all of them.

'We could even record an episode when you get there,' Amanda said brightly.

'Amanda—'

'That was a joke,' Amanda added quickly. 'I'm not that much of a cynical bitch.' She looked over at Lexi. 'Or ... well ... I'm trying to be less of a cynical bitch these days.'

'That's good to hear,' Lexi said quietly.

It was hard even to think about *Your Hot Friend*. The podcast had to have exacerbated things for Claire. What the hell would Lexi do now about the stupid show? She felt bad for allowing such a superficial worry to creep in at this moment, but she couldn't help it. Amanda and Marcus St James would do the shows for now, as agreed. But then what? And what about Jonathan? The house? The maelstrom of worries flooded in.

'Lexi ...' Amanda had obviously seen it all play out across her face. 'Everything will work out. Don't worry, bébé.'

Hearing Amanda's trademark endearment helped lift her anxiety somewhat. So much had happened in such a short space of time, but here was Amanda at her side. The Amanda who'd betrayed her was also the Amanda who'd stood with her every day since they met as kids. Why are all the sad songs and sad movies about couples breaking up? Friendship breakups were far more painful and complex.

CHAPTER 36

Joanne paced up and down on the path outside Claire's building: she'd told Lexi she'd wait and they'd go in together. Lexi had texted to say her dad was coming home from hospital that afternoon and Joanne felt bad for her. The timing was awful.

Finally, a battered jeep pulled up and Lexi hopped out.

'Are you okay?' Joanne called. 'Life is spit-roasting you today.'

'I'm shite, but fine,' Lexi replied, looking shattered. 'Amanda, Shay and Scouty are driving down to Hereford now and I'll get the bus down after this.'

'Ugh, the bus. That's bleak.' They started into the apartment lobby. 'I'll come with you if you'd like? For company,' Joanne offered.

'What about Ted? And Bert?'

'Bert said I should do what I need to do.'

When they'd got out of the airport and were alone together, Joanne had expected Bert to be angry, but instead he'd been apologetic. 'He said that for me to skip the country, he must've really been pissing me off.'

'Right.' Lexi laughed a little.

'Sorry, this is weird.' Joanne grinned as they got into the lift. 'You barely know me. Basically, I've just been absolutely on one since having the baby. I felt like our relationship had totally changed and he was … I dunno … it felt like nothing had changed for him. I guess we have to do some, yanno, work on ourselves.' Joanne mimed vomming just as the lift arrived at Claire's floor.

'Okay.' Joanne turned to Lexi. 'Head in the game. Jamie said Claire's like holed up in their room, insisting she doesn't need to go into hospital.' Joanne checked her watch. 'Her folks are gonna be here in an hour, so we need to help Jamie get her packed and stuff.'

Jamie opened the door the second they knocked and ushered them into the kitchenette of the cramped apartment. He was frying sausages and buttering toast and all the while whispering urgently.

'Claire's in the bedroom – she's safe, she's safe. Those windows don't open. It's something we actually had WANTED the landlord to fix.' He grimaced.

Lexi looked petrified at Jamie's words. 'Do you actually think she's in danger of doing something?'

'I don't know.' He swiped tears away with the back of his hand. 'I don't fucking know. These sausages are taking ages.'

Poor Jamie was clearly addled. Joanne cleared her throat. She was nervous but knew she needed to ask. 'Jamie? Is her medication in there?'

'No!' I took it all out last night when we got her into bed. 'There's nothing in there she could use. I even took her …' Jamie's voice cracked and Lexi, clearly needing something to do, took the pan of sausages and started turning them.

'Took her what?' Fear gripped Joanne like a vice.

'Her craft stuff: her needles and wool and everything.'

'Oh Jesus,' Joanne moaned softly. *Poor Claire.* She felt the sting of guilt as she remembered all the times she'd jokingly called her mad for the fake friend plan. How her words must have hurt.

Then another thought bloomed, like a terrible flower. *That stuff for the soaps. The stuff Claire'd needed gloves and goggles for. Surely she hadn't brought her whole supply to Ibiza?*

'Jamie.' Joanne pulled at his arm urgently. 'Did you take the soap stuff away?'

'The soap stuff?' He looked bewildered.

Joanne didn't wait to explain. She shot across the living room to the door that had to be the bedroom.

'Claire?' She knocked.

'Don't come in —' Claire's voice was flat and quiet.

She felt Lexi and Jamie behind her as she pushed the door open.

Claire was sitting on the edge of the bed, holding a glass of water. She was completely still, no longer agitated. No longer herself at all. She looked up at them but there was nothing in her eyes: they were vacant as a doll's.

'Babe.' Jamie slipped past Joanne and crouched at Claire's knees. Joanne and Lexi hung back while he spoke gently to her. 'The girls have come to see you off. They really wanted to see you before you go into the hospital for a bit.'

'I'm not going to the hospital.' Claire's voice was lifeless.

Claire raised the glass; her movements were mechanical. Jamie was rubbing Claire's legs. 'Sweetie, you know—'

The chill of fear blowing through Joanne grew fiercer.

Something bad is going on here.

And then Joanne knew.

She flung herself at Claire and slapped the glass from her hands. She'd had just enough wherewithal to push the glass away from them all and it landed on the floor, just off the edge of the bed. They watched as the liquid immediately appeared to start eating away at the carpet.

'Oh my god!' Jamie screamed, pulling Claire away. 'What the fuck, what the fuck.'

Joanne took Claire's other arm and with Jamie's help managed to get Claire out of the room and onto the sofa. Joanne examined her for burns, while Lexi leaned into the bedroom to check the spill.

'Careful,' Joanne shouted. 'It's really toxic. Google 'lye spill'. I'm not even sure we're supposed to put water on it. Claire! That stuff would've turned your insides into soup.' Joanne started tearing up. 'You could've ended up on a feeding tube for the rest of your life.'

Jamie was crying and holding Claire, who simply said, somewhat dispassionately, 'I suppose I might go to the hospital after all.'

By the time Claire's parents arrived, the lye had been neutralised. Lexi and Jamie had packed a bag while Joanne helped Claire to get dressed. Claire was saying very little, bar the odd brittle quip.

'Oh, what shall I wear to go to the bin!? I can't remember if there's a dress code.' She'd looked at the jeans Joanne was holding out to her. 'Definitely no belts allowed!'

Joanne couldn't believe how close they had come to disaster. That stuff wouldn't have killed Claire but it could've had life-changing consquences when it came to her health.

'Claire?' Joanne whispered. 'Please promise you will never, ever, ever do that again.'

Claire looked down, but Joanne caught a glimpse of shame marring her features. Oddly, this gave Joanne strange hope. At least Claire was feeling *something*. Though shame was the last thing Joanne wanted Claire to feel – her illness was not her fault.

'Claire?' Joanne picked up the bag she'd left by the door earlier. 'I figured you wouldn't be allowed knitting needles in the hospital, so I brought you this.' She placed the package on Claire's lap.

'Ah,' Claire murmured, examining it. 'A friendship bracelet kit.'

She looked up at Joanne and again Joanne felt she caught a glimpse of the real Claire behind the doll eyes.

'Is this you telling me we're still BFFs?' Claire said, a little sarcastically.

'Yes, it is, you little fucker,' Joanne shouted, startling everyone. She pulled Claire to her feet and hugged her. Lexi joined them.

'We love you so much, Claire,' Lexi whispered. 'We'll be in to see you as much as we're allowed to!'

They drew apart.

'Look,' Joanne said solemnly. 'Fact is, Claire, I just saved your life, so I own your ass, okay? The repayment for life-saving is free babysitting for ever, alright?'

She continued to search for her friend behind the strange mask.

'I know I haven't known you that long, but friendship isn't always about that.' Joanne kept talking, willing her words to penetrate. 'I love you, you know.'

Lexi stepped forward. Her phone, Joanne could see, was open to WhatsApp. 'Hey. This is going to sound weird, especially as I've known Joanne for approximately thirty hours, but can we start a group chat?'

Claire's eyes still had that faraway look, but she nodded slowly.

'Great.' Lexi handed the phone to Joanne. 'Stick your number in there.'

'What'll we call it?' Joanne grinned, tapping in her number. 'Claire? You must do the ceremonial naming, please.'

Claire finally met her eyes and spoke, her voice flat. 'Call it … Claire's in the bin.'

'As in … loony bin?' Lexi looked troubled.

'Uh-huh.' Claire was looking beyond them again.

'I'm vetoing that,' Joanne announced firmly, stepping to her right to try and intercept Claire's gaze, to bring Claire back to them. 'Lexi, call it Operation Friend Escalation.'

Lexi complied, though she looked a little confused.

'It's our first in-joke,' Joanne said, relieved at last to see a smile tired smile break over Claire's face. Joanne turned to Lexi. 'We'll explain it to you on our first visit to the hospital. It's how me and Claire met.'

A knock on the door announced the arrival of Marian and David. Joanne and Lexi went to open the door, and all four of them waited out in the hall to give Jamie and Claire some space to say goodbye.

'So you're Joanne.' Marian hugged her. 'And you're Lexi.' She turned and hugged her too. 'Thank you so, so much for getting her home safely.'

Joanne caught Lexi's eye and a tacit understanding passed between them that they would not be telling Claire's parents just how close they'd all come to tragedy only an hour before. Joanne could still barely believe it herself. How could someone go into freefall so suddenly? It was terrifying.

I need to find out everything I can about bipolar. So does Lexi. And the Bitch Herd, if they're going to step up to the plate.

Marian was talking at hyper-speed about how she and David had made a mistake, splitting up when Claire was still so fragile. Joanne glanced at the short man standing just apart from his wife and felt an acute pang of sadness. In contrast to his wife's frenetic worrying, he simply stood, tears coursing down his cheeks.

Marian turned to him and her words stopped dead.

'Oh, David,' she said, pulling him to her.

He spoke softly, but his words broke Joanne's heart. 'Our baby girl.'

Joanne thought of Bert and Ted, mercifully safe. *But we can't keep our babies safe for ever.* It was the scariest thought she'd ever had.

Behind the apartment door, Jamie's sobs seemed to go on and on, until at last Claire appeared, looking as numb as ever. David stepped forward and folded her to him. Jamie appeared, trying to compose himself and carrying the bag.

The journey in the lift down was silent. Out on the street, David, Marian and Claire got into the car and Joanne, Lexi and Jamie waved them off.

'Jamie?' Lexi looked at a loss. 'Is there anything we can do?'

He shook his head. 'Don't worry – you've done so much. Some of my friends are on the way. I just can't believe I didn't see how bad she was getting ...'

'It's not your fault.' Joanne rushed to reassure him. 'We all thought she was fine. Better than fine – she was so excited about the podcast and everything.'

'I didn't prepare her for how full-on the podcast would be.' Lexi was shaking her head slowly. 'I'm so sorry, Jamie.'

'Look.' Joanne felt someone needed to take charge. 'I know we don't all need another group chat in our lives, but maybe we three should have one too, so that we can coordinate going in to see her and let each other know how she seems after the visits?'

Jamie dragged his sleeve across his red, raw eyes and nodded. He took out his phone and opened WhatsApp.

'Wait,' he breathed. 'No way.' He turned the phone around to show them a notification. 'Aifric's already done it. It's called "Claire's Herd". I didn't even think she had my number.'

'I gave it to her back on the flight,' Lexi said, examining his phone.

Aifric Dwyer created the group "Claire's Herd"
Aifric Dwyer added you

Jamie read out Aifric's text.

Hey gang, I'm making this group so that we can all support Claire as much as possible. Nothing too intense – we don't want her to feel like we're monitoring her. But I think some of us ... well, me ... I think I didn't do enough last year when Claire needed me and I thought this way we could stay up-to-date with how she's doing. Jamie, maybe you can tell us how she is when you visit? And let us know if she would be open to us visiting too?

'Well now.' Joanne was grudgingly impressed. *At least she's trying,* she thought.

'Will you give Aifric our numbers too so she can add us?' Lexi asked.

'Yep.' Jamie nodded. 'Look, thank you both. It might be a few days before I'll be able to visit Claire. The last time she was in, she wasn't allowed off the ward for a while. But I'll let you all know.'

Joanne and Lexi watched him walk back inside and then turned to each other.

'So …' Lexi looked utterly lost.

'Yup…' Joanne nodded. She felt like she was returning from an out-of-body experience. 'I can't believe she was so close.'

'Yeah.' Lexi looked distressed. 'My housemate told me that after the high, it's like just going over the edge into an abyss.' She shook her head. 'I have no idea how I'm going to go and, like, be with my dad and brother and act normal after all that.'

'I could come with you?' Joanne had the same feeling of dislocation. 'I can't imagine going home to Bert right now either. It's like being with anyone who hasn't just been to the brink would be too strange … Does that make sense?'

Lexi nodded.

'Come on. The bus station is like a ten-minute walk. We can get on the bus together and each have a post-traumatic stress breakdown once we're on our way.'

Lexi made a stab at a grin. 'That's the most inappropriate thing you could say right now.'

'BELIEVE me, I'm capable of saying far worse.' Joanne consulted her transport app. 'Next bus to Hereford – that's where you live, right? – is in twenty-five minutes, which will give me just enough time to milk my boobs in the jacks. These things get absolutely enormo when I haven't fed Ted in a while.'

'Will he be okay without you?'

'Yeah, we have bottles – Ted's gonna have to get used to them – and there's a shit ton of tit milk in our freezer. I'm sure after hour three of Ted crying, Bert will cop on that he's hungry.'

CHAPTER 37

The admissions office in St Paul's hospital was a surprisingly banal place. There were no clues as to what the hospital was for, except for the odd poster imploring you to 'GET HELP' and insisting that there was 'NO SHAME' in being ill.

Claire begged to differ. She was rag-dolled on a small moulded-plastic chair, watching her mother giving her date of birth to the kind woman behind the desk. The numbness was starting to ebb and in its place terrible, murky shame – the shame she wasn't supposed to feel – was surging.

Just hours ago I was about to murder this woman's daughter. I was about to ruin her life forever.

She tried to push the thought down.

Would I really have done it?

She examined the events dispassionately.

I didn't down it immediately. I waited to go sit on the bed with it. Was I stalling?

But if she hadn't wanted to do it, then why was she feeling such a profound disappointment at still being alive?

'I don't want to fucking do all this again,' she said to no one in particular. Her mother was now remarking on the weather while the admissions lady printed out some forms. Claire's dad was waiting in the car park. He'd been barely able to speak through his tears.

Jesus, he doesn't even know what I was about to do. Imagine he knew the full truth?

The last time she was here she had been transferred from A&E directly to the ward in the psychiatric hospital. Her memory of that time was very hazy. Ella suggested later that it had been the shock.

Ella.

I'm going to see her and she's going to ask me why I never came back. She's going to say what did I expect would happen?

'I'll take Claire upstairs now,' she heard the woman say. 'Claire will be checked in by the nurses. She won't meet her full team until tomorrow, but she'll be in very safe hands till then. So you two can say your goodbyes and I'll bring you up to St Bridget's ward now, pet.'

Claire stood heavily. Everything felt inordinately difficult. Cleaving her face into a smile for her mother was exhausting. Lifting her arms to hug her was the same.

'You'll get better, sweetie. This is for the best.' Marian stroked her daughter's hair and Claire felt the pity for her mother swell.

She remembered this from last time: the numbness dammed up the emotions for a time but then, inevitably, a crack would form and they'd begin to leak through.

Shame, humiliation, self-loathing and disgust – a veritable buffet.

Claire went through the motions of the goodbye, promising to rest and eat right and do what the doctors told her. Then she shouldered her bag and the admissions lady rode up in the lift with her.

They got off on the second floor. Down a long, bright corridor with windows overlooking a small garden with a greenhouse.

Not high enough, Claire thought. *You'd only break a leg. Plus no windows in the hospital open more than an inch.*

When they came to a pair of double doors, they were buzzed in and met by a young nurse.

'Hello, Claire, I'm Nancy. I'll take things from here.'

The admissions lady disappeared back through the doors and Claire noticed a light above flick from green to red. St Bridget's was a locked ward.

'I'll show you your bed.' Nancy led the way to a small room, where there were four beds with brown curtains serving as dividers. She asked Claire to open her bag and remove the contents, then sifted through the items. Last time, Claire had brought her knitting needles, which had been taken away – she hadn't made the same mistake this time.

Nancy was looking over the bracelet-making kit Joanne had given her.

Joanne. Just her name sucked Claire back into that terrible moment. In her memory, Joanne had looked wild-eyed, angry, flinging the glass from Claire's hands.

Claire shrank from the memory and focused back on Nancy, who was holding up Claire's pill sorter and saying something.

'I'm sorry?' Claire felt detached from her own voice. Derealisation, it was called. She knew all the words for all the things, but it didn't make experiencing them any less frightening.

Nancy was speaking slowly and patiently. 'I'm going to take your medication because while you're here we'll dispense your meds, okay? I see you were here before, Claire? You probably remember the trolley?'

'Yes.' Her voice was an echo. Disembodied and unreal.

'I'll keep your phone charger at the nurses' station for the next few days, okay? You can come up and use it any time, okay? It's just till the doctor says you can have it back.'

'Yes.'

'Right, let's go do your vitals and then you can settle in. The ward's quiet right now because the baking class is on and that's a popular one.'

'Yeah, I remember.'

A foreboding thought suddenly hung like a shadow over her. *What if nothing is real? What if I never actually left the last time? What if I've been here this whole time and Lexi and Joanne and the podcast was all a hallucination?*

She trailed Nancy through the common area, where a couple of men were watching a reality dance show with avid focus.

'That *Hollyoaks* actress has impeccable form,' one remarked.

At the nurses' station, her temperature and blood pressure were taken and then Nancy released her back into the quiet of the ward.

'Dinner is at—'

'Six thirty,' Claire finished for her. 'I remember.'

'Of course. There's some jigsaws in the common area if you fancy.'

'I think I'll just put my things away in my room.'

Back in room fourteen, Claire was met with an unwelcome sight. Her roommate had returned it seemed.

'Hi.' The woman looked to be in her forties, with a full face of make-up and very shiny dark hair. 'I'm Annette.'

'I'm Claire.'

'Do you object to a room diffuser?'

'I … eh, no.'

'Good.' Annette immediately turned on a large glowing orb, sporadically emitting a puff of vanilla-scented steam, and set it down on their communal shelf. 'My last roommate was a fucking bitch who wanted to control everything. Everything. Fucking nightmare. I've found the OCDs to be the most intolerant. Don't you? Wait, you're not one, are you? You don't look OCD – your clothes are filthy.'

'No.' Claire sighed. If these first few minutes were anything to go by, Annette was clearly only going to exacerbate her desire to kill herself. 'I'm bipolar.'

'Ah, that's the handy one, isn't it?' Annette plonked herself down on her bed, covered with chintzy throw pillows. *If ever there was a red flag about a person, it had to be throw pillows,* Claire thought darkly.

Annette was still prattling: 'You bipolars get loads of bits done. Like being on amphetamines without the downsides. Then, poof! It's off the deep end for a bit and then back up! Sounds ideal.'

'Yes, it's ideal. I've won the mental illness lotto.' Claire started shoving her clothes into the locker by her bed.

'They said I've got depression with paranoid features. I said to them, darlings, if you're not paranoid, you're crazy. Look at the pandemic, for god's sake. They sure timed that thing well, didn't they?'

Oh Christ. Claire stashed the last of her belongings. 'See you in a bit, Annette. I'm gonna close this curtain now cos I already tried to kill myself once today.'

She lay curled on her bed staring at the side of the bedside locker for the next hour and a half while images of the last few days and weeks jumbled forwards and backwards in her mind.

I have fucked everything so completely.

The Sweeneys can't let me mind Lila and Frankie and Sonny now. Two hospitalisations in eight months does not a good person to leave your kids with make.

Jamie will never trust me again.

Lexi and Joanne must think I am such a pathetic, attention-seeking drama queen.

Aifric and them are probably just relieved I'm out of the way.

And on and on it would've looped, but for the appearance of Nancy around seven thirty. She was holding a plate of chicken salad wrapped in cling film. 'You didn't come to dinner, Claire,' she said with concern. 'We don't allow food in the rooms, but as it's your first night ...'

The sight of the mayonnaise-coated potato salad made Claire's stomach lurch. 'I really don't want it, thanks.'

'Okay, well you do need to hop up and come out for your meds now. Then you can come back and lie down, I promise.'

Claire hauled herself up from the bed and followed Nancy into the harshly lit common room, where a queue had formed leading to the meds trolley. As Claire shuffled forward in the queue, several people tried to catch her eye, but she resolutely ignored them. She remembered from last time how curious people could be about anyone new on the ward: she just wanted to keep her head down, convince everyone she was fine and get the fuck back out of here.

To do what? She was still undecided. Go back to deranged soap-making? Mine her life for the podcast?

As if Lexi will want to continue with that, she thought, feeling the despair dragging her lower.

Truly from the bottom of my heart, fuck you, bipolar.

CHAPTER 38

It was after dinner time when Lexi, still with Joanne in tow, arrived at her dad's house. They'd accidentally got the bus that detoured into every tiny town between Dublin and Hereford and the sky was starting to darken as they arrived. Annoying though the slow journey had been, it had allowed them to get up to speed on who they each were. Could you forge a meaningful friendship in under three hours while trapped in the fart-fug of a rural bus? Maybe. Lexi certainly knew a lot now about Joanne's vagina – or rather what was left of it.

And Joanne had been a great listener to Lexi's litany of woes. Keeping her voice down – you never knew when a Hottie might appear – she detailed the shared dog custody; the shared podcast custody; the betrayal; the public humiliation; being locked into owning a house with neither person able to buy the other out and a burgeoning crush on a short man.

In the kitchen, Abi was clearing the table when Lexi walked in.

'Hey.' He came over and hugged her tightly. 'I'm really sorry to hear about what happened with Claire in Ibiza. Amanda and Shay kind of filled me and Dad in.'

'How is he?' Lexi asked urgently, lowering her voice.

'He seems good, Lex. I think we got seriously lucky.'

He looked past her to where Joanne was standing in the doorway.

'Oh, sorry ...' Lexi stepped aside and ushered Joanne in. 'This is Joanne, Claire's other friend. We've literally just come from a seriously bleak scene.'

Lexi would probably have cried all the way to Hereford if it hadn't been for Joanne. As well as baring their souls about their current life messes, they'd also bonded over being the kid of a single parent, and Joanne had been very funny about how her mother, Emer, had never had any way of tracking down her father.

'He's out there loose in the world,' Joanne had said. 'Could be anywhere. He might even still be in the country. If Bert's dad was a Frenchman, I literally couldn't have taken the risk. I'll be lucky if I HAVEN'T fucked my own cousin somewhere along the way. I was pretty insatiable in my early twenties.'

Lexi had even caught herself thinking how good Joanne would be on the podcast – a shallow thought that had, in a funny way, helped Lexi realise exactly what she had to do on that front.

'Listen, I'm gonna have to milk these again.' Joanne was cupping her boobs tenderly and Lexi directed her down to the toilet.

Abi looked baffled. 'Listen, do you two want a bit of lasagne? You won't fucking believe this but Amanda actually made it. Like not just "remove sleeve and pierce film": she got lasagne sheets and tins of tomatoes.' He shook his head in disbelief. 'She's been in there for an hour listening to Dad shite on. You know, I am not her biggest fan, but if this is some kind of penance ... well, she's doing it quite well. Shay's been great as well. He's out walking Scout. The guy's obsessed with your dog.' Abi narrowed his eyes. 'Or is it ... ?'

'What?' Lexi folded her arms, trying to arrange her face into what she hoped was scepticism.

'Well, let's just say that the lad is constantly trying to help you out, performing all this menial labour, and Screaming Foetus told me he's been working on lyrics to a song and trying to find something to rhyme with "Lexi" that isn't, and I quote, "sleazy".'

'He's a really good guy,' Lexi allowed. She wanted to ask more questions but wasn't sure it was a good idea to be too obvious, even with Abi. 'He's really sweet. But in answer to your original question, yes, we would love some lasagne.'

In the living room, Eamon wouldn't be dissuaded from standing to hug his daughter. 'Please, Dad, be careful!'

'They told me I'm grand to do a bit of moving about, but just to go easy. You're very good to come. Amanda and Abi explained everything – I hope your poor friend Claire will be okay.'

'Me too.' Lexi chewed the inside of her cheek, then caught Amanda looking up at her.

Amanda stood and tentatively put her arms around Lexi. 'It's been such a rough day.'

'Yeah ...' Lexi relented and hugged her back. 'It got even rougher at Claire's place, but I don't want to talk about it—'

'Of course.' Amanda returned to her spot on the couch. 'It's private. I know,' she said quietly. 'Between you guys.'

'Heya.' Joanne came in bearing plates of lasagne, with Abi behind her carrying cutlery and a couple of Cokes. 'Hi, Mr Maloney,' she chirped. 'I'm Joanne.'

She started handing the plates round while Eamon admonished her. 'Mr Maloney! Call me Eamon.'

While they ate, Lexi felt the anxiety of the day dissipate, replaced by newborn optimism at how chatty and with-it her dad seemed. The place still look tidy, too, even though it had been a couple of weeks now since Claire had cleaned it.

With each passing minute, Lexi felt like she was gaining new clarity on what she needed to do next.

At that moment, the scuffle and bark of Scouty announced the return of Shay. Lexi felt immediately self-conscious: she hadn't been near a mirror since that awful stint in the toilet on the plane with Claire. What the fuck did she look like? What was her hair doing?

But the second Shay appeared at the sitting-room door holding Scout, the worries melted away. From the way Shay was looking at her, she knew he would never notice how she looked. At least not in the way Jonathan always had – with that critical eye.

Shay smiled at her and mouthed, 'You okay?'

Lexi nodded, feeling a sudden and yet not unexpected rush of love. She wanted to jump up and fling her arms around him, but something told her to be measured.

Scouty leapt into her lap and Lexi cuddled her close. She smelled of fresh-cut grass and the unmistakable boy-smell of a drummer in a small-time metal tribute act.

After they'd all eaten a Viennetta Abi had unearthed in the freezer, insisting it must have dated from when their mum was alive, Lexi asked Amanda to come and talk before they all drove back to Dublin. Lexi was going to get more things and come back, but the next day Shay and Abi had work in the morning and Joanne had grudgingly admitted that she'd have to go home some time. In Lexi's room, she and Amanda sat on the floor beside the wardrobe where just five months ago they'd recorded their new year's episode.

Before Lexi could begin, Amanda immediately started to babble and apologise.

'I was a dick, Lexi. A massive dick. I actually don't know what the hell I was thinking. I'm not trying to pass the buck here, but I think me and Jonathan had some kind of shared madness where we'd both convinced each other that it was the best thing to do for the pod ... to secure the Podify deal, I mean. Please, please can things go back to how they were? I hate Marcus St James – he is truly the pits. Such a poser. I miss you so, so much, Lexi.'

'Amanda.' Lexi held up her hand to staunch the cascade of contrition and explanations. 'I miss you too. But I don't miss the podcast. And I don't want to go back to the way things were.'

Amanda looked stunned. 'But Lex. We had our dream job. Just us hanging out all the time. No boring marketing office or fucking hectic waitressing.' She genuinely looked baffled. 'I know I hurt you, but I really thought the last few months were like just a trial separation.'

'Manda, the dream job was destroying us. I didn't see it back then, but now I do. I don't want to mine my life for content any more. And I REALLY don't want to perform our friendship for money.'

Amanda remained silent, but tears filled her eyes.

'Look what happened to us,' Lexi continued. 'It got to the point where you actually thought a "plot twist" at the expense of my feelings was not only totally fine but actually GOOD for the podcast.'

Amanda started to apologise again, but Lexi stopped her. 'Look, I'm not even angry any more. Maybe we ALL had a shared madness. The success was intoxicating. I did stuff every day to get views. I lived my life as this character online. It was getting weird, even before that stupid game. I was anxious all the time, waiting for the next pile-on. I didn't LIKE the controversy, and you didn't take that seriously.'

'I know.' Amanda picked at the carpet where an old stain lay – a red wine mishap after Debs night.

As metaphors go, it's pretty on the nose, Lexi thought, looking at it.

'We could go back to therapy again?' Amanda pleaded. 'I promise I'll take it seriously this time.'

'But Amanda, do you wanna go to save us? Or to save the podcast?'

A silence mushroomed between them.

Amanda's next words were barely audible. 'Can't it be both? It's a lot of money, Lexi. How many thirty-year-olds get a shot at a seven-figure deal?'

'Yeah, it is.' Lexi felt defeated. 'But I guess it's only worth it if that's what's important to you.'

Amanda looked crushed. 'Lex! Please. We'd only have to keep it up for a year. We renegotiate next February. It's nearly June now. It'd be nine months.'

Lexi's anger sparked and then fell away. She was too exhausted for anger. 'Amanda. I'm scared of walking away from the money too – I've bought a fucking house I've never slept in with a man I hate! With money I'll probably be giving back to Podify. But I'm more scared of what nine more months of playing "Lexi and Amanda, your hot friends" on the internet will do to us.'

Amanda chewed her bottom lip.

'It's toxic,' Lexi continued. 'I couldn't see it – or I didn't want to see it. And I dragged Claire into it and now she's in hospital.'

Lexi could see Amanda bristling at the mention of Claire.

'I'm done with *Your Hot Friend,* Amanda. Done. You can keep the podcast feed and the socials. We'll work something out with the Podify deal. I think we were naive to think that all of this wouldn't someday come between us.'

Amanda appeared to be digesting this. She looked like the fight was going out of her, and her mascara was running.

Lexi opened her mouth, but Amanda cut across her.

'I'm not crying about the show.' Her voice was raised defensively. 'I just ...' She looked across bleakly at Lexi. 'Do you have to be done with ME? Because I can't ... I know I mentioned the money, but if it's an ultimatum ...' She held Lexi's gaze. 'It's you. I pick you.'

Lexi nodded. 'Okay.' She reached over for Amanda's hands, still worrying at the carpet. 'It'll take time, though.'

Amanda stared at the stain. 'We never got this out.'

'As I recall, we never even tried.' Lexi tilted her head and gave a sardonic smile. 'Lazy bitches.'

'We'll try this time, Lex. I promise.'

'We're being very poetic,' Lexi remarked.

'Very sincere,' Amanda agreed. 'Very un-Us.'

'We'll get Us back.' Lexi squeezed Amanda's hands.

CHAPTER 39

In the car on the way back from Lexi's dad's house, the man who'd been introduced to Joanne as Screaming Foetus blasted metal unapologetically. Scouty howled along in what appeared to be an expression of appreciation and she, Lexi and Abi exchanged strained smiles every so often when Shay started drumming along on the dashboard or Screaming Foetus tried to sing along.

Joanne was in the back, wedged between Lexi and the door. She was so squeezed, she was convinced it was hastening the leak of milk streaming out of her. Thank god she'd remembered to bring breast pads. She was dying to get home to Ted. And to a lesser extent Bert, even though no doubt the place would be in shit. Plus Bert could very possibly, by now, have unearthed some probably pretty justifiable anger about her sudden flight from their relationship.

When Amanda had seen that the car was full she'd immediately announced she was going to spend the night with her parents, as she was down home. It was, Joanne knew, another elaborate effort on Amanda's part to make it up to Lexi for the various shitty things she'd done in the last three months.

As they passed the sign for Dublin city, Joanne and Lexi's phones buzzed simultaneously. It was the new group chat: Operation Friend Escalation.

Joanne had 'cut the ribbon' on the chat a couple of hours before but there had been no reply from Claire until now:

> *First night is boppin' here. My roommate is Annette, loves a diffuser, hates shutting up. I already know all about 'those bitches' aka her estranged sisters, her sciatica flare-ups, and the lawsuits she's bringing against her neighbour and that 'fecker' who sold her a Nissan that immediately failed its NCT. So happy to be alive for this scintillating content.*

Joanne looked over at Lexi, who shrugged a little helplessly, then leaned in so Joanne could hear her over the music. 'What do you say to a suicide quip?'

Joanne thought for a few minutes. 'You say something,' she replied. 'We can't just ignore reality out of awkwardness – that's exactly what the Bitch Herd wound up doing. We have to be willing to get it wrong.'

She returned to her phone and started to type:

> *I'll be expecting nothing less than a handwritten thank you card for helping you not un-alive yourself.*

Joanne turned the phone for Lexi to see. Lexi shrugged again and tilted her own phone to show Joanne her Google page. She'd searched for 'what do you say to your friend who's attempted suicide?'

They were both lost. Joanne hit send on her glib text. She could only follow her instincts and be her normal self.

Lexi meanwhile sent:

I'm sorry you've been feeling so awful. I'm so glad you're still here.

Joanne quickly typed:

She copy-pasted that off the internet!

Then added:

But seriously, we love you so much. And this chat is here day and night, open 24/7 for any and all thoughts, fears, feelings you need to vent. And funny tiktoks. I demand we have funny tiktoks too.

Claire sent a heart in reply, then added:

Thank you gals. I'm on the mega-meds currently so bit drowsy ... And I'm not allowed my charger so I might not be in touch all the time but just knowing ye're there is nice.

The car and music stopped abruptly. 'Joanne! We're here!' Screaming Foetus announced, and Joanne took in her street with the strangest feeling that she'd been gone weeks rather than a day. Every house was in darkness – it was after midnight. *Ugh, Ted will no doubt be up for the night shift in no time.*

'Thanks for the lift.' She eased herself out of the car and Lexi followed her.

'So ...' Lexi looked exhausted and Joanne felt for her. Having some massive heart-to-heart with her friend on top of everything else must have been draining.

'Well.' Joanne again felt the need to take charge. 'During the day, it'll be easy enough to keep an eye on Operation Friend Escalation, but for the nights I propose that we do a kind of shift, taking turns alternate nights to keep our notifications and sound on. Maybe set alarms to check the chat at two a.m. and five a.m.? Something like that. Just so if Claire messages, we're not leaving her for too long.'

'Yeah, yeah.' Lexi looked relieved to have a concrete plan. 'And when it's allowed, will we both go in together to see her?'

'Yeah, deffo. It'll be a bit less intense than one-on-one.'

'Okay.' Lexi seemed to be stalling and Joanne suddenly realised why. She stepped forward and pulled her into a tight hug. Lexi started shaking in Joanne's arms and Joanne automatically started the soothing shush she always used on Ted. One long, two shorts always did it, for some reason.

'Shhhhh, sh, sh! Shhhh, sh, sh! It's okay, it's okay.'

'I'm sorry. I'm crying all over you.'

'It's okay, my boobs are in floods too! Sympathy tears.'

'I just can't stop thinking about how the podcast must've had a hand in this. I feel like I wasn't paying attention and then she nearly ... We nearly ... lost her.'

'I know.' Joanne's guilt reared up. 'Looking back, I was witnessing some pretty weird behaviour. And I just laughed it off. I was no help. Completely self-involved.'

'Same.' Lexi straightened up and ran her fingers under her eyes to sweep away the tears. 'I'm so shitty …' She hesitated, then continued. 'I'm kinda crying for myself here too. My life is such a fucking mess right now.'

'Yeah, I understand. Mine's a shitshow as well. I've no job to go back to. Getting childcare's a bollocks. I feel terrible, cos I love Ted but I miss work. Anyway, all we can do is be there for Claire and we'll get in to see her in no time.'

'You're right.'

Lexi was halfway into the car when Joanne stopped her and whispered, 'By the way, I think you should get on with railing that Shay guy. It's pretty obvious ye want to. Seriously, it's awkward just sitting in a room with you two. I think we were all worried ye'd spontaneously climax from the tension!'

Lexi laughed tearily and hopped into the car.

Joanne waved until they'd disappeared around the corner. Then she eased the key into her door, desperate not to wake Bert or Ted, hoping Bert wouldn't be up pacing with a screaming baby, having forgotten to feed or change him. She couldn't bear the thought of dealing with either of them at that moment.

Inside, it was mercifully quiet. Truly incredible. She settled herself on the couch. Her breasts were rock hard and extremely painful, but she didn't dare use the pump in case it woke Ted. She rooted out the little manual one.

'Hey.' The appearance of Bert coming out of the gloom startled her.

'Jesus Christ,' she hissed. 'Why are you looming? What are you doing up?'

He ignored the looming accusation. 'I was thinking.'

'Oh.' Joanne resisted the impulse to add a sarcastic 'Wow!' to that.

Stop it, Joanne. If nothing else, you need his half of the rent on this place. Also she had to admit her flight from reason had clarified something for her. Bert had been ready to fight for her, for them. She'd been so busy raging at unwashed rasher pans and how her life had changed, she'd ignored how much he was trying. She disregarded everything he was doing and instead focused on the things she felt he wasn't doing. Taking on extra shifts at work must have been as exhausting as taking care of Ted but he hadn't complained once.

'So.' He stood, cracking his knuckles, which she hated – *Stop it Jo!* 'Your boobs must be in bits. I realised you didn't have the pump. And then I was going to get the bus down after you with it, and then I thought maybe you wouldn't want that … I'm rambling. Anyway, I have a warm compress ready for you.' He tiptoed off to the kitchen and returned with a small plastic tub and two small nappies. 'Let's get you milked.'

'What're the nappies for?'

'Best hot compresses in the biz! I watched a YouTube tutorial.' He unfurled each one and held them against her breasts as she hand-expressed and attempted not to groan with relief. It was bovine enough without her lowing.

'Are they sore?' he asked.

'Depends.' Joanne narrowed her eyes. 'Are you asking in a concerned way? Or a "trying to figure out if we can have sex" way?'

'Jo, c'mon! I'm helping you to milk yourself – I'm not that bad.'

'Oh, so you find me grotesque.'

'I knew it, that question was rigged. It was a booby trap.'

They both started giggling at this and it was as though a presure valve had been turned. They hadn't laughed together in months. They'd barely been alone in a room together in months.

'Listen.' Bert was still cupping her breasts with the warm nappies as he got down on one knee. 'I really wanna marry you, Joanne. And not just because you scared the shit out of me on Friday. I love you so much – there's no one like you. Well, except Ted now, which is pretty cool.'

'Okaaaay …' Joanne felt torn. On the one hand, it would be easy to say 'yes' and hope for the best, but on the other hand … the micro-irritations were a threat to her sanity. She continued to hand-express, pretending she was concentrating on that so she could stall for time.

'Look, I know what you're thinking,' said Bert. 'The frying pans …' He nodded vigorously. 'I got your message and I will never ever leave one unwashed again, I swear to god. Look!' He swept a hand towards the kitchen wall, where he had hung the frying pan with her deranged missive facing out. 'It will be a daily reminder for me of how close I came to losing you. HashtagNeverForget,' he added solemnly as he cupped the nappies even closer around her boulder-like breasts, as if trying to convey the depth of his commitment.

'Bert. This proposal is weird as fuck.' Joanne continued to crank the breast pump. 'But maybe that's kinda what's selling me on it …'

Bert's eyes widened and his cupped hands squeezed with excitement.

'Oww. Chill out. I'm not saying "yes". I'm just not saying "no". Though I still could at any time,' she warned.

'I know. Look. I know I haven't taken into account just how much has changed for you. I didn't take it seriously enough that your job was gone and your friends were being crap. And now this thing with Claire. Look, just let me prove it to you … I can do better at this whole dadding thing. I swear.'

'Bert,' Joanne said gently. 'It's not the dadding thing. You've just been really annoying.'

Again they both laughed and again the pressure valve twisted a little more to the left.

'You can put the nappies down now, thanks – they really helped.'

'Now, I spent some time while you were gone trying to put a plan in place for you getting back to work.' He took out his phone and brought up his calendar. 'All the purple days are interviews for creches that I've lined up. And I also scheduled some with a childminder, in case we'd rather go that route.'

Joanne felt her jaw tighten.

He saw her face. 'What?'

'It's not as simple as that. You didn't even bother to do the maths. My old salary was good because I'd been there six years. Anywhere I start now would be offering way less. With the cost of groceries and childcare, we'd be breaking even. I'd basically be paying for the privilege of going to work.'

'I have done the maths,' Bert insisted. 'I just don't see it the same way. You getting back to work is really important. Maybe we'd be breaking even or operating at a loss for a while, till Ted starts school, but spending money on childcare is like investing in your career. In a few years, you might have your own design studio. Or want to get into a different side of design. We need to make sure family life works for you, Jo. You're so talented and creative. And you love what you do.'

Joanne considered this. She'd come across so many stories where the couple had a baby and it was just assumed that the woman's career would be sacrificed. She had also never ever heard of a man taking on the burden of FINDING the actual childcare.

Before the Your Story closure, it had been a given that she was going back. Because the money could cover the childcare. She hadn't even considered the perspective Bert was offering. That maybe the value in what she did wasn't purely monetary.

'Are you in there?' He waved a hand in front of her face. 'Look, if the money thing is really, really untenable, I can cut back for a while too. It shouldn't all be you doing the sacrificing. Like I said, we'll make it work!'

Joanne looked at him kneeling before her in the semi-darkness and felt a pang of affection. She leaned over and kissed him. It had been so long, she even felt a thrill of pleasure. She pulled away.

'I guess if you don't love me when I am milking my udders then you don't deserve me at my …' Joanne laughed, 'NOT milking my udders?!'

'I love you when you're being milked, I love you when you're being sliced open, I love you when you're hissing at strangers and generally acting like you're in the throes of demonic possession …' He kissed her again.

She pulled apart enough to say: 'This is not a "yes", okay? Like it's not just a case of washing pans and googling creches.'

'Shut up, okay?' he murmured, kissing her again.

CHAPTER 40

The curtain around her bed rippled in the dark. Claire sensed rather than saw Nancy's eyes pass over her before she moved on to Annette. She burrowed deeper in the narrow bed and listened to the squeak of Nancy's shoes and then the tiny whoosh of the bedroom door closing. It was either the one a.m. or the three a.m. check. Claire didn't bother to find her phone to check the time. Time on the ward was a remote concept. The hours were marked out by a metric different to numbers. They were governed by the tick, tick of a checklist rather than a clock.

Breakfast – check.

Morning meds queue – check.

Vitals at the nurses' station – check.

Occupational therapy – check.

Lunch – check.

Midday meds queue – check.

Therapy – check.

Dinner – check.

Evening meds queue – check.

Watch whatever was on TV – check.

Tea and toast cart – check.

Bedtime – check.

1 a.m. bed check – check.

3 a.m. bed check – check.

5 a.m. bed check – check.

Rinse and repeat.

Since she'd arrived a week ago, she'd been through the full checklist routine seven times.

Oddly, it reminded her of her old job in the creche. The day was timetabled in a similar way. Aside from the meds, of course. Sweet, sweet meds. She suspected she was on some pretty heavy-duty stuff: she was sleepy and her brain seemed docile most of the time.

At the creche, she and the other staff checked the babies while they napped, just like Nancy and the other nurses checked on Claire and the other patients through the night.

Claire knew why they were checking and wondered if they had ever come upon a terrible sight. She smoothed her pillow and wondered what you could even do to yourself in the little cubicle. All there was was a bedside locker, a bed and a short narrow cupboard for clothes. Nothing sharp. She squeezed her eyes shut and the fear-thoughts swam into her mind. It had been a week, and she no longer wanted to die. But she wasn't sure that she would ever be free from the terror that she would try again. Two attempts in one year.

It was hard to articulate this when she spoke to her 'team': her therapist Ella, John the psychiatrist and Ingrid the social worker. The best she could manage was, 'What if I am never free of this thing?'

Every day they had tried to explain that she just needed to learn to manage her illness and know the signs. And every day she'd come away feeling afraid. She'd leave the office and would be ushered into the lunch queue or the meds queue while the thoughts roiled in her head.

What if I can't be trusted to manage it? What if I can't be trusted to know the signs?

She turned over in the bed – quietly, so as not to disturb Annette on the other side of the thin fabric. The whole concept of the psychiatric hospital could, it seemed to Claire, be boiled down to this: *We are people who can't be trusted. We can't be trusted to feed ourselves or take our medication or fill an empty hour or stay alive. We must be shepherded from basic task to basic task. Like the toddlers in the creche.*

When she opened her eyes again, the promising light of a summer morning filled the spartan room.

Annette was at the foot of her bed, already dressed.

'Time for breakfast, Claire.'

'Thanks.' Claire pulled herself from the tangle of sheets and put on her joggers.

Annette was growing on her, she had to admit. Though her presence on the ward perplexed Claire. She seemed together in an almost intimidating way. Claire wouldn't be surprised if she wasn't some kind of plant. A 'Normal' stuck in to encourage the rest of them.

They made their way to the dining room, which looked like any old canteen save for the fact that most of the people in the queue were wearing pyjamas and dressing gowns.

'I've developed a theory,' she told Annette, once they'd signed in with the nurse by the door and started queueing for cereal and toast. 'The people who are craziest in here are the ones who get dressed and act like they're totally fine.' She indicated Annette's skinny jeans and Breton top. 'Case in point.'

Annette laughed. 'My psych says getting dressed is a part of good mental hygiene. You should try it.'

'I might.' Claire puffed out her cheeks. 'It's Monday. First Visit Day for me.'

Annette's face seemed to darken, but before Claire could ask what was wrong, Essie, the sweet lady with the toast, was asking what they wanted.

Carrying their trays of cornflakes and fruit, Claire and Annette took a table by the window. Claire watched Nancy help an older man open his tiny box of cereal and felt a gloom of pity descend. A lot of people on the ward were worse than her. Though what exactly constituted 'worse' she wasn't quite sure. Many of them didn't speak. Many weren't allowed off the ward. Others needed help to eat. Some of the rowdier patients had 'one-to-ones' – a nurse assigned to shadow them at all times. She and Annette were in the cohort who she thought of as the people who could be mistaken for staff members. Though when she looked down and took in her stained jumper and pants, she had to grin.

Who am I to think I'm 'better' than anyone else here?

'What's funny?' Annette snapped in her brusque way.

'Nothing.' Claire peeled off the lid of her yoghurt. Yoghurt was a creche staple too She leaned over to Annette. 'Do you ever think this place is just basically a creche for adults? I used to work in one and I swear the whole thing reminds me of how we used to mind the babies—'

She suddenly noticed Annette's face look up. *Fuck! What have I said?*

'What's wrong?'

'Nothing.' Annette's voice was tight. 'Absolutely nothing. I'm going to get to the meds cart, beat the rush.' She stood abruptly, leaving her cereal spoon dripping milk on the table, and hurried out of the room.

Numbly Claire finished the tedious task of feeding herself, then went to join the meds queue. At the top, she could see Annette chatting to the nurses, like they were baristas at a coffee shop serving her a flat white instead of the tiny paper cup of whatever the hell was keeping her going.

The queue moved glacially and Claire was glad when Emily, a girl about her own age, joined behind her. She was a rampant conversationalist and required little interaction from whomever she was talking to at any given time.

'My boyfriend's coming today, can't wait. He's bringing me McDonald's, but so annoying ... he doesn't think he'll get the McFlurry here before it's melted ...'

Emily was being discharged in a few days. That was the other timeline on the ward that was not marked out by hours and days: the timeline of recovery. Ella and John said Claire needed time. And she did – she needed it to pass – but frustratingly they couldn't give her a number in days or weeks. They simply suggested that rather than focus on leaving, she should focus on herself.

'But I hate myself,' she'd wailed.

'Well, maybe that's a good target to work towards,' Ella had said calmly. 'Hating yourself less.'

Not a terrible point, Claire allowed. And if she were being honest, she knew she was where she needed to be. The thought of going back to her life overwhelmed her.

At the top of the queue, she swallowed her pills. Then she walked to the nurses' station to have her blood pressure taken. Everyone called it 'vitals', as in vital signs. Which struck Claire as funny. Are they checking we're still alive?

In that queue she stood beside Benji, forties, garden variety depressive (his words).

'Imagine this was to check how alive we wanted to be on any given day?' she said, and he laughed.

'Like, if the blood was flowing enthusiastically enough, they might say we're cured and just let us out.'

After vitals, Claire looked for Annette in their room to check on her, but no joy. She put on *Your Hot Friend* as she rummaged for something to wear that said 'Look, I'm a mess but I'm a stylish mess'. Not finding that, she opted for a denim pinafore and a stripy cotton top she'd knitted herself.

Amanda and Marcus were talking shit about an Irish influencer and Claire found she just didn't have the stomach for it. She shut it off and put on Bryony Gordon's interview podcast – a show on which guests talked about their mental health called *Mad World*. It was very soothing to her, a citizen of that world.

After she'd dressed, she went to the noticeboard to check the timetable for the day. Visitors would be arriving just after lunch. You could have a maximum of three people: Jamie, Lexi and Joanne were hers. She was desperate to see them and also scared. It had only been a week but it felt like longer.

Luckily, before then she had therapy with Ella and then today's occupational therapy treat, ZenDoodle – whatever that was.

'You look very nice.' Ella guided Claire to the low chair by the window in her small counselling room. Everything was a calming, muted green, right down to the box of tissues on the table.

'Thank you.' Claire forced a shot of cheeriness into her voice. 'I really think I'm coming out of it all now. I feel way better.'

Ella smiled and settled herself in the chair opposite, Claire's file open on her lap.

'As you know, Claire, that's the tricky nature of your illness. You can swing up very fast and swing down equally abruptly. We want to make sure you get a really nice, long, stable period before you go home.'

'But how can I be stable in here when there's so much I need to get back to out there? I can't relax in here, Ella. I have too much to do.'

'And that is a part of the problem, Claire. All the doing.' She indicated Claire's hands, clenching and unclenching at speed in her lap.

Claire quickly quieted them, taking a deep breath. 'But I swear, I'm not feeling racy at all any more.'

'I know,' Ella said kindly. 'But while the mania is bad, it's what comes after that's more dangerous for you. It's only been eight days since you tried—'

'I know, I know.' Claire sighed. 'I know you're right. I guess the manic bit had kind of burned away by the time I was getting the ... em ... plan together. But still, I'd be better getting stable out there, where I can still do my life. I'm letting people down in here.'

'Let's focus on this thought for today's session, okay? I think a lot of fears are coming up.' Ella uncapped her pen. 'List the people you think you're letting down and the reason why you think you're letting them down.'

Claire swallowed and resettled herself. 'Okay, Jamie. I'm supposed to be his girlfriend, someone fun in his life, not this drag. He deserves someone better than me.'

'Okay.' Ella noted this. 'Next.'

'My mum and my dad. I'm their only child and I'm a complete fuck-up. The Sweeneys – they trusted me with their babies and they took me back after the last time and now I've let them down again. There's Lexi and the podcast: I feel like I tricked her into thinking I was this normal person. And there's Aifric: I ruined her whole pre-hen hen do.'

'Okay, Claire. I'm going to ask you a few questions to challenge these convictions. Because sometimes, as a result of your illness, there's a disconnect between your brain and the reality of what's happening. Has Jamie been in touch since you've been here?'

Claire nodded. 'He sends me videos. Twice a day.'

'Right.' Ella nodded.

'But that doesn't mean—'

'Claire, we're talking only in facts here.' Ella was firm. 'Your boyfriend sends you videos twice a day. That is an act of love.' She paused to look at her page. 'Okay, your mum and dad. Have they been in touch?'

'Yes.'

'Daily?'

'Yes.' Claire sighed. 'But you're being overly simplistic. 'They feel they have to …'

'Claire, you have to stop doing other people's thinking for them. The reality is that your boyfriend and parents have been demonstrating their love for you. The feelings and thoughts of others will always be opaque to us, but we have to trust in what their actions are communicating. Let's take the Sweeneys as an example. They "took you back", as you put it. That is big. People don't just trust people with their CHILDREN out of politeness or a sense of obligation. Have they been in touch since you've been here?'

Claire gazed at her impassively. 'Going off this metric of "Have they texted?" is stupid. By your logic, Four Star Pizza really cares about me. They texted last Wednesday to tell me about the Mega Midweek Feast deal.'

Ella grinned. 'So I take it the Sweeneys have texted.'

'Norah said she wants to come visit and that they have temporary cover until I am ready to come back to work,' Claire said sullenly.

'Okay. So tell me, what does your brain make of this?'

Claire glared at the tissues. 'My brain thinks she's just being nice and …' She started to well up. 'And that she's worried that I would've hurt Lila or the boys … and that she doesn't know how to fire me without …' Gasping sobs took over Claire's words.

'It's okay, Claire. It's okay.' Ella pushed her tissues closer. 'The thing with mental illness is it's a liar. It latches onto our worst fears and makes them feel more real than reality.'

Claire pulled a clump of tissues from the box and folded into herself.

Ella continued talking quietly. 'Your brain has been overwhelmed, for quite a long time. And when we're overwhelmed like that, the bad thoughts, the UNTRUE thoughts, can multiply and run amok. But it's not your fault, Claire.'

Claire nodded, trying to rein in her tears.

'This is why it's so important you're here: we need to give your brain a chance to rest and heal. Now, speaking of, ZenDoodle is today's occupational therapy and it's really good for calming the brain. So, you mentioned Aifric – that she must hate you for ruining her hen do.'

'Pre-hen hen do.'

'Right. And, you know what I'm going to ask ... Has she been in touch?'

Claire took a breath. 'Yes. She told me that ...'

'Yes?'

'She said she was going to delay her wedding by a few months.'

'And did she say why?' Ella had the patient tone of someone trying to draw out a toddler.

'She said she wants me there. She said she couldn't imagine doing it without me there.' The sobs rose up again. 'It ... was ... really ... nice.'

'Yeah, that's very nice. It's no picnic trying to reschedule a wedding, Claire. So when people are doing these things and showing that they love you, will you just try and believe them? Try and challenge the negative self-talk.'

ZenDoodle was, as Ella had promised, very calming. Over the course of the hour, the occupational therapist drew a maze of patterns and dots and lines on a large whiteboard while the group followed along, recreating the doodle on their own small pieces of card.

After her sessions with Ella, Claire always felt raw, yet lighter. It was a strange juxtaposition. *It's like cauterising a wound for fresh tissue to grow,* she thought, then grimaced at the image.

After OT, she looked again for Annette, but her side of their room was pristine and deserted. Then Claire had lunch with Benji and a couple of others in the dining room. The queue for midday meds was always a bit shorter, as most people had just morning and evening doses, but Claire still checked there for Annette. No sign.

Claire tracked back over what she'd said. Mentioning visiting day had seemed to nudge a nerve. But it was when she'd mentioned that they were all like babies in a creche that Annette had left. Had she been offended?

Claire's ruminating took her all the way up until it was time to go down to the visiting area on the ground floor: a series of wood-panelled rooms called pods overlooking the grounds. She took the lift with the intensely excited Emily and signed in with the orderly manning the visitor area desk.

'Claire Sheehy,' she told him.

'Excellent, pod 8. One's here already, I'll keep an eye out for the others.'

Jamie had texted to say he was coming first. Claire was nervous. What do you say to the person whose life you almost destroyed? Flashes of Jamie's disbelief and terror when the lye had hit the carpet assailed Claire as she made her way towards the room. She fixed her pinafore and hoped she at least *looked* okay.

All the pods had glass doors and while Claire was conscious that she shouldn't stare, she was curious. Inside each pod she saw others from St Bridget's. In one pod, she saw the old lady who never spoke sitting with a man who had to be her son. He was holding her hands with tears in his eyes. In another was the older gentleman who always wore a suit and carried the *Irish Times* under his arm. Beside him a woman – his wife, his sister? – was squeezing his shoulder and they were laughing. St Paul's was a strange place, full of grief and despair, and yet there was dignity here and even bright spots of joy amid the pain.

Though she'd known them hardly a week, she found she and Benji and Annette and the others had an easy shorthand. Sometimes they could laugh at their grim predicaments: at the fact that EVEN if you got up at six a.m. and went to the tea station, STILL all the chocolate biscuits would already be gone, leaving only the Rich Teas and a scattering of Custard Creams, if you were lucky. There were rumours that there were Bourbons to be found if you got there early enough, but no one had ever seen them.

Further down the corridor, Claire passed a pod with a familiar face inside: Annette. Though she didn't look like herself: her immaculate face was a mask of pain. In her arms she held a small baby, and suddenly Claire realised what had upset her at breakfast: the mention of the creche. Claire hurried on, fearful of intruding on such a private moment, when Annette's usual togetherness was so resoundingly undone.

We all wear masks, Claire realised. *Trying to play a part and pretend we're fine when we're coming apart inside.*

And that, Claire thought, *is how the illness thrives. By hiding ourselves. No one can ever see us if we don't let them. And if we never show anyone our true selves, we are all just left alone inside our heads.*

I'll apologise to Annette tonight, she resolved as she reached pod eight.

Inside, on the other side of the glass, Jamie jumped up, looking as nervous as Claire felt. Claire opened the door and he immediately pulled her into a hug.

'Claire, thank god.'

They drew apart. 'Thank god? For what?' Claire asked as they went to the couch.

'Thank god you're back.'

'What do you mean?'

Jamie rubbed her arms. 'I can see it in your eyes. The farawayness is gone. I can see that you're you again.' His words flowed out on a stream of relief. 'I've just been so scared that you'd never look at me like this again. I know you're not better *better* yet, but you're you again. I can see you in there.'

'Jamie ... I'm so sorry. You tried to help and I pushed you away. I lied to you.'

'Claire, you couldn't help that. You can't help any of this.' He held Claire's face and kissed her long and hard. Claire felt like she was home.

She pulled back: she didn't want to feel home if she was going to lose Jamie.

She took a breath. 'I don't deserve you,' she said quietly. 'And you don't deserve this; you deserve better than me.'

He pulled her close again. 'Claire, you are the only person in the whole world I want. You need to believe me. You. You are my home.'

Something broke in Claire and she sagged. But Jamie caught her.

'Seriously,' he whispered. 'You're the only person as devoted to natural disaster movies as me. You're the only person who can recite *Con Air* word for word. You're the only person for me. Ever, ever, ever. When you get out of here, our whole new life is going to begin. I will keep you safe. I will never let this happen to you again, I promise.'

'You didn't let anything happen to me; I did this to myself.'

'You didn't, Claire. You have this fucker of an illness but also, if you didn't have it ... maybe you wouldn't be you. And we wouldn't be us. Please believe me.'

Claire thought about Ella's words: *When people are doing these things and showing that they love you, will you just try and believe them?*

She found she couldn't speak, so she just leaned in and kissed him. And she believed him.

Soon Claire was giving Jamie a rundown of ward life, feeling a rush of relief every time he laughed. Maybe things would be normal again one day.

'So,' Claire smiled. 'Weirdly, I've actually made a few friends here ... It's kind of nice cos we all have this shorthand. We get each other. We all have the Mads, just different flavours of it. Who knew that the best place to make friends after thirty is the psychiatric ward?'

After another twenty minutes, Lexi and Joanne joined them, bringing with them even more promise of what life could be like after Claire got better.

'Bert,' Joanne announced happily, 'is doing very well at no longer being a wreck-the-head. I may even keep him. You definitely need *bodies* with a baby. I'm applying for jobs and he's reduced his hours so that we're not gonna be completely ruined by childcare costs.'

Lexi was quieter. Claire sensed that they would soon be having some Big Talk. Amanda and Marcus had done Claire and Lexi's episodes of the podcast that week, but no doubt Lexi would be going back to *Your Hot Friend* again soon, most likely with a hot friend that was less of a hot mess than Claire. She tried not to focus on it …

Ella's clear, calm voice came into her head … *Stop doing other people's thinking for them.*

When the time was nearly up, Jamie and Joanne stood and said their goodbyes.

Jamie kissed her. 'I'll be back next week with your mum and dad. But don't think about us, okay? Just rest and do what they tell you here.'

Joanne came forward and hugged Claire. 'I'll see you in the WhatsApp, okay?'

They both left and Lexi pushed the door closed behind them.

Here it comes, thought Claire.

'So …' Lexi took Claire's hand and led her back to the couch. 'I know you're probably worrying about the podcast and I just wanted you to know that you don't have to.'

'I know, I know …' Claire ran a hand through her hair, looking out the window. 'I get it. You're getting back with Amanda. I figured.'

'No.' Lexi found her eyes. 'Well, I am talking to Amanda again. And we're trying to work out a way for us to be friends again. But no, not on mic. Like, never again.'

'Oh?' Claire tried to suss her tone. Did Lexi want to continue with her? She didn't even know if that was what she wanted. She waited for Lexi to speak.

'I want you to know, Claire, this has nothing to do with you. And it definitely has nothing to do with the last week. I just don't want to risk another friendship for a podcast. Ours, like. You mean so much to me.'

'Oh …' Claire tried to believe her.

'Like, we've barely known each other for that long, but so much has happened. You were there for me with my dad. And I just think you're an amazing person.'

Claire cringed. 'I'm not. I'm such a fuck-up. I'm so ashamed about last week.'

'Stop! Don't say that. I love you, Claire. We all do. Look at this …'

Lexi passed over her phone, open to a WhatsApp group called 'Claire's Herd'.

'Aifric and them started it. Me and Joanne and Jamie are in it. We're not talking about you, like. It's all logistics. Who gets to visit and when. That kind of thing. Nadia made a chart, lol. Look, I definitely have my feelings about them but they're trying to show up for you, Claire.'

Claire passed back the phone. 'They've texted me individually here and there but …' She was pretty amazed and touched.

'So.' She turned to Lexi. 'What are you going to do about the podcast?' she asked. 'And the house?'

'We're meeting with Podify on Wednesday morning. It's pretty complicated. Even with everything, the figures have been consistently high since the whole … shitshow. People are probably tuning in in case they miss some tea on it all. It's so hard to know what to do. If we kept going for another nine months, we'd get to keep the money and I could even have a shot at keeping the house. But I really, REALLY don't want to. I feel like I've been living for an audience for five years and it's just not what I want any more. I'm sick of all the speculation online and all the focus being on us. All the "hot girl" shite. It's not who I want to be now. And I just feel like we're not adding anything positive to the world. Amanda is finally starting to get it, I think. We're back in therapy, lol.'

Claire considered this. 'What if you changed tack on the podcast? You could change the name to *Your Hot Mess* and interview people about REAL stuff. You could interview me about being in the bin! Show people it's not the end of the world to be mentally ill.'

Lexi laughed. Then stopped. 'It's actually not a bad suggestion. Though it's definitely not what Podify signed up for ...' She grinned. 'Anyway, I think I'm gonna move back in with my dad for a bit. I need to get money stuff sorted out and mind him better, figure out what I want to do with my life and ...' Lexi paused.

'And ... ?' Claire prompted her.

'I want to kiss Shay so badly it's, like, becoming a health hazard.'

Claire laughed. 'But why would you move AWAY from him if you wanna do that?'

'Because I don't want to live with him the second something starts between us. IF it does. I don't want another Jonathan situation.'

'Oh god, how's that going?'

'Grand? Shite? Depends on the day.' Lexi shrugged. 'It's so weird. We were a couple for five years, but I feel nothing for him now. I feel like the Lexi in that relationship was another person. The one good thing is he doesn't want to share custody of Scouty any more. She was always my dog. So once we figure out the house and the podcast, we're done and I never have to see him again!' She finished brightly. 'Anyway, this has been all about me. How're you getting on really?'

'I'm better,' Claire said thoughtfully. 'Not all the way there yet, but I kind of feel more like I'll get there, you know? I still worry that I'll never be free of this though.'

'You will, Claire. You will,' Lexi said forcefully.

'But maybe I won't. Maybe I'll be back here in a year again. Or two years or three. Will I always be trying to outrun it?'

Lexi took a breath. 'If you do, it'll be different. You have us now.'

'Yeah ...' Claire shrugged. 'But it's hard, Lex. Inside my head, I'll always be alone.'

Lexi moved forward and gathered Claire in her arms. 'We're all alone in our heads ... But if we always tell each other everything, we can do this thing together.'

'Are you suggesting I "reach out"?' She pulled away and gave Lexi a sardonic smile.

Lexi laughed. 'Go for a walk, Claire. Meditate,' she said airily. 'Make sure you drink enough water! That cures mental illness, right?!'

Claire laughed. 'It's so funny when someone says that shit. Go for a walk? I'm like: Babe, I can't get out of bed and a voice in my head is saying I should kill myself! Walks are great to keep a person WELL, but when you're fully in the throes of it, a walk is like throwing a thimble of water at a house fire.'

Lexi grinned. 'I promise I will never suggest you go for a walk. But also, Claire? I promise you'll never have to reach out to me. Cos I'll already have you. I'll reach in!'

'Gross,' laughed Claire. 'But appreciated,' she added.

CHAPTER 41

On Wednesday morning, low granite clouds marred the June sky and rain pounded the windows at the Podify offices.

All very apt, Lexi thought as she waited for Amanda to arrive – they'd agreed that they wouldn't be letting Jonathan anywhere near this meeting and he'd had the good grace not to fight it even though he could've as he still technically managed the show. The receptionist had brought her in to a boardroom and bustled out without so much as offering her a water. Even the fact that they were in the office and not being wooed in some swish hotel spoke to the fact that this meeting was quite possibly about to be unpleasant given all the messing around they'd been doing to the format since signing on with Podify.

'Hey, bébé.' Amanda appeared at the door, uncharacteristically early for the meeting. She slipped into the chair beside Lexi at the long table. 'So … game face on?'

'Yep. Did you see their email about our new show suggestion?' Lexi took out her phone, fully expecting that Amanda wouldn't have been arsed opening it.

'I did.' Amanda rummaged in her bag for her own phone. 'They seemed a bit … non-committal?'

'Yeah …' Lexi agreed.

After she'd left Claire on Monday, her mind had whirred all afternoon and evening about Claire's idea for a new podcast. Yes, she'd vowed never to be on mic with Amanda again, but if the show was actually about something rather than just them… and if they had a guest on every week … things could be different.

She'd been reluctant to call Amanda that day – instead she'd sat with Shay and Abi and Screaming Foetus that night and hashed out the pros and cons. They'd helped her put the idea down on paper and had been pretty encouraging, though all of them had reservations about Amanda's involvement. Could a person really change that much in four months? Lexi felt like she herself had, but one of Amanda's last debacles had literally been mocking a man's mental illness. Then again, Lexi knew Amanda had been rocked by their break-up just as much as she had. Lexi sensed a new-found empathy in her. Anyway, all Lexi was suggesting was doing a test episode.

Amanda pulled two Cokes out of her bag and passed one to Lexi. Lexi accepted it gratefully. *Old Amanda would've brought a White Claw to a morning meeting,* she mused.

'Look, even if they don't go for it, I still think we should.' Amanda was pulling up a doc on her phone. 'There's some really good podcasts about mental health and stuff. But not that many in Ireland. And even the Hotties have problems. I'm positive they'll come along for the ride.'

Lexi smiled nervously. *Was this a mistake? I won't know unless I try,* she decided.

A clamour in the hallway announced the arrival of the head of development, Mark and a few other Podify executives.

'Girls!' Mark walked in, carrying his tablet. Lexi was finding it hard to gauge his tone. Was it a 'Girls – how are you the biggest flop decision I ever made?' Or a 'Girls – I don't hate your new idea'?

Everyone got settled and Mark called for the receptionist.

'Dee? Will you ring down for some coffees, please? Maybe some pastries?'

That seemed promising, Lexi thought. If he was about to read them Clause 5 Section 14 of the contract detailing the financial implications of disbanding the show in the first year, it would surely be a pretty quick meeting ... not requiring niceties like pastries.

'So.' Mark cleared his throat. 'We read the new proposal with great interest. *Your Hot Mess*. I think we can all agree that, yes, it's been a bit of a hot mess on the show for a few months now ...' He grimaced. Or was it a wry grin? Lexi couldn't tell.

'We've discussed the new direction in depth and I have to say, we think there's something in it. Of course, without a pilot, we can't be certain that the tone would work. Amanda, you in particular have a reputation for being—'

'An insensitive bitch?' Amanda supplied helpfully.

'Yes, exactly.' He nodded. 'We all agree here that the figures on *Your Hot Friend* are still excellent – whether that's because of your very public break-up or the actual content remains to be seen, of course. But the audience is there for you two and it'd be a real shame to throw that away this early in the partnership.'

Lexi leaned forward and even Amanda sat up straighter. This was sounding positive.

'I'm proposing you two record the pilot. Lexi, Aine said your co-host is still under the weather, so if Amanda could steer the ship with Marcus for a couple more weeks while we explore the new idea further, that would be great. Lexi, I gather this is something of your baby, so I trust that you can arrange for your first guest and liaise with our marketing team to discuss a possible new look for the show? We want something still in keeping with the *Your Hot Friend* identity but communicating the slight change in tone that *Your Hot Mess* will have. I liked the feud merch look very much, so perhaps engage that designer again?'

'No problem.' Lexi nodded.

'Regarding the financials. If the pilot works and the transition to the new format goes smoothly, and IF the figures stay roughly the same as they are now, we are happy to continue with our original agreement. However, if in six weeks you haven't delivered a consistent listenership on *Your Hot Mess*, we'll have to take another look at this. Ultimately, the money handed over at signing was provisional on a year's partnership, and if that were to dissolve earlier ...'

Beside Lexi, Amanda was nodding furiously. Lexi felt more sanguine. If they liked the new show, they liked it. Either way, she and Jonathan would be selling the house. She was sad but also accepting. That house held a future she no longer wanted. She was moving her stuff down to Hereford later that day. On paper, it was going backwards, but in reality she understood now that life didn't follow a straight line.

'I propose we schedule a separate meeting to get into the nuts and bolts of the contract side of things, but basically what I'm saying is a tentative ... okay. Let's give *Your Hot Mess* a shot.'

'Amazing!' Amanda turned and flung her arms around Lexi.

The rest of the meeting was devoted to logistics and spitballing ideas about possible segments. An hour later, Lexi was saying goodbye to Amanda on the street outside.

'I'll see you at therapy tomorrow,' Amanda called, hurrying away under her umbrella.

Lexi hopped into the taxi that had just pulled up. She was feeling the mounting optimism that always came with the promise of a fresh start. Though there was still more logistics to get through before then. She gave the driver her old address in Dún Laoghaire – Jonathan had managed to extend the lease. The car pulled out into the sluggish traffic and Lexi gathered herself for what could well be a tricky conversation.

Jonathan opened the door, with Scouty yelping and circling his feet. He looked stunned to see her.

'Oh, hey. I assumed Abi or Shay would be collecting her.' He stepped aside as Lexi, pausing to scoop up Scouty, made her way into the living room.

'Yeah, I just figured, as it was the last time …'

She trailed off, taking in the changes to the apartment since she'd last been there. There was a new tan leather armchair by the window and a fancy sound system had been installed.

'Place looks great.' She put Scouty down again and turned back to Jonathan. 'Did you have a nice last few days together?'

'Yeah.' He dug his hands into his pockets. 'It was nice, but you're right, she's your dog. I was only digging my heels in on the joint custody thing out of spite. I'm sorry.'

Lexi nodded. She truly felt no animosity towards him now; in fact, she felt a flicker of pity. She was going to have a better life than Jonathan. She had real friends.

'So I gather from Aine that you and Amanda are getting back together.'

'Yeah … tentatively.' Lexi knew where this was going.

He shook his head. 'I can't believe you would choose her over me.'

'Really?' Lexi cradled the dog. 'Why's that so hard to believe? She tried harder than you, Jonathan. She showed up for me and my dad, even when I wasn't speaking to her. You didn't even go to him the day I asked you to, and we were still together then.'

'I did,' he argued. 'I did a drive-by. The lights were on, so I figured—'

'The lights were on? That means nothing.' Lexi shook her head. 'He was in a bad way. I trusted you.'

Jonathan shifted uncomfortably, raking his hand through his hair. 'Amanda cheated too, you know.'

Lexi rolled her eyes. 'Yeah, we're working through that. We're in therapy.'

Jonathan scoffed. 'You're back doing couples' therapy with your friend?'

'Yes, because we want to make our relationship work. We want to fight for our relationship. Just because it's not a romantic one doesn't mean it's less important. It's actually more important. Lots of people stay together after cheating in romantic relationships. Why is it so crazy to stay together in platonic ones? Even after everything, I love her and she loves me.'

Jonathan shook his head, but Lexi carried on.

'She's a part of me. When I was a teenager, she was like my sister and my mother and my best friend all rolled into one. She taught me how to use a tampon. She came to my abortion with me. She watched all four seasons of *The O.C.* with me, over and over. So yeah, I pick her, Jonathan.'

He folded his arms. 'We've still got the house to sort. My share of the Podify deal is still mine, even if it is sunk into that place.'

'I don't care, Jonathan. I really don't.'

'Amanda will fuck up that new show.'

'If she does, she does. I'll get a real job.' Lexi shrugged. 'I am ready to fail at whatever happens next. I'm living my life for me now. I don't care how it looks from the outside.'

Jonathan at last started to look contrite. 'Look, I'll ... I'll get the ball rolling on the sale.'

'Thank you,' Lexi replied courteously.

'It shouldn't be too hard to shift.'

'Mmm.' She nodded, eager to leave now and get on with the move. She wanted to be down at her dad's for dinnertime.

'Will we engage the same gal who sold it to us?'

'Do.' Lexi picked up Scouty again and started for the door.

'I'll cc you on the email.' Jonathan sounded defeated.

'Thanks.'

'I suppose I'll definitely have to get a real job again.'

'Well, tour manager wasn't exactly the most permanent, pensionable job.' She smiled, with a patience she wasn't feeling. Then she pulled open the door.

'Lexi ...' He looked up at her. 'I didn't mean it about the money. With the way things went down ... with what I did ... I don't deserve my cut.'

'Jonathan, will you just not? When we shift the house you take it – you cut the deal. I don't want your share. I just want to leave!'

He nodded sadly.

By late afternoon, Lexi was sweaty but had, at last, finished stuffing the car. The thud and bang of Slip'not practice had provided the soundtrack to her work. She checked the time again. Five past four. Only five minutes since she'd last checked. The band knew she had to leave, and they'd be up any minute to say goodbye ... but she still hadn't figured out how to say goodbye to Shay. Sudden silence from the house set her mind racing. What would she say to him? She wanted to get him alone.

I could ask him to check my room with me?

Or maybe come for a quick walk with Scout before putting her in the car?

Or I could just cry and beg him to kiss me?

Before she could decide on an approach, the band started streaming from the house. They were also drenched in sweat, pulling off their masks. They were going on tour in a couple of weeks and when shows were coming up they practised in the full get-up so they could, as they put it, acclimatise.

As Lexi hugged them each in turn, she realised Shay wasn't there. She knew he'd been at practice as she'd been hearing the drums all afternoon – Lexi had to admit she'd become a fairly committed Slip'not fan since staying in the house.

She stepped back from them, trying not to get upset.

Maybe he's had to take a call or something. Anyway, it's not like I won't see him. He's my friend now.

The last thought kicked off an unexpected fear.

But maybe he doesn't want to say goodbye because he knows I like him and he doesn't like me after all and he doesn't want things to be awkward ...

Just then Shay hurried out the front door and elbowed his way through the band. 'Wait, Lex!' He came towards her and Lexi caught her breath: his sweet eyes and messy hair. And those lips. 'I have something for ...'

Me?! she thought, hope leaping in her chest.

'... for Scouty! Here, girl.' He called the dog over and produced a black dog collar with small spikes. 'Honorary member of Slip'not,' he said, fastening it around her. He stood up, raking his hair back, and turned to Lexi. 'Her band name is Hitler's Lover. Only joking.' He winked. 'That name's taken. No, we're gonna call her "People = Shit", you know ... after the song.'

As a matter of fact, Lexi did know.

'That's beautiful,' she grinned, trying to mask her disappointment. This wasn't going to happen. She could just tell.

'So ... ehm ... yeah ...' He turned back to the band and she thought he was about to join them and just wave her off like the rest of them. But then she saw him motion at them and they all turned as one and appeared to start talking amongst themselves.

Then Shay turned back to her and moved closer. 'Lex. Can I tell you something?'

'Yeah,' Lexi breathed.

'You're my favourite person in the whole world.'

'Yeah? Even including Joey Jordison?'

'Yep,' he laughed. 'And Jay Weinberg.'

Lexi backed up a little, the car now directly behind her. A bit of 'hot girl' vibe was required sometimes. 'Do you wanna kiss me?' she asked.

'Uh-huh.' He nodded and came even closer.

'Well, you better then, cos I'm leaving now.'

He pressed her against the car and then his hands were in her hair and his mouth was on hers. He pushed himself closer, running his hands down her body, and Lexi felt a thrum of pleasure deep inside her.

Shay pulled back a little. 'Fuck, Lexi, I've wanted to do that for so fucking long.' Then he started kissing her again.

A faint strumming caught Lexi's attention and Shay turned sharply. Screaming Foetus was holding his guitar and advancing slowly.

'No!' Shay started waving him away. 'No, man! We vetoed the song idea, remember?'

Screaming Foetus ignored this, smiling serenely and continuing to play. Lexi recognised it, one of Slipknot's few ballads: 'Vermilion, Pt. 2'. Behind him the rest of the band had turned and started to sing, arms around one another.

Shay turned back to her, shaking his head and laughing. 'They've been really rooting for us!'

'Good.' Lexi pulled him closer again. 'I have been too.'

EPILOGUE

Claire stood at the doors to the ward and felt the tug of apprehension. Beside her were Nancy and Ella, smiling.

'I will see you next week, Claire,' Ella said firmly. 'I will see you,' she repeated, her eyes boring into Claire's. 'Do not cancel. Don't neglect your health – this illness is too dangerous.'

Claire nodded. *Was it finally starting to sink in? She had an illness. It was an illness that could be fatal.*

One that had come very fucking close to being fatal twice now.

'We'll miss you.' Annette stepped forward.

'I'll miss you too.' Claire smiled. It was only a semi-lie.

'Okay. Down you go, now. Reception rang up: your friends are waiting.' Nancy handed over Claire's bag of medications and phone charger. Then she gave her a brusque yet loving hug. 'Try not to come see us again.' Her eyes crinkled as she smiled at Claire. 'But also: we are ALWAYS here.'

Claire went down the lift nervously. The last time she'd been discharged, it had been a chilly autumnal morning and Jamie had collected her alone. Now it was the middle of July – how?!

She was out of the lift and across the reception in a matter of seconds, and there they were. All three of them were leaning rakishly against Lexi's car in the sunshine, looking like they were springing her from prison.

'Claire!' Jamie rushed forward to grab her and kiss her. It was so good to smell him again. Whenever Jamie had visited her in the last six weeks, the smell of the hospital had overpowered the special and essential Jamieness that Claire had always been addicted to.

Next, Lexi and Joanne buried Claire in a hug.

'You're a free woman!' Joanne exclaimed.

'Where do you wanna go first?' Jamie asked.

'Bearing in mind,' Lexi added with a twist of mystery in her smile, 'that there's like twenty people waiting in Lavine's for a celebratory welcome home lunch.'

'No way!' Claire relinquished her bag to Joanne, who began stuffing it in the boot.

Jamie stepped in front of Claire. 'That's IF you feel up to it? There's absolutely no pressure – everyone will understand.'

'Yeah, I wanna go. Who's everyone?' Claire asked as they piled into the car.

'Well, there's the Bitch Herd, your mum and dad, the Sweeneys, Bert and Ted, Aine, Abi, Shay, Screaming Foetus.'

'Oh. Wow. That's like tons of people.' Claire felt shy but undeniably happy. All of them had come for her. And they all knew everything, and yet they were still there waiting for her.

The drive to Lavine's took them along the coast road heading north, away from the city. The sea dazzled and Claire felt an almost palpable recalibration in her body. The air, the light, the space was everything she hadn't had on the ward in the last six weeks. Sure, she had walked outside in the grounds. But this was freedom. Her head felt as though it had been released from a vice: the terrible stew of shame and unreality and terror had at last drained away and her mind felt as open and clear as the blue sky above them.

At the restaurant, the banner said 'WELCOME HOME!' and Claire cried. She didn't get to sit down for at least twenty minutes, while every single person in her life hugged her and rained kind and gentle words down on her. It was as cleansing as spring rain.

The sprawling group had been allocated two long tables. Claire sat with Lexi and Joanne.

'This is so crazy.' She looked around. 'It's so funny to see Screaming Foetus talking to Aifric!'

'Yeah, it's a bunch of weirdos for sure.' Joanne munched on the breadsticks while they waited for their meal. 'I'm into it, though. And Aifric's wedding will be like a reunion. She invited me and Lexi this morning!'

'Ah, that's deadly.' Claire started on her own breadstick.

'I actually said I'd do the favours in the end, so it was the least she could do,' Joanne remarked.

'Oh god, the favours, please don't remind me! What did you do?'

'I designed a bookmark for them. Twee bullshit, but she was delighted.'

'Thank god it got sorted.' Claire cringed at flashes of the Ibiza trip and that grim morning in her bedroom the day after. 'I can't believe my manic episode revolved around something so ... mundane.'

'Ha,' Lexi barked. 'To be fair, there was a lot more going on than soaps. The friend stuff, the pod stuff.'

'Yeah.' Joanne nodded vigorously. 'It was a super-fucky time.'

'Still, it's so embarrassing. I wish there was a tee-shirt that just said, "I'm sorry for what I did when I was manic" so everyone would know without me having to say it.'

'There could be!' Joanne sat up. 'I love that idea! Super-niche merch for the mentally ill! Forty-six million people have bipolar, appara – I looked it up back when you first went into the bin.'

'Not sure that's a good business idea, trying to coin it off mental illness.' Lexi winced. 'Though maybe that's what people think we're doing with *Your Hot Mess*.'

'Not a *business!* A *charity*. We could raise money for education around mental illness ... And then we'd just do some light embezzling on the side.'

'Perfect!' Claire laughed. 'Also, only I and my fellow binmates may call it the bin.'

'Lol, my bad.' Joanne held up her hands.

'So, how is *Your Hot Mess* going?' They'd kept her up-to-date on the WhatsApp over the last month and a half, but it was so much easier and more relaxed to chat properly outside the hospital. Claire had listened to the first four episodes of *Your Hot Mess* and had found them funny and reassuring, but who knew if that translated into listens?

'It's going amazing, Claire.' Lexi beamed. 'You have to come on. If you want, that is. And whenever, not like this week or anything. As you know, we're interviewing a different guest every week and doing Q&As with mental health professionals on the Patreon.'

'The reviews have been so good,' Joanne enthused. 'Especially the ones of my episode about trying to go back to normal after having a baby!'

'So modest, Jo.' Claire grinned. 'And how is being back at work?'

'A fucking godsend. The new agency is great and I get to leave the house every day! Unreal scenes! Plus Aoife and them really copped on after they heard my interview on *Your Hot Mess*, so I'm seeing them a bit more.'

'That's so good. I can't wait to go back to work.' Claire looked across at Norah and the kids, smiling. 'I start back in a couple of weeks. It's amazing.' She turned to Lexi. 'And how's your dad, how did this week's check-up go?'

'Really good. The doctors have him scared straight. No more beers, lots of rest. He won't let me pay rent, thank god. I'm broke until the house sells, but I'm earning my keep as his live-in butler/chef/chauffeur. We've gone back to the bridge class as well. Did I tell you Shay comes too; he's bizarrely into it.'

'So that's still going well?'

'It is.' Lexi smiled shyly. 'We're going on dates. And having ... sleepovers!'

'So cute.' Claire smiled, then leaned closer to them. 'I can't wait for me and Jamie's first sleepover back. There should be conjugal visits in the bin!'

Just then a tinkle of steel against glass interrupted them. It was Jamie, standing to make a speech.

'Gang, we are, as you all know, gathered here today to celebrate Claire. We're so happy to have you home. It's been a tough time for you and for all of us who love you, but you made it. We're so proud of you. I'm not great with words and I'm an even worse singer, so Screaming Foetus is gonna help me out here ...'

Screaming Foetus produced a tuning fork and whacked it against his knee, then listened to it closely for a moment before singing a couple of 'me, me, me's, apparently to give Jamie his note. Jamie took a breath and began to sing 'Que Sera, Sera', with the whole table soon joining in.

Claire burst out laughing at the spectacle of everyone she knew singing about a future that wasn't theirs to see. By the second chorus, the entire bemused restaurant was singing along too.

And Claire realised then that while she couldn't know if the darkness would descend again, there were two things she knew for certain:

I know that what will be will be, and I know that everyone at this table will always be with me.

LETTER TO READERS

Hello Hi Hey Hello,

Firstly, thank you so much for reading *My Hot Friend*. It means the absolute world to me that you are. This letter is possibly not for you and I am very very happy if it isn't – you see, this letter is for anyone who is on the precipice and needs to know that better days are coming. If you are in pain. If you are scared. If you are losing hope. This letter is for you.

I have been in that sunken place. I have been so sick in the head that death has begun to look like a solution, a solution to a problem that I thought was without end.

In the autumn of 2007, I was planning to end my life. I had been living in the torment and terror of mental illness for three months and had decided that there was no other way for it to end but for me to go. While I felt bad about what I was about to do to my family and friends, what I really felt was overwhelming resignation. I simply believed that there was no way I would ever be ok again. To be clear, I didn't even want to be *happy* again, I just wanted to be *not* terrified and *not* trapped in the vice of anguish that was my head.

That year psychiatric care and the love and acceptance of my family and friends saved my life.

I came back from the sunken place. I was more or less me again. Kind of. But recovery is not linear. We can sink again. But we can also be saved again. And again. And again.

In 2014 psychiatric care and the love and acceptance of my family and friends saved my life.

In 2018 psychiatric care and the love and acceptance of my family and friends saved my life.

In 2020 psychiatric care and the love and acceptance of my family and friends saved my life.

Today, and every day, psychiatric care and the love and acceptance of my family and friends save my life.

There is no cure for my mental illness, it can only be managed. But there are no certainties in this life. Basically, mentally ill or not, there is no 'cure' for life and it all has to be 'managed'. In a way, I think those of us with the Mads might even be better off. When the shitstorms hit, no one's better equipped than us!

If some of the events of the book are difficult for you or make you feel unsafe please free call Samaritans on 116 123. They are ready to listen and help, 24 hours a day, 365 days a year.

Better days are ALWAYS coming. I promise you. I am living proof of this.

Hold on, hold on, hold on. Please hold on.

All of my love,
Sophie

ACKNOWLEDGEMENTS

I am so, so lucky to work with the most brilliant, wise, patient and creative editor, Ciara Doorley – she always has the most incredible vision and insightful feedback. I would be utterly lost without her. I would also like to thank Joanna Smyth – her keen eye frequently saves me from myself! Also I am so lucky to have Elaine Egan in my corner, she takes such good care of me. Thank you to all at Hachette Ireland. Also a massive thank you to my fab agents, Tanera Simons and Sheila David who big me up and are such huge supporters through the whole book-making process. Also my deepest thanks to the whole team at Darley Anderson.

I'm especially grateful to the wonderful teachers and staff of St Matthew's School and the loving, caring gang at Giraffe IFSC.

Thank you to all my (hot) friends: Jen O'Dwyer, Cassie Delaney, Louise McSharry, Emer McLysaght, Liadan Hynes, Lisa Coen, Sarah Davis-Goff, Esther O'Moore-Donohue, Sooby Lynch, Gemma Fullam, Jane Doran, Mary Kate O'Flanagan, Alan Brady, Yvonne Hogan, Madeleine Keane, Leslie-Ann Horgan, Regina Lavelle, Alan English, Bill's pals, the Creeps and the *Mother of Pod* crew.

Thank you to Orlaith and to Tim Donlon for your help with the particulars of lye – any errors on this one are my own. Thank you also to the Samaritans for their guidelines for writers – these were invaluable when writing about sensitive issues.

To the early readers of this book: Louise O'Neill, Marian Keyes and Rebecca Murphy. There really is no greater generosity than reading drafts when a work is in progress. It always is so reassuring to the deeply panicked author ;)

Thank you to the OG Bitch Herd who are nothing like the Bitch Herd in the book! Jess Pierce, Rebecca Coll, Clodagh Hynes, Kate Gorey, Rachel Griffith, Heather Irvine, Clara Kelleher, Niamh Bannon, Suzanne Byrne and Orla Lawton, you made school and many years since so much fun <3 <3 <3. Big love XXX.

I'd like to thank all the readers and everyone on Bookstagram – you have supported my work so generously and I appreciate it so SO much.

Thank you to my family: Anne Harris, Constance Harris, Mungo Harris, Nancy Harris, Kwasi Agyei-Owusu, Vivianne White, David White, Hilary White, Viktorija White, William White and Triona McCarthy.

All of my gratitude and love to my nearest and absolute dearest: Mary O'Sullivan, Kevin Linehan, Sebastian White, and Rufus, Arlo and Sonny White.